TRULY *Madly* PLAID

ELIZA KNIGHT

sourcebooks casablanca

Published by Sourcebooks Casablanca, an imprint of Sourcebooks
P.O. Box 4410, Naperville, Illinois 60567-4410
(630) 961-3900
sourcebooks.com

Printed and bound in Canada.
MBP 10 9 8 7 6 5 4 3 2 1

To all of the essential working women and men in the world who put their lives on the line for others. You make this world a better place.

Dear Reader,

When I first imagined the concept behind this series, I knew I wanted to create a cast of incredibly brave heroines who would have to risk nearly everything for the good of their country and their future king. The Jacobite era of Great Britain's history is the last civil war fought on the united soils of Scotland and England, ultimately coming to rest in a rather tragic ending for many. Throughout the tumultuous years were born many heroes—dozens of which were women.

I wanted to incorporate their bravery, tenacity, and enthusiasm for their cause and their loyalty to a prince they wanted to be king, so I used many of their stories when creating those within this series. In *Truly Madly Plaid*, you will find Annie's story to have a flavor of the lives of Anne MacKay, Anne Leith, and Lady Winifred Maxwell, mixed in with a generous helping of my imagination.

There is also a fun rumor that the Christmas carol "O Come, All Ye Faithful" was in fact a Jacobite call to arms, and that the line "come and behold Him, born the king of angels" was code for "come and behold him, born the king of the English"—who just so happened to be Bonnie Prince Charlie. Allegedly the Latin verse was actually a celebration of the prince's birth rather than of Jesus's, all connotation of which was lost when it was translated in the nineteenth century. Learning that his people were nicknamed angels, it seemed a fun theme to incorporate into the series: Prince Charlie's Angels.

I do hope you enjoy reading this book and the rest of the series as much as I have enjoyed writing it!

Best wishes,
Eliza

Prologue

January 1746
Bannockburn House
Scottish Highlands

Icy rain had pelted the earth, threatening to freeze everything into a single slickened crystalized mass, and for now, it had waned at least enough that Lieutenant Craig MacLean felt safe moving out of his tent.

While most of the men were celebrating their victory of the most recent battle, the rest of them were battling the ferocious weather, exhausted and simply looking for a place to get warm.

Craig was of the latter group and trudged toward the house to check on the prince, who'd come down with the ague that had seized a number in his own company. The closer he drew to Bannockburn House, the more certain he was that he could hear someone retching. Dear God, how many more of them were to catch this illness?

Then he saw her, bent almost all the way over, a hand holding her balance on the stone facade of the wall.

Her brow was slick with rain or sweat or both, dark tendrils of hair plastered to her forehead and temples. At his approach she stood up straight, swaying. Her pallor was gray and ghostlike. He stood for a moment watching her, recognizing in an instant who she was. Sister to his friend Graham, Annie MacPherson, the prince's own healer and a healer to many of the soldiers within camp. Yet it appeared she was the one in need of healing now.

She leaned her back against the stones, stared almost through him, and then turned slowly, pressing her forehead to the cool outer wall. The lass was seriously ill. Craig edged closer.

Och, he'd never seen so much vomit in his life, not even from a drunken soldier. She'd vomited up the entirety of the last meal she'd eaten and perhaps what she'd consumed for the last sennight. Over and over again, so much so he'd begun to think it an unholy thing.

"My lady," he started, standing only a few feet away now, arm outstretched as though to aid her somehow. She might have been ill as the devil, but he had to help her.

Annie wiped her mouth and then pulled a dagger from her boot, brandishing it toward him with wild eyes. "Get away from me, *Sassenach*, or I'll cut off your ballocks and shove them down your throat if ye come another step closer."

Craig held up his hands in surrender, brows raised nearly to his hairline. Had the illness caused her to be addled? He was clearly no *Sassenach*. "I only want to help, my lady."

"I said leave me, ye savage *Sassenach* bastard. Run back to your butchering friends." And then she bent over again, convulsing, her body not done tormenting her.

Craig glanced down, wondering what part of his attire—kilt, frockcoat, boots—made her think that he was a *Sassenach*. He'd yet to bathe after battle, not wanting to freeze to death, and it had been many days since he'd shaved his face, but if anything he just looked more like the rest of the bearded rebel Highlanders.

When Annie was finished retching, she brandished the knife toward him again, swinging it so wildly he feared she'd end up hurting herself. And then she threw it at him. Though he dodged, the tip nicked his lip before falling at his feet. Craig growled at her, the taste of blood on his tongue. Finished with this nonsense, he moved to turn away when she started to sway uncontrollably, stretching for the stone wall, not finding it, and pitching forward.

With her weapon at least discarded, he reached in then, an arm around her back, another beneath her legs, lifting her up into the air. She collapsed against him, weak as a lamb just born and hotter than fire with fever.

Annie struggled meekly. "Put me down. Do ye know who I am?" And then she fell into unconsciousness.

"I know exactly who ye are," he said to her unaware face. "And your brother would have my head if I left ye here. I'm taking ye inside, lass. Get ye some help." He carried her to the front door and managed to open it with her in his arms. "Is there someone who can help?" he called. But no one came. "Bloody hell."

Craig carried her up the stairs and found a spare bedroom, laying her down on the mattress when footsteps sounded behind. He turned around to find a wee maid brandishing another knife in his direction.

"What the bloody devil with so many of ye trying to

kill me when I'm only trying to help." This one looked to have a worse skill with a knife than wee Annie, and she lunged at him, but Craig was able to block her, grabbing her wrist and applying just enough pressure that she dropped the weapon. But then she tried using her fists. "Oh, for bloody hell's sake." He held her tight in his arms, staring down into her face.

"What have ye done to my mistress?" she demanded, wrestling against him.

"I was helping her, ye bloody fool. I ought to have ye whipped."

Her face paled. "Please, I didna realize..."

Craig let her go, and she scrambled backward. "I'm no' going to hurt ye any more than I was hurting her, ye pair of mad fools. I was only trying to help your mistress, who was outside getting ill against the side of the manor."

"Oh no, she's caught the prince's ague."

"Aye, and a bit of madness too." Craig backed away, his thumb brushing at the fresh wound on his lip. "Take care of your mistress. And dinna attack anyone else with the damned blade. Either of ye."

One

April 5, 1746

This was a mistake.

Every hair on the back of Lieutenant Craig MacLean's neck stood on end, as though each one wielded its own sword against the enemy.

Without the protection of the fortress walls, they were sitting ducks tromping through the forest. An army with most of its men on foot would not be able to escape should a legion of redcoats cut off their path.

Winter had not stopped the sieges. Winter had not stopped death.

A vulture flew overhead, accompanied by two cronies as they cut a wide circular path in the graying sky. Were he and the men the dead meat they sought?

"We should go back," he said to Graham MacPherson. "Your invitation was appreciated, but I've no' got a good feeling about this."

There was no telling when Cumberland's men would make their move, and if the men were inebriated from drink and tired from too much celebrating, they'd not be ready for an attack.

Graham chuckled and tossed the end of a stick he'd been chewing at Craig. "Ye're afraid of a few birds, are ye?"

"I'm no' afraid of anything."

"Let loose, MacLean. The men need to have some fun, and so do ye."

The very last place that Craig wanted to be was riding toward Cullidunloch Castle. It wasn't that he didn't like castles or his host or the warm feast that Graham had promised or the ale that was certain to be flowing.

Craig liked all of those things quite a lot. More than a lot, if he were being honest. Toss in a bonnie wench or two to flirt with, and he'd be in his own version of heaven. But Cullidunloch Castle wasn't only home to his best mate. It also happened to house a woman he'd been working hard to avoid for months. Graham's sister Annie was very beautiful and very irksome. She was as brilliant as she was irritating, and despite that brilliance, the lass had conveniently forgotten the single encounter the two of them had shared.

He hadn't forgotten. How could he? And now he was descending upon her home—her and Graham's home—to partake of their hospitality. *Her* hospitality. If she was willing to give it.

Hospitality he would really like to have, considering he hadn't had a warm bath in weeks. He'd only managed to keep himself from smelling like a chamber pot by swimming—when the lochs weren't covered in a sheet of ice. His clothes were getting stiff from use, and he was fairly certain that his last good pair of hose now had a hole where his big toe was greedily trying to squeeze through.

At least right now they weren't dealing with snow,

though it was only early spring and another storm was inevitable in the Highlands. The temperatures had been rising steadily, enough so that the men in his regiment weren't so fearful of freezing to death anymore. Unless of course it snowed tonight and Annie MacPherson tossed him out with the last of the evening's rubbish. He wouldn't put it past her.

Craig would have to make nice with her, though he found the very idea absurd. Graham didn't need to know what a termagant his sister truly was. He'd never told his friend what had happened when he'd found Annie retching after battle.

To everyone else she encountered, Annie was sweet as sunshine. Even the men she had to stitch up while they writhed in pain called her their angel—men in his own regiment, men he'd trained and led into battle. She was lauded for her nursing skills and her bedside manner, which stung even more. Of course he sent his men to her to be mended; she was the best damn healer he'd ever seen.

And that was about all the amount of niceties he'd extend. Why had he been the only unlucky fellow to have encountered her waspish side?

He would never be caught openly acknowledging the bonniness of her face. The way her chin curved into a petite point or the way her eyebrows arched delicately over her mesmerizing eyes. Eyes that were the most incredible amber color.

Bloody hell.

Every time he looked at Annie, every time she smiled,

he saw that derisive sneer she'd flashed at him the night he'd tried to help her. He'd seen a side of her he was certain no one else had, and he'd run as far as he bloody could—after making sure she was safely taken care of, that was.

He wasn't a complete monster.

But he was quite all right with her believing he was, if that meant she'd stay the hell away from him.

"Is the pottage breakfast no' agreeing with ye?" Graham's teasing voice cut through Craig's thoughts.

He snorted. "I've an iron stomach, lad."

"Lad? I think I've got a year or two on ye. And ye forget we've been living together on campaign for months. Bean pottage is no' your friend, mate."

Craig snickered. "Are ye saying that ye're in need of a latrine?"

"Debatable."

Craig was glad for his friend's distraction. Though he didn't want to talk about beans or what happened after he ate them.

"Annie's sure to have a hearty meal for the lot of us this evening." Graham sounded so wistful, as though he were talking about something more fantastical than food. Like the war ending with Prince Charles Stuart sitting on the throne. Now that was something to long for.

Craig's smile faded, and he nodded, having hoped to avoid any further conversation about Graham's chit of a sister.

"I'm honored to be your guest." This much was true.

"Honored?" Graham let out a guffaw. "Ye're my brother in arms, mate."

While they'd known each other for years, they'd become closer friends after having saved each other's arses at the battle at Falkirk the January past.

"I'm certain Logan will want to spar with ye," Graham was saying of his younger brother, who'd been sent home from the front with a grave injury. "And Annie, she'll be there to sew ye up."

Craig laughed, but only half-heartedly. If he had his way, he'd keep Annie the length of a jousting stick away from him—preferably farther—at all times.

Some said that the measure of a man was the sum of his parts. His courage, his honor, his strength. But what was the measure of a woman? Her ability to be a mother? A wife? To be sweet and obedient? To run a household without faltering? If these were the elements by which Annie MacPherson were to be measured, then she would fail. She was used to that. She'd failed at many things in her life. She wasn't as skilled with a sword as her friend Jenny. Nor was she as brave as her friend Fiona, who dared the woods at night alone to deliver important messages. Annie was also not a mother and certainly had never been a wife, though the topic had come up more than a time or two.

But if she were to be a wife, then there would be just another person to tell her she could no longer spend her time in barracks full of wounded men or attending those on campaign, sleeping in tents surrounded by soldiers.

A healer's job seemed risqué to some. Those were the ignorant folks who didn't see her when she was up to her elbows in blood.

Running a household was easy; that was perhaps the only thing she hadn't failed at, but she didn't enjoy the work. And sweet and obedient? The answer to that depended on who was asked. She had been the light in her father's eyes and could do no wrong by him, whereas her mother had always seemed to be huffing and puffing when Annie was in attendance.

Annie stood in the great hall of Cullidunloch Castle, arms crossed over her chest, surveying the work that had been done under her direction. She was surprised she'd been able to pull it off in so short a time. Less than twenty-four hours ago, she'd been riding hell-bent for leather from Inverness. Now, here she was, smudges of purple beneath her eyes from lack of sleep and feeling just a wee bit shaky from lack of food but utterly triumphant.

The whitewashed walls gleamed, and even the black soot stains above the massive hearth had been mostly scraped away. The carpets and tapestries had been beaten to within an inch of their life in the courtyard. The brass handles, sconces, and candelabras had been polished to a bright shine. The few spring flowers that had decided to bloom early despite the hideous weather had been scoured from the moors. They now sat mixed with greenery and herbs in vases to lend a sweeter smell to the ancient stones of the great hall.

No one had done any redecorating in the many years since her parents had passed, and the great hall looked exactly the same as it always had. Annie's gaze was drawn to one of the castle's most prized possessions, an armada chest that had been designed by an ancestor of theirs more than two hundred years ago. Made of heavy iron and wood, there was a dummy keyhole in the front to trick unsuspecting thieves, while the true latch was embedded in a mystery of complicated locks and levers on the top, disguised by decorative emblems and embellishments. She'd spent hours with her brothers trying to break into the coffer while their father watched with pride. They'd been told it was filled with Spanish gold and jewels.

Annie ran her fingers over the top of the chest, along the pattern that led to its opening. It had only taken them a few weeks of nightly attempts before they'd figured it out. Annie had always been good at solving puzzles, taking things apart and putting them back together. There'd been no Spanish treasure inside, of course, but instead three tiny trick-lock chests that they could hold their own prized possessions in. Annie and Logan still had theirs, and she wondered if Graham had his, too.

"Ye miss Da." Logan's approach—none too quiet, given the wooden false foot painted to look like a boot—surprised her all the same. She gave a little jump, glancing beside her.

Her younger brother had the same eyes as her own, the same amber as their mother, and his hair was just as dark. Lanky and great in height, he even towered several inches over their brother Graham. But what Graham lacked in height, comparatively, he made up for in musculature.

Logan put his arm around her shoulder, pulling her in for a sideways hug. She rested her head on his shoulder and glanced up at him. "I do."

"Me, too."

Annie shoved playfully away from her brother with a little laugh and swiped away the tears that had started to fall. "Enough of this ninny stuff. We've work to do."

Over a year had passed since they'd last had guests at Cullidunloch, and Annie—though exhausted and battle-weary—was exhilarated at the thought of entertaining. For a night or two the men would convalesce at the castle, sleep beneath a sturdy roof surrounded by thick walls, and have savory meals prepared by proper cooks before they made their way back to the war camp.

"Ye never stop." Logan shook his head. "I'm exhausted just thinking of all ye've been doing."

Annie shrugged. That was who she was. Always moving, never slowing down. When she did rest, her mind wandered to places she didn't want to go—like ruminating over the thousands of dragoons crawling around their country, putting people in harm's way. Keeping busy let her shove away the thousand worries pummeling against the inside of her skull. "Rooms have been prepared for the titled men and for the officers in Prince Charles's army. The remainder of the men will cluster inside the barracks and the great hall and share the hospitality of those in the village."

"The men will appreciate no' having to suffer another night out of doors. And I will enjoy seeing them again."

Logan was part of the reason why she'd worked so

hard and been so amenable to Graham's idea of the men returning to Cullidunloch for a wee sojourn. He'd been isolated since the battle at Falkirk Muir in January, thanks to a sword in the hand of a bloody *Sassenach*.

Oh, what Annie wouldn't do to get her hands around the neck of the man who'd maimed her brother. Better yet, to take a cleaver to that bastard's ankle as he'd done to Logan, pulling him from his horse on the battlefield. Logan had suffered the loss of his foot from the blasted redcoat who'd cut it off.

It'd taken a good solid month before the wound had healed, but from the moment he'd woken in bed to find out what had happened, Logan had plastered a smile on his face. He'd not broken down, not in public, and truth be told Annie wasn't certain he'd broken down in private either. Which left her constantly on edge. At any moment he could succumb to madness over the injury, and she wouldn't blame him. What had happened was horribly unfair, something she'd seen again and again in this war. For men who made their living as soldiers, being left alive but taken out of the fight was as much a death sentence as a final blow.

Logan still trained with the few men who remained at Cullidunloch, using a wooden boot that fitted to the bottom of his leg. And Graham had made Logan steward of the castle and master when Graham, laird of clan MacPherson, was away. The position was well respected and seemed to give Logan purpose, but it was also obvious that he missed the thrill of battle and camaraderie of other soldiers.

"Aye," Annie said wistfully, recalling years past when Cullidunloch had been the liveliest place in all the Highlands. "'Twill be nice to have a full castle."

"Any other lady would do without a barrage of soldiers descending on her home," Logan teased.

Annie bumped her shoulder against his and passed him a soft smile. "Aye, but ye know me. I'd rather be stringing my needle and mending soldiers' flesh than embroidery."

"This is true." Logan wrinkled his brow. "I suppose Jenny and Fiona too would be happy for the rowdy company. They were always up for whatever scheme ye had going when we were children."

Annie laughed with a sound that was unexpected even to her, hard and sharp and full of joy. "The three of us certainly did enjoy tormenting ye back in the day."

"Torment is an understatement." He wrapped an arm around her shoulders, tugged her against him, and then mussed her hair with his free hand.

Annie wiped away the tears of laughter. "Be glad, brother, that I've no' yet had Eppy fix my hair, else I'd have no hesitation in pummeling ye."

"I'd like to see ye try."

This was an age-old exchange between them that hadn't stopped for long after Logan's injury. At first she'd been unsure, not wanting to hurt him, but her brother had insisted she treat him no differently. Since that one moment of hesitation, she never had one again—including now, which was why she gave him a swift jab in the ribs, calculated not to be hard enough to truly hurt.

"I would, but Graham and the men will be here at any moment, and I've yet to make myself presentable in a way that willna have our dear brother up in arms." She rolled her eyes to the rafters. Graham had often made comments about how she managed her appearance while on campaign. Annie loved her brother dearly, but the man was so unrealistic. Remaining awake at all hours to tend injuries did not lend her time for preening, a fact she pointed out quite often to Graham. At least he had the decency to be apologetic about it—until the next time he asked her to make herself presentable.

Logan chuckled. "Best get on with it then."

With the fires roaring in the kitchens, bread being baked, venison and grouse roasting, vegetables being chopped, and pies being whipped up, she felt safe to say that no one would go hungry.

Not all of the men could return at once, for the regiment numbered in the hundreds, and if something should happen closer to the prince's camp, they needed to have warriors at the ready. Instead they'd had to draw straws, and Graham had promised that they'd take shifts in convalescing at Cullidunloch, which was less than a day's ride from their current encampment. The prince too had been invited to the castle, but he'd declined, feeling his presence needed in Inverness at the latest fort they'd taken. There was always the fear that loyalists would get some sort of bug up their arses to retake the strongholds.

An action Annie wouldn't doubt they'd take, the bastards.

With everyone working to get the castle ready, Annie

climbed the stairs to her bedchamber and stared longingly at the dry tub where she'd soaked the night before. She'd had enough time to get scrubbed but not long enough to work the kinks out of her muscles. It had been months since she'd had a proper bath, but at least the act of a good scrubbing had given her energy enough to keep going.

Annie stripped out of her dirty clothes and splashed water on her face, rinsing the grime of housework away. She donned a freshly washed chemise over clean hose and drawers. Eppy tied on the hoops around her waist and hips, underpinnings she'd mostly gone without in the field. A petticoat and a clean wool gown in shades of light green and blue went on overtop. The effect of the hoops and gown made her feel elegant, a definite difference from the blood, sweat, and muck of the battlefield. Annie wasn't one to desire being elegant often. She was much more comfortable with her hands steeped in healing herbs or working tidy stitches.

Eppy brushed out Annie's long locks until every knot had been detangled, and then she sprinkled a bit of scented rose water along the length. And when it was nearly dry, Eppy took hot tongs to her hair and curled it until ringlets formed around her face before piling those curls atop her head. There was a certain femininity in preparing oneself in this way, with hair done up, a fine gown, and silken stockings that felt unnatural to Annie. Though many likely considered her plain, at least in this moment, staring at her reflection in the looking glass she felt... like an impostor.

The men wouldn't even recognize her. They were used to her working looks—her hair hastily tied up in a knot on the top of her skull, her skin sallow from lack of sleep, dark smudges smeared beneath her eyes. The smudges lingered even now, but Eppy had attempted to hide them with a bit of powder.

Och, what did she care for the men's opinions of her anyway? She had no plans for any sort of clandestine affair or any intention of wooing a man. There was no time for any of that. But she might not deny a simple flirtation over dinner, if only to forget for a moment all the horrors of war.

It was difficult to think of the turmoil of their current existence. But for a few brief moments while the Jacobite soldiers were here, they'd know something of what it was like before the king had sent his son to butcher them all.

That put quite a damper on the festivities, and she felt almost silly for having Eppy curl her hair. Here she was primping and preening when at any moment a cannonball could rocket through their walls.

"Ye look beautiful."

Annie jerked her gaze up, catching Eppy's beaming reflection in the looking glass.

Drawing in a deep breath, she mustered the gumption to say, "Thank ye."

Annie glanced down at herself, feeling suddenly self-conscious. Though she thought she looked pretty...perhaps she looked *too* pretty. "I feel overdressed." Annie held up her hand when Eppy reached forward with a jar of tint. "No rouge."

"At least a scent then?"

"All right, but that is it, and then I need to get back to work. I've spent plenty of time being fussed over while the rest of the castle is working their fingers to the bone." As if to echo that point, there was a thud from somewhere down below. Likely the servants bringing in benches to the great hall.

Eppy held up two familiar scent bottles, one that was more an essence of spring, with floral notes, and one of autumn that was decidedly earthier.

"Given it is spring, I shall go with that scent."

"Wise choice, my lady."

Eppy plucked the cork from the vial, and Annie dabbed droplets of lavender, jasmine, and chamomile onto her wrists and to the spots behind her ears, wiping the excess along the back of her neck just beneath her hairline.

"Ye smell heavenly." Eppy put back the bottle.

"I'm glad to no longer smell of campfires and as though I've gone months without a bath."

Eppy nodded vigorously, disappearing from the room and leaving Annie a moment to herself. With a final sigh she descended the stairs, rounding the winding staircase, the hoops squeezing her for space on the narrow way down. Out one window, she caught a glimpse of approaching riders on the moor. The MacPherson crest waved proudly on a flag, the hissing cat unmistakable. As if to echo the crest, Pinecone hissed and batted at Annie's legs as she passed the old cat on the stairs. Graham's own pet was an elderly and notoriously angry gal.

Annie hissed back and then laughed at her own silliness. Down the rest of the way she went, pushing open the wide oak doors to the courtyard in time to see the men riding through the gate.

Two

"Who is this playing mistress of Cullidunloch?" Graham teased from atop his horse before swinging down.

Annie descended the front stairs of the castle, her shoes crunching on the courtyard gravel, and rolled her eyes. "Would it hurt ye greatly to give a lass a compliment?"

"Nay, of course no'. But I see no lass here, only a sprite." He smiled ruefully, and it was all she could do not to pinch the back of his arm when she embraced him.

"Brother!" Logan rushed from the stables where he'd been helping make room for the extra horses. His gait was a wee bit wobbly now but strong all the same. Annie felt a surge of pride at his progress.

Annie watched their reunion briefly before her gaze slid to the man who'd been riding at Graham's side. She recognized Craig MacLean from the campaign, though she'd often been too busy to say much to him. Any time she'd approached to speak with her brother, MacLean had turned around and gone the other way. She could only assume he either found her displeasing in some way or didn't like her being on the battlefield. Whatever his reasoning, she found his behavior unnecessarily rude.

The soldier swung his leg over the back of his horse in one fluid movement that left her momentarily stunned.

His plaid rose up just the barest amount, but enough for her to view several inches of the back of one well-toned thigh. Quickly she averted her gaze, instead taking in Logan's excitement; no doubt he was overjoyed finally to be in the company of his compatriots again.

"My lady."

A low, rumbling voice jerked her attention back to their new guest. When had he approached her? And why? He was nearly half a foot or more taller than she was and broader by two. He bowed swiftly, a movement so quick she barely had time to take in that it was happening. When he straightened, he reached for her hand. She'd been too stunned in the moment to offer it but quickly righted the situation.

He assessed her with cool eyes the color of emeralds ringed in sapphire. Ginger hair curled out from under his cap. He brushed his lips over the air half an inch above her hand, never quite touching her skin, more a perfunctory obligation than a sincere greeting. It marked her all the same. Lord, but he was even more handsome up close. He had a strong jawline, high cheekbones, and a broad forehead. There was a smattering of freckles across his brow and cheeks that gave him an impish look. If not for the cool way in which he regarded her, she might have expected to see his eyes dancing with mirth.

"Jasmine?" he asked, a slight twinkle in his eyes. "Reminds me of spring."

Why was he so solicitous now when he normally ignored her? Was it to show off in front of her brother? Annie snatched her hand back, trying as hard as she could not to frown in his direction. How dare he comment on her perfume? “That is the idea,” she retorted.

“Lieutenant MacLean, my lady, at your service. I thank ye for allowing us into your home.”

Annie frowned. “We are no’ strangers, sir.” Did he not remember seeing her—and avoiding her—for the past several months?

His eyebrows rose. “We are all strangers, my lady. For who can truly say they know another person well?”

Annie resisted the urge to roll her eyes and knock on the side of his head to see if there was any brain left inside all that brawn. And how did she say to him, *That's a load of horse—*

Annie shook those words from her head. “I've been on campaign with all of ye the last several months. And though it is true we've no' been formally introduced, we have sat in the same circles and eaten the same fare. I've even mended a few of your men.”

The lieutenant did not look shocked at all at her reminder. In fact, was that a smirk? His gaze swept over her appreciatively, sending an unwanted shiver of pleasure along her spine. “I know who ye are. And there've been more than a few of my men at your mercy. Ye clean up nicely, my lady.”

Oh, the insolence! “Aye, well, I've had a bath, a luxury no' afforded in the field of battle.”

“If only a bath were to make us all—”

“MacLean, are ye daring to speak to my sister about bathing? No' at Cullidunloch more than thirty seconds and already ye've forgotten about propriety.” Graham's tone was full of teasing, but heat still blasted Annie's cheeks.

"I was trying to remind the lieutenant that we are no' strangers," Annie said.

Graham laughed. "I'm only teasing, sister. Ye're bonnie as ever."

Annie watched MacLean nod, a slight twitch of his full lips the only non-smirking smile she'd seen on him. Even when he'd been in her brother's company at camp, he was always brooding. He reminded her of a man who took life a little too seriously, a man who wanted and needed to be the strongest in the room.

Despite his attitude, Annie was intrigued by him. She wasn't certain if it was more from his lack of interest in her so far or an innate urge to dig deeper into his mind—to unravel the mystery of this man and figure out what exactly was going on behind those eyes.

"A bonnie surprise," MacLean admitted, touching his fingers to his cap. "Forgive me, my lady, for not having noticed sooner."

A bonnie *surprise*? Did he have to take the compliment out of a compliment? Was he doing it on purpose?

Annie's chin rose three notches, if that was possible, and she assessed him with as cool a gaze as his. "Will ye no' come inside? Our housekeeper will show ye to a chamber. Or do ye prefer to bed down in the barn? Perhaps ye may feel more at home in such accommodations."

MacLean's impossibly defined brow arched high, and Graham gave her a stern look.

"My thanks for the offer, my lady, but I think I'll stay in the barracks with my men."

"Dinna be silly," Graham said, slapping him on the

back. "Annie is only jesting. We've plenty of room. Besides, ye're only here for a night. Ye might as well sleep comfortably."

Only one night, thank the heavens for that bit of luck!

MacLean glanced at her and then back at her brother. "If ye insist."

"I do. Come now, dinna insult our wish to bestow hospitality on ye." Graham flashed Annie a questioning stare, to which she simply looked the other way. What could she possibly say to her brother about his friend? That he'd ignored her for months and now when forced to acknowledge her was passing her barely veiled insults?

Unfortunately for her, looking away from her brother turned her gaze directly into MacLean's cool stare.

Straightening her shoulders, she reminded herself that even rude soldiers needed to enjoy an evening away from grief and strain. With that bit of charity lodged into her brain, she plastered on a syrupy-sweet smile that she was certain her brother would see through.

"Well, then, that's settled. Graham can show ye inside." The desire to flee rose within her, and she decided the role of host was better put on her brother's shoulders.

Had it been the same for MacLean when he'd come across her at the camps—this need to get away? Probably not. Disgust was not exactly the problem because he was not…disgusting. In fact, he was the opposite of disgusting. So what was it? She couldn't figure it out exactly. But whatever madness was leading her to a lapse in judgment was strong.

Her palms slickened, and no matter how much air

she sucked in, she never quite felt like she was getting enough. For some reason, MacLean's stare was giving her a fit of nerves. Nay! A strong and emphatic nay at that. Annie could not have stomached the things she'd seen if she was prone to fits of nerves.

Annie started to turn around, to walk away. To put as much distance between herself and this man who was unsettling her with every look.

"Wait, sister," Graham said.

Fists clenched as tight as her jaw, Annie turned slowly around to face Graham. He gave her an apologetic look and then flicked his gaze to Logan and the other men. "I've still to show the men to the barracks. Will ye take MacLean inside, please?"

Please? Her brother never used words like *please* or *thank you* or *sorry* with her. That had never bothered her much before now, but in that moment, the *please* set her ire on fire. It suggested that she had some sort of choice in the matter, and even she, who loved to take agency for herself, knew that she could not very well deny his request. He was, however, going to owe her a big favor in return.

Annie nodded curtly and began to march toward the door to the castle, her gaze flashing perfunctorily over MacLean as she indicated for him to follow her. MacLean followed, not making a sound, as though he were a ghost or very good at skulking about. At first, she was tempted to turn around to make certain he actually was behind her. Only she discovered that she didn't need to. She could feel him, as though the air around them both curved and bent with their movements. Her skin prickled but not with fear; if anything, it was awareness, which was confusing in itself. The sheer presence of him threatened to overwhelm her, and her lungs kept up with their stupid act of forgetting how to breathe.

Peace washed over her as soon as she opened the door, and though it didn't completely calm whatever attack of madness she was having, it did soothe the edges. This was her home, and this very door was the one through which she and her brothers had chased each other as children. She was safe within these walls.

The other reason for her relief was that their housekeeper, Mrs. Hannigan, was standing right beyond the threshold. *Thank all the saints in heaven.*

"Lieutenant," Annie said dismissively. "Mrs. Hannigan will show ye to your chamber."

"Thank ye, my lady." MacLean stepped around her to follow the housekeeper up the stairs. The scent of him—masculine, spicy, and rugged with just a hint of sweat—enveloped her as he passed. Heavens… How was it possible he didn't smell like a latrine like the rest of them?

"'Tis *our* pleasure," Annie said, not wanting to say the pleasure was hers, for it was most certainly not.

He turned around to give her one last glance before he rounded the corner, the gesture surprising her. That same intense stare slapped against her like a door being slammed in her face. Once he was out of sight, she was able to let out her breath, shaking her head at her own ridiculous antics. What the devil had gotten into her?

She glanced down at her usually steady hands only to see them trembling.

"Oh, for the love..." She did not finish that sentence, afraid that others might overhear. And if she gave voice to her reaction, she might make it linger.

Nay, what she needed to do was get that irksome Lieutenant MacLean out of her mind. And fast. With no wounded needing tending to, the kitchens were her best alternative for distraction. She would go see how the meal was coming along. The men would be hungry and thirsty. The sooner they were served a hearty meal, the sooner she could escape what she'd previously hoped would be a joyous evening.

Less than an hour later, a line of servants passed her carrying jugs of ale from the cellar and tankards in which to serve it.

As the guests filed into the great hall, Annie stood between her two brothers to greet each and every one. There had to be at least a hundred of them present. Every extra table, chair, and bench had been brought in to create enough room to seat them all. And tomorrow they'd do it all over again with the next set as the men traded places.

MacLean was one of the last men to enter. Though he'd not been covered in muck from the journey, she could tell he'd taken the time to wash. His face was clean and his hair still slightly damp. He'd changed his clothes too, out of his kilt and frock coat into a pair of well-fitting leather breeches and a crisp linen shirt. Did the man have to look so incredible in everything he wore? As he approached her in the line, her heart kicked up a notch, and she shifted on her feet, still uncertain why his presence made her belly do little flips.

"My lady," he murmured, his voice a low rumble that skated like a caress over her limbs.

"Lieutenant." She offered her hand in dazed confusion, her fingertips grazing against his callused palm, and then the heat of his mouth was fanning over her knuckles. Once again his lips didn't touch her skin, but she felt scorched all the same. And she didn't have the strength to pull away. The intensity of this man left her feeling a little dizzy.

"MacLean, sit with me," Graham said, breaking the moment, and immediately Annie's face was awash with heat.

She ducked her head, glancing out the sides of her eyes to see if anyone had noticed her overreaction.

He was going to sit at their table. Next to Graham. *She* always sat next to Graham, between her brothers. With luck he meant to put MacLean on the other side of them, and she wouldn't have to talk to the man at all. But as they approached their table, her brother pulled out her chair, indicating for her to sit. She did so quickly, avoiding eye contact with their guest. Instead she tucked in her skirts, scooted in the chair, and fiddled with the linen napkin laid out on her plate, wishing she could count the actual fibers that had gone into creating the fabric square. Then her brother did the exact thing that she had feared he would—he sat MacLean down right beside her on the left, taking the chair on MacLean's opposite side for himself, but not before he whispered, "Be nice to our guest."

Zounds…

That entire side of her, where MacLean took up the expanse of his chair, felt like it was aflame. What in bloody hell was wrong with her? How could this man make her feel as though she were not herself within her own skin? It was unsettling and confusing and…*hot.* And even if someone were to douse her with a bucketful of cold water, it would not extinguish whatever this flabbergasting heat was.

Was this how Jenny had felt about her husband Toran before they'd fallen in love? And he'd been an enemy of hers, not just her brother's friend. How much more difficult must that have been? Comparing their situations was silly, of course. She was not in love with this man. Nor would he ever be interested in her. The man was full of animosity toward her, even if he wasn't her enemy.

He was her brother's friend, and he fought for the prince. The same side as she was on. The same goal. The same values. And yet she was so…*unsettled.*

"My lady? May I?" He offered to pour her a glass of wine, and she nodded, shifting her glass closer to him.

Annie narrowed her eyes at his look of surprise. Had he not expected her to accept the offer? "Unless ye plan to poison me, sir?"

To her own surprise, his expression never wavered. His cool gaze locked on hers.

"I am no' the one with extensive knowledge of herbs, my lady, though we both know well how to kill a man."

Annie raised an impressed brow and gave a small grin. "Alas, I am in the business of keeping men alive, whereas ye, sir, are in a trade where deaths are collected as trophies. But—" She wiggled her glass. "I'll take my chances."

Her voice did not sound like her own. It sounded softer than usual, silkier, and that made her all the more irritated. She'd promised her brother she'd be nice, but why should she? MacLean had only been rude to her for months. Well, she supposed she could look at it as wanting to have a bit of fun. She could pretend he wasn't Craig MacLean but some other dashing soldier.

Annie was not a practiced flirt. This was a good opportunity to get some practice in. She knew how to sew up skin and pack a poultice full of healing herbs. A fever was her domain; she could wipe out the heat and sweat. If a tisane was needed, she could whip one up that would cure vomiting, headaches, and any other ills. She'd birthed bairns and cut off limbs destroyed in battle.

And yet the idea of talking with MacLean seemed an effort. It was thanks to his behavior on campaign, the way he'd run from her every time she'd drawn near. Had he imagined he was being respectful?

Or...did he dislike her for some other reason?

"Will ye return with Graham to Inverness?" he asked, as if he'd been thinking the same thing.

She glanced at him, lifting her glass to take a sip as if the wine might bolster her or provide her with an answer. It did neither, and so she set it back down.

"No' right away," she said. "But soon."

He nodded, frowning into his cup.

"May I ask ye something, Lieutenant?" She was going

to regret drawing his attention. She already regretted opening her mouth and forming the words.

He glanced at her, and she had the unsettling feeling that he knew what her question was going to be. "Aye," he drawled.

"Why do ye suppose it is we've no' been formally introduced before? Ye've been campaigning with my brother for months, and I know the two of ye to be good friends."

His gaze flicked away from her, and he took a hasty sip of his wine, the same way she'd done only a few moments before.

"I may have misspoken previously, but I did no' want to overstep."

What in the world was he talking about? "Pardon me?"

He wouldn't look at her, and she craned her neck to look into his glass to see if a fly or some other pest had flown into his wine.

What he said next stunned her. "We have met before, my lady."

Annie cocked her head to the side, puzzled. Impossible. "When?"

"'Twas—"

Graham slapped MacLean on the back, breaking the flow of their conversation and turning his attention away from Annie. "Logan was just asking what happened at Fort William. Care to tell him the story?"

It was on the tip of Annie's tongue to demand that MacLean finish their conversation first, but she didn't want to embarrass herself, nor did she want her brothers to overhear whatever explanation the man might have had, so she forced the need away.

MacLean laughed, a raw, low thrum of a sound that tickled its way along her spine. "Och, aye. The men easily surrendered, knowing that the last of their forts had already been taken, and so we scoured the stronghold only to find a woman sitting inside the great hall before a fire..."

Annie closed her mind to the story and wondered if there was any way she could escape this current awkward situation.

The men were behaving jovially, and the kitchen service was under control. She could always complain of exhaustion. That was one of the reasons that Graham had sent her back to Cullidunloch, after all, and it wouldn't take much to convince him. All she had to do was fake a few yawns, let her eyes droop, and sway as though she might collapse at any minute. Mind you, that was a tactic she'd often used when they were children to get out of a chore, so her brother might actually recognize it. Then again, he'd been concerned for her health of late, so he might not.

Annie faked a long yawn, tapping her fingers to her lips. No one noticed. Perhaps she needed to be a little louder. Loud yawners always got the attention of others. But she didn't want to gain attention from anyone other than Graham so that he'd send her to bed.

Och, for heaven's sake, this was ridiculous. She was a grown woman, had battled demons in red coats, and she couldn't simply stand up and say she was leaving the table?

Oh aye, she could. She was going to stand up right now and march out of this great hall. And she wasn't going to let her brother say she couldn't. It was either that or stand up and demand in front of everyone that MacLean finish explaining himself.

But then everyone would hear how he believed he knew her, and there was something in the way he'd been avoiding the topic that caused her to believe it wasn't for anyone else's ears. If that were the case, then perhaps she didn't want to know the truth after all.

Three

He'd been avoiding her for months. Ever since their first encounter, one she clearly didn't remember, but Craig did—quite thoroughly.

To make matters worse, Craig hadn't been lying to Annie when he'd said she was a bonnie surprise. The lass was more than bonnie, she was a downright goddess. Used to seeing her dressed for work at camp, he'd not anticipated the way her semiformal attire cinched at the waist and pushed up her ample breasts, just begging for him to look—which he was working mighty hard not to do. But every time he glanced toward her, there they were. Plush, silky-smooth breasts that he wanted to lay his head on. Breasts he wanted to taste. Breasts he wanted… *Christ!*

He had to stop. Now. Right now.

His breeches made his visceral reaction all too obvious. Not to mention that the lass was more likely to stab him through the heart than she was to accept him with willing and open arms. After all, she'd already tried to do just that a few months before, and he had the scar on his lip to prove it.

That thought was the perfect dash of cold water he needed to remind himself exactly whom he was sitting beside.

He gave Graham a suspicious look. Did his friend know what had happened between Craig and his sister?

Was that why Graham had sat them next to each other? To see if she would try to kill him again?

Either the lass was an excellent actress or she truly didn't remember their first rather…tempestuous encounter in January. Hell, she'd been acting as though she couldn't tell the difference between him and any of the other soldiers ever since. Was that a performance, or did she truly not remember?

Och, but the circles he was dancing in his head were a ridiculous torment.

There could be no doubt that he admired her. But he also thought her to be completely mad not only for her dedication to the men on the battlefield when most other women were safe at home but also because she legitimately did not seem to remember their encounter.

She stirred beside him, drawing Craig's attention back to her close proximity. He stiffened, glancing down at her, noting the stark-white knuckles on her hands, now folded in her lap. Was she just as uncomfortable as he was?

Perhaps she remembered more than she was letting on.

"This meal has been delicious," he murmured, glancing her way and trying like hell to keep his eyes pinned up to hers. "I thank ye for your hospitality."

Annie glanced up at him, a curious glint in her gaze. She looked about to speak, and so he sat back at little further, his attention fully on her.

"Ye're welcome, sir. If ye'll excuse me." She pushed her chair back abruptly and murmured a good night to her brothers, who waved her off as though they barely noticed she was taking her leave.

The lass didn't wait for their acknowledgment either as she made her way from the great hall, nodding at this person and that as she went.

Craig wished he wasn't watching her leave. Because his eyes followed the path of her swaying hips, exaggerated by the hoops at her sides. The abundance of fabric swaying around her bottom did nothing to curb his recollection of what she'd looked like in a pair of trousers. He'd seen that precisely once, and the memory had never faded. Most of the time she wore plain working gowns, but that one day he'd come out of his tent to see her leap from her horse, trousers clinging to her curves in a way that had made his mouth water.

A swift elbow in his ribs jolted him from his continued inspection of Annie's curving hips and bouncing bottom.

"I know that look," Graham said. "And ye'd best no' be giving it to my sister."

Craig groaned and rolled his eyes. "I dinna know what the hell ye're talking about."

Now it was Graham's turn to roll his eyes. "Drink, friend." And he poured him a large mug of ale.

Several hours—and many mugs of ale—later, Craig managed to make his way up the winding staircase, counting the doors and corridors along the way. He could have sworn that when the housekeeper had shown him to his room earlier in the day it had been on the fourth level. Or was it the third level, fourth door?

He paused a moment, swaying slightly, and leaned

against the stone for support. He tried to remember exactly, but the only thing about the day that really stood out to him was how disturbed he had been by Annie's presence. Not the type of disturbing that meant danger... Well, perhaps it *was* danger he sensed. The danger of falling into her bed—if she was willing. He'd avoided her for months, and now all he really wanted to do was get closer to her.

"Ye blasted cat, get back here!"

The shout came from above, the voice distinctly female and undeniably belonging to the very lady in question. Craig grinned to himself but was attacked by a feral tabby as it bolted down the stairs, batting at his legs with a hiss in his direction before disappearing into the dark.

He started up the stairs again, only to run straight into a very irate Annie. She'd been running down at top speed and hit him like a boulder crashing down a hill. Instinctively Craig's arms went around her, tucking his body so that he could protect her from the fall as he went backward and trying to land against the wall instead of end over end down the steps.

They crashed against the wall of the stairwell with a thud, her body, the curves, sinking into him and instantly sobering him from his boozy state. *Mo chreach,* but the lushness of her was delicious against him.

Bloody hell...

Craig glanced down at her face, taking in her amber eyes, wide with surprise, the long, sooty lashes, the pink of her cheeks, and the shocked gape of her plush lips.

"What happened?" he asked.

Annie pressed her hands against his chest, her gaze going to the places she touched. A shadow of curiosity flashed across her face before her expression went blank.

She pushed away slowly, and he kept his hands on her waist to be certain she was steady. He kept himself against the wall, the hard stone at his back an anchor for his body.

"My brother's cat… She's a termagant." Annie turned her arm over to reveal slashes in the white fabric, marred with growing splotches of red blood.

And it was also then that he noticed she was no longer in a gown but a thin night rail. That was why he could feel her so completely. His gaze dipped for the barest second to her breasts, pink flesh just barely visible but discernible enough beneath the fine linen that he was… Craig stifled a groan.

He focused on her face. "Ye shouldna be walking around the halls dressed this way with an army of men accepting your hospitality."

Her cheeks colored bright pink in the pale-lit stairs. "I did no' expect to run into anyone."

Craig tried to keep his gaze centered on hers rather than scanning the length of her body, taking in the way she looked in thin linen. He wanted to pull her back against him, to savor the feel of her barely covered body all over again. To burn into his memory all her heat and curves.

But, alas, she was starting to back away.

He grabbed hold of her hand, gently pulling her arm straight so he could look at the still-bleeding wound.

"Why did she claw ye?" he asked.

"Pinecone is a bit of a witch," Annie said with a roll of her eyes, tugging her hand. He didn't let go, smoothing the fabric up over her arm to take a closer look at the injury. "I dinna need ye to play nurse. I can take care of it myself. 'Tis just a wee scratch."

But it was more than that. There was a deep gash on her arm, two inches long, centered between two other, shallower scratches.

"We need to get these cleaned." He spoke the words despite recalling exactly what had happened the last time he'd tried to help her. He was willing to be skewered all over again. What did that say about him?

That he was clearly drunker than he thought. That was it.

"I dinna need your help." Though she said it, she didn't pull away this time.

"I know ye can mend yourself, lass, I've seen ye mend a hundred men or more. But sometimes it's just a wee bit easier to allow someone else to help."

She seemed to think about it for a minute and then tugged her hand away in earnest. "'Tis just a scratch."

"Ye really are stubborn." A lazy grin curled his lips. His earlier fear of her faded away to amusement.

"Pardon me?"

Craig shrugged. "We both know 'tis more than a scratch, and that middle one could likely use a few stitches. But rather than accept my help, ye'd prefer to suffer in silence."

She moved to cross her arms over her chest but winced when her arms made contact.

Craig reached for her hand once more. "Let me help ye, as a thank ye for all ye did for the men in my regiment. Ye can tell me exactly what to do the entire time if that makes ye feel better."

She frowned up at him. "Dinna make me out to be as much of a termagant as that blasted cat."

"Ye're the one who said it."

She frowned at him harder, and he half expected her to hiss at him. Instead she said, "Fine." She turned on her heel, marching up the steps with as much vigor as a soldier marching into battle. "Ye can sew me up, and then ye must leave my chamber."

"I had not planned to stay." Although he wouldn't have minded, and if she invited him, he was in just the kind of mood where he'd say *aye* with relish.

Annie mumbled something under her breath that he didn't quite catch. As they continued up the stairs, he kept his gaze centered on the back of her head. Instinctively, he followed the line of long, silky hair against the length of her spine to where it brushed the top of her rounded bottom. And right at the perfect eye level…that very attractive arse, swaying pink and free beneath the gown. *Bloody hell…* She was wearing *nothing* beneath the night rail. The lass was practically naked.

Craig jerked his gaze skyward. He wouldn't look. He couldn't look. As much as he wanted to. And oh God, did he want to.

Annie shoved open her chamber door and continued inside, but Craig paused on the threshold and took in the four-poster bed with its pile of lush, pale-pink-colored blankets and matching pillows. Decidedly feminine and not at all what he would have expected from her. The lass lived it rough most of the time in a camp filled with men and came home to a chamber fit for a princess of the blood rather than the daughter of a laird.

Settled before a hearth were a settee and two chairs. Along the opposite wall, interspersed with windows was a dressing table, a wash basin, and a screen for privacy. Beside the hearth was a large wardrobe that she stood before right now, staring at him over her shoulder.

"Are ye coming in or no'?"

"Aye," he croaked, feeling suddenly entirely too large and too male for this prim and dainty room.

She opened the wardrobe and pulled out a wide leather bag, the one he'd seen her carrying around the camp. She took out a few vials and then needle and thread and set them on a table. Then she disappeared behind the screen, and when the white chemise was tossed over the top, his mouth dried up completely, and he struggled to stand upright.

Behind that screen, she was naked, pink skin all on display. All he had to do was step behind it. A second later she emerged in a fresh night rail and raised a brow at what had to be his stunned expression.

"It had blood on it," she said by way of explanation, treating it as casually as if she were pointing out that it were night outside and that's why stars were in the sky. "All right, I need to wash it first." She approached a table set with a basin and pitcher, poured water into the porcelain bowl, and then rolled up her sleeve.

Craig came up beside her, picked up a linen cloth that lay beside the basin, and dipped it into the water.

"I can do it myself." She reached for the linen, but he didn't give it up.

"I know ye can." That was all he said, and to his surprise she quieted, thrusting out her arm and allowing him to gently wash the cut. He curled his fingers under her arm, holding her in place. Her skin was warm and softer than he'd imagined, given the roughness of her hands.

It did occur to him that he should leave. Being inside her chamber, washing her wound, was not his place. If her brothers or any of the servants happened upon them, he would be justifiably called to task, even though what he was doing was a favor to the woman who'd mended so many of his own men.

Craig was gentle in his ministrations, and Annie was brave, not making a sound, though he was certain the chill of the water on her torn skin had to hurt. Their eyes locked for a brief moment, and he stilled. "I'm sorry if this hurts ye, lass."

She lifted her chin. "There is nothing for ye to be sorry for, unless ye somehow managed to get that blasted cat to attack me."

"Afraid even my powers of persuasion are no' that persuasive. Why did Pinecone decide to give ye the claw?"

She snorted, a sound that was both unexpected and adorable.

"What's so funny?" he asked.

A twinkle of laughter flashed in her amber eyes. "'Tis funny to hear such a silly name coming from a man like ye."

"A man like me?" *A man who despises ye one moment and lusts after ye the next?*

"Aye. All…tough and strong."

He raised an eyebrow at that, a devious curl to his lips. "And the name Pinecone is not tough and strong?"

"Well, no' when ye say it."

He chuckled. "How did your brother come up with such a name for a cat anyway?"

"We found her in the woods about eighteen years ago, curled up among the pinecones. She'd been abandoned or run away from her mother, we'll never be certain which. But we couldna leave her there."

"So ye rescued her."

"Aye. But it was quickly evident that she preferred Graham over all others. This"—she nodded toward the gashes on her arm—"is not the first wound she's inflicted upon me, and she's only become more crotchety as the years have passed. Most recently she's decided that my chamber should in fact be hers, and so she didna like me coming in and lying down on what she considers to be her bed."

"Ah, and when ye chased her out, what were ye going to do with her?"

"I considered tossing her out the window, but cats have nine lives, and she'd only make certain to gouge my eyes out the next time 'round." Annie laughed. "I was trying to catch her so I could take her to Graham's room. He'd have soothed her hurt feelings."

"And yours?"

"My what?"

"Your hurt feelings, lass."

Annie shrugged. "I've no' got hurt feelings."

"Just hurt skin." He rubbed his thumb along the tender inside of her arm, just above the wound.

Annie regarded him for several moments, eyes squinted as she studied him. What was she looking for? "Aye."

She led him to the table and pulled the stopper from a vial, tipping it over, pouring several droplets of oil onto the tip of her finger, and dabbing it into the wound.

"What is that?"

"'Tis an ointment that will numb my skin as well as stave off infection."

"Ah." Craig used the water basin by the window to splash cold water on his face, and he wiped off the excess with his shirt in an effort to make certain he was completely sober before taking on the task of piercing her skin with a needle. He watched the way her fingers moved over the wound and took note of the slight tremble in them. "Allow me, lass." His voice was softer than usual.

"'Tis finished." She handed him the needle and thread. "But this task I will concede to ye."

He smiled as he took the needle in hand, his fingers steady. Craig was not a stranger to stitching. When he was on campaign—which was the better part of his fighting years—he had to stitch not only himself and his men if needed but his clothing as well, which his hose were currently not thanking him for.

Threading the needle, he stared down at her wound and hoped to hell whatever numbing agent she'd applied to her skin had taken effect. He did not want to be the one who hurt her.

She laid her arm in his palm, her soft skin warm against the callused surface.

Craig lifted his gaze to hers. "I'm sorry for any pain I am about to cause ye."

Annie shook her head but did not speak at first. She bit her lip and returned his gaze. "I am certain that ye'll do a good job."

"Are ye?"

She shrugged. "Ye'd no' have made it this far if ye didna know how to sew a decent stitch."

"That is no' necessarily true."

"Ye're right." She laughed softly. "But I dinna think ye'd have offered to help unless ye planned to harm me for some past transgression." Suddenly her mood shifted, and she tugged away from him. "Is that what ye were planning?"

Craig scoffed. "I should be offended ye'd even suggest such a thing. And let me remind ye, lass, as much as ye dinna like me, your brother and I are good friends. I'd no' ill use his family for anything."

Annie let out a long sigh, her shoulders relaxing. "I'm sorry for having implied it."

And for the very first time he actually saw the lass looking contrite. Now that wasn't saying much, since he didn't exactly know her all that well. It was enough, however, to give him pause.

Craig inclined his head and, with the needle threading complete, held the tip to her arm. "Are ye ready?"

Annie drew in a long deep breath and then nodded, her face the flawless image of pathetic subjugation. How funny he found that, given that she was used to being the one on the other end of the needle! She knew she was about to be put back together, not sacrificed to pagan gods, and yet she looked so much like a martyr right then and there that Craig had to repress a laugh. The lass obviously had a hard time accepting help from anyone.

"Well?" he asked, as she'd not actually answered him. He didn't count the sigh as speaking.

"Do as ye must."

Craig paused. "This is as we both must."

She shrugged. "I could just let it heal naturally."

"Ye could, and it would stay open twice as long as well as be more prone to infection. Ye know this better than I do."

"Also true."

Craig shook his head, took a firm grip on her arm, and pierced her skin with the needle. He worked as gently as he could to pull the thread through her flesh before piercing the opposite edge, tightening the wound until the edges were flush. He cut the thread with her tiny scissors and tied the first knot before starting the process again. Neither of them spoke, though Craig was breathing heavily through his nose and she was breathing heavily through her mouth. The two of them made a fine pair, each of them breathing with the force of a gale wind.

"Do ye need a break?" He was about halfway done.

"Nay. Do ye?" She arched a brow at him in challenge.

Truth be told, he could have used a pause for a

moment. Though he'd stitched up men in an emergency before, he'd never stitched a woman, and she was being so brave. But he was breathing hard, his head starting to ache around the edges, and his heart was pounding something fierce. And every time he pierced her skin he winced at the pain he was causing her.

"I dinna," he said at last.

"Keep going and let us be done with it."

"Are ye certain ye dinna need a dram of spirits?"

"I'm certain. Please proceed."

Craig continued with the job until the very deepest gash was closed. When finished, he clipped the final thread and inspected his work.

"What do ye think?" he asked.

She examined her arm. "I think ye've done a decent job of it."

"Only decent?" He raised a brow. The stitches were tight and even.

Annie smiled up at him. "Ye did well, sir. I am confident I will have only a minor scar." She popped the topper of another vial.

"Allow me."

She didn't argue, but he almost wished she had. With the ointment on the tip of his finger, sliding over the stitched wound, he was more worried than ever he might unintentionally hurt her. She didn't make a sound, nor did she wince.

When he was done, she pulled out a thin linen strip from her bag and started to wrap it around her forearm on her own.

"I am right here, lass. Just ask." He took the linen from her hand and finished the job. "Now what should we do about the demon cat to make certain she doesna try to gouge out your eyes next?"

Annie laughed at that. "I'm no' certain there is much we can do. She is mad."

Craig raised her fingers to his lips, and though he'd avoided touching his mouth to her skin earlier in the day, right then he couldn't help but brush his lips against her in truth. She smelled so good he was certain to taste her scent on his mouth. "Good night, my lady."

And then he let her go and turned on his heel. *Get the hell out of here afore ye do something ye regret.* The sooner he got away from her, the better. He'd have to make extra careful he didn't suffer any injuries tonight or before he left for Inverness in the morning. He was fairly certain he could keep himself away from her otherwise. Her and all her temptations.

MacLean ducked through her open door, disappearing into the corridor and sucking all of the air from the room with him. Annie stared down at her bandaged arm, stunned at what had just transpired.

She never let anyone help her. She was the one who helped people, not the opposite. And now when she'd been perfectly capable of taking care of herself, she'd allowed this man to do something she could have easily done herself. And he'd done a fine job of it, at that.

"Huh." Her arm barely even hurt, a dull throb that was diminished greatly by the ointment—and by the tingling on her skin where he'd kissed her.

There was a tinkling sound in the distance, which she knew to be Pinecone's wee bell, and Annie rushed to her door to shut it. She supposed Pinecone had gotten used to using her room while Annie had been away on campaign, but she was not about to fight for territory again tonight.

But when she peered out into the corridor, she saw something truly amazing. MacLean had crouched, lowering his great height down, and his hand was held out to the cat. Pinecone rubbed her face against his knuckles. Was that a purr? That traitorous cat.

And what was he saying to the animal? She couldn't make out the words.

"Careful or she'll think ye've a mind to take her to bed," Annie teased.

Pinecone hissed. Annie winced, the pain in her arm suddenly flaring as if the wee demon now had a power over her.

MacLean chuckled, looking back at her over his shoulder. A lock of his ginger hair had fallen over his forehead. That grin, the laziness of it and an almost sensual curl to his lips had her staring hard at him and at a loss for words. Slowly he rose to his full height, sending the cat running down the corridor in the opposite direction. Annie's breath went the way of her speech. He started toward her. Annie's feet remained rooted to the floor. How could she move? Should she? Aye, she should. Right now.

And yet she couldn't.

The closer he drew, the harder her heart pounded. Then as swiftly as he'd left her room he was back, standing on the threshold of her door, staring down at her with a look that both puzzled and intrigued her. His eyelids drooped, but not in a way that made him look tired. In fact, the way he was staring at her she suddenly felt very, *very* alive.

He was close enough to touch. Close enough to feel the heat of him.

Annie stared up at him, intensely curious and also incredibly cautious. She should back away and shut the door. And yet she wanted to reach for him. Which was extremely strange given that she should be annoyed by him. Whatever was coursing through her was the opposite of annoyed.

He reached for her, coming ever closer, and she sucked in a breath that lodged in her throat. His fingers grazed her arm, and just when she expected him to kiss her, he stopped his forward motion.

Belatedly, she realized he had taken the handle of the door behind her. That he'd leaned down to grab it, not to kiss her.

"Good night, lass." The words, said with a promise of something else, sent shivers racing up her spine.

"Good night." Annie backed into her room as he closed the door behind her. It shut tight, and she still didn't move, staring at the grains and knots of the wood where his face had been only moments before.

What was that all about?

Something was different. *Very* different. MacLean,

the man who'd avoided her like the plague while on campaign, had been kind. And then he had been solicitous, possibly even nice—to a cat that was likely a handmaiden of the devil.

And when he'd come back… His body had been so close, and she'd wanted to lean into him. Wanted to feel what it was like to have his lips pressed to hers.

She'd not kissed a man before. She'd often wondered if she would go through the whole of her life never having kissed a man. Devoted to Prince Charles and the Jacobite cause, the idea of men, of kissing and marriage, had been the last thing on her mind.

Of course she'd be lying if she said she had never fantasized about the moment. The prince had played a part in those fantasies when she'd nursed him back to health in January after the battle at Falkirk. Alas, his mistress would have had Annie's head for it, and that would not have allowed her to keep her age-old vows to help.

And when MacLean had stood and approached her just now, when he'd leaned down… Goodness, but her entire body was flushed. Annie pressed her hand to her beating heart, willing herself to calm. What must he think of her, the way she'd been standing there like a fool, her face upturned, lips parted, eyes wide?

"Idiot," she murmured to herself.

Why the hell would she have thought he would kiss her?

Why the hell did she want him to?

Annie backed away from the door and headed for her window instead, tugging it open. The chill evening air washed over her, cooling her skin and slowing the racing of her thoughts.

Tomorrow it would all be over, and he'd go back to Inverness. If she was lucky, she'd never see him again. Was that likely, though? Especially given his close relationship with her brother?

Annie had the sinking feeling that she was doomed.

Four

Four days later

Annie jerked awake, groggy and confused, at a shake of her shoulder. It felt like she'd only just fallen asleep. She blinked several times, trying to make out the shadowy figure looming in the darkness, and realized it was Eppy.

"What is it?" Annie asked, rising panic chilling her to the bone. "Has someone been hurt?"

She was often woken in the night when someone was in need of healing, but there was something about the way Eppy held herself, a stiffness that suggested fear.

"My lady," Eppy's voice held a nervous edge that woke Annie fully, and she blinked the sleep away. "The king's troops are outside the castle gate."

Nay! Annie bolted upright and swung her legs over the side of the bed. She'd made a habit of sleeping in her clothes while on campaign and wished it was one she'd kept at home as she rushed to dress.

Royal troops had not been to Cullidunloch since she was a lass of fourteen, but she'd never forget the foreboding sound of their fists on the door. The way they'd walked right through the lifted gate and threatened her family, the too-keen interest they'd paid in anything that looked of value, including Annie's young body. Annie shuddered at the memory. At least she'd had her mother and the great hall filled with Highlanders to protect her then.

"My boots." Annie searched the foot of her bed, hands swinging in the dark, hoping to connect with leather.

"I have them already." Eppy held them aloft and went to light a candle.

"Dinna light it," Annie said. "Let them think they have the element of surprise."

Annie tugged on her boots, lacing them only halfway in her haste, and was about to ask Eppy for her cloak when her maid set it on her shoulders. The bedchamber was frigid, but nothing compared to what it would be like outside.

Loud, panicked voices carried through the glass in her window.

"Where is Logan?" Annie asked. Graham had ridden out with the men and remained with Prince Charles to help him in laying siege to the forts in Inverness, and Logan had been left in charge of their family's castle. He might be in charge in name, but Annie still felt the need to protect him. She'd dealt with redcoats before; she would deal with them now and save her brother from their taunts.

"I dinna know, my lady. I woke ye as soon as I heard what was happening outside. I could see Cumberland's standard in the moonlight."

The Duke of Cumberland, in charge of King George's army, and the sworn enemy of every Jacobite who'd ever drawn a breath. That his men wore coats the color of blood seemed not to be a coincidence.

Annie tucked her loaded pistol into the belt looped around her waist and stuck a dagger in her boot. It wasn't enough, not if the English loyalists were able to break through the gates, but it would do some damage. She wasn't a particularly good shot or an expert in fighting, but she'd been lucky enough to do some training with her dear friends Jenny and Fiona, and there'd been a few occasions that those lessons had been put to use. She'd not had cause to kill anyone yet, but she'd had to ward off a few enemies on a battlefield—and a few drunken Scotsmen, too. The way her gut churned right now, she was certain tonight would be no different.

The corridor was dark when she left her room. She and Logan had made the decision to keep the sconces unlit at night so as not to draw the attention of any redcoats on the march, but that didn't seem to have helped this time. It was well past midnight, and yet the castle had been found. Which meant that in all likelihood, Cumberland's dragoons had been ordered here specifically.

Two guards, Seamus and Jameson, stood sentry at the base of the stairs, barring her way down. Annie had known them since they were small children, and they were both close friends of Logan's.

"My lady, Master MacPherson has ordered ye to remain above stairs."

Annie frowned. "In case ye've forgotten, I dinna take orders from my wee brother."

The men glanced at each other as though they'd been expecting just that response from her. "Alas, 'tis too dangerous outside, and Chief MacPherson did give Master

Logan the power to protect the castle and those within it," Jameson said.

"Stand aside," Annie ordered, ignoring their explanations. "Else ye'll be waking with a headache and no way of explaining it."

This was a false threat—she wasn't likely to knock out either of them with the other there to fend her off. But Eppy came to stand beside her all the same, as if she'd be any help felling these two well-trained soldiers.

Seamus and Jameson exchanged yet another glance.

"Och, will ye just spit it out? Ye know it is no' that dark in here and I can see the two of ye looking at each other."

"My lady, please, we beg ye. Dinna go out there."

"I have as much right as my brother to defend my family's house." This wasn't exactly true, as Graham had given Logan the authority. But she didn't want Logan to go out there, not when he'd only been so recently brought down. Still, the guards did not back down, puffing their chests as if to broaden themselves enough to block the way entirely.

Annie stepped off the bottom stair, into their space, and the two of them backed up a pace to give her room. She stared up at them, frowning. "Ye realize I was on the field of battle with Graham at Falkirk just a few months ago, aye?"

Neither of them made a move or sound.

"And after that I traveled with Prince Charles and his entourage, which included my eldest brother, as they lay siege to Fort Augustus and Blair Castle?"

Again, blank stares—not a single nod nor a syllable uttered.

"If my brother would allow me to accompany an army,

then I should think he'd be fine with me helping Logan shoo away a few dragoons."

"'Tis no' a few, my lady. 'Tis an army of hundreds of men. Maybe a thousand."

Annie's heart did flutter then. When Eppy said she'd seen Cumberland's standard, she'd not been able to tell her how many men stood beyond it. That number of men outside their castle gates could only mean one thing.

Visions of what Annie knew the redcoats were capable of left her breathless. Plundering, beatings, rape. Neither the age nor the sex of their victims mattered; they sought to humiliate all, strip them of their humanity and pride.

For some, unfortunately, that worked. The dragoons would tear apart the castle, steal their food, take their livestock, and then burn it all to the ground. Those who were strong enough to pick up the pieces would. And she prayed they were all strong enough because it was too horrific to think about the alternative.

Would their tenants have had time to hide from such a vast army? She swallowed hard, beads of sweat prickling beneath her arms. Cullidunloch didn't even have fifty soldiers at its disposal. Fighting back was not possible. It would be an annihilation.

"Our people?" she managed to say without choking.

"I dinna know, my lady." Seamus's face was tight. Did he truly not know, or was he hiding something?

The doors to the castle burst open then, and another of her brother's guards stopped short upon seeing her. "My lady, Master Logan sent me to make certain that ye and the other women in the clan were hidden well."

Blast! She'd not beaten Logan out. Annie squared her shoulders. "I intend to join my brother outside."

The warrior shook his head vigorously. "That is no' possible, my lady. He is going to have to let the dragoons inside."

"What?" Annie's voice was breathless with fear. She knew Logan wouldn't do it if he had a choice, that it probably was the only way to avoid any kind of battle, and yet it was also the worst of ideas. Once inside, there might be no getting them out again.

"We will no' stand for a siege," he explained, "and they have promised no harm to our people if we give them a night's lodgings on their way to Inverness."

Annie felt her veins running cold, her body as frozen as though she'd been doused with a bucket of icy water. No good could come from the enemy breaching their walls, even if they made promises of peace. No good could come from the enemy sleeping here. Every woman was at risk.

Graham and his soldiers had left but a few days before. If only they'd been able to stay a few days longer... Ironically she'd been happy to see the back of Lieutenant MacLean, and not just because she liked to watch him walk away. Part of her had been jealous that the men were headed back to the war camp. That was where she belonged as well, but Graham insisted she stay and rest a bit more.

"My lady," Seamus said. "We need to protect Logan. We'll have a harder time doing that if we have to worry about ye standing beside him."

Annie slowly nodded because if Logan was insistent on it, then that meant there was something bigger afoot. And Seamus made a good point. She didn't want them worrying about her instead of Logan.

"Where are the other women and children now?" she asked.

"They're preparing to find shelter, my lady."

"Very well, have them come to the crypt and I'll join them there."

The guards all gave a single nod.

"We'll make certain they come to the crypt, my lady," Seamus said.

"Aye, I'll gather them myself," Jameson added.

Having two men she trusted seeing to the women, Annie glanced at Eppy. Her maid's face had paled considerably, understanding in her eyes. Eppy had been with Annie on the fields of battle, had seen the aftermath in the villages ravaged by redcoats. She was not naive to the dangers they would be exposed to upon opening their gates to Cumberland's men.

Without a word, the two of them hurried through the keep. They avoided going outside by way of the butlery and down the steep dark stairs to the musty cellar that connected to the crypt of the kirk. It was dark inside, but Annie had spent hours down there as a youth during games of seek and find and knew the hallways well. She headed straight for the place she knew there to be a candle and lit it with a flint, lighting up the dank space.

Eppy's face loomed before hers, eyes wide as though permanently pinned open.

"Everything will be fine," Annie said, grateful to hear her voice reflecting a confidence she didn't feel.

Eppy nodded and then set about dusting off an old crate. "For ye, my lady," she murmured and then stood sentry beside it.

"I've no need to sit just yet, Eppy, but my thanks for the consideration."

Eppy murmured a reply, but it was lost in the rush of blood in Annie's ears.

She strained for any bit of sound above them. A murmur of voices. Shuffling of feet. Scraping of boot-heels or chair legs. Anything. *Something.* But all was silent. As a child, she'd sat down here for hours, hidden in the corner, waiting for the same hints of life beyond these dank walls. Back then, she'd been rewarded with plenty of sounds. The eeriness of the silence now was terrifying.

Hours seemed to pass in what was probably only minutes, the silence dragging on interminably. Annie tried to distract herself by checking the small shelf for extra candles and finding three. She checked the door to see if it was locked—it wasn't. Where was Jameson with the clan women and children?

Growing weary of waiting, Annie stood abruptly. She had to go find them and make certain everyone was all right. The guards had heard her say the crypt, hadn't they? "I'll be right back."

"I'm coming with ye."

Annie was about to argue but then decided against it. After all, she wasn't going far. Up the stairs she crept, toward the kirk, and then slowly turned the handle and pushed the crypt door open just a touch. No sounds filtered down from the kirk, and so she crept up the open stairs that led into the nave only to find the chapel dark, empty, and silent.

"Where is everyone?" she whispered.

Annie could just make out Eppy's face, and she looked ready to be ill.

"They should be here."

Annie took a step forward, but Eppy put a hand to her arm to still her. "We should go back down. I've a bad feeling."

Annie's stomach churned, the same uneasiness sweeping through her, but she shook it off and gently squeezed her maid's arm. Annie went toward the stained-glass windows to see if she could make out what was happening outside.

The closer she got, the colder she felt. A draft blowing from somewhere reached its cold fingers up the skirts of her gown. Her fingers tingled, and even her toes were going a little numb. The pulse point on her neck jumped. Was that smoke? She drew in a deep breath, swearing she could smell something burning.

In the bottom corner of the glass, where it wasn't colored, orange flames danced across the courtyard. Fire engulfed the roof of the keep and lit the spaces behind the windows. The smaller outbuildings attached to the keep, the kitchens—all were wreathed in flames. Livestock and horses ran to and fro...among the bodies on the ground.

"Oh my God," she said, her hand coming to her throat, and bile burned in her chest.

Eppy brushed up beside her, peeking through the glass. "We need to go back into the crypt, my lady." Her voice sounded chilled. "In case they come in here next."

They would, Annie knew. They'd have beaten whoever dared defy them—which would have been most if not all of her brothers' men—and then they'd set the castle to flames. The church was next, the most obvious place for anyone to hide. Except no one else had come.

Her people. *Oh God, the people!*

Annie nodded, though she couldn't make her feet move. It was as though they'd been bolted to the floor. She couldn't seem to draw breath either. Where was Logan? Seamus? Jameson? Where were the women and children? Had they found safety elsewhere?

A sound from near the chancel had her squinting her eyes. She glanced up, expecting to see the roof burst into flames from a lit arrow and pieces of the rafters falling down around her. But instead, several shadowy figures shifted about on a balcony.

"Who's there?" she hissed. "Come out."

Slight figures of women and children emerged from the darkness. Where were Seamus and Jameson? Fear for her guards ripped through her.

"Ye're no' safe here," Annie said. "Come down to the crypt."

"We dinna want to be stuck down there with the dead," replied the tear-choked voice of a woman.

"Better to be stuck with the dead than be dead," Eppy replied. "They're going to burn the kirk just as they are burning the castle."

Several wails from the chancel followed that bit of news, and mothers hurried to hush their children. Rather than argue more, the women and children stood and made their way down to the nave and the door that Annie held open to the crypt.

"Go down," she said when they paused. "God will be with ye, and so will Eppy."

Before anyone could pick up on what was happening, Annie shut the door behind them, and ran to the back of the church where a small door led outside to Father Mac's private garden. Aye, she knew it was madness to go outside when their assailants were all around, but how else was she going to see what was happening? Annie had never been one to sit idly by. She was often right there on the fields of battle with the men, dragging the wounded away.

The peace of the garden was broken by the thick scent of smoke and shouts of panic. Groans of pain. People running. Angry barks.

Every fiber of her muscles strained to run to the keep, to make sure that her brother was all right. To check on everyone. But if she were to dash straight into the chaos, her brother would be very angry with her. She'd be defying a direct order.

Annie stood stock-still in the garden. The right side of her yearned to go and take care of the wounded. The left side rooted her in place, demanding that she return to the crypt and care for those who had yet to be harmed.

She listened, closing her eyes a moment to make out any patterns to the sounds. Listening for the obvious and the not so obvious. Crying. Shouting. Screaming. Crackling rush of an out-of-control blaze. What she didn't hear was the clash of steel on steel or the sounds of men fighting. Not even a warning shot from a pistol.

Annie opened her eyes. Had Cumberland's men left already? Come only to set her home afire?

To her right was a tree. In two steps she was at the base. Annie reached up to grab a branch, the cold bark cutting into her fingers, and swung herself up, climbing as high as she dared. From there, she stared out over the wall to see for herself how many of Cumberland's men had come to torment them.

Not a single redcoat was in sight. She squinted her eyes, certain the dark had to be playing tricks on her. But her eyes had not lied. Having brutalized the people, no doubt stolen their stores and ravaged the castle so no survivors had a place to be safe, they were gone. They'd been doing this across Scotland—pillaging and burning as if they'd all gone back to the dark ages without a care to the cost to those who remained behind.

She started to climb down when something else caught her eye. On the ground outside the garden, in the field, was a lumpy sack of cloth or… She squinted again. A person. There was a person—fallen and… She didn't want to think about whether they lived or died, only that she needed to bring them back within the walls. Where was her brother? Where were Seamus and Jameson?

Annie hurried down the tree, her hair catching on a broken twig and yanking painfully at her scalp, but she ignored it in her haste. Ignored, too, the ripping of her skirts. She leaped to the ground as soon as it was safe, her feet pounding hard on the earth. She toppled forward slightly, catching herself on her hands before bouncing back up and running at full pace toward the gate and out to the road.

Behind her, the heat of the fire warmed her back.

She skidded to a halt, dropping to her knees beside the man, knowing instantly from the dark curls it was her brother.

"Logan!" she shouted, touching his shoulder and rolling him onto his back. His eyes were closed, one of them red and swollen. The rest of his face was in the same battered state, and his clothes were torn and bloodied.

She pressed her hands gently to the sides of his face, palpating the injuries and then doing the same to his arms, his legs, his ribs. He groaned when she pressed his sides, clearly feeling several broken ribs, and then she felt the warm gush of blood. The wound was a circular hole. They'd shot him. They'd *shot* him! Annie yanked at his shirt, ripping the fabric and pressing the freed scraps to the wound.

"Dinna die on me, brother."

With one hand holding the cloth in place, she checked the rest of him. Luckily his other limbs were not broken, save for several fingers on his right hand—his fighting hand. She hoped whomever he'd gone up against had been given a similar beating.

Logan's eyes blinked open and then rolled closed once more.

"Wake, brother. Wake up!" she demanded.

"Seamus…" he murmured. "He was taken."

Dear God… Their men in the hands of those monsters. Thinking about it made her want to vomit. The dragoons would surely not keep them alive for long. How realistic was it to think that he'd allow the prisoners to be bartered back? And what could she possibly give them that they'd want?

"Can ye stand?" she asked. He was badly hurt, but without broken limbs, he might yet be able to walk—at least limp—to safety. The men had left without burning the kirk; they could go there and rest. She needed someplace safe to get the bullet out.

"I can try."

Annie worked to pull his right arm over her shoulder, avoiding touching the broken fingers on his right hand. She was able to get him to sit up, but he hissed in pain.

"Come on, ye're almost there," she said.

"Just leave me here." Logan tried to lie back down, but she wouldn't let him.

The ground rumbled with the thunder of approaching riders. "Come on, Logan, they are coming back." Her voice held a note of hysteria.

"Run, then."

The defeat in his tone made her want to scream obscenities, and she never used vulgar language. "Dinna let those bastards beat ye," she said.

"They already have."

"Ye're alive, which means they didna."

That seemed to get him moving, and he put more effort into standing.

They'd made it almost to the arching gate of the keep when the horses were nearly upon them. "My lady! Master Logan!"

Annie had never been so relieved to hear Jameson's voice. She turned slowly, her brother's weight making it hard to stand up straight. Jameson had returned with a dozen or so burly Highlanders, crofters wielding shovels and pitchforks.

"He asked me to get help," Jameson said. "We're too late."

"No' at all," Annie said. "Ye came back just in time. The kirk is full of the women and children, and I'm going to get my brother cleaned up. He's taken a bullet." She glanced behind her at the burning keep, a heaviness beyond Logan's solid weight making her spine curve.

"Once Logan's wounds are dressed, I need ye to take him and the rest of the clan to my cousin Ewan at Cluny Castle. He'll keep them safe."

"My lady, that's all the way in Aberdeenshire."

"Aye. Far from Cumberland's army and the fighting."

Jameson looked like he wanted to argue, but she pursed her lips and jutted her chin forward to forestall his complaints.

"Where is Seamus?" he asked instead.

The weight on Annie's shoulders grew tenfold. "He's been taken."

Jameson didn't speak, but the way his features tightened was enough to break her heart. Seamus and Jameson were a pair, one not often seen without the other.

"I'll get him back," she promised.

"What?" Jameson looked puzzled, and then understanding dawned. "Nay, ye must come with us."

"I'm no' coming." She shook her head. "I need to go to Graham. To tell him what's happened here, about Logan, Seamus, and the others. There has to be a way to get the men back, and since Logan is unwell, I intend to see it done myself." As if to prove that point, Logan collapsed, taking her down with him.

Five

"CUMBERLAND'S ARMY IS ON THE MOVE," CRAIG TOLD his men as they gathered for the first morning muster in the large bailey at Inverness Castle four days after having left Cullidunloch Castle. "And so we must also be ready. We travel to Culloden, where we will meet them on the battlefield tomorrow."

They'd been making camp at the castle for the past month, along with other soldiers in Prince Charles's army. The cold and snow had not kept them from their campaign, nor had a shortage of food, which left them with rations that never quite filled their bellies. In fact, the best meal they'd had in the past month had been when they'd convalesced at Cullidunloch, partaking in the hospitality of a certain lass he was trying to forget. His belly growled at the memory.

They weren't going to let a little thing like hunger stop them, however. Not when they needed to retake as many of the stolen properties from the English as they could. The goal, as always, was to oust King George and to get the Stuarts back onto the throne. Weather couldn't put a stop to progress.

Since the Battle of Falkirk Muir in January, when they'd crushed Cumberland's fancy redcoats, they'd continued on a course that the chicken-livered royal army hadn't been able to match. They'd retreated to the west coast, the lot of slimy weaklings, or back to England awaiting better weather.

And Craig supposed that "better weather" was now. The snow was newly melted, the ground only a wee bit soggy, though there was still a brisk wind that could put a chill in a lesser man's bones. They were most likely in for another snow as well.

"Prepare for battle, men. For tomorrow we're going to kick those bastard arses back to hell."

His men let out whooping cheers, echoed from across the moor by their fellow clansmen who prepared for exactly the same thing. Several hours later, those clans arrived at Culloden, building up their camp around the manor house, which the prince had claimed as his headquarters.

Outside his tent, Craig stood and stretched, pleased to see that the men seemed mostly in good spirits. At movement in his peripheral vision, Craig glanced to his left. Graham MacPherson approached him, his brow furrowed into tight angry lines. Immediately Craig was on alert.

"What is it?" Craig asked.

Graham nodded his head to the right. "A word."

Craig stepped out of earshot.

"I've just heard from Lord Murray that we're going to attempt a predawn attack. Take the loyalist bastards by surprise."

Craig nodded. Lord George Murray was a general in the prince's army. Though he'd voiced often that he thought the prince was a reckless adventurer, he felt strongly enough for the cause that he continued to lead the Jacobite army. "Good, we'll annihilate them before they wake to sip their morning tea."

Graham smirked. It was a running joke among them that the dragoons woke in the morning and preened about their campsites with cups of tea, sipping like ladies in their drawing rooms, while he and his men woke to a dram of hearty whisky or a mug of stout ale.

"We'll be ready to move whenever 'tis necessary." Craig turned back to the camp to look over his men, the best of the best and always prepared.

Graham grinned. "Just think, in a week's time or so we'll all be back home with our feet up, a warm bowl of stew on the table, and the bloody loyalists back in England where they belong."

"Is that what ye dream of? A warm bowl of stew?" Craig teased, rubbing his elbow into Graham's ribs. "I myself dream of a willing wench or two rubbing my aching bones, and—"

"I dinna need any more details," Graham interrupted with a snort. "The stew comes after I've had my way with a half dozen pretty lasses. Or just one feisty one." His voice turned wistful, and Craig had an idea about whom Graham was waxing nostalgic—a lass who was now entirely unattainable, as she'd wed only a few months prior. Jenny Mackintosh, a warrior in her own right and a renowned beauty. All the men daydreamed about her.

Craig, however… Lately he found himself fantasizing of a certain termagant. A brave and maddening woman. He'd lied when he'd said he'd dreamed of a willing wench or two because in truth, these past few nights, there'd been only one woman filling his nighttime imaginings. And she was just as unavailable for him as Jenny Mackintosh was to Graham.

"Colonel Jenny is spoken for, man. I think Toran Fraser would put up a deadly fight if ye tried to take her," Craig taunted.

Graham chuckled. "A man can dream. And to think I'd known her since we were both bairns. So many missed opportunities." He clucked his tongue. "What about ye? Have ye a woman at home?"

Home with the MacLeans was not something Craig talked about. Indeed, Craig rarely shared anything personal with anyone. For him, home was on the field with his men. Home was riding his horse into battle. Home was protecting the lands so that other people could sit before their roaring hearths while he stayed out in the cold. Home for him was not home at all.

And truth be told, there were no women back home who interested him. Not unless Doctor Annie was going to make a house call.

Craig stared at his men, who sat in clusters talking over their morning ales. Those who'd grown up with him knew his story, the struggles of being a lad with a demanding father. A lad who didn't grow into his own until much later. No one who looked at him now would think he'd once been thinner than a blade of grass and shorter than a mushroom stump. He'd been cursed with a tiny frame from birth until he was about thirteen, and before his body had somehow conjured a miracle, he'd been teased and taunted for it. Tossed into the ring with lads twice his size by his own father, a well-respected hero within their clan until the day he'd died.

Then, the summer he'd turned fourteen, things had started to change. Craig had suffered terrible pains in his limbs, waking him at night and making him think he might be dying. The only thing that had made the pains ease was movement—to run, to toss weighty stones, to lift anything heavy he could get his hands on, to work his body to the point of collapse, as if training to fatigue somehow overpowered the pain of his bones deciding they were ready to grow. Months later people were gawking at him, and when summer faded into fall that year, he'd been easily five inches taller and a stone heavier. The same thing happened the next summer and the next until he was eighteen years old, taller than most of the men in his clan and easily two stone heavier, his body strong and agile. Those who'd picked fights with him at his weakest shook with nerves when he asked for a rematch—and *won*.

Craig had swiftly worked his way up through the MacLean army after that, but he never found the one thing he sought—approval from his father. The man had died that summer, leaving Craig to wonder if he ever would have gotten that respect, if he'd ever have seen his father look on him with pride.

To mull over those memories of home when there were things to be done here at camp was a useless waste of time. And so Craig did what he always did: he smirked at Graham and turned the conversation into a jest.

"Nay, I've no' got a woman at home. But I heard your sister was in the market for a man."

Graham slugged him on the arm, as was expected, and Craig barely wavered, laughing his arse off and brushing away the sting of the blow.

"Dinna touch my sister." Though Graham frowned, his eyes danced with humor.

Thank God Annie remained at home for the time being, and probably with good reason. Because after having spent time with her at Cullidunloch, Craig wasn't certain he could continue to avoid her. He'd been relieved to get back to Inverness Castle and away from temptation.

Graham was relieved for different reasons. The man had fretted for months over his sister's safety and her virtue both when she rode with them. From the dragoons and from the many Jacobites who wished to woo her.

Before that evening at Cullidunloch, Craig had barely spoken two words to the lass since their first encounter. Would he ever see her again? Why did the idea of not seeing her make his chest tighten uncomfortably?

Och, what did it matter? He wasn't in the market for a woman. Lover or wife, didn't matter. Both were distractions for a man who made a battlefield his home. He'd have to keep her protected because Annie could hardly protect herself.

But, nay, wee Annie MacPherson was never going to be his. And all the flashes of memory that revolved around her needed to leave him the hell alone, else he was never going to get another good night's sleep. Shaking away her haunting image, Craig chuckled and rubbed his smarting arm.

"Dinna ye fash, man. Annie is the last woman on earth I'd ever see myself attached to."

Now Graham frowned at him even more. "And why's that?" Offense laced his words.

Ballocks. Craig grinned and shrugged. "Because I fancy living. Though she'd probably tend my wounds after running me through. Just doesna seem worth it."

Graham chuckled. "Aye. Ye might just be smarter than the rest of these bastards."

If he was smarter, he'd not be dreaming about a lass who was so unattainable, but he couldn't very well tell Graham that.

"Now, that is a sure thing." Craig clapped Graham on the back. "Where are we headed?"

"Culloden. We'll meet up with other Jacobite forces there for a predawn attack like we did at Prestonpans, only this time in Nairn. Word has reached us that Cumberland has set up a camp there."

Back in September they'd been victorious against the king's forces in their first major military action since the prince had landed. If they could duplicate that victory, then this war would be over before the end of the week. "We'll be ready when ye make the call to move out."

Graham nodded and started to walk away but then turned back, his brow furrowed with curiosity and something a bit deeper. "Can I ask ye something?"

Craig shrugged, studying his friend's odd behavior. "Ask away."

"If tomorrow—"

Craig cut him off. "No *ifs*." He crossed his arms over

his chest, showing Graham he meant exactly that. Victory or death.

"Fine. Let us say I should fall and ye do no'."

Craig's arms fell, and he opened his mouth to interrupt again, but Graham held up his hand. "I'm serious. I need ye to promise me that if I should fall, ye'll be the one to tell my sister. Protect her. Logan will be devastated, and Annie…"

This was not at all what he'd expected to hear, and the great responsibility Graham was giving him was an honor he didn't even want to consider having to fulfill.

"Of course I will."

Graham nodded again and started to move away, but Craig stopped him this time. "Why me?"

Graham flashed him a confident grin. "'Tis simple. As ye said, ye're the last man on earth to want her. I know she'll be safest with ye."

Craig laughed, feeling the lie all the way to his toes. "I'm the safest bet, then?"

"Aye."

"Better no' fall under those bastards, then."

"I dinna plan on it." Graham took two steps and then stopped again, his face serious this time as he spoke. "Truth is, MacLean, ye're the best of all of us. I canna think of anyone else I would rather have as protector to my family."

Craig held his fist to his heart. "Ye have my word."

When Annie reached Inverness Castle the day after the fire, the evidence of the men's camp was all around them. Dozens of campfire circles had been abandoned, socks that needed mending deserted in the muck along with other rubbish. The air was thick with their smells, not all of them good.

Eppy and the two guards Jameson had insisted she take sat on their horses beside her, the four of them staring down at the abandoned camp, frowns on their faces.

"Perhaps there is someone in the castle who can direct us," Annie suggested.

Thomas and Gregory nodded, one of them peeling off in that direction, with the three of them following. Annie's insides were twisted into knots. Extreme guilt lodged in her chest for not remaining with Logan as he and those left from the wreckage of Cumberland's onslaught headed east for their cousin's castle and the safety his walls could provide.

She feared him succumbing to his injuries along the way or a murderous highwayman intent on stealing what meager possessions they had, which were few. They were lucky that the fire had only burned the keep, the kitchens, and a few of the outbuildings but they had not touched the stables except to steal some of the horses. Though the enemy had torched the armory, small barracks where weapons had been hidden beneath the floor had remained untouched. They'd been able to gather some supplies and weapons to protect themselves.

Jameson had not wanted to leave her, but she'd insisted he go with Logan. How else could she live with the idea of not going? Of not being with her brother when he needed her most? She had to know he was protected by one of the best.

Despite Jameson's reservations, it only felt right that she be the one to tell Graham what had happened. Annie couldn't have stayed at the burned-out castle, and she wasn't going to journey across the country away from the prince's army where she belonged. She needed to be in the thick of it, beside Graham.

Graham and the other Jacobites had to be warned that Cumberland's army was on the move, that they were pillaging and murdering their way through the countryside. Aye, she knew her home had been a target specifically because of what it represented, but the MacPhersons weren't the only ones fighting against the loyalist government. They were not the only ones who wished for Prince Charles Stuart to take his rightful place.

The Jacobite armies had been fighting for decades for the Stuart line to be put back on the throne. None of them were loyal to King George, sitting on his fancy throne in his fancy castle back in England, a country that was not even truly his, the lineage that put him there far behind the Stuart line in precedence. The Protestants in the courts couldn't imagine a Catholic on the throne again, however, even though it was his right.

As if allowing Prince Charles to act as regent for his father King James was going to take them back to a time when those of differing religious beliefs had been burned at the stake. As if King George wasn't punishing them already for practicing what they believed!

They just wanted a king who wouldn't persecute them at all. Annie wanted to be able to ride across the moors to see Jenny and Fiona without worrying that some arse-hole in a red coat was going to leap from the trees and rape her until she wished she were dead. King George didn't care that they were vulnerable. They held no value for him other than as vessels for the depraved pleasures of their tormentors.

The centuries-old war of English versus Scottish still thrummed in the veins of everyone, even after their king-doms had been united by King James VI of Scotland, I of England in 1603. It didn't matter. One king, one man, couldn't wipe away hundreds of years of torment.

Thomas returned from asking his questions at the castle. "They've ridden for Culloden, my lady."

"Culloden." Annie rolled the word around on her tongue, fear prickling her skin. "Did they say why? Have they gone to battle?"

Thomas shook his head. "I dinna know, my lady. 'Haps we should stay here until they return. We can protect ye better within castle walls. I dinna like the idea of heading in the direction of the fighting." He looked over his shoulder. "Even now the loyalists could be behind us, in front of us."

"We have to keep going." Annie shook her head. "I'm no' staying here. My brother—" Her throat closed on a near choke. "My brother needs to know what happened to Logan, to our home. And I need to be there to…to help after the battle, if there is to be one. I made a vow to this country, to the prince, and I'll be damned if I'm going to let that butcher make a liar of me."

"My lady," Gregory said. "What happened will still have happened after the battle. They could just be out on a raid. The servant in the castle said that food was becoming scarce. If we wait, there's a chance they will return shortly."

What happened will still have happened after the battle. Harsh words, though she knew them to be true. Still, they stung. Frustration coiled inside her. If Jenny could ride into battle, if Fiona could traipse the countryside unnoticed, why couldn't Annie ply her trade as easily? She had never been one to sit idly by, and she wasn't about to start now.

Straightening her shoulders, she looked right into Gregory's eyes. "I am no' a wee miss, nor am I a soft lady who needs to hide. I am no' unused to battle, and I dinna need ye to remind me of the dangers. I am going to Culloden. I am going to tell my brother what happened at Cullidunloch, and I am going to resume my duty in the prince's camp. And I dinna need your permission to do it." She couldn't put voice to the fear in her chest or the visions in her head of Graham going into battle and not coming out of it again. It was a fear she felt upon waking every morning and had since she was a child and it had been her father riding into battle.

Annie's chest tightened, a flicker of warning at just how close she was to the breaking point. How many more terrible things had to happen before this war was over? She shoved that flicker deep down, burying it. There was no time for fear.

The strained look on Gregory's face softened. "My

lady, 'tis my duty to keep ye and your family safe, and if that means I accompany ye to your brother as ye wish, then I will do so. I would no' seek to keep your skill from those who need it."

"Thank ye, Gregory."

He inclined his head toward her.

Annie glanced at Eppy. "If ye have reservations, I would never demand ye attend me. If ye wish to stay here, I will leave ye with some supplies."

Eppy rolled her eyes, a small grin on her lips. "I've been with ye during battles before, my lady. What's another?"

"I know, but this one…" Annie swallowed. This one felt different. Cumberland wasn't going to let his army fail without harsh retaliation. The people would pay for it, not the soldiers themselves.

"This one is no different." Eppy straightened her spine and looked just as stubborn as Annie felt.

Except her maid was wrong. Somehow, this one was very different, and something deep in Annie's bones felt very unsettled by it. Aye, the battle at Falkirk had been horrendous, the injuries extensive, and she'd worked tirelessly to bring men back from death's door, but they'd won.

However, this evening, staring over the wrecked fields before them, an ominous mist rolling over the abandoned camp and circling around the hooves of their horses, had her blood running colder than the melting mountaintop ice caps.

This battle was a culmination of all the battles, it

seemed. And Cumberland, raging across the Highlands, burning houses, terrorizing women and children, maiming men who might fight against him without taking any prisoners… He wasn't going to simply lie down.

I am as brave as any soldier. Sucking in her fear and burying it deep inside her, she said, "Let's go."

"My lady, it will be dark soon. Perhaps we just stay here for the night, and we will head out at first light. Or just before dawn, if ye prefer."

Annie almost agreed, but something in her gut told her they needed to leave immediately. Believing in her instincts had gotten her this far, and she wasn't about to change that now. "Nay, we will ride through the night."

"As ye say, my lady."

They rode across the camp, back onto the road, and toward Culloden. With every step, Annie's skin prickled, her nerves jumped. She tried to shove aside the violent images that kept flashing into her mind, scenes of battle mixed with Logan's bloody, broken body and the burned-out shell of her home.

It was just as well they rode tonight because she was going to get no sleep until everyone she loved was safely together again.

Craig and hundreds of his men hid in the woods four or five miles from Nairn, having walked nearly seven or eight miles on empty bellies, in boots that were too worn, and on feet that had seen better days. The journey to this point had taken twice as long as they'd expected. The moon was not bright, and they had taken a path off the road, over areas that were not well traversed, overgrown with thistles and brambles that clutched at their skin and clothes. It meant that by the time they arrived at the meeting point, they were all more tired than they should have been and hungry to boot.

Their love of country, their desire to see the rightful leader in his place, was what drove them forward through the dark, else the lot of them would have deserted this misery long ago in hopes of finding food and warmth.

Loyalty.

That was something the bastards in red coats did not have. They were the traitors to the true crown. It was the Jacobites who would win this day.

They *had* to.

Craig passed off his rations to his men, preferring to see them eat rather than eat himself. It was something he'd done many times over the past few months. He would host a feast for the ages when this war was over.

It was hours before dawn, and they awaited the rest of their army. They'd split in two lines for the journey, and Craig's group had been the first to arrive. He and his men had followed General Murray, while the other half of their army had followed the prince. The purpose of the predawn attack was to assault the traitors while they slept, teach them to run and to never come back. But they couldn't do it with only half an army. Where the hell were the others?

Craig allowed his men to take shifts napping, to sustain their energy, while he went in search of Graham.

He found his friend sitting with Jenny, her husband Toran Fraser, and several other soldiers. Toran passed him a flask from which Craig took a hearty swig, passing it back as the warmth soothed his throat and quelled the gnawing hunger in his belly.

"Thanks. What's the word?" Craig asked.

"We have to turn back," Graham answered, irritation rife in his words.

"What the hell do ye mean we have to turn back?" Craig sat down heavily on the ground in their circle, stretching his legs out in front of him, exhausted from the hours they'd traveled through the night. "Where is the prince?"

"He and his men have fallen behind." Jenny bristled. "By the time they get here, it will be daylight."

"Murray's sent a message for them to turn back to Culloden." Toran took a long swig of whisky. "We'll arrive by the time the original battle was to take place."

Craig frowned, an unsettled twist in his gut. "Turn back? How the hell is the messenger even supposed to find them in the dark?" They'd been having difficulties themselves, finding it hard to traverse the land, rivers, croft walls, and fences in the dark. Craig let out a harsh expletive. "Christ, they've traveled for hours. This will crush whatever's left of their morale."

"Aye, it's a goddamned bloody mess," Graham growled.

Craig was weary all the way to the marrow of his bones, exhausted, cold, hungry, in pain. His feet throbbed, and even his blisters had blisters. Every muscle ached from overuse. His legs and arms were covered in bramble scratches from their mad journey through the wilds, and his stomach was raw from hunger. He accepted another swig of whisky to forget just how damn miserable he was.

With a resigned sigh, Craig said, "If we turn back now, at least we'll get to Culloden before the enemy reaches us there."

"It'll be a miracle if we all make it back." Jenny glanced at her husband and then the rest of the group. "We've had several desert us on the way here, in search of food."

The woman had a good point. Craig stood, wishing there was something more than promises he could offer them now and knowing at the same time he couldn't. "Let us all pray for a miracle."

Hours later, feet numb from cold and sores, the men stumbled into their camp at Culloden. Fortunately it was still before the dawn, and the darkness meant his men could rest their drained bones for an hour or two before Murray mustered them all to arms.

Just as he collapsed into a heap against a tree, a ripple of activity went through the men at the edge of camp, arms pointing toward them. Craig's eyes went wide.

He rubbed his eyes, certain his vision and lack of sleep were playing tricks on him. But the hallucination was still the same.

Riding through the throngs of tired men with her maid and two guards was Annie MacPherson, a vision in the firelight, golden shadows bouncing off her figure as she passed the campfires.

Craig swallowed hard, his mouth suddenly dry, as he

tried not to take in the curve of her fair cheek or the way her dark hair seemed to sparkle golden in places from the light of the flames. He stood, the shock of seeing her giving his body renewed energy.

She sat astride her horse, her shoulders back and straight, and she looked from man to man, a frown creasing her usually smooth brow until she finally spotted her brother.

"Annie?" Graham said beside him, confusion in his tone, then more brusquely, as he leaped to his feet, he asked, "What the hell are ye doing here? I told ye to remain at home."

That was the point at which Craig took in the parts of her that looked crumpled and defeated. The weary wrinkle in her brow, the way her lips didn't even twitch in so much as a semblance of a smile. Something was gravely wrong. He wanted to go to her. Reach for her. Tug her off the horse and wrap his arms around her. Protect her as he'd promised Graham he would do. But Graham was there, and he could and should be the one offering her comfort. Besides, she'd likely knife him if he tried.

"Graham," she said, her voice tired, cracking with emotion. "There is no home."

Everyone stood or sat silently watching Annie. Even Graham, who must have been impatiently waiting for her to continue and now seemed to be in shock at her words. No home? What had happened? Craig stared from Graham's stunned expression back to Annie.

She dismounted her horse, walking slowly toward them. Had they ridden through the night? She glanced up at Craig, her eyes filled with sadness as she passed him to reach her brother. It took everything inside him not to touch her, pull her to him. Instead he turned as she went, following her path just a few more feet to her brother.

Graham stared down at her, hands on his hips. "What do ye mean?"

Annie looked down at the ground, and Craig wanted to yell at his friend to embrace his sister, but he knew this side of Graham, the side that matched his own need to hide his emotions from anyone around them.

"Cumberland burned Cullidunloch, Graham. Logan was badly injured." She was abruptly silent, her hand coming to her chest as if she were bracing the beat of her heart. Craig, his chest clenching as he imagined his own sister having to go through something like this, wanted to reach out and take the weight from her. "I sent Logan with Jameson to Ewan at Cluny, but Seamus—he was taken by Cumberland. He has several others of our men as well."

Graham let out a hiss and an obscenity, followed by a string of curses that didn't faze anyone present. In fact, the litany was one they all would have shouted to the stars above if it would have made a difference.

"I had to tell ye." Annie's shoulders slumped. "I had to come."

Graham nodded, his hands at her shoulders as he searched her somber expression. "Did they...hurt ye?"

She shook her head vehemently. "Nay, Eppy and I were safe in the crypt with the other women and children."

Graham finally tugged Annie into his arms, hugging

her so fiercely Craig was certain they could both hardly breathe from it.

"Good." That was all Graham said, that single-syllabled tight word.

There was much left unspoken, but they all knew what everyone was feeling. Rage. Pure and simple. Rage and vengeance.

"We will beat him on the field," Craig said to them both. "We will burn him to the ground."

Six

A light rain drizzled over the men in camp, an unwelcome addition to the already-miserable dawn. With their night attack aborted, the men were just as exhausted as he'd expected. Some of the men on their way back from Nairn had dispersed to various places, deserting the cause, and a third of their army had yet to return from being backtracked. To say that frustration was high in the camp would be an understatement. But so too was the desire to beat Cumberland and his troops into an early grave. To be done with all this.

A few of the men were grumbling that Bonnie Prince Charlie should have left the battle plans to the experts. And others complained that Murray was making decisions without consulting the prince, whom they all should be following. It would seem that the general had decided the *reckless adventurer* no longer needed to be heeded, but the last thing they needed right now was a breakdown in leadership.

Rumors spread like morning mist across the camp that the king's forces had spent the night cavorting and drinking brandy, which only made Craig's men more irate. They'd spent the night suffering in the woods when they could have attacked the bastards head-on and been done with their drunken arses for good. Craig reminded his men that they'd only been half an army the night before, but that didn't assuage them.

From a few yards away, Craig spied Graham with Annie. She was huddled beneath a blanket, her maid beside her and her two guards flanking them. Even at this distance he could see that her nose was red from cold. Her unexpected arrival in the hours well before dawn had lightened the mood of many of the men and left Craig to mull all over again how disturbed he became at her presence. The men admired her, had enjoyed her company when she'd been on campaign with them before and hosted them at Cullidunloch. They also trusted her.

And Craig… He couldn't stop thinking about the feel of her soft skin beneath his palm, the way she'd been so brave as he sewed up the wound on her arm. The way her eyes had danced with humor one minute and all seriousness the next.

How much he wanted to be back there now, sitting alone with her, far away from the melancholy of battle. The danger of the army before them. The sadness of the loss of her home. God, they must be heartbroken over it. And Pinecone… Had the cat made it to safety? Was he being ridiculous for wondering?

The black of night had turned to a muted gray, made foggy by the rain. In the distance, a horn blew—Murray sounding the troops to rise. Finally. Craig pulled his gaze away from Annie and directed it toward his men.

"To arms," Craig said. "We've been waiting all night for that signal. Though we're a few hours behind, tonight we'll celebrate our victory!"

Cheers resounded in the predawn haze, and the

men moved in a blur as they dressed and prepared their weapons. Within a quarter hour, they were marching the couple of miles toward the moor that the prince had deemed to be the place of battle.

Graham turned his horse toward Craig, and unbidden, Craig searched for Annie. He expected to see her with her brother, but she wasn't there.

"The prince has ordered my sister to remain behind preparing beds for the injured," Graham said, somehow having guessed that Craig had been looking for her. He didn't want to read into that observation.

Craig cleared his throat and gave a perfunctory nod. He hated the idea of Annie remaining behind. She would be in more danger in such a remote place where Cumberland's men could get to her than if she were near the battle and Craig's help. But he bit his tongue to keep himself from saying anything. It wasn't any of his business what the lass did anyhow. Her brother would make the right choices to keep her safe.

"Murray says Cumberland's men are already advancing on Culloden," Graham said.

"Then we'll meet them halfway there, before they get close enough to Culloden House." Craig wouldn't put it past Cumberland to decide to put an end to this war by killing the one man he blamed for it—the prince—instead of taking him prisoner.

"Aye." Graham nodded and then said softly, "And ye remember what I asked of ye, MacLean?"

Ye're the best of all of us. I canna think of anyone else I would rather have as protector to my family... Protecting

Annie. Craig swallowed, his voice coming out gruff as he said, "I remember."

Graham flashed him a confident grin. "We'll celebrate tonight."

"With a cask of whisky for every man, we'll toast again and again until we fall down drunk."

"And for every man his own roasted goose," Graham added, exaggerating as there were no geese to be had. Somehow, they'd find a way.

"Ten loaves of bread with freshly churned butter." Craig's stomach growled at the thought.

"Oh, but it will be a grand feast. We fight today for the glory of having that feast and no bloody dragoons hovering over us, threatening our livelihoods. Burning our houses."

"Aye. Those bastards will never hurt our own again."

After months of battling, after years of torment, it would finally be coming to an end. King George's youngest son, the Duke of Cumberland, was the one leading this battle. If the Jacobites won against the king's son, surely it would bring an end to war. Craig had to believe it. And there was one man in particular he hoped to face on the field: Captain Thomas Boyd. The man had been terrorizing the Highlands for years. Craig himself had come into contact with him only once, and that had been nine years ago, but it was a day he'd never forget.

Craig's father had been captured during a raid on an armory held by the English, caught stealing gunpowder and weapons. Craig had been on the lookout, whistling like mad when he saw the line of red jackets marching toward the armory. Somehow his warning had been misunderstood on the inside, for only half the men had escaped. The others met the bayonets of the dragoons. Despite fighting fiercely, they were arrested and taken back to Boyd's garrison.

The captured men had been beaten and tortured for information, and they were given a choice—which one of them would sacrifice his life as an example and a warning to the others.

His father had loudly proclaimed that he would give up his life for his men. Craig had been on the outside of the walls for the execution, about to signal a gunshot for the rebels to attack and help. Only the gallows broke when the stool was kicked out from under his father, and so instead of letting him die by hanging, Boyd shot him once in the heart.

His father's body had not been returned to their family. When Craig had tried to batter his way into the garrison with his shoulders and fists, his men had held him back. They'd already lost one MacLean, they'd said. They weren't willing to lose another. But Craig had been lost to them for months after, and part of him still was. Though he'd always been afraid of his father, he'd still also wanted his acceptance. To know that he'd never achieve that goal left a crater in his soul. From then on, Craig had made it his business not to feel. Only to fight. To win.

And today would not be any different.

He was the stone-cold warrior who won battles. Who survived. That wee lad who wouldn't let the bigger, older lads take him down. Victory or death.

They marched, the beats of the drums behind them urging them forward, until they reached the battlefield. And there they waited. Their numbers had dwindled from men who'd gone in search of food and not come back. Men who'd lost consciousness from exhaustion and not mustered when called. Men who'd not returned from the night's excursion. Would enough come back in time?

Hours later, at what Craig guessed was close to noon, the first signs of men in red coats smeared the horizon. They stood in neat ordered rows, like the toy soldiers a bairn might play with. They looked well rested, not wavering on their feet, nearly five hundred or more men to a regiment and cannons between them. Did they have more cannons than the rebels? How had the redcoats gotten their guns through the bog?

Craig wasn't certain if he was more nervous about the cannons or the still readiness of those men as they waited to be sent on the attack. He took the last moments he had left to examine the hundreds of men assembled on the hill, his division fighting under Lord John Drummand's standard.

Frasers and Mackintoshes were fighting together under Colonel Jenny and her husband. Farquarsons. MacLachlans. Chisholms. And his men, the MacLeans. They were nearly twelve hundred strong on their side, with both infantry and horsemen. All of them were heavily armed with their long swords, muskets, and long daggers. But the exhaustion on their faces and the stoops to their shoulders belied their readiness. The Jacobite army was tired, and their lack of morale sent a cold shiver of dread along Craig's spine. If only they hadn't tried for the night attack, his men could have rested and been ready for battle.

Culloden moor was a stretch of boggy land that tried to swallow their horses' hooves, just south of Culloden House. The prince should have remained locked up tight inside but had joined them instead, against the advice of his generals. Purple heather and grasses attempted to sway in the breeze but couldn't seem to lift themselves from their trampled graves. The sun was hidden behind dark clouds, and mist shivered in ghostly portent around them.

The collected armies and soldiers were on the front line, facing the king's army across the moor.

The prince, riding on a white horse, wove his way in and out of the men, giving instructions and inspiring words to the thousands who'd come to fight for him. Rain came down in drizzles at first, growing in volume as it splattered against their heads. A chill wind came with it, making the men more miserable than they already were. Craig found himself pumping up those in earshot with promises of whisky and fresh roasted meat when the battle was over.

"Remember Prestonpans!" Craig bellowed. "We defeated them utterly there, and we shall defeat them again. We'll leave them running with their cocks between their thighs and stripped of their red coats."

His men cheered at that, wanting some bit of hope to grasp onto.

"We beat them at Falkirk. We will beat them again.

Their cannon fire, their straight lines are nothing compared to the heart of a Highlander."

From down the line, an energy shuddered through the men.

"We'll be the first to let the redcoats' blood run," Craig bellowed. But his words were too quickly uttered. Cannon fire erupted from somewhere among their ranks, the massive ball of destruction crashing through the enemy's ranks and spraying earth and limbs up through the air. Six volleys were fired back in prompt answer, smashing into the Jacobite ranks and sending up screams of pain. Massive gaps were punched through their lines.

This was not the victory his men had been promised.

Charles had given the order for a cannon to be fired with no warning. And then a second. The loud booms of Jacobite cannons shuddered the earth, cannonballs landing at the feet of the king's army.

Holy Mary Mother of God… Craig looked on in horror as each cannon was fired, waiting for the orders to come down for the regiments to attack, and yet nothing came. They remained rooted in place when they should be charging the enemy. Only silence came from their leaders, which had him questioning whether they still lived. In the haze of the smoke, he tried to see, as men slowly looked back and forth in fear and confusion. Should they charge or not? To go before the order was given would be to create chaos, and yet to stay left them vulnerable.

"What the bloody hell?" Craig growled.

"I dinna know," Graham said, equally confused. "We should be leading the Highland charge."

Craig strained to study the landscape. "We canna let our men just stand here and be crushed by more cannon fire."

"Aye."

The cannons' devastation left them vulnerable and thinly stretched in the middle. Men shifted in confusion, waiting for the order yet to be called. Craig worked hard to keep the morale of his men up. They would be the first to charge, whenever the order came down from Prince Charles.

But the call to attack did not come.

Craig, making eye contact with Graham, nodded. They couldn't allow their men to continue falling and not fight back. They'd lost valuable time. And so, with a final signal, Craig raised his sword and let out a bellow to rival all battle cries. The sound echoed in the throats of the other men down the line. With Graham by his side, Craig led the Highland charge, riding their mounts through the boggy moors, their men running behind them.

The line of the English army raised their weapons, a thousand or more muskets firing at once. Balls of lead shot lodged themselves in the moors near their feet and, for the less fortunate, into their waiting bodies. The redcoats reloaded and not twenty seconds later fired again. And again. Men fell all around Craig and Graham. The right flank was approaching the English line faster than the left, who had to slog through wetter ground, their forward motion slowed, leaving them wide open as targets.

The bloody bastards were taking the Jacobites out by the dozens, and the more ground Craig had to cover, the farther away he felt. And then the cannonballs stopped falling, replaced instead with cannons full of grape shot, firing deadly pellets at the men. For several breaths Craig was certain they would never make it to the enemy's lines. Men running beside him fell, and those who took their places fell. Nearly half their men gone already. *Mo chreach*... This wasn't supposed to happen!

Prince Charles's army was unprepared for the volley of firepower that came at them, cannons and muskets alike. But they couldn't stop now; they had to recover their wits. A bullet grazed Craig's cheek, but he barely flinched. The crash of bodies and weapons thundered in echoing booms as the Jacobite advance finally reached the line of firing redcoats.

Craig sliced through one man and then another. He blocked blows with his targe, slamming the small shield into his enemies, and slashed at them with his long sword. Frenzied Highlanders sliced and diced at the enemies around him. Wild rebels fell as the government troops cut to the right, stabbing at the vulnerable places exposed when a soldier blocked with his targe on one arm and raised his sword with the other. The bloody bastards had figured out their weak spot and were taking advantage of it.

Graham bellowed orders and warnings to his men, cursing the redcoats as he went. "Watch your ribs. Cut forward!" He swung his blade to and fro, cutting down one man after another, as though he were slicing through a thicket in the woods.

The Highlanders had the advantage now. Better fighters with swords, they were overpowering the enemy one by one. But there were just so many of them. And the men were tired.

"Stuart! Stuart!" Craig shouted with every blow of his that landed, and soon his men too were shouting Prince Charles's name.

A man jabbed at Craig's leg with his bayonet, but Craig jerked at the last second, giving Craig only a minor slice along his shin rather than impaling him against his mount. Craig thunked the soldier on the head with the hilt of his sword, kicked his body away, then wheeled his horse around, and rose him up on his hind legs to kick out at two approaching English.

Impaling a man on his left through the chest, he pulled out his pistol and fired off a shot to the right, killing a man who was attempting to skewer Graham. Pistol discharged, he tossed it to the ground, knowing he wouldn't have time to reload. He fought atop his warhorse until some bastard brought his mount down with a nasty thrust of his bloodied bayonet. Craig ended that man's life with a single slice to his neck.

All around him men fought, bellowed, bled. Several of his men fell beside him, though those still standing held their ground against the government troops. He gritted his teeth, fighting harder, and leading his men through the broken first line of redcoats toward the second. But as they ran, the second line converged on them in overpowering numbers. Cumberland's men had been terrified by the Jacobite bellows and cries during the first charge, but no longer. Despair tried to sink its teeth into Craig as another volley of fire was aimed at them.

They were losing. Not just losing.

It was a *massacre.*

Craig swiveled to his left, fighting off a jabbing redcoat, missing the blur of motion at his left as a bastard attempted to slice at his gut with the tip of his bayonet. Craig leaped backward and thrust his sword through the man's throat at the same time as something, the butt of a gun maybe, bashed him on the head.

Another round of fire.

He fell to his knees, dizzy. Something hit him, and he jolted backward, settling on his heels, the burn of shot in his gut. Craig gritted his teeth at the pain, his insides feeling as though they'd been ripped out. He'd clapped a hand to his belly in reflex and drew it away, covered in blood. He watched the front of his shirt soak through. The air around him stilled, the sounds turning muddled.

He'd been shot.

His men were being shot down all around him.

Craig reached for the dagger at his side and searched the sea of faces in front of him, eyes settling on a soldier still holding the smoking musket. With the last bits of energy he could muster, Craig aimed and threw the dagger. The tip sank deep into the bastard's eye, killing at once the redcoat who had likely just ended his own life.

Clutching his stomach, Craig blinked and tried to stand. Fell back to his knees. Tried again, only to be knocked down by a blow to his back. Craig collapsed onto his stomach, landing face-first in the bloody, rain-soaked earth. He had enough forethought to turn his face to the side, to avoid drowning before he bled to death.

He blinked, watching footsteps dancing haphazardly around him. Something heavy fell on his back. The sounds of battle faded, and his breaths seemed to be all he could hear. Shallow. Low. And then he heard nothing.

Annie had remained at Culloden House long enough to prepare the beds and, with Eppy's help, tear hundreds of strips of linen to be used as bandages. But after a time, as she normally did when a battle was at hand, they left the comforts of camp and made their way toward the battlefield, to be there when the time came to save lives.

Loud cannon fire shattered the peaceful silence of the moors and rumbled the ground beneath them. A volley of gunfire spooked their horses. Gregory grabbed her mount's reins when he rose up on his hind legs, and Annie had to struggle to hold on.

"My lady, I insist we find shelter."

Annie was about to argue, but in between bouts of cannon fire, she could hear the distinct sound of unison marching, the chink of metal. They were about to be set upon by Cumberland's men. And so she nodded, not wanting to risk others' lives for her sake.

But they couldn't go back to Culloden House, as the sounds of marching were coming from that direction, and they couldn't ride toward the battle, else they'd be caught. That left only one choice: to ride east of the battlefield.

They rode hard for about a mile, following a small

stone fence until they came to a gate. In the distance a small cottage with a smoking chimney beckoned.

"Pray they be Jacobite," Annie muttered as Gregory unlatched the gate, and the four of them rode through. They drew closer to the cottage, and the hackles raised on the hound standing guard outside the door. He began to howl and bark something fierce.

"Shh..." Annie tried to soothe. "We are friends."

But the hound did not stop.

The door swung open, and the barrel of a musket was shoved through the opening, leaving the woman holding it in shadow.

"What do ye want? I'll no' hesitate to shoot ye."

Annie swallowed, holding out her hands to the side. "We come in peace, I swear. We seek shelter for an hour or more, that is all."

"God save the king," the woman said.

"And his bonnie son," Annie replied, a line often given among the Scots to see which side they were all on.

"Come in."

Thomas and Gregory took the horses to a small barn just to the side of the cottage while Eppy and Annie entered the cottage. The echoes of cannons and gunfire thundered all around them even there. The more time that passed, the louder the sounds seemed to be, and the more she thought the battle was headed their way.

Their host, Mrs. Sullivan, kept up an endless stream of chatter, but none of it served to distract Annie from what was happening just a mile down the road. She paced the main room of the cottage, wearing thin the already-threadbare rug that covered the roughhewn wood floor.

Mrs. Sullivan was sitting by the banked hearth mending a shirt and watching Annie nervously. She had two sons and three grandsons in the fight. The womenfolk who lived at the cottage had hurried away when they heard of the impending battle, to shelter with family they had in Perth. Mrs. Sullivan remained behind to tend to the men despite the protestations from her female relatives. She was old, she said, and her old bones wouldn't do well on the road. Besides, she wasn't going to let those nasty dragoons take away her home. She'd been born in this cottage, had married an Irishman to spite her father just outside the threshold, and had birthed her children in the loft above them. This was where she belonged, she said, and she would see no other way about it.

Annie admired the woman for her courage and thanked her profusely for letting them stay. She had offered her a handful of coins to allow Annie to use the cottage as a base for caring for the wounded. Mrs. Sullivan was pleased to let them, as she knew she'd be getting excellent care for her own men once they returned.

"Shall I make ye some tea to calm your nerves?" the older woman asked.

Annie shook her head. She had her box full of medicines and a large grain sack full of linens that could be used for wounds, and tea was definitely not going to calm her nerves. The only thing that would serve to calm her now was to see her brother's face and those of all his men. Of MacLean.

"Have ye a bigger pot?" She eyed the cast-iron pot on the hearth that bubbled with a pea soup that had likely been simmering there a few days.

"Aye. I think so, out in the barn. What do ye need it for?"

She needed something to do, even if it was small. Searching for the pot and filling it with water would distract her for a time. "Can I bring it in for ye? Ye'll need to boil water and the dirty linens, for when your men return."

"Of course." Mrs. Sullivan smiled at her. "Thank ye for being so thoughtful."

Annie reached for the door, but her guards followed.

"One of ye is quite enough," she murmured, and Thomas sat down, leaving Gregory to follow her out. "The fighting is happening elsewhere," she reminded him, though a rumble of distant cannon fire nearly had her jumping out of her skin. "And I'm perfectly capable of finding a pot on my own."

Gregory nodded but didn't reply, her words not deterring him from his task in the least.

Out in the barn, several empty stalls were filled with supplies—chopped wood, discarded and broken furniture. There were a sad old cow, two sheep, and a pig, but no horses save for the few they'd brought with them. Either they'd been stolen by the English, they'd been taken by the women who rode to Perth, or they'd not resided here in a long time.

The pot was not easy to find, and so she dug around the broken pieces of furniture until she found the massive thing, rusted around the hinges that held the handle in place. She feared that pulling at it might cause the whole thing to break, but a test lift showed it was strong enough despite the coppery-orange flakes that showered down.

"May I, my lady?" Gregory offered to take the pot from her.

"All right." She passed it over. "Let's find the well. We might as well fill the pot with water now."

They searched the yard but found no well, and upon asking Mrs. Sullivan, they found out they would have to make a trek to the creek that ran just inside the woods behind the house. As they marched through the slickened grass, weighed down by the weight of the rain, Annie tripped not once but twice on a hidden stick or rock—and not because she was so jumpy from the sounds of battle still moaning on the moor. She couldn't imagine someone Mrs. Sullivan's age having to walk out there day in and day out to get her water. It was a wonder she'd not managed to break her legs doing so.

Back at the cottage, everyone was in exactly the same positions they'd been in when Annie had left, as though time itself stood still. She fussed about, asking Mrs. Sullivan for other things that she could do, and busied herself with more household chores.

Then she stopped, her busy fingers stilling as she listened. Something had changed. She could no longer hear the shots from muskets and pistols or the boom of cannons. The screams she'd heard before had dulled into a muted roar that only echoed in her head.

"'Tis over." Annie brought her fingers to her neck,

feeling her throat bob as she swallowed hard. "Now we must go."

"We'll go," Gregory said. "Ye stay here."

Annie scowled at him. "Since when have I ever done such a thing? I'm no' about to start now."

"My lady, please," Gregory begged, pure terror on his face. "At least wait an hour afore we go."

"An hour will be too late for some men."

"Any sooner could be too late for ye."

He might be right, but she'd made a vow to protect the prince's men, and if she could do that, she had to. Even now the prince would be expecting her on the field, searching for wounded and directing which men were to be brought back to Culloden House. "We'll wait a quarter hour and nothing more." She turned to Mrs. Sullivan. "And I'll be certain to ask after anyone named Sullivan."

"Thank ye. God be with ye." Mrs. Sullivan crossed herself.

The men didn't argue with Annie any further, apparently realizing that to do so would be futile. She was just stubborn enough to go out on her own.

After a quarter hour, the four of them mounted their horses and headed in the direction she'd watched the soldiers take earlier. Please God, let her find Graham alive. Better yet, see him riding off with his men. And Lieutenant MacLean, who'd sworn they'd burn Cumberland to the ground—she hoped to see him riding off, too, as they raced toward Culloden House with the prince to celebrate their victory.

But the air was thick with despair, and the closer

they drew to the battlefield, the more eerie it became. Random horses ran past, frightened and wild, their coats smeared with blood.

What she didn't see was a single soldier running toward her. Not one Jacobite or redcoat. It was as though the entire battlefield had simply been annihilated.

They were close now, the scent of burning shot singeing her nostrils. Death was all around her, making her limbs go heavy. Nearly there… Fear gripped her spine, begged her to turn around. Told her she didn't want to see what they were soon to expose.

Rain dripped down her face, ice-cold, and mingled with the warmer slide of her tears. She was happy then for the rain, for it kept anyone from knowing she was crying. From learning that the aftermath of battle never was any easier to see, no matter how many times.

Seven

No amount of battlefield experience could have prepared Annie for the carnage spread across Culloden's moors.

Bodies lay everywhere. Men. Horses.

Rain spilled on the fallen, mixing with their blood and mud in a swirling, frothy muck. The earth looked as if it had exploded with the dying, and no amount of rain could wash away the bloodshed.

Annie gagged at the reek of death and butchery. Every prone body was one of her brothers and their friends, their clan, their family. Every body was that of someone she'd smiled at, talked to, loved. So many dead…

And yet decidedly lacking in variety.

She scanned the battlefield, which seemed to pulse larger in her mind's eye than it truly was, felt her body sway with the strain of it. Beyond the carpet of carnage, beyond the ravens laying claim, she could make out no survivors.

No one ran. No one crawled.

It was as though those who had were already gone before she arrived.

This was utter devastation, over a thousand men down at least. Were there any survivors? Where had they gone? The prince's army had been at least five thousand strong. Not a complete crush, though a single glance might make one think so.

There was not a king's man in sight, save for the few who'd fallen, their red coats split open and their wounds gaping wide. Those who'd survived had already marched off, and she imagined the resounding cheers of the victorious, for she was certain it was they who had won. The vanishingly small number of red coats compared to plain clothes and plaid was a devastating giveaway. Amid the overwhelming number of her countrymen lying dead, only a handful of the dead lay in red.

The sight was enough to bring her to her knees, and she was glad for the horse beneath her to keep her from falling.

Wind whipped against her face, stabbing her with pellets of rain and causing her hair to flap about her head as though it wished to escape the sight.

Perhaps on the far side of the moors she might spy more bodies dressed in red, but she doubted it. If the victory they'd been hoping for had been real, then her brother or his men would have come to find her. The Sullivans would have come home to greet their matriarch. And yet there had been nothing, not a single sign of a living Jacobite.

A painful lump lodged in her throat. Where was Graham? Lieutenant MacLean? What about her dear friend Jenny, who was to have led a charge with her husband Toran at her side? If she were to succumb to battle, then where would Annie and Fiona be?

Annie stilled her tongue when she wanted to scream, fearing that any voice she put to words would bring out the phantom redcoats who wished to rip her heart further from her chest.

Please dinna be here. Please dinna be here.

"Oh dear God," Gregory murmured, crossing himself. Thomas followed suit, and Eppy let out a gasping sob.

"There was no God here," Annie said, the harshness of her blasphemous words not lost on her. "Only the Devil and his Butcher."

Across the rain-swept moors came moans of pain. As mournful a sound as it was, it was also one that gave Annie hope because it meant there were some survivors. Though many of those lying in the muck of battle were still and quiet, it would seem some were still alive. Every woeful cry cut into her skin as though she'd been sliced by the enemy as well.

Emotion, however, had no place in healing. She had a job to do. A task. A goal. Find her brother. Find her men. Find MacLean. Find Jenny and Toran. Help people. To make sure that every man or woman that the loyalists had tried to kill survived. They needed to bring about another generation of people who would fight for what was right. She could not let them die.

"We need to help them." She slid her gaze to Thomas. "I need ye to go back and fetch a wagon from Culloden House."

"We canna go back there," Thomas said. "If they've won here, they will be sacking the prince's headquarters next."

Annie swallowed down her panic. "Mrs. Sullivan, then. She had a wagon."

He started to argue, but she ignored him, dismounting and searching for a source of the sound. The first man she found wounded and moaning had a massive gash in his head and blood covering his entire face, and his arm was badly bleeding. She wrenched open his coat and tore at his shirt, using a length of linen to tie off the end of his arm to stop the bleeding. At first he started to panic, begging her not to kill him, as though he fully expected an execution.

"I'm no' going to kill ye. I'm here to help."

"Bless ye, angel," he murmured.

"I'm no angel, sir," she whispered with a smile. "No need to bless me. Just stay strong. We'll get ye to safety. What's your name, soldier?"

"I… I…canna remember."

She wrapped another bandage around his head, while Eppy dismounted to find the next downed soldier they could help.

"'Tis all right," Annie soothed. "Ye'll remember soon enough."

Thomas watched for only a moment before he took off for the help she'd ordered.

Gregory joined Annie and Eppy, calling out when he found someone alive and carrying the soldier to Annie if he were able. Four were all they found in this first part of the fields, and there were so many more dead. Some of whom looked to have been killed by a single blade to the heart—as though the redcoats had indeed come through the field after the fight, killing survivors. Each time she wiped a face clean of blood or mud or turned a man over, she expected to see someone she knew and loved.

Thankfully, she'd not yet recognized anyone. From

what she did learn, she was among the MacLean and MacLachlan men, which meant that Graham's men wouldn't be far from here. It also meant that any of the men she found here could be the lieutenant.

The wounds she found were horrendous, and though she tended each one, a subtle shake of her head at Gregory told him which men should be left in peace where they were and which ones should be moved to the group of those she'd bring back to the Sullivans' croft.

On the far side of the field, people moved about the bodies. Annie spotted them and urged her three companions to duck down, afraid it might be Cumberland and his men come back to finish off the survivors. But after a moment it became clear that the others were about the same purpose, checking the wounded.

Thomas returned with the wagon, and he and Gregory worked to load in the four men they'd rescued before Thomas left once more to take them to Mrs. Sullivan's small cottage.

Movement to her right caught her attention, but no moans or calls for help came from that direction. Was it ravens already pecking at the bodies of the fallen? The birds of prey circled overhead, but none had landed so close to her yet. Though it was only a matter of time. Nature had to take its course.

There, again, just a subtle movement. A hand. She edged closer. The moving appendage was attached to an arm buried beneath an unmoving body. Dear God, a soldier fallen in battle and another man landed on top of him. He was lucky not to have been suffocated by the pile of bodies.

Annie heaved at the first body, unmovable in its dead weight. Eppy knelt beside her and helped to roll the poor sot off the other. Lying on his belly, blood covering his face, the wounded man had a shallow gash across one shoulder blade that could use some stitching but was not itself life-threatening. They managed to roll him over. The soldier had a massive gash on his forehead and a wide hole in his jacket, burned at the edges and oozing blood from a gunshot.

"Can ye hear me?" she asked.

He groaned in answer.

"I'm going to help ye." She palpated the wound and grimaced. The bullet had gone in deep, as if he'd been shot at point-blank range. It would cause him a lot of pain when she dug it out.

The soldier blinked, eyes red and filled with pain as he stared up at her. His features were difficult to make out in the fog and covered in muck and blood as he was. Recognition seemed to flare in his eyes, though. Poor sot probably was hallucinating that she was someone from his family, perhaps his sweetheart or wife. The thought struck her right in the chest. Would she ever feel love? Always on the move for the cause, going from one battle to another, one sickbed to the next. She was Doctor Annie, or so they called her. She wasn't a real doctor, not in the sense that most men would acknowledge, save for the dying and wounded, who believed in her more than she even believed in herself.

The closest she'd come to any sort of thoughts of romance had been most recently with Lieutenant MacLean, when he'd sewn her wound.

Annie wrenched herself out of her thoughts, concentrating on her patient. He was in bad shape, but she'd seen men survive worse.

She wrenched open his coat, lifting his shirt to get a better view of the wound, whispering soothing words. The pulpy, reddish-pink flesh of a gaping wound faced her. Annie tore a piece of his shirt and pressed it to the wound.

"Ye're lucky this didna kill ye," she muttered. The gunshot seemed to have hit him closer to his ribs than his guts, deep and dangerous but not as deadly as it would have been had it penetrated another few inches over.

She poured some whisky on his wounds to clean them. He stared up at her, his teeth bared in a silent growl at the pain she'd caused, but he didn't make a sound. After a heavy indrawn breath, he let it out and seemed to calm. "We'll take ye to a safe place where I'll stitch ye up and get that bullet out." She wrapped linen tightly around his middle and another around his head to calm the bleeding on his forehead, swiping at the muck covering his face.

As she cleaned him, she stared into his cool emerald eyes, ringed with blue. That was when she recognized him. Had it not been for the rinsing of blood and muck from his face, she might not ever have seen him for who he was. But those eyes… She knew those eyes. And now they seemed to touch her soul.

"MacLean," she said.

He grinned up at her, but his eyes started to roll back into his head. He'd wasted so much energy trying to be brave about her ministrations. She couldn't let him fall asleep now. When men slept, that was when they let their lives slip away.

"Lieutenant," she said, prompting him back awake. "Stay with me."

Green-blue eyes blinked up at her, glassy with the need to sleep, the body's natural defense against such trauma. He opened his mouth, licked his lower lip with a dry tongue. His lips moved, but no sound came out, and then his eyes rolled into the back of his head and closed again.

"Nay, nay!" Desperation sounded thick and heady in her tone. "Wake! Where is my brother?" Annie pressed her hand to the good side of his face and gently prodded him, hoping to rouse him. "Wake and tell me! Where is Graham?"

But he didn't stir, and she felt foolish for trying to coax information out of a dying man, even if she was desperate.

Eppy's gentle touch on her shoulder pulled Annie from the panic she'd allowed herself to fall into. There was no need for words. Annie nodded, sitting back on her heels, her palms pressed to the tops of her thighs as she worked to calm herself. As Gregory and Thomas lifted her brother's friend—*her* friend—to carry him to the wagon, her gaze fell on a familiar head full of brown curls, shot through with blood.

Her hand flew to her mouth, and she barely choked out, "Graham."

Eppy must have seen him the same time Annie did, and both of them scrambled to get up. Annie half crawled, half stood as she tripped forward in her panic. Gregory and Thomas set down MacLean and ran toward Graham, all four of them reaching him at the same time.

Graham's handsome face was pale, his lips a light shade of blue. Panic crashed into her chest like a hammer's blow. Annie's heart shattered. *Nay! Nay!* His vacant stare was cast permanently at the sky, eyes the same amber hue as her own now glazed over with death. But she couldn't, *wouldn't,* accept that.

"Graham, wake up." Her voice shook, but the tremble in her throat was not as bad as those in her hands as she frantically searched his body for a wound. She found two. Either could have been fatal, one near the top of his thigh and one clear through his belly. "No," she sobbed. She pressed her hands to the wounds that still seeped a small amount of blood; the majority of his life's essence had already spilled into the earth around them.

But still, in her state, she felt the need to stop the bleeding. That was what she did. She healed people. Eyes blurring, she thrust out her hand toward her maid.

"Eppy, I need more linen. I need to bind his wounds."

"But, my lady—" Thomas started; however, Eppy cut him off with a loud rip of her own underskirts and a hiss in his direction.

"Here ye go, my lady." Eppy placed the linen in Annie's outstretched hand.

Annie took the strip of linen with trembling hands and first tied off the wound in Graham's leg, having to make the attempt more than once when her fingers didn't want to work. Hand pressed over the wound, she stared at Graham's face. Her older brother. Her champion. A scream bubbled up in her throat, and she caught it just before it escaped, a keening sound coming out instead. She cut it off abruptly when her hand flew to her mouth, realizing too late that her brother's blood covered her palm.

Keep going. Keep going. She chanted in her head, sucking in a breath and forcing herself to press the wadded linen against his belly. But there was no need, for the bleeding there had ceased.

"He's..." She tipped her head backward, gazing up at the sky and then letting her head fall back forward. "He's gone."

All of them sat quietly, surrounded by their people's dead. An ache so deep and potent that it could not be borne filled Annie's chest, and she fell over onto her brother, hugging him tightly. In the span of just a few days, Cumberland had threatened the lives of both of her brothers and succeeded in ending one. Possibly two if Logan didn't make it. Och, but he *had* to!

She sobbed into Graham's bloody coat, her body too heavy to lift. Too heavy to move at all.

If she'd found her brother like this...what was to say that Jenny was not in the same condition? Or Toran?

"We canna leave him here," she said.

"Of course no'," Gregory said softly, his face strained with grief. "We'll take all of our men."

She nodded, swiping at the hot tears that mixed with the rain on her face. "We'll take him back to the Sullivan croft, and I'll wash him up. He should return to the castle—" There was no castle to return to anymore. But there was still the kirk and their family burial ground.

"Aye, my lady," Thomas said. "I'll take the wounded and your brother back to the cottage and return in case ye've found more."

Annie nodded, but the weight of her head made her neck feel brittle. She stood on numb feet, watching as they carefully carried Graham's body to the wagon, both men standing over his figure with heads bowed. She held her hands out in front of her, palms up, his blood washing away with the rain. But she was certain. Forevermore, when she looked at her hands she'd see the stains of his death there.

Thomas mounted his horse, and the wagon jolted forward, eliciting a few groans from some of the wounded. She watched until the cart disappeared and then turned around. Eppy and Gregory had already resumed their searching. She stumbled through the piles of bodies, searching for any familiar forms. Though she never found Jenny, she did find many of her clansmen. And like Graham, they had been forever silenced.

A hush came over the moor, and her skin prickled. Those who'd been searching for the wounded on the far side had disappeared, like woodland animals when a hunter was in their midst. "We need to leave," she said. "I fear we've stayed too long already."

They mounted and were headed back to the cottage when she heard the approach of marching boots and horses' hooves. The redcoats had come back to finish off those who remained on the battlefield, and Annie wanted to take up every weapon she could find and run them through one by one. If only she had the power to do such a thing. If only she could harness the wind and blow them all away.

Graham... She wanted to wail. To fall to the ground and never get back up again.

But she couldn't. And the powerlessness that ate at her insides reminded her of her youth. Annie had been a child when her father had died from battle wounds. Much like Graham. A lump lodged in her throat, making it hard to breathe.

Their healer had been away from the keep, all those years ago. Annie had watched everyone scramble to do something to save their clan chief, but no one had had the skills. It had been on that day, when he'd drawn his last painful breath, that she'd decided to become a healer. And even though she'd trained for it, she still hadn't been able to help her mother when she'd fallen ill some years later.

And now Graham. She'd been too late.

If only she'd listened to her instincts and come right away instead of waiting a quarter hour. Maybe then she could have saved him... But the extent of his injuries made that an impossibility. The only thing that would have helped was if she'd taken the shots herself. And if she had it to do all over again she'd make that happen—in a heartbeat.

She stared down at her hands on the reins, barely recognizing the leather straps across her palms.

Tears spilled down her face, and all she wanted to do

was curl up in a ball and hide, to mourn. But she couldn't. There were men in the cottage who needed her. Men she could save, even if she'd been too late to help her brother. Why hadn't he let her go into battle with him? If she'd been there, she might have been able to do something, anything!

Even as she thought it, visions of the horrors she'd just seen lashed at her mind. She'd have been lucky to make it off the field alive and likely would not have. Aye, she could hold her own in a skirmish. Could wield a sword, shoot a pistol, fire an arrow. But not well; she was not a warrior. Not like Jenny. Her power was in her ability to heal.

By insisting she stay behind, Graham had saved her life. Still, knowing that didn't take away the pain that lanced at her as sharp as a redcoat's bayonet.

The Sullivan cottage came into view. The smoke from the chimney was dampened by the rain, but she could still smell it. Gregory sped ahead to help Thomas carry in the last man from the wagon—her brother.

Annie halted her horse where she was. If she didn't move forward, didn't enter that cottage, then she could make believe for just a little while longer that Graham was still alive somewhere. She could believe that this war hadn't taken away more than half of her family. Could believe that somewhere else in Scotland Graham was smiling, laughing, running, teasing a lass into giving him a kiss.

"My lady?" Eppy said it softly, and Annie could feel the question in her maid's voice, feel Gregory's question at her back.

Why have ye stopped?

Why do ye no' go forward?

"I'm no' ready," Annie whispered.

"Go on," Eppy told Gregory. "My lady needs a moment of privacy."

But Annie was certain no number of moments would prepare her for what she had to face inside.

Eight

An angel was singing to him with soft, sweet words. But with every melodic incantation came a visceral bite of pain. Craig tried to open his eyes, but the very act of moving his eyelids proved to be too much. Everything hurt.

When he'd first heard the angel, he'd thought he must be dead and in heaven. But a man like him didn't go straight to heaven. Nay, he'd have to labor in purgatory for a long time before he was allowed beyond the pearly gates. Perhaps that was where he was now, purgatory, for every bone, every muscle, every inch of skin screamed out in agony.

Thirty minutes or thirty seconds went by, he wasn't sure which, and wherever he was didn't seem to be a place where time mattered. With every moment that passed, however, he worked to open his eyes. When one finally obeyed, he was blinded by light. Nay, not light, flame. There were flames everywhere, and just beyond them, golden eyes looked down on him. The singing stopped.

"Go back to sleep," the angel murmured.

Without knowing why, he closed his eyes as she bade him and fell back asleep. The next time he woke, there were no sounds of angel voices but the screams of men in pain and torment.

Definitely purgatory.

Craig didn't need her to tell him to go back to sleep

this time. He did so willingly, wishing the screams would stop.

The next time he woke, there was silence. He opened both eyes, though they didn't seem to be inclined to pry themselves wider than a slit. The flames were gone, and all around him was darkness. He tried to sit up, but a cold hand on his arm stilled him.

"Lie down." It was her, the angel, sitting beside him, watching over him.

"I'll take heaven or hell, but I'll no' lie here in purgatory."

"Neither of them want ye today, sir. Here, drink this." Her fingers left his arm, but warmth remained where she'd touched him even though her touch had been cold. How odd.

Metal pressed to his lips, and he forgot about her for a moment, a sudden thirst overtaking him. He gulped, barely tasting what it was until too late. Poison. The ale was bitter with herbs.

"Ye've killed me," he growled, thrusting away the cup.

"No' yet, but ye might end up doing yourself in if ye keep this up. Lie back down. Go to sleep, else ye'll end up tearing out your stitches."

Stitches? Stitches meant that he was only wounded.

Not dead. Not in purgatory.

Craig did a mental check of his body, unable to pinpoint exactly where a wound might be because everything hurt so goddamned bad.

He'd suffered many an injury in battle over the years and had experienced plenty of pain. Why was this so different? And then he knew. Because he *should* be dead. This angel had found him and brought him back to life. While his mind was alive, his body wished him on the other side.

"Thank ye," he murmured, and then let the darkness take him once more.

Time did not exist in his state. What felt like mere moments later, he blinked open his eyes, no longer blinded nor in the dark. Shirtless and without his kilt, he lay on the floor of what looked like a cottage. Beneath him was a folded tartan, probably his own, to keep him from lying on the hardness of a wood-planked floor. Overtop his legs and hips was another blanket. He rolled his head to the side, seeing several other wounded men lying beside him, plaid blankets concealing their bodies and wounds from him. There was no sign of his angel. Where had she gone? Who was she? He turned in the other direction to see several other men laid out sleeping, most of them in the same state, a few others with their shirts on.

He was in some sort of makeshift infirmary. The rafters were thick bands of woven sticks likely covered with thatch. Two small windows were opened to let in light, but the room was still very dark. A fire burned in a hearth, and he thought he could smell some sort of pottage simmering, but he couldn't make out what. An old woman, dressed in a plain wool day gown, sat in a low chair beside the hearth, knitting something and humming.

Had he imagined the young woman who'd tended him? Or had it been the old woman? For she was the only one here now, and in his state, he wouldn't be surprised if he had somehow seen the older woman as a mirage of her youthful self.

Craig opened his mouth to speak but found his throat tight and dry. He coughed and tried again, staring at the old woman as he spoke. "Where am I?" His voice was scratchy and low.

The old woman stopped knitting, setting aside the bundle. "Ye're in my cottage. I'm Mrs. Sullivan. Let me get ye a cup of tea."

Craig struggled to sit, pressing his hands behind him and pushing, but his body did not want to cooperate, and his head and insides rebelled.

"Best no' do that," she advised. "Else Doctor Annie will have my head."

Doctor Annie. A wash of relief hit him unbidden, and he lay back down. She'd been the one tending to him? The angel he'd seen.

Flashes of nonsensical memory bombarded him. Her lips moving, her eyes fierce on his. Scenes from the battle clashed with the memories of her sweet singing voice. He reached up and touched his forehead, his fingers brushing over a bandage on his face.

"Ye were pretty bad off," Mrs. Sullivan said as she approached with a steaming cup of tea. "But the lass, she fixed ye up."

The older woman pressed the cup to his lips, and he sipped slowly, this serving tasting sweeter than the last cup he remembered.

"Where are my clothes?" he croaked.

The old woman clucked her tongue. "I've been mending the shirts of most of ye as they were cut off what wasna blown off or sliced off. And your kilt, ye're lying on it. I've no' got a bunch of beds, ye see, only the one for myself. The lads, they slept upstairs with their women in the loft on hay."

Craig grunted. He had the overwhelming need to piss, and he was not going to ask this elderly woman to help him up nor risk giving her heart a scare when she saw his cock. He rolled his head toward the other men, looking for anyone who might be able to help him besides her. But then she placed a chamberpot beside him and nodded.

"Dinna be embarrassed, lad. Ye'll no' be the first."

When he finished, she swept away the pot and a moment later was asking him, "Are ye hungry? I'm certain Doctor Annie wouldna mind if ye had some broth. I gave some to another lad earlier."

"Where is she?" He needed to see her. Right now. Had to know where Graham was. Where all of his men were. Craig closed his eyes against the onslaught of battlefield memories. The calm coolness of the redcoats as they raised their weapons and fired.

The old woman's face saddened. "She had some family to attend to."

"Is Graham MacPherson here?"

Mrs. Sullivan shook her head slowly. "He was, but not in the sense of which ye mean."

Craig frowned. What the hell was she talking about? "I dinna understand."

Mrs. Sullivan pressed her hand to his shoulder. "He

died in battle, son. She's gone to bury him at their family kirk. And to arrange a deal to get the men taken from her castle returned." She turned away, leaving Craig gaping at her back as she shuffled back to the hearth.

Graham had died… The truth slammed into him like he'd been shot at point-blank range once more. Craig dug the heels of his hands into his burning eyes. *Gone. Gone. Gone.*

It should have been him. Graham was a leader of his clan, had Annie and Logan to look after. Craig was not a leader of his clan, and his sister was well taken care of, needing him for nothing. If one of them were to die, he had less to lose.

Memories swept him back to that dawn before they'd marched into battle, Graham making him promise to take care of Annie should anything happen. Craig's arrogant response that they were going to kick the army's arses all the way back to England. And now… His friend was gone. And he'd a promise to keep, which meant the agony he felt in his gut, in every wound on his body, had to heal, and had to heal fast. Because Annie had one brother in the grave and another far away and healing from his own injuries. Which meant he was as close to a family as she had. And damned if he was going to let her down. Especially after he'd not been able to protect her brother.

He gritted his teeth against the internal pain of loss. How many of his own men had perished? It had been a slaughter, and it shouldn't have been. If they'd only gone in for the attack in the middle of the night, they might have won.

But one could not live a life speculating in *if only*. One could not wish for time to turn back; one had to make peace with the past and move forward. Yet he didn't want to. There was no making peace with what had happened, and he was certain none of the other Jacobites wanted to move on either. They would all want to make a different choice. To see that blade coming before it landed in their hearts.

He touched the bandage on his forehead, glad that the blow hadn't got him in the eye. Small favors. Craig continued to explore his injuries, assessing the damage. He had vague memories of being shot. There was a bandage across his middle covering the wound, and he had a flash of being knocked down from behind. Originally he'd thought he'd been kicked, but now from the sting over his right shoulder blade, he thought he must have been slashed by the end of a bayonet. Other than aches and bruises, those three bandages were covering the only wounds that appeared to have needed stitching.

Craig rolled his head to the side, searching out Mrs. Sullivan. "When will she be back?"

"Later today, I suspect. In the meantime, she's left me strict instructions on how to help ye, and her maid too."

Craig rolled his head to spy the maid but didn't see her.

"She's gone out to fetch more wood."

"Alone?" He tried to struggle up once more, finding his arms to be overly weak. Good God, how long had he been lying there? "Have ye no one else to help ye? To protect ye?"

Mrs. Sullivan's eyes grew sadder then, and Craig wished he hadn't asked. Of course she would have had, before the battle. But like most of the families in the Highlands, they would have lost someone. More than one.

"No' anymore." Her voice was so small, so childlike that Craig's heart broke for her.

"I will repay ye this kindness for watching out for me," he swore.

"Nay, son, ye dinna have to." She bent over the shirts she was mending.

"I know, but I will." She didn't respond, almost as if she didn't hear him. "How long have I been here, madam?"

"Six days now."

Six days had gone by, and he'd barely been conscious of the time passing. Six days of his men languishing on the battlefield, suffering or dead… He prayed most of them were lying low. Awaiting orders. Craig's eyelids dipped, and he struggled not to succumb to sleep. He still had so many more questions.

The door to the cottage opened, filtering in more light, which had him momentarily closing his eyes against the sudden brightness. The air shifted from musty, scented with burning peat and the wounded, to all of that plus the crispness of spring air. He drew it in deeply, the cold, fresh air filling his lungs.

"I've brought the wood," said Eppy. "And my lady has returned."

Annie was back. Craig willed his eyes to adjust faster and watched a bonnie lass enter the cottage, a wool cloak buttoned up tight, arms laden with wood. She went straight to the hearth, not looking at any of the men lying about, but he didn't suspect she would. It was her mistress who tended them.

Before he could ask where she was, Annie swept into the cottage, her manner as cool and crisp as the air whipping by outside. Her cheeks were flushed a pretty shade of red, no doubt from riding. She removed the hood of her riding coat, revealing that her long locks were swept up in a plaited bun. What he wouldn't do now to have the energy to rise up and pull her into his arms.

Mrs. Sullivan helped her take off her coat. Beneath the plain woolen garment she wore a gown as simple as the one her maid wore. She was tall for a woman, he knew, but seemed taller now with him lying there on the floor. Wisp thin, no doubt from months of being on campaign, and he guessed taking in little food the past six days. But despite that, there was a steadiness to her shoulders, a strength about her arms. The woman worked hard. She was not one for sitting around, and he should know. He'd watched her for months.

Now, in the quiet of this cottage, he observed her unabashedly as she spoke in low tones to their host and to her maid. Her expression was quiet and without too much outward show of emotion, but there was a sadness about her eyes that matched the one in his heart. A dull ache thudded in his chest that had nothing to do with any physical wound.

Annie glanced over her shoulder and met his gaze. Her lips stilled, and the other two women turned to look at him too.

He felt on display, and he sort of was, lying there practically in the nude. She'd seen the worst of him, his bloodied, mangled body. She'd taken him off that field of battle, and she'd put him back together. Graham might have begged him to watch after Annie, but it would seem she'd taken up the task herself.

Annie turned to face him fully now, slipping her gloves off her long, slim fingers. She took a tentative step forward and then one more, assured as she approached him. Her skirts swirled about her ankles, and her shoulders were squared. Hands that had been at her sides reached out to him, touching his forehead, pressing to his chest.

"What are ye doing?" he asked, uncertain how he felt about the delicate touch of her soft hands on his body.

"Checking your fever and heartbeat." She closed her eyes, her lips pressed together in concentration. He counted the seconds that she rested against him, felt his heart kick up a notch, and willed himself to calm.

Craig grasped her hand in his, giving a gentle squeeze. "I'm alive, lass."

Nine

Annie had touched thousands of men in her lifetime, rested her hand against various body parts. Seen men in so many different states of undress and duress that to see another, to touch one more injured body, should have been just like any other day. She should be immune to the heat of a man's skin, the way the hair on his chest prickled her palm. But for some reason she wasn't. This was not just any man but MacLean, Graham's best mate.

Tears welled in her eyes as she stared down at him, and she blinked them away. He was a link to her brother, gone too soon. Annie pulled her hand away from his grasp as though she'd been seared.

"Ye're still slightly hot," she murmured.

"Is the fever bad?" he asked.

She shook her head, straightening. "No' as bad as it was."

Annie turned away from him, making a pretense of gathering a few items from her valise, but truly it was to get ahold of herself. This was war, and men died all the time. But not her brother, just not him. She couldn't believe that he was gone. And Logan was still recovering from the beating he'd received. Lord, if she lost them both! She swallowed around the lump in her throat, gave a little cough, trying to knock out the grief that threatened to consume her. The one consolation was that MacLean was healing well. He was a link to Graham she wasn't going to lose.

"I'll be right back," she said, her voice tight.

"Wait." His voice held a note of pleading. "Please."

Annie turned back slowly to face him, lying out as he was, his eyes tender as they settled on hers. He beckoned her forward, and without giving her feet permission, she moved at his request.

"I'm sorry." The words tumbled from his lips. What felt like a tidal wave of emotion came crashing over her, and Annie could not hold back her tears. They fell in massive, quick-spilling drops down over her cheeks, rushing forth unbidden and with no way for her to stop them. Those two simple words, *I'm sorry*, held so much meaning within them that she couldn't contain herself.

"What did ye learn of your people?"

"My friend Jenny—she has a large network of Jacobites, and she has added the MacPherson men to the list of those she needs to recover. My people are in her capable hands."

"Good, they should be free soon then."

She pressed her hands to her face to hide her tears. To hide her sadness. Her grief. The pain had not lessened in six days but remained stagnant and solid like a knife buried in her chest. Only that morning she'd bid a final farewell to Graham where he had been laid to rest in a freshly dug grave in Cullidunloch kirk. Thomas and Gregory had accompanied her, but she'd not allowed them to accompany her back to the cottage. While on the road, they had learned that Jenny and Toran were arranging a trap to reclaim those Jacobites arrested, and they needed men. Thomas and Gregory were able-bodied and strong. They would be put to better use in the rebel army than acting as her bodyguards.

So here she was, quite alone save for her maid, their kind host, and a chamber full of broken men, one of whom didn't even know his own name.

There was a tug on her gown, and she looked down to see that MacLean had clasped her hem and was pulling her forward. Just as suddenly as he'd grabbed ahold of her gown he dropped the fabric, as if only then realizing what he'd done in touching her like that.

But she didn't care. She would have let him tug harder, if only to distract her for a moment and also because he seemed genuinely bereft and as much in need of comfort as she was.

In an instinctive move, she knelt beside him, draped herself over him, careful of the wound to his belly. The heat of his body seeped into hers, and she squeezed her eyes shut. Tentative fingers stroked her back, bringing her more comfort than she would have guessed. Annie wanted to curl up beside MacLean and stay there for the rest of the day and all of tomorrow too. The comfort she received from him was a surprise and a relief all at once, as if for a few blessed moments, this fallen soldier had taken away some of her pain.

But the longer she remained there, the harder it would be to pull away. Annie lifted herself up slightly and, on impulse, kissed him on the forehead before gazing into his eyes. "He loved ye, MacLean," she said. "He told me more than once what a great man ye were. A brave soldier and a good leader. Know that he was proud to have called ye friend."

"Och, lass, 'tis I who should be saying this to ye. Graham was forever talking about ye. He was so proud to call ye sister." His hand grazed her cheek, and that simple touch was enough to nearly undo her all over again.

It had been so long since she'd felt the comforting touch of another, and though he was lying there nearly dead from the battle, she felt inexplicably safe with him. Which was completely absurd because if a troop of redcoats came at them right now, he would barely be able to get up off the floor, let alone protect her. And yet here she was allowing the stroke of MacLean's hand to calm her.

They remained like that for several moments, until someone behind them cleared their throat. She lifted herself away from him, swiping at her face and clearing her throat of the last few sobs.

"Thank ye," she whispered to him.

"Dinna thank me, lass. I do my duty by your brother. He was a good man, and I will honor him. Protect ye like a brother."

There seemed to be so much more to those words than what he was actually saying, and she wanted to ask him to explain himself but was distracted when she noticed the bandage on his middle had a few dots of red seeping through.

Damnation, this was her fault.

"I'm so sorry," she said, gently peeling back the binding. "I shouldna have touched ye. Ye're bleeding again. Eppy, bring me new linens and hot water." A moment later her maid had brought her the supplies. Though once she'd removed the bandage, his wound did not look as though it were infected.

"'Tis no' your fault, lass, but my own. I may have poked at the wound afore ye returned and also attempted to get up."

Annie frowned, seeing where a couple of stitches had torn loose. "Och, but why?"

"I didna know what happened."

"Foolish man," she muttered.

"'Tis no' the first time I've heard that." He flashed her a grin that was more teasing and definitely more suited for a drawing room or tavern than a makeshift hospital bed in a hidden croft too close for comfort to the field of the massacre.

"I'm certain it will no' be the last." Annie rolled her eyes, teasing him back. "Fortunately it doesna look like ye've reopened your wound, only torn a few stitches."

He opened his mouth to speak, but she started to wash his wound, and his lips clamped shut.

"Here." She offered him a flask of whisky from her bag, which he gulped until he reached the very end. Good. That ought to help him sleep or at least numb the pain she was causing. He made no sound, though it had to hurt like the devil. Beads of sweat formed on his forehead, and he gripped the folds of the kilt he lay on as though to stop himself from bolting upright as she fixed the stitches.

MacLean was brave, which she already knew, but somehow seeing him this way gave her a whole new respect for him that she hadn't had before.

"How are your stitches?" he asked.

Annie glanced down at her covered arm. She'd removed the stitches just the night before since it had been nearly a fortnight since he'd put them in place. "Healed quite nicely, thanks to ye."

MacLean nodded. "What of the cat?"

Her heart broke a little thinking of the wee termagant. "She's likely taken over what's left of the castle." Annie cleared her throat of the emotion welling there. "The ointment will help to numb the wound. Though that does no' give ye the freedom to walk around just yet." She hoped her words could soothe him, though to be honest she wasn't certain he'd even heard her. When dealing with pain most of her patients found a place deep inside their minds to preoccupy them.

As gently as she could, she dabbed the ointment onto his stitched belly and then wrapped him up again. "Let me know if it continues to weep. I'll have to make certain it's kept clean. Ye were lucky that the bastard who shot ye didna aim just a smidge more to the left, else ye'd have had your guts spilling out."

"Do ye woo all your patients with such honesty?" He passed her a pain-filled flash of a smile.

She grinned down at him, a comforting hand on his shoulder. "I wouldna say I woo anyone."

"Perhaps 'tis a talent ye've yet to discover. I find my heart leaping quite a bit right now."

Annie patted his cheek. "That is the whisky talking."

"Nay..." His voice trailed off, and his eyes drooped before flinging open once more. He took hold of her hand, his fingers surprisingly strong for the state he was now in. "Ye're stuck with me, lass, I promise ye."

Annie would have laughed, but he seemed so serious, and she didn't want to hurt his inebriated feelings. "Ye dinna have to make any promises to me, sir. When ye're well and healed, ye'll go on your way and continue to fight for our prince, and I'll continue to help in the best way I know how."

"Nay… A promise is a promise." His grasp loosened, and she let her hand fall away from his hold.

Annie was unsure of why she felt so stunned right then. She'd heard plenty of bedside promises from soldiers, but this one… It struck her in a different way than the others. "I am honored ye'd make such a promise, but I willna hold ye to it."

But MacLean was already asleep, his lips partially open, his breathing deep and heavy.

"How many is that?" Annie asked Eppy.

"I'd say 'tis the two hundred and eighty-third man to promise his life away to ye, my lady. Ye sure do have a way with the gentlemen."

Annie did laugh now. "There is something so very special about saving a man's life. They all want me to remain by their side forever." Her gaze slid back to MacLean's sleeping form. Dark lashes splayed over his cheeks, and his lips parted in sleep. She had the sudden urge to kiss those lips, just a small brush of her lips on his.

"As would I, my lady, for fear I might endanger myself again." The mumbled words came from MacLean, though his eyes had not opened.

Annie grinned as she put away the vials of medicines she'd used on MacLean and handed Eppy the dirty linens to boil and dry for the next man.

She leaned down and whispered into his ear, "Ye'll no' be endangering yourself on my watch."

His lips curled into a boyishly handsome smile, and it was hard to pull herself away from him, but alas, she did.

Annie made her rounds and checked on the rest of the men, but her eyes kept drifting back to MacLean. He slept so peacefully, one hand on his heart and the other arm haphazardly at his side and well off the makeshift pallet—the true sign of a man in deep sleep. She passed by, shifted his arm back onto his plaid berth so no one tripped over him, and then drew his blanket up farther toward his chest, pausing to stare at him again. Watching him almost made her forget the pain in her heart.

There was a connection between them. Not just because she'd treated his wounds and not just because he was her brother's friend, though that connection was one she never wanted to part with. There had been something between them that had started months before and that had been growing in the days leading up to the battle. Perhaps the most poignant was when he'd tended the scratch on her arm. Careful, kind, and gentle. To think she'd imagined he was going to kiss her.

Annie let out a long-suffering sigh and stood. If she kept staring over him like this, Eppy and Mrs. Sullivan were bound to start asking questions she wasn't certain she could answer.

An urgent knock sounded on the door, and the three

women froze. The hound who'd been keeping watch outside had never made a sound. Annie pulled the small pistol from her boot, thankful that she'd made certain it was loaded before putting it there this morning. She approached the door. Eppy took up a place in front of Mrs. Sullivan, holding a poker.

"Who is it?" Annie asked through the wood, her hand on the bar that locked them all inside.

"Annie, 'tis me, Fiona."

Annie jerked back in shock at the familiar voice and then quickly recovered, yanking open the door to find her dear friend Fiona MacBean standing on the threshold. Her flame-red hair was swept up under a cap, and her violet eyes watered from the wind. Her fair skin was even paler than usual, making the freckles on the bridge of her nose stand out.

Annie ushered her friend inside, fearful of anyone who might have seen her come.

"How did ye find me?" Annie peered outside and then quickly closed it when it was clear Fiona had not been followed.

Eppy and Mrs. Sullivan set down their makeshift weapons, their bodies sagging in relief.

"I trailed ye back from Cullidunloch this morning, but I promise that I wasna followed." Fiona's gaze roved around the cottage, taking in the sight of the recovering men.

"Did ye speak with Jenny? Is she all right?" Annie asked.

"Aye, she and Toran made it to a safehold," Fiona said

with a sad shake of her head, "but many of their men are lost."

"Oh, Fiona." Annie tossed herself into her friend's embrace, breathing in her familiar earthy scent. "Graham… is…"

"I know, I know." Fiona hugged her tight. "I'm so sorry."

"I canna believe he's gone." Annie's voice caught on a sob.

"He was a fighter. Ye can damn well be promised that he took down more redcoats than got him in the end. Those bastards will rot in hell." Fiona was fierce in her words and expression as she stood back at arm's length, her hands firmly gripping Annie's shoulders. "We will no' give up until we are rid of them."

"I'm no' giving up. We made a pact, and I intend to see it through until my dying day. They can keep taking away the things I love, and I will still continue on my path."

"As will I."

"What pact?" They were interrupted by MacLean, who'd woken again, craning his neck to look behind him at the two of them. "What do ye intend to see through to your dying day?"

Annie moved away from Fiona to hand MacLean a flask of whisky. "Dinna concern yourself with the mumblings of women. Drink this."

He chuckled and waved away the flask. "Dinna think a man canna be concerned with what a woman has to say, my lady, for I promise I am."

There he went again with promises. Why did every

word he uttered make her belly do a little flip? "Ye should drink this." She thrust the flask back toward him.

"Ye want me drunk and passed out."

"Aye." She felt no need to beat around the bush with that truth. "Sleep."

With a grin on his lips, he took the flask. "If it makes ye happy."

Annie pressed her lips together and watched him, like a mother tending her toddler and wishing their movements were just a wee bit faster. "My happiness is of no concern to either of us, but your recovery is. Now drink. Sleep. Get well. Forget what ye heard. Forget your promises."

"Aye, aye, Doctor Annie." He flashed her a wink that in different circumstances would have made her knees go weak. Eyes still on her, he took another long sip of whisky and then another. "'Tis good stuff."

"Thank ye," Mrs. Sullivan said near the hearth, her voice tight with emotion. "My boys made it. We've plenty."

MacLean handed her the flask back. "I may sleep now, lass, but I will remember when I wake."

"Nay, ye willna."

"I will. I've said it, and it will happen."

She rolled her eyes. "Fine, I believe ye." But she didn't. The man was full of whisky by now, and she hoped that the liquor and his slight fever would scrub from his mind any of the conversations they'd had.

Fiona glanced at her with a brow raised. "Who is that?" she whispered.

"A friend of Graham's."

"The two of ye… Are ye well acquainted?"

Well acquainted… That depended on who was doing the speculating. Outside of the two of them, no one knew that MacLean had been the one to sew up her wound. The fact that he'd been alone with her in her bedchamber and she in nothing but a thin night rail… Well, one might think they were very well acquainted indeed. But from the outside—and all she was willing to admit? "No' well, but we have met before. Several times."

A vision of the way she'd draped herself over him moments ago and the way she'd fussed with his blanket came back to her. Perhaps more than "acquainted." But she didn't need to admit that, at least not now, for soon they would part, and while she wished it weren't true, it was likely she'd never see him again. She'd want to remain close with those who'd been close to Graham, but she had Logan and the rest of their clan for that. Yet knowing that didn't sit right with her, and she found herself staring down at MacLean, her brother's closest friend of late, as he fell back into sleep.

"He is verra handsome," Fiona murmured.

"What has that got to do with anything?" Annie asked, feeling a sudden and uncharacteristic spark of possessiveness at her friend's observation.

Fiona shrugged, nonchalant, though there was a hint of teasing in her blue-violet gaze. "Nothing, just noticed. He is very striking. And large."

Oh, heavens, but he was. The man could walk into any room—or any field or tavern, didn't matter—he could walk anywhere, and women would stop what they were doing to stare at him. Annie had seen it happen. Had done so herself. Even now, Fiona was staring at him, enamored so much by him that she'd yet to tell Annie why she'd come.

"We forget ourselves," Annie said.

"Sometimes forgetting yourself is all right. If it means ye get to stare at a beautiful man." Fiona let out a long dramatic sigh followed by a giggle.

"Oh, come now." Annie waved away the silliness.

With a theatrical turn away from the man, Fiona faced Annie, her face gone serious. "Enough distractions. I came to relay a message. The redcoats are searching the countryside for any remaining Jacobites. They've received orders from the Butcher to slaughter anyone with allegiance to the prince."

"Nay..." Annie felt her heart leap into her throat. But even as she denied the possibility, in her heart she had known this was going to happen. Cumberland wanted to wipe any drop of Jacobite blood from the earth.

"Aye. They went through the field and killed those who'd yet to be rescued, and at a neighboring cottage that housed many of the injured they—" Fiona choked on the last of her words.

"Ye need say no more. I understand."

"Ye're no' safe here. I want ye to come with me. I'll give ye a few moments to pack up your things." Fiona gazed around the cottage with regret deeply set in her features. If her friend was desperate for her to leave now, to leave the men behind, then danger was truly imminent.

But danger or no, Annie had a responsibility to those she'd rescued. "I canna leave the wounded at the mercy of the Butcher's men. I canna leave Mrs. Sullivan. I brought the soldiers here, and I put her in danger. They are my responsibility. One of the men is no' even sure who he is."

Fiona looked around the cottage, at each of the men who lay beneath blankets and a couple who were sitting up, leaning against the walls for support. Still healing, but not as badly injured as those who lay asleep.

"How are ye going to remain safe?" Fiona's voice was strained.

Annie shook her head, rubbed her temples where an aching pulse had started. "I dinna know. But we canna leave yet. No' until everyone is able to stand and walk out of here."

Fiona took her hand, squeezing. "Please, Annie. Ye must leave afore then. Some of these men willna be able to stand for weeks."

Annie squeezed her friend's hand back but then let go. "I canna leave without them, Fiona. I willna. I know the risk of remaining behind."

Fiona looked ready to argue. She pressed her lips together and then opened and closed them several times, squinting as she studied Annie—perhaps to see just how serious she was. Finally, she said, "I will be your eyes and ears, then. I'll make certain ye're the first to know if they are coming closer."

Annie shook her head. There was no way she was going to pull Fiona away from her important work. Without Fiona, the Jacobites would be less an incredibly important messenger. Fiona had spent years cultivating routes and establishing contacts across Scotland. It was because of her that messages were sent and received in a timely fashion from Jacobite factions in all cardinal directions.

"Nay, ye've got to get your messages out. I canna take ye away from your duty. We'll be fine. Eppy and I can manage."

One of the men in the corner pushed himself to standing, and Annie started to rush toward him, but he held out his hand in silent supplication for her to stop. "My lady, allow me to help."

Annie shook her head. "Jared, please, sit back down. Ye'll bust your stitches." She glanced at MacLean. "We've already had one of ye do so today."

But Jared ignored her, remaining on his feet. And then another man stood. "Ye can count on me, Doctor Annie."

Annie glanced at Fiona, Mrs. Sullivan, and Eppy to see if they were witnessing the anarchy underway.

From his place behind her, MacLean's voice rang out stronger than it should have for a man who was both drunk and feverish. "I promised to keep ye safe, Annie, and I mean to keep my word."

She wasn't certain what she should be more surprised about—his conviction or his use of her name. The way it sounded rolling off his tongue made her insides warm, but just as quickly, knowing the reality of their situation, she was back to worrying all over again. A wash of emotion cascaded over her. She was so overwhelmed and exhausted. But there was no room for such feelings or for falling down now. She had to buck up. There were people who needed her, and giving up wasn't in her nature. Nor was allowing anyone else to take up her responsibilities for her.

Annie's gaze fell on MacLean, following the line of his long nose and the jaw hidden beneath a thick mat of stubble. Maybe it was none of those things at all. Perhaps what had her most worried was that she would lose *him*. That the redcoats would come back and take his life like they'd tried to do already. Like they'd done to her brother.

And as much as she was loath to admit it, MacLean was a link to her brother she didn't want to lose. To a redcoat, to a wound, to battle, to anything or anyone else.

That realization struck her straight in the chest, and she had to lock her knees to keep from stumbling. She barely knew him at all. To have such a strong feeling rushing through her was nonsensical. It was the heightened emotions around what was happening, the fear, the grief, all of it, that were making her latch on to a man she barely knew. A man she wanted to know all the more.

Who was she fooling? She'd had those same feelings two weeks ago at Cullidunloch when he'd come for the feast.

"I thank ye, Lieutenant, but I would much rather ye lie abed and get well than worry about having to keep me or anyone else safe. Ye've done enough already. Rest. Heal."

She turned away from him to find Fiona staring at her in a way she'd seen before and didn't like. It was her friend's way of seeing through her, knowing that she was lying—not only to everyone in the room but to herself as well.

"Let me pour ye some pottage before ye head back out on the road," Annie said, trying to change the subject and shake the expression from Fiona's face. "And ye must be exhausted. I've a cot in the loft. Shall I make it ready for ye?"

Fiona cocked her head to the side. "I am hungry and in need of a few minutes' rest, but truly, Annie, I would like nothing more than for all of us to leave right now. However"—she stared at the men lying on the floor—"I can see that would be unwise at the moment. Perhaps I can take at least the men who can move and deliver them to a safer location?"

Annie bit her lip, looking to the two men who'd stood. "Aye, I think that would be a good idea." It was better to lower their numbers while they could. Fewer men would be easier to remove, and since they'd come here just over a week before—she'd lost count of the days—they'd acquired several more than their original number. "I'll prepare them to leave with ye. The rest will remain here with me until I can get them to safety."

As she said the words, she met MacLean's eyes. He'd somehow managed to push himself up on his elbow. The man was determined to help her for some reason, and he was going to hurt himself in the process.

"I'll let ye help me," she said to him, "if ye promise to lie back down. Ye'll tear your wound open again."

He grinned. "As ye say, Doctor."

Why did she feel like the man was nothing but trouble? And why did that warm her heart?

Ten

Craig woke with a headache that had nothing to do with his injuries and everything to do with the amount of whisky the lass had plied him with the day before. Granted, he'd needed it to sleep. He kept waking with a jolt and imagining redcoats banging down the door. One time he even woke thinking himself at home and swearing the image of Cumberland himself was looming over the bed when it had only been Mrs. Sullivan.

He'd nearly taken the poor woman's head off, but luckily he'd come back from his unconsciousness before he'd done any damage other than scare her out of her wits.

Despite the headache, his body was not in as much pain as it had been the day before, and he felt the intense need to get up and walk around. A quick scan of the cottage showed no women present, and so as gingerly as he could, Craig pushed himself up to sitting. The room spun a little as he did, as a result of either the alcohol or having been lying down for days now. His muscles screamed with the effort and yet tingled with the ability to finally stretch.

Recalling that he was naked as the day he was born beneath the blanket, he wrapped wool plaid around his waist, tying it off and not spending the effort to actually pleat it. Standing up, he wobbled all the more, slapping his hand against the wall to steady himself. He'd been injured before, and yet every time he moved after lying still for so long, he was surprised anew by the effort it took to move his feet once more. Like a bairn learning to walk all over again, he shuffled forward. A wave of dizziness overtook him, and he paused a moment to rub the sides of his head and regain his balance.

"She'll have your head." The words came from behind him, and Craig turned to find another man on the floor, also struggling to sit up. He was the nameless one. The one who some of the lads were starting to whisper might be a redcoat spy.

"Aye, she might." Craig grinned. "But I had to get up."

He needed to take a piss, and he was tired of going in the chamber pot beside him. He wanted to go out into the woods and leave his mark on a tree like a real man. Or at least like a man who didn't have to piss into the chamber pot that the woman he was sworn to protect had to clean up.

Craig reached for the door handle.

"I wouldna do that if I were ye," the man from the floor warned again.

"Aye, she'll be angry," said another.

Craig rolled his eyes. The few patients who'd been able to walk out of here had done so with Fiona the evening before, and now the rest of them had lain there with a bit more than a wee worry over whether the redcoats were going to find them and murder them in their sleep.

"I'm no' going to lie there like a weak bairn any longer, just waiting for my death to catch up to me. 'Tis time to build up my strength again, even if it just means walking out this door, breathing in fresh air, and facing the wrath of a Scotswoman."

Several faces stared back at him, blinking as though he'd gone mad. They'd understand soon enough when they had ample strength to stand. Craig had never been a man to laze about or to have anyone serve him, care for him. He was his own man, and he wasn't going to continue being an invalid. Warriors didn't have time to be invalids.

He shuffled forward, his unpleated kilt brushing against his ankles. Where were his boots? He looked around the small cottage, noting piles of men's belongings set aside by one wall. There were many pairs of boots, all of them scrubbed clean of the muck of battle. Another thing he would have done himself had he been allowed. There were weapons beside the boots and rucksacks, too, along with a neat pile of mended shirts and hose.

"Doctor Annie willna be happy that ye're moving about." 'Twas the sound of the old woman's voice that had him pausing mid-reach for boots.

Craig turned around, squinting toward the hearth where she sat very still in her chair, hands moving over her knitting. How had he not seen her sitting there before?

"She'll understand. The woman has seen enough battles and mended enough men to know their needs."

Mrs. Sullivan raised a brow, continuing to knit with her gaze on him, and he could feel the judgment in that look. She thought him foolish and stubborn. And she wasn't wrong.

Craig reached for his pair of boots.

"Might want to put on some socks at least," the old lady said. "'Tis frigid out this morning."

Craig grunted. "A little cold never hurt a man."

"Suit yourself."

He would suit himself, *thank ye verra much,* and he felt more than a wee bit petulant about it—a sentiment he only found to be more irritating than anything else. He lifted his foot to slip it into the first boot, gritting his teeth at the pain in his belly that came from the sheer effort and agony of the simple move. The wound on his belly wasn't deadly, but damn did it hurt. He lifted his left foot, shoving it into the other boot, feeling his world tilt as he did so. For the love of…

He wasn't bending down to lace his boots. Forget it.

Craig grabbed one of the clean, folded shirts and gingerly tossed it over his head, the length of it coming down to his knees. If he wanted, he could drop the plaid wrapped around his hips and walk outside in just the shirt without fear of showing too much. But just the slightest breeze might lift the hem of his shirt, and then, well—anything he might have wanted to remain a mystery would be revealed.

What he wouldn't give for a pair of breeches at that moment. Where were his breeches? Squinting toward the pile of folded garments, he thought he could make out several pairs, but the effort of going through them all to find his own seemed like too much.

He was taking too long. The more time he spent searching for his things, the more likely it became that she would return and force him back to bed. And to hell with that. Well, to hell with it while she wasn't here anyway.

Craig shuffled toward the door, feeling as though he'd aged thirty years since he'd been charging redcoats on the battlefield. A week before? The sheer effort it took to reach for the handle, all these small movements he'd taken for granted, was annoying the hell out of him. Why wouldn't his body work the way he needed it to?

His head hurt, he was slightly dizzy, his mouth was dry, and he felt like his guts were about to bust out of his abdomen. He probably was stupid for trying to do so much all at once, but there was no use lying in bed. A man didn't get better by lazing about. That was perhaps an exaggeration, but he didn't care. He was determined to walk out that door and piss on the first tree he saw, no matter who chanced to witness it happening.

The door creaked open, letting in dull dawn light and a blast of chill spring wind. Craig closed his eyes and drew in a deep breath, relishing the smell of fresh air and grass.

A hound looked up from where he lay outside the door, patiently guarding the cottage. Craig bent down despite the pain to pat the animal on the head.

"Good lad," he murmured and then stood up again, grinding his teeth at the tug on his belly.

He looked around the yard. Not a soul in sight. And there was a tree not ten feet away. That was a good goal, and so he focused his gaze on that and shuffled forward, the tips of his boots growing wet and dark with dew from the grass. The hound followed behind, cautious.

"Did she tell ye to watch me?" he asked, knowing he wouldn't get an answer.

At last he reached the tree, tugged the plaid out of place to allow himself a moment of victory at a goal met, and relieved himself.

Not ten seconds in, a deep sigh sounded from behind him that was decidedly more female than it was hound. Craig looked up at the sky, certain he could also hear her toe tapping on the ground.

"Look away, lass," Craig said. "I've no intention of stopping."

"Ye've made it this far. I'd no' take the pleasure of marking your territory away from ye."

He snickered and then watched the hound trot around to the other side of the tree, lift his leg, and participate eagerly.

When he was finished, he let the plaid fall back into place and turned around to face his nursemaid—or captor, whichever suited him better.

But Annie didn't look angry; nay, she looked ready to engage him in a challenge. Her arms were crossed over her chest, brows raised, and there was a slight lift to the side of her lip as though she found him amusing—and likely childish. He found himself studying her hand to see if there was a weapon clutched in her grasp.

"Do ye feel better?" she asked, her gaze darting at the gate and road beyond as though she expected them to be ambushed by dragoons at any moment.

"Infinitely." This was an exaggeration. He felt like throwing up and also like dropping to the ground right now. Lying on the cold, wet grass would be much better than standing. He was fairly certain that if the attack did come he would not be able to avoid the dragoons, and his own weakness disgusted him. Everything hurt, and he was famished. Even his vision was blurring in and out. Ballocks, but he felt like a bloody mess. And yet he stood there, tall as he could, reminding himself that he was Craig MacLean, soldier, leader. He didn't let anything or anyone put him down.

"Mrs. Sullivan worked hard to get the bloodstains out of that shirt. I hope ye've no' ruined her efforts with this foolishness."

Craig slanted his head slightly. "I promise to clean the stains myself next time."

She huffed and then pointed at him, swinging her arm back toward the cottage. "Back inside with ye, ye look ready to drop."

"Nonsense," he said, but she wasn't wrong. His limbs were shaking, and his vision was blurring more than it was focusing.

The lass took his arm casually, as if the touch were perfectly normal, allowing him to settle some of his weight on her. He would have preferred it be the other way around. When they reached the door, he let go of her, determined to make it the rest of the way inside on his own. Pushing it open, he swayed forward with the momentum but righted himself before she noticed. Then, with the steadiest steps he could muster, he made his way to his makeshift bed and dropped gratefully to the floor.

"Anyone else interested in being brave today?" she asked. "Might as well do it now afore the dragoons find us. Else ye'll find bullets in your arse."

From where he lay, he watched several hands shoot up.

"Ye've started a revolution, Lieutenant," Annie said, a bit of dry humor in her tone.

All he could do was grin as he laid his arm over his face and let darkness envelop him.

Foolish man.

Annie shook her head at the sleeping form at her feet. If she'd not come upon him when she did, he could very well be facedown in the grass right now, likely asleep in his own mess. She rolled her eyes and let out a deep sigh, grateful that she'd not found him like that and that she'd not seen any flashes of red in the perimeter beyond.

Fiona's warning was not far from her mind. They were sitting ducks out here, just waiting for the enemy to come knocking at their door.

"We told him no' to go," said the nameless man, which earned him a muttered threat from one of the other patients for being a snitch or a spy.

They were all starting to feel the walls close in around them. Tempers were rampant, and the men were bickering more often than not.

"'Tis hard to tell an old dog new rules," Annie said and then shook her head. "If any of the rest of ye would like to take a wee walk, then I'll be glad to help ye. As much as I want ye all to rest and get better, a bit of fresh air and exercise may help. It's been a week now. It'll do some good to remind your muscles what they are supposed to do."

She gazed down at Max, a young man who'd lost the lower part of his leg, several inches below the knee. "Even ye, Max, if ye're up for it."

Logan had been eager to get out of bed and move about after losing his foot at the ankle, trying to pretend as though nothing had happened.

"I'm a bit tired still, my lady."

She nodded, not wanting to argue with him. There was so much he had yet to deal with, she wasn't going to push him. Not when it was likely they'd all have to get up and move out soon. Her hands started to tremble, and she gripped the sides of her skirts hard to hide it from everyone in the room. No need for them to realize she was trying not to panic.

How much time did they have?

Which reminded her—she had to check on the wagon to make sure it was secure. Not that she knew much about wagons. She turned a quizzical look on the men.

"Have any of ye ever driven a wagon?"

"Aye, my lady," Max replied. "Many times on my family's croft."

"Well, when ye're up for it, I could use some help making certain it's fit for travel."

Max closed his eyes for a moment and then nodded. She could feel his nerves in that one look, and her heart went out to him, but it was better to work through anxieties than to be held at the end of a dragoon's bayonet.

"I've got a crutch that my husband used when his knees started to bother him. I'll fetch it from the barn." Their host stood from her usual post by the hearth.

"Thank ye, Mrs. Sullivan," Max said.

After assisting those who wished to in walking about outside, her eyes and ears perked for any sign of an attack, Annie got them all settled again and took a moment to breathe before launching into the next task. The busier she was, the harder it was to remember everything she didn't want to think about right then.

"Who is ready for some soup?" Annie marched to the hearth and started to ladle the savory-smelling meal into bowls for the men.

Eppy took the bowls to the men, nudging awake those who were sleeping. "Eat up, lads. Ye must regain your strength."

MacLean was the last to be woken, and he greedily slurped at the soup. A few of them, including him, asked for seconds, and she cautioned them to slow else they vomit up what they'd consumed. Too late... MacLean doubled over, gagging.

When he was finished, she wiped his brow with a cool cloth. "Slower next time," she said softly.

"Seems our roles are reversed," he said sheepishly, taking the cloth from her hand to clean himself up.

"What do ye mean?" Annie cocked her head to the side, studying him.

Craig shook his head. "My punishment for pushing it, I suppose."

"Nay, only for eating too fast."

He grunted.

"I can get ye another bowl if ye're still hungry."

He lifted a brow as if to question her willingness to tempt fate. "I think I'll wait just yet."

Annie smiled gently, taking the messed cloth from him. "Tell me when ye're ready."

Frustration filled his eyes, and she could well understand how he was feeling. She'd seen many a man go through this same struggle. To be once so hardy and strong and then to be weak and rely on others for help.

"Ye're getting stronger every day."

MacLean ran his hand through his hair. "No' fast enough."

She shrugged. "I think plenty fast."

"We need to leave here. I need to heal faster." MacLean's tense shoulders and tone gave away nearly everything he felt, and she wished she could help him, wished there was some sort of herbal concoction she could give him that would help him heal faster. But there wasn't anything other than good old-fashioned rest and getting plenty to eat. Nature would have to take its course.

"We're fine for now," she lied. She wanted to assuage his fears and her own; the only problem was she knew the truth. They were living on borrowed time.

From the way his brow furrowed, she could tell he didn't agree.

"Listen, MacLean," she started, but a low growl and bark sounded outside the door, sending a shiver of fear running down her spine.

No' fast enough…

Annie stood from where she crouched and turned around to see that Eppy and Mrs. Sullivan had both grabbed hold of the nearest fire poker and candlestick as weapons. The dog would not have howled for Fiona, who'd returned only the day before to the dog's repeated silence. Annie reached for her boot and pulled out her pistol.

"Everyone stay put," Annie whispered as the entire cottage seemed to become alert. The men tensed, those who could stand coming to their feet, prepared to battle to their last breath. She tucked the pistol at her back and went to the window, peeking out of the curtain to peer into the courtyard. In the waning afternoon light, she made out three burly men heading their way. They were covered in muck, and their faces looked as though they'd been dragged through a bog. Fear raced through her veins, not lessened any by the fact that they were wearing kilts and not redcoats. A kilt did not necessarily mean they were not here for nefarious purposes. There had been plenty of Scots on King George's side. Plenty of Scots killing their own countrymen.

"They've come for us!" Eppy whimpered.

"Ballocks," she murmured under her breath, too late remembering her company.

Thank goodness she'd thought to bar the door when she brought the last man back to bed because whoever had come calling was now jiggling at the handle trying to get inside.

Two loud bangs rattled the door on its hinges. "Grandma, 'tis us."

"Oh, Mary Mother of God!" Mrs. Sullivan leaped so

forcefully from her chair that she knocked it against the wall. It would have tumbled into the hearth were it not for Eppy grappling with it at the last moment.

"Wait!" Annie called as Mrs. Sullivan reached for the bar on the door. "Please, look out the window and make sure 'tis truly your lads come home."

"I'd know their voices." The old woman glared at her.

Annie had no doubt that she did, but she didn't trust anyone. It wouldn't be the first time she'd heard of someone lying about who they were to gain access to another's home.

"Aye, but make certain 'tis only them and no others," Annie said in hopes that would convince Mrs. Sullivan to check.

Their host frowned but agreed, and Annie moved aside to allow Mrs. Sullivan a view out the window of the men on the other side of the door.

"'Tis them." The old woman nodded. "And I see no others."

Someone pounded on the door again, and the dog barked; however, this time his bark was happy and excited with no bite in it at all.

Annie let out a sigh, her heart pounding so hard it sounded like drums in her ears. "Good." She removed the bar herself, and the three men tumbled inside, grappling up Mrs. Sullivan in massive bear hugs. The tears flowed from all four collectively.

Annie smiled, though watching the happy reunion was a blow to her already-crushed heart. She would not have that same moment with Graham and Logan.

"Where are your das?" Mrs. Sullivan asked.

The lads took a step back, all of them, heads bowed, shaking. No words were needed to explain to their grandmother what had happened to her sons. As one, the room collectively crossed themselves, and several whispered prayers sounded in the crackling of the fire.

"How did ye survive?" Mrs. Sullivan's voice croaked.

"Our das made us go to the back of the regiment. When we were hit with a blast, they were the first... Our commander told us to retreat, but we couldna leave without making certain they were all right. We leaped into the crater with the men, and..." The lad shook his head, tears streaming down his face. "We've been on the run, hiding out. Didna want to lead the bastards straight back to ye. We lost so many..."

"Ye need say no more. All that matters is ye're alive."

"We are."

"Oh, my lads." Mrs. Sullivan tugged all three of them back in for a hug.

After several moments, one of the men glanced up from where he bent over his grandmother and met Annie's eyes. Previously oblivious to the audience, he straightened, seeming then to take in the rest of the men recuperating on the floor.

"What's this?" he asked, which drew the attention of his brother and cousin and they too turned around to look.

"I'm Annie MacPherson," she introduced herself. "I served as Prince Charles's nurse, and now I'm caring for these men. Your grandmother was kind enough to take us all in while they heal." She glanced at the men behind her, who nodded their heads in the Sullivan lads' directions.

"They served the prince too?" the oldest of the trio asked.

"Aye, as did ye?"

"Aye."

"Then we can help each other," Annie said. "For I have it on good authority that this cottage will soon no' be safe for any of us."

The lads nodded. "No one is safe anywhere." There was torment in their eyes, and she hated to think about the horrible things they'd seen. Hated to think about what Cumberland and his men were doing to the countryside, tearing it apart as they tore men limb from limb. "We're going to be taking our grandmother away with us now, to Perth to meet the others."

Annie nodded, choking up at the thought of Mrs. Sullivan leaving. They'd grown quite close over the past week, and she wanted to make certain the woman was safe. Though she supposed she would be safer with her grandsons than she would with Annie and a bunch of wounded warriors, given the redcoats converging on them. Perhaps it would be a good idea for Annie to muster the men into riding with the Sullivans. They would do better in numbers.

"Ye're welcome to stay here as long as ye like," said the older Sullivan, making no offer to take them on the journey.

Disappointment stung deep. "Thank ye for that kindness."

"I would have it no other way," Mrs. Sullivan said, tugging her into a hug. "Ye're so verra brave, lass. Stay safe."

"I will." Annie swallowed back tears.

"And keep in touch. When this war is over, I want to see ye again." Mrs. Sullivan was so genuine, Annie had not the heart to tell her that such a fate was highly unlikely.

Annie smiled and pressed a kiss to the old woman's forehead. "I count on it."

The lads worked to help their grandmother pack, but when it came time to leave, Annie knew for certain they would take with them the wagon that she'd wanted to use for the men. There was no way that Mrs. Sullivan with her old bones could ride all the way to Orkney on horseback. Annie couldn't begrudge them that, even as it frustrated her. The wagon wasn't hers, and the lads had been through enough without her needs making their lives more difficult.

Annie and the men would be on their own for weeks until everyone could travel by foot again or they could figure out a way to get a new wagon and horses.

And so it was, with a sour belly and fear gripping her spine, that Annie watched the family roll away using the only means of transportation she'd had. Who knew, now, when, or if, she'd be able to get these men to safety.

Eleven

Inside the cottage, Annie sat in the chair that Mrs. Sullivan had occupied and stared at the five men across from her. While a couple were definitely sound asleep, at least one was faking it, and two were watching her in return.

The cottage air was stifling. Since the departure of Mrs. Sullivan and her lads, Annie had broken up a fight over a plaid blanket and endured at least an hour of bickering between Max and Leonard over whether they should be melting down any bits of lead they could find, or even the buttons of their coats, for bullets, or whittling sticks into arrows.

And then there was the man who couldn't remember his name and the vicious stares the other men were starting to give him. Was he a redcoat spy as they suspected?

"We're no' melting down anything, and if ye go looking for sticks in the woods, ye'll likely just find yourself at the end of a dragoon's blade," she interjected. "Ye need to rest so we can get out of here."

The men looked stunned at her raised voice, and she apologized and then went silent.

Her eyes were drawn to MacLean and the color coming back to his cheeks. Cheeks that were quickly becoming covered with a thick ginger beard. She cocked her head to the side, squinting her eyes at him as he slept. There was something so familiar about him, and not because she'd seen him for months at camp or at Cullidunloch. Something else niggled at the back of her mind, and she couldn't quite put a finger on it.

Their conversation at Cullidunloch came back to her, how he'd said they'd met before and never once explained.

When?

Something about that beard, though, the way it covered his face, making him look all the more rugged, all the more...sensual somehow.

How did she know this man before she'd known him?

"What will we do, Doc? How will we survive this?" Andy, propped up against a wall, looked toward the door, fear on his features. He shot the nameless man a look of fury.

Andy had suffered a bullet to the back that had narrowly avoided his spine. He was well on his way to being mended.

The men weren't going to give up, and she wasn't going to give up on them either. That was part of her vow made with Fiona and Jenny. They were the angels of the prince, and no matter what, they wouldn't give up. Their fathers, grandfathers, uncles, cousins, hadn't fought for the cause in order for them to give it up. Annie was lucky that her brothers both fought on the side of right, for Jenny had been battling her own brother for years. In fact, Hamish was still held prisoner within Jenny's walls, the prince having given her the wardenship over him.

"We will survive. That is what we do." Annie straightened her shoulders, daring any of them to contradict her.

"We are Highlanders. We are Jacobites. We fight for the Stuart line and a better country. We fight for our people and for our beliefs. We fight to remove a pretender from the throne and rid the country of his hounds."

The men who were awake started to clap, and the one who'd been pretending to sleep sat up to join in. Those who'd actually been asleep woke with the sound and looked about, confused, including MacLean, who met her gaze with intense curiosity.

"Right, Lieutenant?" she teased.

"Whatever ye've said, I'm certain 'tis true," he agreed with a slow wink aimed only at her.

She grinned. "Such confidence."

"How could I no' have confidence in the woman who has orchestrated our safety? We'd have all died on the battlefield were it no' for ye."

This was not necessarily true but highly likely. And they were not out of danger yet. Her skin prickled, and inside she was quaking, fearing a pounding on the door at any moment. Still, she wasn't going to claim all the glory. "We have many to thank besides me," she said. "Eppy was with me the entire time."

Her maid bowed her head modestly.

"And Mrs. Sullivan, too. My men who helped carry all of ye. We thank them all and keep them in our prayers."

"And we pray for ye, too, our angel," MacLean said.

Heat rose along Annie's cheeks. They were going to need a lot more than prayers in the coming days.

"How about some more soup?" She and Eppy went about serving the men another round of soup. They would need to take over the cooking now with Mrs. Sullivan gone. There still seemed to be a fair amount of oats and peas in storage and plenty of dried herbs, but no one had been hunting. There was no meat, and what the men truly needed to regain their strength was bone broth.

She would have to hunt. She was somewhat familiar with the task, but she was hardly an expert. Annie glanced at Eppy, who was carrying bowls to the men. The lass was also not skilled at hunting.

First their horse and wagon were gone, and now she had to worry about food. If they weren't going to be killed by dragoons, she couldn't very well let them all starve to death. The feeling of helplessness made her heart seize. Annie was normally the strong one, the one who did the helping. Annie had come this far; she wasn't going to let a little thing like shortage of food stop her. This was just another challenge she would have to overcome, and she could do that. Aye, she was going to provide.

"I think I shall try to hunt before it gets dark," she announced to no one in particular. "Eppy, will ye be all right staying here with the men?"

"My lady." Andy pushed up to his full height. "Allow me to do it."

"I couldna."

"My wound is better. I can do it. I used to hunt for my family every day."

"Me too." MacLean sat up.

"Ye canna," she started, pointing at the ginger-bearded soldier and then, not wanting to hurt his pride, she added, "Some men must stay behind to protect the others who are not yet well." Like Max, who would likely not be able to escape the cottage for weeks to come.

MacLean looked ready to argue, but Leonard, standing up beside Andy, interrupted. He'd lost an eye in the battle, and the white bandage over his face covered the stitches that closed the empty socket. "I'll go. The two of us will be sufficient. Ye're needed here, Doc." He grinned. "Besides, the bastards only took my bad eye."

Annie stared at the two men, their bandages clean, their skin color better than the day before. They would be ready to leave with Fiona when she came back. What if her friend returned before the men did? What if they were captured out in the woods? What if one of their wounds opened up and they couldn't get back?

Annie started to shake her head, but the men all erupted into protest. Her ears pounded, and the walls seemed to vibrate with her nerves.

"We canna lie here like invalids forever." Leonard had a very good point.

"All right, but no guns. Ye need to use arrows so as no' to draw attention."

Andy nodded. "A bow is my weapon of choice."

"Mine too," added Leonard.

Annie cringed on the inside, apprehension running deep. This was a bad idea, but a necessary one. "Hurry back before nightfall, even if your hunt is no' fruitful. 'Tis better to be within the cottage than roaming about in the dark."

"Aye, my lady, we will."

Fortunately for them the Sullivan lads had not divested them of all their weapons and boots, so Leonard and Andy dressed and flexed the bows, choosing the ones that suited them best before heading out.

"Godspeed, lads."

They tipped their hats to her, and she tried to ignore the way her belly flipped over. Watching them walk out the door felt like she was sending bairns out to the slaughter. But there really was no other choice. They were running out of food, and any day now—possibly even tonight, when Fiona returned—she'd lose their strength of arms.

Annie pressed her hand to her heart, feeling the erratic beat of fear beneath her palm. Goodness, but how she wished she could reverse time. But to when? Scotland had been fighting redcoats since before she'd been born, even before her own parents were born. This was a fight that was generations long and had never showed any signs of waning, not until now when Prince Charles had finally amassed an army that had beaten the king's troops more than once. Aye, this last battle had been epically devastating, but that didn't mean it was over. Jenny was right now renewing the troops. Fiona was traversing the Highlands delivering messages, and Annie was to do her part to make well the soldiers who would raise up their arms once more against tyranny.

Indeed, the English and Scottish thrones had been fighting over rulership of their lands for centuries. War was inevitable when men believed only in their own rights to power. War was inevitable when men did not believe in the freedom to choose one's own religion.

Prince Charles Stuart was the rightful heir. His direct line dated back to James I of England and the VI of Scotland, son of Mary Queen of Scots and nephew to Elizabeth I. And yet the throne had not been passed to him because he was a Roman Catholic and an edict passed in England—without Scottish voice—had deemed papists ineligible for succession. As if blood were not a factor in the divine right of kings! And so it was that the Stuart line, which had ruled for over three hundred years, was superseded by the House of Hanover, a bloodline that was neither English nor Scottish, save for a few drops.

Annie stabbed at a burning log in the hearth with a poker a bit more violently than what was called for. How dare mere mortal men decide they had the right to choose who should be king? And if they thought such a right was theirs, then they should suffer at the end of a Jacobite blade.

"Might ye be murdering that log?"

Annie turned around to see MacLean sitting up, facing her. His torso rippled with muscle still despite having lain about for the past week. She supposed a mere sennight was not enough to deflate muscles that had taken years to build. All the same, why should he be so beautiful, even with a bandage wrapped around his middle and another about his head?

"Do ye think it sufficiently dead?" She glanced behind her with a sarcastic sigh.

MacLean chuckled. "I've seen ye wield a blade afore, lass, and I'd say if ye wanted it dead, the beast would be."

She whipped her head around. "Ye've seen me with a blade?" Shoving the poker back in place, she stalked toward him and rested the back of her hand on his forehead. "Ye dinna have a fever, and yet ye hallucinate. Was this a dream ye had? While here? Because I assure ye, Lieutenant, ye'd no' have seen me with a blade. I've only drawn a pistol and have yet to use it."

He lifted a brow, which made her question even herself—and she knew very well she wasn't the violent type.

"I am no' mistaken, lass."

She studied his face, the way his thickening beard covered up his strong jaw and framed his wide, full lips. His upper lip had a faint scar on the right side from top to bottom, as though he'd suffered a slice there once. Thank goodness his assailant had not cut off his lip completely, for she couldn't seem to recall a more perfect pair that she'd ever seen.

Again that sense of familiarity ate at her. Where did she know him from—*before*?

She itched to touch him. To feel the bristles against her fingers. Was on the verge of moving toward him but quickly caught herself, curling her fingertips into her palm. "Have ye had a beard afore?" she asked, hoping he hadn't noticed her falter.

MacLean's lips twitched in a just barely noticeable smile. "Aye." His voice was soft, intimate.

Annie licked her lips, wiped her slickening palms on the front of her gown. That one word uttered on his beautiful lips had the power to make her shiver. Had the power to make her forget for a moment where they were, who was around them, and what was happening in the world. "Do ye mind if I ask when?"

He shrugged. "Several months ago. I found it helped keep my identity hidden from the enemy. Plus it keeps me warm." He winked, and she felt a sudden spark of desire swirl in her belly from that slow dip of his eyelid.

It was madness, she knew, and yet she wanted him to wink at her again. Wanted him to tease her and smile. Wanted to touch his lips with her own. She was supposed to hate him...but the truth was she didn't. And she hadn't ever since he'd come to her castle. Truly, she hadn't hated him before then either, couldn't remember why she'd set her mind to do so. Except for his rudeness, which he'd not displayed since that day at Cullidunloch.

"Why do ye ask?" He pushed up to stand, wearing trews now, *thank goodness,* because she feared the plaid blanket would fall away and he'd be standing there nude before her. She'd seen plenty of naked men in her line of work, but never one who made her heart pound so.

Annie swallowed, uncertain how to answer as her mind was now going in a very different and inappropriate direction. She gave a slight shake of her head and then tucked a loose lock of hair behind her ear. "'Tis nothing," she said. "I just... Ye seem familiar with a beard, and I canna remember ye at camp having had one."

He grinned and stroked his beard. "Ah, I see. But the truth is, lass, when we first met, I looked much the same as I do now, minus the bandages, I suppose." After a second, he said, "And I was more fully clothed."

Annie laughed nervously at the mention of his lack of clothes, her gaze dipping to take in the corded muscles of his arms, the sprinkle of ginger hair over his chest that tapered into a line dipping beneath his trews. He seemed closer to her than he'd been a few moments before. When had he moved? He was only a couple feet away now. A respectable distance, and yet she felt oddly enveloped by his presence.

"I dinna remember meeting ye." Why did her voice have to sound so strained?

"Och, lass, but 'tis a meeting I've never forgotten." The intimacy of his voice had deepened to something warm…sensual, even.

Annie chewed her lip a moment trying to decide if she should flee now, end this conversation, or ask him to explain. Why did it seem like something incredibly intimate had happened between them before? If so, she needed to know what he knew. "Tell me, MacLean."

He liked the way she said his name, calling him MacLean, the way it rolled off her velvet tongue. And he shouldn't. For he was supposed to be looking after her as though she were his wee sister, and that was most definitely not the way he was thinking of her right now. Thinking like this was not going to help him in the task her brother had laid at his feet. Perhaps if she called him by his given name as his sister did.

"Call me Craig, lass." He wanted to reach for her, slide

his fingers over her face, where she worked so hard to keep her emotions at bay.

"All right, Craig."

Ballocks. That was worse. Her voice was like a warm caress, and he imagined her saying his name over and over against his skin—a thought that was entirely inappropriate, but he didn't give a bloody damn.

He hobbled toward the shelf that housed the whisky and opened a bottle, pouring a dram each into two cups and then handing her one. He leaned casually against the wall and sipped. When she took a taste, he spoke. "It was after the battle at Falkirk."

She narrowed her eyes, watching him, and took another tiny sip of her whisky. "I was in the prince's entourage. He was ill then and asked me to look after him."

"Aye, and when I found ye, ye were alone, outside Bannockburn House and growing quite ill yourself."

She licked a drop of whisky from her lips and cocked her head at him, challenging. "I rarely get sick, Craig. Why should I believe ye?" There was an edge to her voice.

"I recognized ye from the gathering before the war, but at the time, Graham and I..." He paused a moment, his throat tightening, the loss of his friend, her brother, still so fresh. "We'd only just met, and I'd yet to be introduced to ye. I thought to leave ye be, but then ye started to...retch."

Annie's cheeks grew red as she stared at him now, her beautiful amber eyes wide, the same ones that had been reddened by fever when first they'd met. "Please tell me it was no' your neckerchief I kept?"

Craig grinned. "Aye, lass, I'm afraid it was. I had nothing else to offer, and ye were sorely in need of it. Ye tried to refuse me, but I insisted. I offered to help ye inside, and that was when the situation took a more serious turn."

Annie's brows rose together, and he wanted to stroke her reddened cheeks, smooth his thumb over those arched brows. "More serious than vomiting?"

He couldn't help but chuckle at that. "Aye. Ye wiped your mouth and then pulled a dagger from your boot."

"Nay..." She tightened her grip on her cup, her knuckles growing white.

"Oh, aye. Ye told me to get away from ye, swore to cut off my"— *ballocks, and feed them to me*—"well, ye swore to cut me to pieces if I came another step closer. Called me a savage *Sassenach* bastard."

Annie's mouth fell open wide, shock on her features. "Ye're jesting."

"I wish I was. Ye called me every unmentionable thing known to man, told me to run back to my butchering friends before ye started retching again." He paused to sip his whisky, a movement that she mimicked. "In any case, I caught the tip of your blade with my lip." He touched the faint scar. "When ye dropped the dagger and started to sway on your feet, I picked ye up, weak as a lamb just born, and carried ye inside. Found a spare bedroom to put ye in and was nearly accosted by your maid, who clearly learned her knife work from yourself." He made erratic slashing movements with his hand. "I'm lucky to still have my eyes."

It would have been easy to take her advice and

disappear back then, the lass could have made a lesser man fall to his knees with that mouth, but he wasn't a dishonorable man. What man of honor would leave a lass to her own devices outside the walls, in her retching, delusional state? Craig chuckled at the memory.

"What are ye laughing at? This story is…" She pressed a palm to her reddened cheek. "'Tis preposterous."

"Dinna be embarrassed, lass. I remember it fondly now that I know ye. I confess, before I thought ye a mad termagant."

She groaned. "I dinna blame ye. I have no recollection of that. How could I no' have recognized ye? For shame…"

"Well, to be fair, lass, I shaved the beard immediately, fearing another lady might take me for a wild man."

"Oh, nay…"

He chuckled. "I jest."

"'Tis no wonder ye avoided me after that."

"Well, I did want to stay in one piece. Though ye were feverish, I was a wee bit concerned ye might turn out to be the madwoman ye portrayed even once well. Besides, my lady, ye have seen many of us at our worst."

"I never did return your neckerchief."

"Nay."

"I will have a new one made for ye, I swear it."

"I've no' much use for a cravat these days." He touched his bare neck.

"All the same, 'tis no' right that I kept it for so long. I should have returned it to ye. But I didna know who ye were, and now…" She let out a little frustrated mewl. "'Tis I who should apologize."

"Never apologize for who ye are."

She jerked her head up. "Is that a jest, sir? Ye think me a mean-spirited vomiter?"

Craig's lip twitched into a small smile. "I would never say that. And if we're being honest, I didna want the neckerchief back after what I saw ye wipe off onto it."

Her mouth fell open, and though she was silent, he could almost hear the groan in her eyes. "I'm going to need another drink, sir."

Craig poured her another dram. "Dinna drink too much or else—" He stopped abruptly, about to have said *Else Graham will have my head for getting ye tipsy*.

"What?"

He shook his head, swallowing around how close he'd just gotten to making a major faux pas.

"Ye're thinking of Graham."

His heart lodged in his chest. How did she do that?

Then she was touching his hand, squeezing his fingers. The slimness of her hand was engulfed in his grasp. Her skin was not soft but rough from working, and her fingers were callused as well as her palm. This was not a lady who sat idly by but a woman who woke before the dawn and often fell asleep mere hours before she had to wake and start all over again. She was strong, not only physically but mentally.

Craig stared down at her for several moments, taking in the flush on her cheeks, the way the bones of her face were subtle—not sharp, but solid. Her eyes met his with a slight challenge in them. There was a haughty tilt to her chin that made him want to smile. All this smiling in a man used to brooding, and so he forced himself not to even try.

"I miss him so much, and I know ye must as well," she said.

"Aye." Craig let her hand fall away, afraid he'd pull her into an embrace. He drained his cup and poured another. "He was a good man."

"The verra best." She took a small sip of her whisky, eyeing him over the cup. "Do ye have any siblings?"

Craig nodded numbly. "A sister, Marielle. She is younger than I am."

"Do ye get to see her often?"

"No' of late."

"That is verra sad."

But not permanent…

"Aye, for the both of us, as our parents are gone. And though she's with a relative, there is something no' quite the same about being gone from one's siblings." Until that moment he'd not truly realized how much he missed his sister. He'd always thought her better off without him, and now he wondered if that were the case.

"This is true. I fear I willna be able to see Logan for a long spell, and I fear how he is doing, how he will take the loss of our brother…"

"Logan is strong. So are ye."

"We were stronger together. The Butcher has decided to take us out, one by one. First he tried with Logan and then succeeded with Graham, and now our home burned… I have nowhere to go and all these men here to help." She looked beyond him to the other patients in the croft. "I shouldna admit it, but I confess… I am fearful for what's to come. Does that make me weak?"

"Och, lass, weak? Nay, no' ye. Ye marched out onto the battlefield while dragoons still circled and dragged men to safety. Ye've risked your life over and again for the cause. When the Butcher burned your house, ye didna run, ye rode headlong toward the enemy. And even now, when ye could leave to save yourself, ye've stayed. That is the opposite of weak."

Her lips quirked in a small semblance of a smile. "Thank ye for saying that. I am no soldier. I admire my dear friend Jenny for taking up the calling of leading an army."

"Colonel Jenny?"

"Aye. I fear I've no' got her talent for battle."

"She's an amazing leader and soldier, but, lass, without healers, where would all the broken go? I admire *your* talent. I've no' the patience or knowledge for much beyond wielding a sword. Besides that, the way I've seen you swing your dagger, any enemy ye come upon should be scared. Dinna discount that," he jested.

"Thank ye, Craig."

A pretty blush had started on her neck, rising up toward her chin—a result of the whisky? Or perhaps the striking intimacy of a conversation between two people who only weeks before had been mostly strangers. The urge to touch her was overwhelming, to trace his fingers over her collarbone, to feel her pulse beneath his caress. Memories from Cullidunloch, of her in her night rail, so trusting as he'd stitched her up. And then when she'd called to him, and he'd come back to her chamber… He'd wanted to kiss her, had started to before he came to his senses. Now he wished he had, to at least have the memory of her soft mouth on his.

Something about the lass's presence seemed to calm and excite him all at once, and he couldn't figure out why. Rarely did he come across a person who he genuinely liked, especially someone who'd drawn a knife on him. But Annie was different. He liked her very much.

"No matter what happens, I will be right here beside ye," he said. "Ye're no' alone."

And then the door rattled, reminding them just how *not* alone they were.

Twelve

EVERYONE IN THE CROFT STILLED, STARING AT THE door. The wind howled, rattling the entire building. Annie's trembling returned full force, and her heart felt as though it had leaped into her throat.

They were outside. She could feel it. Prowling around the property. Taunting them. When she'd gone out on patrol earlier in the morning with Eppy, they'd searched as thoroughly as they could and found no signs of dragoons in the immediate vicinity. But now they'd come.

Another gust blew against the house, and everyone grabbed whatever they could within reach that could be used as a weapon.

The door shook. Outside thunder rumbled, and a gust of wind blew beneath the door, making the candles flicker. Whatever sunlight had been there quickly dissipated as a storm brewed.

The men were silent, as were Annie and Eppy.

This was it. A storm raged, and they were going to be ripped out of the croft by the Butcher's henchmen. Well, she wasn't going to go down without a fight.

And she wasn't going to wait for them to knock down the door.

Annie marched forward, ignoring the hissing of her men to stay back. She reached for the handle, prepared to wrench open the door when a massive gust of wind blew it open, cracking it against the wall.

Rain pelted inside, splattering Annie in the face. They all stilled, waiting for the march of men dressed in red to stain their doorway, but there was no one there.

Taking a shaky breath, she took a step forward, only to have Craig's hand on her arm stopping her.

"Dinna go out there," he mouthed.

"I have to," she mouthed back. The dragoons were either going to come in, or she and her men were going to have to go out. One thing was for certain, their enemy wouldn't just go away. They would not be so lucky.

A flash of lightning lit up the fields, showing that dragoons were not on their doorstep, but figures were edging closer in the distance. And then the light was gone, and she felt like a child all over again thrust into darkness.

"Did ye see them?" she asked, her throat dry and tight.

"Aye," Craig said. "They've returned."

"They will kill us."

"Why would they do that?" He sounded genuinely confused.

"The Butcher's orders."

"But they are with us."

"What?" Another flash of light showed the men drawing closer, and she nearly collapsed with relief when she spied not dragoons but Leonard and Andy returning across the field carrying a stag they'd felled. They were greeted with whoops and cheers by the small party in the cottage, and she did run out into the rain then, eager to hug the men who were not in fact murderers.

"We can make a hearty stew with that," Annie said. "Well done, lads."

All of them worked together to prepare the food. Large succulent chunks of venison were added to the pot with turnips, potatoes, and herbs. Just the act of preparing food, the way the air was scented with it, brightened the somber mood of the cottage. The men seemed in better spirits, even Max, who took a walk outside with Eppy's help.

For a few brief moments, they were all able to forget where they were and what had brought them together. Well, mostly. For they all kept a part of themselves on alert for any outsiders coming near.

"We should dry the rest of the meat," Craig said. "I know the thought of eating jerky from here on out is no' exactly exciting, but it will keep us fed if the men should be leaving soon and if we're in a hurry to escape ourselves."

While the men prepared the meat, Annie refused to let any of them dig the hole they were going to use for a makeshift smokehouse, instead doing the work herself, groaning at the way her muscles ached from the exertion. She slammed the old shovel into the ground, wincing as a fresh splinter pierced her skin, and tossed the scoop of dirt she'd unearthed aside.

Annie huffed, then turned at Craig's approach, and wiped at the sweat prickling on her brow.

Craig grinned at her, drawing closer. "Ye've some dirt..." He lifted the hem of his shirt and wiped at her brow while Annie stood there speechless.

The touch was soft and intimate, and at the same time he'd exposed the muscled ridges of his torso. She'd not seen that expanse of sensual flesh since he'd started wearing clothes again, and the sight of him was...breathtaking.

Annie cleared her throat. "Thank ye," she murmured softly.

Craig looked like he wanted to say more but instead nodded as he backed away. He made himself busy elsewhere, disguising the gate with fallen branches and other bits of nature's rubbish. Annie scanned the fields in front of them, the road behind the stone wall covered in brambles. Hiding the gate would not deter anyone who wished to enter, but it might at least slow them down enough to give those within a warning. She couldn't help but worry that every second he spent trying to hide the gate was another second when dragoons could see him there and ask what he was doing.

She wished that the Sullivans hadn't taken their hound with them when they left. At least when the dog was there, it had been able to give them a warning of anyone's approach.

Later that evening, while Annie sat and ate a bowl of stew on a log before the makeshift fire, Craig came and joined her. He smelled good, and the heat of his body warmed her on that side. She bit her lip to hold in the sigh that wanted to escape. They'd not had a chance to speak privately since he'd looked her in the eyes and told her she was not alone.

Annie spared him a glance and a small smile before returning her gaze to the smoking meat, feeling foolish for avoiding eye contact but at the same time needing some measure of distance between them.

Craig had no idea how deeply his words had touched her. As soon as they were out of his mouth, caressing her ears, she'd backed away, pretended a personal need so as not to hear him say another word. And now she found herself craving something more. To hear more, savor that personal connection. She'd just lost her brother, and the wound was so very deep. Was that why Craig's words had been so endearing? Was that why she wanted so desperately to latch onto the promise they held and never let go?

Grief had to be the reason. She barely knew Craig, and yet whenever he was near, asleep or not, he moved her in ways she couldn't understand and dared not try to explain. Almost as if she had this being trapped inside her chest that fought to be released the moment he appeared.

Annie shoved a hot bite hastily into her mouth, breathing harshly around the hunk of meat that was burning her tongue. *Zounds!* Eating while nervous was not a good idea.

"The stew is perfection," he said, blowing the heat from his spoon.

Annie managed to swallow her food without having done too much damage. "Thank ye." She reached for the cup of watered ale at her side, easing some of the burn in her mouth.

"How is the meat coming along?" Craig peered into the pit.

"This batch looks near done." She glanced over at him. "Ye should be inside resting. 'Tis getting chilly out here."

"I'm done resting." Craig took another bite, and she watched his jaw moving, working the meat.

"Ye canna be done resting. Ye've still got wounds and need at least a few more days afore ye can truly move about."

"They are mostly healed." He grinned at her wolfishly. "Shall I show ye?" The maddening man started to lift his shirt once more.

"Nay," she huffed, feeling like a sour nursemaid because as much as she personally wanted him to strip, she also needed to be serious. "There is still a chance you might reopen the wounds."

"Only if I were to perform some great exercise, such as running or building a new barn or...never mind."

Annie rolled her eyes, ignoring the bawdy tone of his *never mind*. "Building a new barn? Have ye ever built a barn?"

He shrugged. "I've helped with a few."

"I'm certain the Sullivans' barn is still standing. However, ye may just have to run should any dragoons sniff us out. Hence, my edict to rest is still valid."

"I'll no' allow any dragoons around my meat." He waggled his brows and took a hearty bite at that, grinning at her widely as he chewed.

Heat rose to Annie's cheeks. She was worldly enough that his reference to meat was not lost on her. Flustered, she gave a short chuckle and patted the pocket in her apron where she was storing a pistol. "Me either."

"Are ye a good shot, lass?" Craig set aside his bowl and boldly reached into her pocket, pulling out the pistol. His fingers brushed against her thighs.

Annie worked hard to suppress the shudder his touch

elicited and pretended to be staring very intently at her own pistol in his hands. "Depends on the target."

"A moving target then?"

"Depends on the speed." She shrugged. "But I'm certain to hit some part of a dragoon, whether it be his ear or his toe."

"I fear if ye're aiming for either of those spots then we're all doomed. On the other hand, if ye wield the pistol as well as ye wield a dagger, I'd run."

Annie laughed, enjoying their easy banter back and forth.

"Nice weapon." He handed it back to her, the wooden handle smooth in her palm, and she put it back into her pocket.

"Thank ye. 'Twas my mother's."

"Was she a good shot?"

"I dinna know." Annie wished she'd paid more attention when her mother was alive. No pocket of her memory carried an image of her mother even holding the weapon. Annie'd found it in a trunk in her mother's bedchamber after she'd passed, among other items that looked to have been from her wedding trousseau.

"I'm no' certain about mine either," he said, wrinkling his brow. "She died shortly after birthing my sister."

"I'm so sorry." Absently, she touched his arm, giving him a subtle squeeze. He placed his hand over hers, warm and gentle.

It was funny to think of Craig as gentle. He was so big, so broad, and she knew him to be a hearty, fierce warrior. And yet he handled her with a touch that was almost delicate.

"I'm sorry about your mother, too," he said. "Seems we are both orphans."

"This war has made orphans of many. At least we're old enough to care for ourselves."

"Aye." Craig opened his mouth to continue but then closed it again. He patted her twice and then removed his hand from hers.

He leaned forward, scooping up a piece of meat from the makeshift grill and bending it in half, the fibers of the dried venison breaking. "'Tis done. Try a bite?" He handed her a piece, and she popped it into her mouth, surprised at the intensity of the flavoring. They'd actually done a good job—shocking considering none of them had ever made it before. "Perfection."

"Aye, perfection." His words caught her off guard, especially the way he said them, and she glanced at him to see that he was staring at her with a look on his face she couldn't decipher.

An intensity shimmered in the blue-green depths of his eyes. Annie's insides warmed, and so did her face. That heated look had her breath catching, and she found herself momentarily at a loss for words.

"Are ye flattering me, sir?" she asked, trying to keep her voice calm when she was fairly certain she squeaked like an adolescent lad.

"Merely stating a fact." He winked slowly and then looked down toward her mouth.

Oh goodness... She licked at her lower lip, feeling that same frisson of heat from weeks ago when he'd stared at her mouth on the threshold of her chamber door. The same regard that made her think of kissing… *Snap out of it, Annie!*

"Ha," she said with a snort. "Ye were no' saying such a few months ago. You called me a madwoman."

"Ah." Craig chuckled, the sound utterly sensual. "But I was thinking it."

She playfully slapped at his arm, trying to breathe like a normal person rather than one who'd forgotten a basic function. "No, ye were no'. Dinna tease." But the last of her words came out so close to a purr that it shocked her as much as it appeared to shock him, for Craig stilled, his gaze intensifying.

Then a slow grin curled his lips. "I was thinking ye were a perfect madwoman. Does that no' count?"

Annie rolled her eyes with exaggeration, groaned, and slapped her hands to her chest as if he'd wounded her. She leaned back on the log, just to the point where if she leaned any further she would fall. Craig's hand came swiftly to the small of her back, as though he thought to catch her. She bolted upright, feeling the searing heat of his intimate touch through her gown where his hand remained.

They both paused, staring at each other in the swiftly fading light of day. All this playing around, the teasing that wove its way between heated looks—there was no denying what they both wanted. What they'd both been thinking about. And now, with their eyes locked, Annie's breath caught, the heat of his palm against her spine.

Kiss me…

Craig leaned forward, and without hesitation she did

the same. As though his simple movement was a beckoning call to her entire body, the culmination of a game of chase.

Only he didn't kiss her—he spoke instead. "We should go inside," he murmured only a few inches from her face. "'Tis getting dark, and there's more meat to dry."

"Aye."

But neither of them made a move to retreat. All Annie could think about was his perfect lips, how his top lip dipped in the center, creating a heart shape with a tiny scar. How would his lips feel upon hers? Would the ginger hair of his beard tickle her skin? Would he be a passionate kisser? A sensual kisser? Would he taunt and tease, or would he take her breath away, or all of it at once? Would all the daydreaming she was doing right now be ruined when he did finally kiss her and it was too wet or too abrasive?

"What are ye thinking?" he asked, his voice so sensual and smooth she thought she'd melt just from the sound of it.

Dare she tell him what she was truly thinking about? Annie's gaze flickered up to his. "Kissing." The word was out before she could pull it back.

A slight twitch at the corner of his mouth drew her gaze back to his lips. "Do ye often think of kissing, lass?"

"What if I do?"

He laughed softly, gravelly. "I'd say 'tis a good thing ye're wicked with a blade."

Annie giggled at that, hoping he wouldn't take his hand away from her back. "And what are ye thinking about?"

"Kissing."

Oh my… She swallowed. "Do ye think of kissing often?" Her voice was breathless, heady, oh God, she wanted to kiss him so much.

"Whenever ye're near."

No sweeter words had ever touched her ears. "Oh, Craig," she whispered. "I want ye to kiss me."

"God, I thought ye'd never ask." The space between them closed at an interminably slow pace that only made her want to grab onto him, to tug him closer.

Annie's eyes dipped closed, and she breathed out slowly, waiting, her pulse leaping. And then he was there, brushing his lips ever so gently against hers. They were warm, soft, and the bristles of his beard prickled her skin in a way that made her smile and gasp.

"Does it tickle?" he teased.

"Aye," she sighed.

"Do ye wish me to shave it?"

Annie opened her eyes, staring into his gaze. She reached for the bristles the way she'd wanted to earlier in the cottage, letting them tickle her palm. The sensation was at once sensual and amusing. She rather liked the way it felt. "Dinna shave it."

He grinned. "Perhaps for ye then, lass, I'll keep it."

Craig leaned in again, his lips touching hers, but no longer the soft brush of moments before. Now he pressed them to hers in earnest, and her heart pounded, her breath catching. *Aye, this was a kiss.*

His hands came to rest on either side of her face, his warm breath fanning over her cheek. Languidly he slid his mouth back and forth, sending sparks of excitement coiling through her. The kiss was not at all carnal, and yet it set every inch of her skin aflame. Annie slid her arms about his neck. She threaded her fingers into the long hair at the nape of his neck, softer than the bristles at his cheek. He slid his mouth over hers again and again, catching her up in a whirlwind of lips, breath, and heat.

Shivers raced along her spine and limbs, and she started to feel a pulsing ache in places she'd never known could pulse or ache. Her breasts felt warm and full, and her nipples hardened into tiny, tingling points. Between her thighs, a spark—and all she could think of was what it would be like to taste him, to climb onto his lap and devour him whole.

Against her lips, he murmured, "I shouldna, I canna."

All she wanted was to shout, *Why, why no'*? Except she knew why… Soon she'd be on her way and he on his. He couldn't stay with her forever, even though he'd said she'd never be alone, even if this was the most amazing kiss any two people could have ever shared. He was a soldier, and she was a healer, and while they'd likely wind up in the same places of carnage, she couldn't allow anything to get in the way of her mission for the prince. What if his current injuries didn't heal as well as she hoped or a future injury made it so that he could no longer be a soldier? If she were with him as his wife, would she not feel an obligation to remain at home by his side rather than following the prince into battle?

Aye, she would.

"Oh, what nonsense."

"What?" Craig pulled away an inch at her shocking grumble.

Dear God, had she said those words aloud? Annie shook her head, both of them breathing heavily. She touched the heat of her cheek, mortified to have actually uttered the words. She could not tell him the line of her thinking or that she was calling nonsense on herself. One kiss did not mean they had to marry. Utter folly.

"I am only thinking that 'tis nonsense for ye to think ye canna kiss me. I gave ye permission. I wanted it."

"Aye, but..." He furrowed his brow. "I made a promise..."

She didn't want to hear him say anything about her brother because she could sense that was the way in which this conversation was headed, and she didn't want to ruin the moment or the memory of how amazing it had been to finally kiss this man. The perfection of it would be what kept her going through the long nights to come.

"Shh." Annie gently pressed her fingertip to his lips. "We kissed. We enjoyed it. And that's it." She didn't wait for him to say anything else. Annie leaped to her feet and marched toward the perimeter, every nerve in her body on edge for the dragoons who could leap out at them and for the emotions Craig elicited inside.

Even marching the grounds as the sun set all around them, a stern look on her face, Annie made for a mesmerizing sight. Normally he'd attribute his behavior and seeming fascination with her to too much whisky, but the truth was it'd been hours since he'd had any, and even then he had consumed very little.

Craig had not meant to kiss her. In fact, he'd refrained for quite some time. But in that moment where she'd spoken it into being, he'd been lost. Bloody hell, but it had been amazing. She'd felt so good against him, soft, lush, and her eagerness to kiss him back had nearly undone him. Craig had kissed many a lass, but truth be told it had been a long while since he'd last indulged. He was too busy with the demands of war, of country. Too busy in proving his worth to the world, that he was not merely the son of a great man but a great man himself.

And so he'd not indulged in the baser needs of the flesh, instead managing to force himself to set aside those desires. He was probably addled for thinking he could go on as long as he had or longer.

But didn't that make the two of them perfect for kissing one another? Two people joined in their own madness.

She whirled on her heel, rushing back to him as the sun faded further and shadows leaped from the edges of the grounds.

Craig thrust his hands into his hair, remembering too late about the wound there and letting out a gasp of pain as he contacted it, knees buckling.

"Are ye all right?" She rushed toward him, concern etched on her features as she knelt before him.

"I'm fine," he muttered, embarrassed at having been

such a fool and for appearing so weak before her now that he was supposedly recovered.

"Let me see." She edged closer, leaning toward him, her hands moving over the bandage.

But all he could focus on was her scent surrounding him, the heat of her body, how close her breasts were to the tops of his thighs, and how all he would have to do was shift slightly to feel them brush against him. How her mouth was dangerously close to his and how much he wanted to kiss her some more. Ballocks, but he was a cad. He no longer felt any pain, only the rising ache of his groin tightening against his trews. Perhaps he'd been a fool to go without a woman's touch for so long, for now this one woman was making him pant with desire like a rabid, lusty dog.

Craig took her wrists in his grasp and gently pushed her away. "I'm fine, I swear it. Besides, ye can barely see out here."

"If ye say so…" She sat back on her heels and stared up at the evening sky, exposing the long expanse of her neck. "'Tis getting dark out rather quickly." There was an edge of worry to her voice, the same one he felt.

"Aye. Let's go inside." He stood, lifted the basket of dried meat, and then held out his free hand to her, which she took as she rose. As they walked, she brushed at the leaves and grass that stuck to her skirts.

The door to the cottage opened before they reached it, and Eppy popped her head out. "Ah, good, I was coming to see if the meat was ready."

"It looks delicious, aye?" Annie said, holding out the basket.

Eppy nodded, eyeing Craig narrowly. No words were exchanged, but he had an idea of what it was she was saying to him with her expression: *I saw everything—stay away from my lady.*

Eppy had likely been watching them from the door all along. He wasn't surprised. The two women had looked out for each other for years. It would be odd if they didn't continue doing so now.

They were lucky already that they'd not been found out. Fiona had shared the news of the dragoons searching the Highlands for Jacobite sympathizers. It was only a matter of time before they came knocking. Craig turned around then, staring out into the waning light, feeling as though a thousand eyes were staring back.

He didn't need to remind Eppy and Annie of the redcoats' vile nature. She was well versed, from both her battlefield efforts and having been herself a victim of their brutality. What he wouldn't give to turn back time and go back to when he'd visited her castle, to have extended the men's stay a few more days so that they could have been there to protect her, Logan, and the rest of the clan when the Butcher's men had come calling.

Now settled inside the cottage, Craig watched Annie from the place that he'd taken up before the fire, turning a roast of meat over the fire. It would be the last such before they were subjected to days of dried jerky. Annie was buzzing from one man to the next, checking their wounds and giving them draughts. The click of her boot heels against the dusty wood and her murmurings were the only sounds in the cottage over the faint crackling of the fire.

Did she ever sleep? Come to think of it, he wasn't certain he'd ever seen her at rest. When he was awake, she was awake, and when he slept, he felt her watching over him like an angel.

She came to him last, marching toward him like a general, a no-nonsense look on her face that he wanted to kiss away. "Now that we are in the light, surrender your pride and let me see the damage ye may have caused your head."

Craig chuckled and resisted the urge to tug her close. "I assure ye the only damage to my head has to do with my pride."

Annie grinned and clucked her tongue. She held up a clean linen bandage and a vial of clear liquid. "Allow me to clean the wound and apply this. It will help with healing."

Craig quit turning the meat and tipped his head up toward her, allowing her to clean his wounds and feeling significantly less pain than any of the previous times she'd done so. Magic hands… This close to her and now in the firelight he studied her face, taking in the deep purple smudges beneath her eyes, the weariness in the crease of her brow, the pinch of her lips. She looked utterly exhausted.

"Are ye sleeping, lass?" he asked, voicing his concerns.

Annie paused in her ministrations, those beautiful amber eyes locking on his. "Aye." She frowned. "Why?"

Craig shrugged. "Ye seem always to be awake."

She pursed her lips and went back to dabbing at his wound. "Some of us need less sleep than others."

"Ye'll wear yourself thin."

Her fingers stilled and she slid her gaze back to his. "'Tis my business if I do so."

Craig wanted to tell her that Graham had asked that he look after her, make sure she was well, but that was a secret he'd take with him to the grave. He didn't want her to think his interest in her stemmed solely from her brother's dying wish, when it was so much more. So instead, he said, "Who is looking after ye?"

"I look after myself. I also have Eppy."

"And that is all ye need?" *Dammit!* He wanted to tell her he would look after her, that she couldn't do it all on her own, and that someday Eppy was going to want to have a family of her own too. "'Tis no' a crime to ask for help."

A long, soft sigh escaped her parted lips, and it took every ounce of his willpower not to press his lips to hers. To kiss her once more, pull her down into his lap. With a thoughtful glance, she took a step away from him. "Ye're healing verra well," and he knew she wasn't going to answer his question.

"I have a good doctor," he said with a wink.

Annie smiled and patted him on the shoulder. "I am no' really a doctor. We both know that."

"Ye heal people. That is good enough for me."

Thirteen

Just as the first fingers of dawn reached up to scrape her nails across the land, Fiona gave the signaled knock on the door.

"Ye must leave now," she said, staring behind her into the distance. "I was discreet, but there is a contingent of dragoons not five miles away. They will reach here before the day is through. I've a new package to deliver, and I'll no' be able to return. Please, Annie. Go now."

Annie stifled a cold shudder that started at the base of her spine. The farm fields stretching away behind Fiona were bare of life, reminding her just how alone they truly were. She'd known this day was coming, but she'd faced down the enemy before. She could do it again.

"Can ye take Leonard and Andy with ye? I'll get the rest of us to safety."

"Aye, but why do ye no' come with me now?" Fiona glanced behind her again, her nervous energy spreading quickly through the room.

Annie tugged her inside, shut the door, and then beckoned Fiona to follow her into the back room of the house, a bedchamber that she and Eppy had shared with Mrs. Sullivan. With the door shut, she said, "We will only slow ye down. Andy and Leonard are the most healed. Ye've a package to deliver, ye said so yourself."

Fiona started to shake her head, but Annie pressed her hands to her friend's shoulders and whispered, "We will only slow ye down. I promise, I will be safe. We will figure out a way to meet soon so that ye can see for yourself."

"I dinna like it." Fiona pressed her lips together in a frown. "We are supposed to be doing things together."

"Nay, we're no'. We vowed to help the prince, and each of us has our own talents for that." Annie tossed her friend a winning smile in hopes of changing the subject. "Before ye go, will ye eat some stew? 'Tis quite good."

Fiona shook her head, sadness making her eyes droop. She did not return Annie's smile, which sent Annie's belly into a swirling storm of apprehension.

"There is no time, my friend," Fiona said. "Leave the stew. Ye must escape, and ye must do it now."

"I will." This time Annie didn't bother to hide her fear behind a smile. "And I'll see ye soon."

Fiona nodded, thrusting a small velvet bag into Annie's hands. "Keep this in case ye need it."

Annie unwrapped the packet as Fiona opened the door. The men in the main part of the cottage were quick to appear busy, most likely having been listening at the door to every word exchanged.

In her hand, Annie held a jeweled brooch in the shape of a Tudor rose, pearls, rubies, and gold forming the white and red petals and the golden center.

"What?" Annie shook her head. "I canna take this."

Fiona glanced at her. "Aye, ye can, and ye will. It should be enough to free ye if ye're caught."

"Or get me arrested for thievery."

Fiona shook her head, a soft smile on her lips. "Nay, my friend, it will gain ye safe passage. Trust me."

Annie wrapped the jewel back into the soft velvet and tried to thrust it back at Fiona.

Fiona held up her hands, refusing to take it. "I meant it for ye. Keep it. And when this world is put to rights, if ye still have it, put it in that treasure box ye kept hidden at Cullidunloch."

"If no one has stolen it already."

"Ye hid it well."

"Aye."

Fiona pressed a kiss to Annie's cheek and then turned to find Leonard and Andy having already collected together their meager belongings.

The two soldiers approached Annie, standing before her sheepishly, heads ducked, their equally brown hair hanging low over their faces.

"We shouldna be leaving ye," Andy said, and Leonard proclaimed his agreement.

"Aye, ye should," Annie said brightly. "The two of ye are well enough to travel back to the prince and devote your time to the cause. That is a soldier's mission, is it no'? Ye're no' to remain behind doing chores for me. Besides, I will see ye all again soon when the prince establishes a new camp." Despite what propriety might call for, Annie pulled them both into an embrace. Though she had no children of her own, she thought that seeing them off would feel a lot like this, like she was tearing off a piece of her flesh and letting it walk away. Aye, it was a strange feeling to have for men she'd not known all that long, but when she'd found them on the field, they'd been on the brink of death, and she had nursed them back to health.

Prayed for them. Feared for them. And to see them stand, walk, smile, all of it was like watching a man be reborn from the grips of mortality.

Before she started to cry, she tugged Fiona into a hug, squeezing her tight. Fiona's duty to the cause was dangerous, perhaps more so than Jenny's, who rode into battle with hundreds of men at her back. Fiona was often traversing the Highlands alone, delivering important and dangerous messages to Jacobite rebels. If she were caught, hers was an offense punishable by death. But she was good enough not to get caught, often called a phantom by those who suspected her existence—able to get through walls and doors that should have been impassable to a human.

"I will pray for ye," Fiona whispered fiercely. "Please dinna delay."

Annie squeezed her hard one more time. "I will no'."

"Head west," Fiona said. "To the Isle of Skye. There is a fisherman by the name of Murtagh at the docks of Loch Alsh who will take ye across if ye give him my name. He'll give ye information on where to hide as well."

"Thank ye."

"See ye soon." Fiona, Leonard, and Andy stole into the dawn, sticking to the shadows where the sun had not yet touched, and then they were gone.

Annie listened for a minute to the quiet morning. The mist rose up on the ground, almost as if none of this was truly happening. And then, in the distance, she thought she could hear the sounds of horses on the road. Was it her imagination? So many times over the past few days she'd heard that sound, and it had never materialized into a true threat.

She turned back to the men left in her care and to Eppy who stood beside the table looking very worried. How many arrows did they have left? How much gunpowder and shot? Who could wield a weapon?

Besides Craig, there were Max, the stump of his leg healing cleanly, and three other men. One whose name she was yet to learn—he'd suffered some sort of brain injury upon the field and couldn't remember who he was. She suspected his fever—which had lasted for nearly a sennight—might also have had something to do with it. The two others were in similar shape to Craig, with bullet and bayonet wounds that were nearly healed but did not allow for swift travel. Without a wagon, it was going to be difficult to get them out of here. They still had two horses, but with seven of them, there would be several who had to walk.

"The nights will be cold if we dinna find shelter," she told the men. "Pack an extra blanket, and put a packet of jerky in everyone's roll. And in case we are…attacked or separated, keep going. Dinna stop."

The men worked to gather up their things, and she did her part, putting as much of her supplies as would fit into a bag she could carry on her back. They'd not be able to take everything without better transport options, but between her and Eppy, they had enough.

"My lady." Craig came before her, his face intense, brows drawn. Why was he being so formal?

"Aye?"

"Go. Take Eppy, take the horses, and run. I will be certain to get the men to safety."

Annie shook her head, uncertain she'd heard him correctly. Did he honestly think she was just going to leave them all here without her? Leave *him* here? "What? Nay, I canna allow ye to do that. I will no' leave all of ye to be caught."

Craig pressed his lips together in frustration and took her shoulders in his grasp, ducking his head to look her in the eye. "Annie, ye'll be arrested for harboring fugitives. 'Tis madness. I canna allow it."

Annie scoffed, growing quite tired of all the men in her life telling her what she could and couldn't do. She brushed his hands away and stood tall. "Do ye forget that I too am a fugitive already for what I've done? Do ye think me incompetent?"

Craig shook his head vehemently. "Nay, 'tis no' that. Ye're the smartest woman I know. But we will slow ye down. Ye have a chance to be saved, and ye're being stubborn about it."

Had he heard the confession she'd so quietly made to Fiona about how they would slow *her* down and that was why Annie refused to go with her? God, she hoped he hadn't.

"I willna ask ye to understand my decision, but I will ask that ye respect it. I have spent years putting my life on the line for those who fight for a better Scotland. I'm no' going to stop now."

He pressed his lips firmly together, considering what she'd said. "I do respect ye."

"Thank ye." She turned to the men in the cottage. "They are coming. We will head to Skye."

"Wait," Craig said. "I have an idea."

"What? We must leave." Annie started to gather items.

"Fiona said we should go to the Isle of Skye, but that is clear across the country and too arduous a trip for some of the men. We are closer to your castle. The men will be safe there. As it is burned down already, the dragoons will not bother with it again. They will think no one is there."

Annie started to shake her head. But she knew he had a point. And there had to be someone near her castle who would aid them.

"At the verra least it allows us time to get a wagon," he added.

"Aye, ye're right."

"There are seven of us, including ye and Eppy," Craig said. "That is too many in a party if the men are on our backs now."

"So what are ye saying, that we should split up?" Annie shook her head. "That is also too dangerous. And my castle is at least a day's hard ride from here, but we are most of us on foot. That means four or five days. We canna wait that long."

"If I may." Max rose, using a long staff that he'd carved from a fallen branch to hobble toward them. "My family's home is no' far from here, a quarter of an hour's ride. We could make it there on foot in an hour or less."

"We couldna put your family in danger," Annie said, shaking her head. "We'll attempt the journey to Skye."

"They would help us," Max insisted. "At least give us a

safe place to rest for the night and a few horses. We need horses to make the journey to Skye."

Annie didn't like the idea of putting Max's family in danger, but the only other option was to seek hospitality from strangers or camp out in the woods. There was no guarantee they'd find anyone, and being out in the open left them vulnerable not only to dragoons but also to the elements. The April nights were still bitter and freezing, and lighting a fire in the woods was like a beacon calling enemies to their location. Though the men were all on the mend, they were still in a weakened state and could be brought down by something as simple as a frost.

"All right, then. Let us go to your family."

Annie opened the door to the cottage and quickly shut it again, her heart pounding and bile rising in her throat. She muttered an expletive before realizing that every man in the cottage had likely heard her. They were too late. The sound of horses was loud and clear, though she could not yet see them. "They approach," she whispered in a panic. "I can hear them on the road."

Craig peered out the window. "They are no' yet in sight. We must hurry. Everyone out, and to the rear of the cottage, to keep our retreat hidden. I'll fetch the horses."

Max led the string of men out, Eppy at the end of the five. Craig ran to the barn with Annie on his heels.

"What are ye doing?" he demanded, grabbing two bridles off the wall.

"Helping." She took one of the bridles from him, and they quickly tugged them over the horses' heads. "Go."

They'd just barely skirted the building when the

dragoons were pounding on the front door. Had they spotted them?

"*Run,*" she mouthed silently, helping to shove Max onto a horse with Eppy behind him. Two of the other men leaped onto the other horse, taking off toward the woods and crossing the creek with Annie, Craig, and the unnamed soldier on their heels.

Highlanders were trained to be silent, but she feared in their weakened state they would have trouble doing so now. She need not have worried, however. They were quiet, even as they splashed through the shallow water of the burn, and she concentrated all of her own energy into remaining as quiet as possible as they raced across the fields toward the forest. The safety of the trees would cloak them, should any dragoon happen to look out a window.

At any moment Annie expected to hear the firing of a pistol at their backs, to feel the agony as a bullet ripped into her skin. Crashes and bangs echoed on the moors, likely the cottage being ransacked for the supplies they'd had to leave behind. When they reached the other side of the narrow flowing burn, she turned around and peered through the tree branches long enough to see that they'd lit the cottage roof on fire. Annie refused to imagine what would have happened had they not made it out in time, though her mind kept trying to go there.

A dozen dragoons on horseback circled the cottage, one of them staring hard at the field where they'd been only moments before. Could he see the path they'd taken? See the lines of trampled grass? Distinguish their shapes in the woods beyond?

"We need to keep going," Craig urged, brushing his fingers on her arm. "They will come this way if they are smart."

"Let us no' flatter the bastards," Annie said.

Craig smirked and took her hand in his as they fled.

Despite missing part of his leg, Max was making good progress. Sweat dripped down the sides of his face as he learned how to ride, holding onto the horse with his thighs. The effort for him was extreme, she could tell, and she was glad that he had Eppy at his back to help him.

"We're no' yet followed. We can slow down if anyone needs to," she offered, not singling him out. Every one of them refused, Max being the first to deny her suggestion.

After a quarter hour of speeding through the forest, Annie insisted they stop. Not because she couldn't keep going, but because she truly did fear for the men on foot. Craig and the unnamed soldier had been running to keep up. They'd all been on their deathbeds not two weeks before, and now were fleeing for their lives. Would this never end?

They stood in a tight circle, panting, staring at the forest behind them. The next bit of their journey was going to see them out in the open again. The unnamed soldier leaned against one of the horses, sweat dripping down his face, which was growing paler by the moment.

"This is your fault."

Annie jerked her head up to see Paul pointing his finger at the nameless man. He blanched, lips twisting in horror.

"Nay."

"Aye, ye're the reason they came. Admit it! Ye're one of them, and they've been looking for ye."

"Paul, please," Annie said. "He's no' a spy or a redcoat. When I found him, he was among the Scots, his clothes those of a rebel."

"Then why does he no' remember his own name?"

"Because he had a head injury," Annie said. "Sometimes that happens to a man."

"'Haps he willna remember us leaving him here then." Paul hobbled toward the nameless soldier.

The man held up his hands, which trembled, and Annie feared his knees would buckle at any moment.

Craig came to stand between the two men. Paul looked ready to push his fist through the unnamed soldier's gut, and if he'd had a pistol in his hand, he'd likely have fired it, too.

"Paul, we are all allies here. We canna start fighting amongst ourselves. We canna lose sight of what needs to be done—getting the hell out of here."

Paul seethed, his teeth bared, looking more like a rabid animal than a worried soldier.

"I've been trying to remember," the soldier said. Fingers at his temples, he slapped his head, and Annie winced. "But nothing is fucking working." The last of his words were said in a frustrated shout.

"Give yourself time," Annie said soothingly. "And the rest of us will be patient with ye, too." She pointedly looked to Paul and then slid her glance to Max, whose face was pinched, but he kept silent.

The men had long suspected him of being a spy, but

she didn't believe it. She knew what she'd seen when she'd found him on the field; the other men didn't. And they were likely to be suspicious of a squirrel if it showed up wearing red.

"I'll hold off on killing him for now," Paul muttered.

And Annie had to take that as a win, for she wasn't going to be able to convince him otherwise, nor did she have time.

Annie passed around an old water canteen she'd found stashed on a shelf in the cottage. They all drank thirstily from the vessel, draining it completely. Hopefully they would come across a spring soon so that she could refill it, else the journey would become even harder.

Again they were off, Craig taking her hand in his. She didn't know who was leading whom anymore. He seemed to be passing his strength to her, which was utterly wrong, given he was the one with battle wounds still healing.

The sun was fully risen now, and they were in full view of anyone who might happen to look over the field and see them running. Annie longed for the cover of the woods or the cover of darkness, something that would make them less vulnerable. She wasn't certain if her heart pounded harder from running or from the fear that the dragoons would catch up with them.

When next they stopped, it was at a thinly trickling burn. The men dropped to their knees, Eppy helping Max dismount, and they all drank greedily, water dripping down their chins and wetting the fronts of their clothes. Still panting, Annie filled the canteen once more.

"How much farther?" she asked Max.

"We are close." He pointed to the mountain in the distance. "Just there."

Annie nodded, staring into the distant rise of land. Mountains always appeared closer than they were. They could be a mile away or five.

"How are ye holding up?" she asked each of her patients, checking their bandages. Only Paul had any blood seeping from his wounds, but it was a minimal amount.

"We can rest a little longer," she said.

Paul shook his head. "Nay. The sooner we are there, the better. 'Tis only a wee bit of blood, my lady. There was a whole lot more of it there before, aye?"

There was. He'd been shot not only in the hip but in the ribs and was fortunate that none of his innards had been destroyed.

"Aye," she agreed.

She checked Max, finding that the place where the end of his knee rubbed against the horse was irritated. She frowned, reached under her gown, and ripped a long strip from her underskirt, binding an extra bit around the amputated end. "Ye'll toughen up in no time, and riding will be easy again."

His face colored slightly, but he inclined his head, his expression grateful. "Thank ye, Doc."

Annie grinned. "Ye're a lot stronger than I think anyone gives ye credit for."

"I'm the youngest of six brothers," he said with a laugh. "I've always had to keep up."

Last she approached the unnamed warrior, whose coloring had improved. He eyed her warily, eyes like those of a cornered animal. "I'll no' let anyone hurt ye," she whispered as she checked his head. "Ye've a friend in me."

He didn't reply.

Less than a quarter hour later they were greeted at Max's home by the end of a long smoking gun, the bullet fired from it landing about six feet in front of them as a warning. Hauled up short, Annie squinted into the distance to see who'd fired.

Fortunately, Max shouted, "Ho, there, brother. Would ye kill me when the bastards didna get the chance?"

A shouted curse was the reply, followed quickly by "Ma, Da! Max is home!"

"'Tis my brother, Jed Gair," Max said, dismounting with Eppy's help. The unnamed soldier handed Max back his staff, and he hobbled forward to embrace Jed, who lumbered toward them.

If the gun was their way of greeting, Annie could only assume the dragoons must have come by more than once already.

"Where the hell have ye been? We thought ye dead." Max's brother grappled him up in a bear hug, forcing Max to drop the staff that held him upright as he was crushed into his brother's embrace.

"It was a near thing, but Doctor Annie saved me."

Jed faced her, tears glistening in his eyes. "Thank ye for saving my wee brother."

"Ye're welcome," Annie said, so many other words

tumbling through her mind that didn't quite make it past her lips.

Three other hulking Highlanders greeted them on the doorstep, and waiting inside was a tiny woman whom Max greeted as his mother. It was shocking to consider that she might have been able to birth those large lads, but given the size of her husband, it made more sense.

"We'll no' be long," Annie said. "And we'll leave if ye ask us to. The cottage where I was tending the lads after the battle was found out by dragoons." She glanced over her shoulder toward the shut door. "They could have followed us here, though we tried to stay hidden."

"Nonsense," said Mr. Gair. "We'll no' be letting the bastards get to ye. And what kind of thanks would we be giving if we took our Max and thrust the lot of ye out?"

He ruffled Max's hair like he was a lad of twelve, which only made the color rise in the young man's cheeks all the more. Annie sucked in a breath, trying to hide her visceral reaction to this family reunion. Sadness had a way of seeping in, though, and she ducked her gaze to hide her quickly tearing eyes. She missed her brothers so much, and Graham... His life had needlessly been cut short. Anger replaced grief, drying up her tears. She shuddered, squeezed her eyes shut, hands clenching to fists at her sides. Craig brushed his fingers surreptitiously against hers, giving her the bolstering support she needed to face the happy family.

"Thank ye so verra much," she managed, forcing a smile that quickly became genuine. She couldn't begrudge them their happiness or their reunion. This was what her calling was, after all—to keep men alive.

"What do ye need from us?" Mrs. Gair asked. "We are happy to help."

"Besides a place to stay the night? Some boiling water and clean rags if ye have them. I need to tend to the men's injuries before we settle in and make sure that Paul's wound has no' opened more than it appeared on the road."

"Here, come with me." Max's mother led them to a chamber off the side of the main room, where there was a bed, a wardrobe, and a small table.

"We canna take your bedchamber," Annie protested.

"'Tis fine. There's been more than one night that I've bedded down with my husband before the hearth, and today will be no different."

"Ye have no idea how much this means to us. Ye have saved lives, madam."

The older woman colored in her cheeks. "I would do anything for my lads, and to know ye saved one of them, it is the least I could do to provide ye a night's shelter." Tears brightened the woman's eyes, and she pressed her hand to her mouth. "Thank ye."

Annie nodded, trying not to get choked up herself. Mrs. Gair ducked out of the room, and Annie let out a ragged breath, grasping the bedpost and leaning against it for a minute to get ahold of herself.

"Are ye all right?" Eppy stopped on the threshold, linens draped over one arm and a pot of hot water grasped in the other.

"Aye." Annie forced another smile and waved her maid in. "Are there coals in the water to keep it warm?"

"Aye."

"Good." Annie took off her satchel, pulling out the healing supplies she'd stuffed inside. Emotions needed to be set aside, and the work needed to begin.

One by one the men came in to have their wounds examined and cleaned and fresh salves put on them. They were a battered group, but none too much worse for the wear. As usual, Craig came last. When he entered the room Eppy left it, almost as if she were trying to give them privacy.

The wound on his head was healing nicely, the skin having grown back together in a puckered, pink, jagged line.

"I can probably remove the stitches soon," she said. "A few more days is all ye need."

She dabbed a salve onto the wound and then re-bandaged it. He reached for her hand, engulfing her palm with his own long, strong fingers. Every time he touched her, no matter the circumstance, a buzz of excitement washed through her. When this was over, when he was back with his men and she was following the prince's camp, Annie was certain she'd never be the same again. No one else had the power to make her still. She was a bundle of energy, constantly moving, but when he touched her, that need to rush about turned to calm, and she felt like she could breathe.

"How are ye holding up?" Craig's voice was soft, his eyes full of concern as he studied her.

With so much going on, Annie hadn't given herself time to think about her own situation. And she didn't really want to. The moment she started to think about herself was the moment that she might break down.

"I'm well," she lied, shifting on her feet at how uncomfortable it felt to tell him anything less than the truth.

Craig raised a brow, clearly knowing that was a falsehood.

Annie huffed a breath. "I'm alive," she added, which wasn't a lie at all.

"That is true, and we must all be grateful for that." He rubbed his thumb back and forth over her knuckles, and she bit her lip to keep in a sigh.

"Aye." Annie let go of his hand, needing to put some distance between them, even if it was only an inch. They were alone in this back chamber together, and thoughts of kissing him were quickly invading her mind again, if only to steal a few moments of that bliss she'd felt by their smoking pit. Alas, kissing was not meant to be. Not now. She cleared her throat. "Take off your shirt and coat," she ordered.

Craig's eyes widened slightly at that, a slow, wolfish grin curling his lips. "Och, my lady..." he teased with a wiggle of his brow.

Annie rolled her eyes, realizing too late what her request might have implied. "Ye know I seek to tend your wounds, no' to woo ye."

"I confess I prefer the latter."

She laughed softly. "Dinna all men?" *Didn't she?*

Craig took his time removing the jacket and shirt. "I'd fight off any man who tried to woo ye, lass."

"What if I wanted them to?"

His eyes darkened, as if he'd not thought of that possibility, and she could tell he didn't like it. Craig reached up and tucked an errant lock of her hair behind her ear, smoothing his knuckles over her cheek, pausing right at the corner of her mouth. "Do ye want another man?"

God, nay! She wanted him…desperately. Annie shook her head, finding it hard to breathe. Hard to think. "I've no' time for that."

He grinned, said softly, seductively, "There's always time for kissing."

Och, but she felt light-headed. What she wouldn't give to collapse right then onto this very convenient bed and let him kiss her until they were both breathless. Let him show her all there was to be enjoyed between a man and a woman. Pleasure, endless, glorious pleasure—for that was what the look in Craig's gaze promised. Infinite bliss. Long, languid days of entangled limbs and nothing else.

Annie faked a cough that she hoped would snap them both out of whatever it was they'd been drawn into. "Are ye feeling sore?" She used her most nurse-like, no-nonsense voice.

That seductive grin still tipped the edges of his mouth. "Nay. Just savoring the time I have with ye."

She didn't know whether to believe that line or not, so she did the next best thing, which was to ignore it, else she fall limp into his lap. Ignoring his words might have been possible, but disregarding the expanse of muscled chest in front of her… *Heavens.* No naked torso had ever been so riveting. Her hands itched to stroke over the ridges and plains. To touch his flat nipples and see if they perked like hers did.

Utterly shameful, she was. She was not at all behaving like a woman in her position should. She was a healer, lauded by Prince Charles himself as one of the best in her field, and yet the sight of Craig's rippling chest and belly, the slope and coils of his shoulders, had her breath catching and her mind going back to those moments by the smoke pit when he'd kissed her. When he'd pressed his chest to her breasts. What would if feel like for her to press her naked breasts against all that muscled flesh?

"Is it bad, Doc?" he asked, a note of teasing in his tone bringing her back to the present.

"What?" she asked, a little breathless.

"Ye're staring. I fear ye willna touch me because I've taken a turn for the worse."

Annie shook her head, forcing herself back to the task at hand. Heat flamed her face. "Nay, I was…I was simply somewhere else."

Craig cocked his head. "Where?" The way mischief danced in his blue-green eyes, she could tell he had an idea of exactly where she'd been.

Annie jutted her chin. "A lady doesna have to divulge her mind if she is no' so inclined."

"Is that a fact?" The wicked grin grew by a factor of two.

Annie wanted to roll her eyes at herself. She was not that type of lady. In fact, she was so used to working with soldiers over the years and having grown up with two brothers that she was more often blunt than subtle.

"Hush," she scolded, peeling back the bandage at his torso. The wound in his gut was healing even better than the one on his head. It had taken her hours to dig out the bullet and fragments and then sew the wound tightly closed. "I could remove these stitches now, but I fear with more of our running, it might be too soon. Another day or two." She took a clean cloth and washed the star-shaped scar. "Ye were lucky this one didna puncture any of your organs. I found the bullet resting just beside one, as though teasing whether or no' it would go in all the way."

Annie rubbed a salve on the wound and placed a clean bandage over it.

"How do ye feel?" She knelt on the bed beside him to look at the wound on his shoulder blade. "Incredible," she murmured.

"I'm alive." He repeated the words she'd used before.

"And I think we can all just be grateful for that right now, aye?" She rinsed the wound with a wet cloth.

He nodded, sitting still as she administered more salve. But when she went to move away, to clean up the supplies, he took her hand in his again. She paused, one knee still on the bed, very aware of how close she was.

"Do ye know how brave ye are, lass?"

"I'm no' brave." She planted both feet on the floor but didn't let go of his hand. "I merely do my duty. I can tell ye that more times than no' I've been scared so much my knees knocked together and my teeth chattered as though I'd been left outside in a winter blizzard."

"Being brave doesna mean being without fear, lass."

She stilled, his words washing over her. "Are ye scared?"

"Sometimes."

Annie smiled. "I never would have guessed that would be your answer, Lieutenant."

"I learned a long time ago that fear in the face of danger can often be an ally."

She cocked her head at his cryptic statement, watching him intently. The muscle at the side of his face flexed, the only sign that he wasn't completely calm.

"What happened to make ye so scared?" Absently, Annie sat down on the bed beside him.

Craig chuckled. "Do ye think it possible to use the same line as a lady and say a soldier doesna divulge his mind if he is no' so inclined?"

"Of course." She shrugged, making to pull away, but he tugged her closer, and the heat of his body made the chill she felt in her limbs warm some.

"But I find myself wanting to share with ye, lass."

And a very large part of her longed to hear his innermost thoughts, to know what went on in his mind. Who was Craig MacLean, and what was it about him that drew her so?

"I want to hear," she said, suppressing a shiver. They'd run for hours, and despite the exertion keeping her heated as they moved, now that her body was cooling and the sweat still clung to her skin, she was finding herself chilled. That was one excuse for her shiver. The other, well…

"Ye're cold." Craig's touch went from her hands up to

her arms and back down again, sliding over her in a way that was soothing and warming all at once.

Annie sighed. "Much better. Thank ye." But she wasn't much better. Every inch of her prickled with anticipation and want.

"'Tis my pleasure, lass."

The way he said *pleasure* had her staring at his lips, distracting her once more, but she *did* want to hear about his times of fear. Was he distracting her on purpose? Perhaps he wasn't ready to share that information with her. Should she leave? Should she go back to the others? The thought of leaving this room to go sit in the main room as they waited throughout the day for night to fall sounded dreadful.

Craig chuckled softly and pushed the sleeve of her shirt up over her arm until he could see the scar from where he'd stitched her up. Cool air touched her exposed skin. It was no longer as pink as it had been, though not nearly white yet, either. He rubbed his thumb gently over the scar, and gooseflesh rose on her arm.

"Before I was your healer, ye were mine," she teased.

"How many more do ye think your wee cat has tormented in your absence?"

"Dozens, I'm certain. We will likely have to fight her for a place to sleep when we rebuild."

He chuckled, deep and throaty, bringing her hands to his lips where he gently kissed them. As gentle as that kiss was, it sent a rioting shiver throughout her body.

"Still cold?" he teased, though he had to know that the reason for her shiver had nothing to do with being chilled.

"Aye," she lied.

"We're going to get out of this alive, Annie," he said, meeting her gaze. "I promised Graham."

Fourteen

Craig knew he shouldn't make promises he wasn't certain he could keep. But this was a vow he'd made to her brother and now he'd made to her. He would keep Annie safe. Until his dying breath, he'd make certain the lass was unharmed. Even if it meant never kissing her again.

Every day he was getting stronger, and though he had a damnable headache that didn't seem to dissipate, it dulled noticeably when she was near. Especially when she allowed him to touch her.

He wanted to kiss her again. To sweep her into his lap and press his lips to hers. To taste her, to pleasure her, to hear her gasp with delight as sensation poured over her. But to do so now, when anyone could walk in, would be to put her in a compromising position he was certain she didn't want. It was one thing to kiss her in front of a fire when no one was about, save for her spying maid, but for total strangers to come upon them kissing in a bed-chamber… Well, he didn't want them to get the wrong impression of her or think that he was taking advantage. *Was* he taking advantage? *I want ye to kiss me*. Her whispered words were clear as day in his mind. Nay, he had only done as she asked. As they *both* wanted.

Now it was Craig's turn to clear his throat to shake himself from his thoughts. "Let us join the others."

There was a flash of disappointment on her face, and

it was on the tip of his tongue to say, "*Me too, lass, me too,*" but he refrained. Once this war was over and she was safe, then he could devote more time to kissing…to more than kissing. To pleasuring her until she cried out again and again. Until then, he needed to just make sure they survived this.

"I need to clean up a bit. I'll be there shortly." She slipped away from him, and this time he didn't grapple her back toward him.

"As your friend, lass, I do hope ye rest today and sleep tonight." Craig stood, stretching out the kinks in his body, amazed that he felt so limber compared to nearly a week before when he'd tried walking and none of his body parts had wanted to cooperate.

"What are ye saying, Lieutenant? That I look bedraggled?" She shot him a challenging grin, the slight twitch to her lips showing that she was teasing.

"I told ye to call me Craig…" He tugged on his shirt, the fabric going over his face just after he saw her look of disappointment. He grinned into the linen at that, for he too was disappointed to be dressing again.

"Aye, ye did, but it felt like a Lieutenant moment." She tossed his dirtied bandages into the hot water pot.

"A Lieutenant moment? Lord, but ye're full of fire, are ye no'?" he teased.

She cocked a coy shoulder and capped the vial, putting it back into her valise. Then she handed him a flask. "Drink up."

"Mayhap ye should too, lass. Ye fuss about all of us, so someone needs to fuss over ye."

"We've had this conversation before."

He held up his hands, took a swig, and pressed the flask back into her grasp. Backing toward the door, he kept his eyes on her, willing her to call him back. He paused at the threshold and tugged on his jacket, watching her put away her supplies and stir the bleaching pot with the long-handled wooden spoon.

Would she still aim to go to Skye as Fiona had suggested, or would she travel east to where her brother Logan was convalescing with their cousin Ewan at Cluny Castle?

The thought had never really concerned him until now, when the following morning would mean time to make their choices. On the morrow they would move on with their journey. If she wanted to remain in the prince's retinue, she would go to Skye. But if she would rather go to Logan after losing Graham, he would understand that too. Selfishly, he wished she would go to Skye, for that was likely to be his direction now that he was nearly ready to get back on the campaign.

"Ye dinna have to watch me work, ye can help," she chided without looking up. "Come and get this pot."

Craig jerked forward, taking the heavy pot from her. Any other woman reproaching him might have rubbed him the wrong way, but not Annie. He would walk to the ends of the earth if she asked him to. "Apologies, lass."

"Och, 'tis nothing." She grinned at him and then waved him away, and he took the pot outside to dump the dirty water behind the house.

He stood there for several moments, scanning the farmlands around them, the mountain behind. The steep cliffs would give them a good hiding spot, as the dragoons weren't accustomed to climbing. And given the lay of the land, they'd have ample notice if anyone were to come upon them.

Craig turned at the sound of footsteps behind him, seeing that Max's father had come outside to gather wood. He loaded a few logs into his arms and then stopped, eyeing Craig. He put down his burden and approached Craig, a curious expression creasing his brow.

"Max Gair," he said reaching out his hand. The man was the spitting image of his son, only a few inches taller and all gray in the hair. His bushy eyebrows rivaled the hair on his head for thickness.

Craig shook the man's hand. "Craig MacLean."

"Ye strike me as a leading sort of man."

"I am a lieutenant in the prince's army."

"Was my lad in your regiment?"

"Nay."

Mr. Gair nodded. "Still waiting on a few more of our kin to come home."

Craig hadn't the heart to tell him that he was lucky that even Max had returned, that it would be a miracle if the others did.

"I owe your lass a great deal of gratitude," Old Max said.

Craig shook his head. "She's no' my lass."

"Oh. Really? Pardon my saying so." Mr. Gair grunted. "Just seen the way the two of ye look at each other. Besides the fact that ye took a lot longer in that bedchamber than anyone else." Max raised a scrutinizing brow.

Craig gritted his teeth. It was a subject bound to come up, though he'd hoped it wouldn't. "She is a lass to be admired and respected."

Old Max chuckled. "Ye're sweet on her."

Craig shrugged. "She's bonny." *And smart and brave and full of passion…*

"Aye." The man looked off to the distance nostalgically. "Well, have ye need of anything, just ask."

"What is your plan, sir? Should the dragoons come calling."

"We've had many come up before now. We tend to scare them off."

"And what if they canna be scared?" What if there were two dozen of them? Fifty? The family would all be skewered on the spot.

"The day they canna be scared is the day we should be."

Craig grunted.

"Help me with the wood?" Old Max asked.

"Of course." Craig allowed the man to pile firewood into his arms, the iron pot dangling from his hand. He rather liked the fact that Old Max didn't treat him as an invalid despite the bandages.

Inside the crofter's cottage everyone gathered in the small main room, some on stools, others on plaids that had been laid about the floor. A few of the men were playing a game of dice, while Eppy and Annie appeared to be helping Lila, Old Max's wife, prepare a meal.

"Pardon me, lassies," Craig said, setting his wood down before the hearth.

Annie smiled at him, and it was a vision he could have stared at for the rest of his days. Damnation, but that thought alone was a slug to the gut. He was getting mighty attached to a lass he'd imagined to be a complete madwoman only a few months before. What had come over him? Was it because she'd saved his life? Or because Graham had bid him watch over her? Was it guilt over his friend's death? Recompense for what she'd done for him? Or the fact that he genuinely admired and desired her?

Whatever the reason was, he couldn't allow it to stand. This was certainly one of those situations in which he could not allow himself to become emotionally embroiled. Graham had asked him to keep her safe. To protect her, should anything happen. The best way for Craig to see that through was by making certain she made it to her family in the east country—far away from the prince and the Isle of Skye. She'd be angry at first, he was sure of it, but in the end she'd understand that her safety was what mattered above all else.

Which meant he could no longer kiss her. Touch her. Watch her. Think of her… Wish for her to stay by his side. All of those things led to a desire he wasn't certain he could contain. For aye, he wanted her, like a drowning man wanted land.

Craig turned away from her, heading toward the men playing dice. Better to get involved in a game of chance with his men than a game of chance with a woman he could never have.

Annie pretended that she was extremely interested in the preparation of the thick pottage that Max's mother Lila was making, but in truth all she could think about was the look that had crossed over Craig's face when she'd smiled at him just now.

Flashes of disgust, confusion, and surprise battled with one another on his countenance. At first she'd touched her face to make certain she didn't have anything on her that might be disgusting, but when she felt nothing, she flicked her tongue over her teeth to see if a bit of jerky might have gotten caught between them. Again, nothing.

So what had warranted that look from him?

She frowned down into the pottage, feeling as though she'd been thrust several months back, the same way he'd avoided her on campaign.

"Is ought amiss?" Lila stared into the pottage, too, and then back at Annie. "More salt, ye think?"

"Oh, sorry, my mind was elsewhere, and I just so happened to be staring at the pot." Annie smiled and waved her hand absently as though that were a good enough excuse for her distant behavior.

Eppy frowned at her, knowing her well enough to see through her act, but Lila giggled.

"I confess it happens to me often," the older woman said.

Annie managed a grin that didn't feel entirely like a grimace.

"Will ye help me make more oatcakes?" Lila asked. "With so many extra mouths, I fear we're going to need more, and they're always better-tasting when warm. Make them a wee bit thicker than usual, too, lassies. We like our bannocks to be hearty."

"Of course." Annie and Eppy mixed together the oatmeal flour, rendered bacon fat, and water.

They rolled out the dough into rough batches about an inch thick and then followed Lila's lead by laying them onto a grate in the hearth.

"They'll bake nicely."

Annie's mouth was already watering, her stomach giving a little grumble of approval. None of them had eaten since the night before, having woken before the dawn with Fiona's warning.

"Are ye hungry? I can make ye some eggs if ye like," Lila offered.

"I can wait for the bannocks to be ready."

"I've a delicious marmalade."

Annie didn't have the heart to tell her she didn't like marmalade and instead nodded, taking a rag to clean up the scattered flour from their baking. She kept stealing glances toward Craig, hoping he'd look up, but he didn't. Was it her imagination, or was he avoiding her gaze for some reason? Why?

"Ye look verra tired, my lady," Eppy whispered. "Ye should rest."

So many people telling her to rest, as if she actually had time for that. Madness! Annie stared down at the table's surface, gleaming from where she'd wiped, and did a mental calculation of her body, if only to prove them all wrong. But each muscle and limb she ticked off grew heavier at the thought. All at once, exhaustion hit. She felt as tired as everyone had been telling her she must be.

"I think I will go lie down if 'tis all right with ye."

Eppy took the rag from her, and Lila pointed her in the direction of the back bedchamber. Annie was slow to move, her feet somehow having gained a stone each. Walking across the cottage felt more like she was dragging dead weight, and by the time she made it to the bed, all she could manage was to collapse facedown onto the mattress. In her weakness, she struggled to tug on the blanket, making it only halfway before she gave up, letting her mind and body fall into unconsciousness.

Her sleep was anything but restful. With every sound, she bolted upright, swearing they were being attacked. By the sixth time Annie jolted awake, she was covered in sweat, her breath heavy. She sat up in the bed, feeling like the world was spinning.

Rushed footsteps sounded outside the door, and then Eppy was pushing into the room. "Are ye all right? We heard ye yell."

"Yell?" Annie didn't even know she'd made a sound. She wiped at her brow and tucked her hair up onto the top of her head, allowing the air of the room to cool the back of her neck. "I didna realize. I'm sorry if I scared ye."

"Was it a night terror?" Eppy came and sat down on the bed beside her. She touched Annie's forehead. "Ye've no' got a fever."

"Thank goodness," Annie mumbled. "Aye, a night terror."

"Do ye want to talk about it?"

"Nay." There had been more than one, and all the memories slammed back into her at once. "I think I should like a dram of whisky afore I plan to sleep again."

Eppy nodded, studying her face with concern. "That will definitely help." Her maid disappeared into the other room and returned with a wet rag and a flask. Annie took the proffered rag, wiped her face, neck, and chest, and then greedily sipped at the flask—probably more than she should have.

The spirits burned a path down her throat and then immediately warmed her belly. Within a few moments, she started to feel a little more herself. At least her pounding heart had calmed, and she was no longer in a cold sweat.

"Better?" Eppy asked.

"Aye." Annie bit her lip and took her friend's hand. "We've no' discussed this until now, but I think it needs to be said."

"Dinna say what I think ye're going to say."

"Ye're no' to be a martyr for me, Eppy. I've already lost too many people in this war. Should it look as though ye have a chance to save yourself, take it."

"I canna leave ye, my lady."

Annie rolled her eyes. "Eppy, we've been friends a long time and witnessed more than many lasses our age have. I think 'tis time ye start calling me 'Annie' and also start thinking of yourself."

Eppy shook her head. "Annie, I'm no' going to be selfish. I admire ye, and when have ye ever been selfish? That's no' in your nature, and neither is it in mine. If I was scared or wanted to run away, I'd have done it months ago. If not then, certainly when the Butcher burned down the castle."

Annie pulled Eppy against her with an arm around her shoulder. "Ye're a good friend. What an honor it has been for me to know ye."

"The honor has been all mine."

Annie passed Eppy the flask. "Cheers, my friend."

Eppy took a tiny sip and passed it back. Annie took another pull, though this one smaller than the last, feeling the effects of the whisky calming her nerves.

Someone knocked against the open doorway, and she glanced up to see Craig standing there, his face full of concern.

"Is aught amiss?" she asked.

"I...um..." He cleared his throat. "I wanted to make sure ye were all right."

Eppy stood up and excused herself. Annie wanted to call her back, needing the safeguard of her friend's company—not because she was scared of Craig but because she didn't want to explore all the emotions that washed over her from his presence in the doorway alone.

"I'm all right. Only a night terror."

Craig nodded, looking almost embarrassed—or in pain, she couldn't quite figure him out, and she shouldn't be interested in trying. Except that she was. "What is amiss with ye?" she asked before she could make herself stop. "Ye've been acting strange since I cleaned your wound."

"I think we should head east, to your cousin's castle. And not to Skye."

Fifteen

There, he'd said it, and now she was most assuredly going to agree.

In a world in which fantasies reigned…

In reality, Craig watched her face go from curious to confused to downright irritated. Lord, but she was beautiful in any mood. Her amber eyes flashed, her high cheekbones colored, and her brows, so expressive, moved with each and every mood.

"What?" Annie stared at him, incredulous. "Why would we go so far away from the campaign? Away from the rendezvous with the prince?"

We… Craig could not think about "we." He'd made up his mind, and this was for the best. Graham would have wanted it that way. Ballocks, but it felt a lot better to hide his own cowardice behind a promise to a friend.

"I think it best ye return to your family for now, until the threat has passed," he continued, but she interrupted him, her brows pulled so close together they nearly met as one.

"Are ye *drunk*, Lieutenant?" There was so much bite in her tone that he felt it tear into his flesh. 'Twas enough to make him want to turn around and run from the room. By some miracle, his feet remained rooted in place.

"Drunk?" He was frowning now. What did whisky have to do with anything?

"Aye, for certain ye would no' have suggested such a

ridiculous notion if ye were sober." She ran her hands angrily through her hair, already flying all over the place from her restless sleep. With every passing moment, she was looking more and more like the mad lass he'd first encountered. And perhaps sounding a bit like her, too.

"My notion is no' ridiculous. Dragoons are now murdering at will. If they find us in the woods on our way to Skye, they'll no' hesitate to kill us on the spot. And worse, they'll..." He couldn't make himself say what they might do to violate her. "Needless to say, it'll be hell, and they will no' be asking questions or accepting any answers. We'll be guilty by the sheer fact we're out and about."

"And what do ye think they were doing before now?" She shoved herself off the bed and marched toward him, eyes of fire and the stance of a general. For a moment, he thought she might slap some sense into him, but she stopped short two feet away. She was close enough that he could easily grab her and pull her toward him, far enough away to make him pause before taking such ridiculous action.

She did have a point. The damned redcoats had been abusing their power for years. Now, they just had open permission from King George's son himself.

Should he tell her what Graham had asked of him? Perhaps if she knew what he was attempting and at whose behest, she might be better equipped to understand.

"I am doing what is best for ye. What Graham wanted."

"How the hell do ye know what Graham wanted?" Her face grew red with anger as she stared him down.

So that hadn't worked out the way he'd hoped. Craig felt

the directed fury like a slap. The lass didn't need to connect with his flesh; the air between them was charged enough.

He couldn't back down now that he'd started. "Graham asked me, should anything happen to him, that I see to your safety. I think it best that ye go to Cluny to be with your cousin and your brother, far away from the Butcher and his hounds. Ye're all that Logan has left. Why would ye want to risk another of his siblings' lives? Especially when ye have the chance to save yourself."

Now it was Annie's turn to look as though she'd been slapped. "How dare ye?"

Craig could understand her anger, but he was mightily confused by her question. "Dare I what?"

"How dare ye bring my brothers into this? How dare ye try to make me feel guilty for doing my duty to country? What of ye and your family? Do ye no' think it best *ye* get away from the danger and heal? Ye nearly died before I dragged ye off that field. What makes ye think that your duty is any more important than mine? How dare ye, Lieutenant Craig MacLean, believe that I should go and hide, and how dare ye try to use my brother's death against me?"

Craig held up his hands, taking a step back as every word was hurled his way, hitting him like stones.

"I made a vow," Annie continued, "that I would do all I could to help the prince win his throne. I have no' the skill to fight in battle, but I have the skill to save the men who do. I dinna need your help nor your permission, and I didna ask for your protection. Graham is dead, and ye can consider his request dead too."

Stunned by her vehement words, Craig barely had time to react as she stormed past him and marched out the door. He whirled around in time to see her leave the cottage, his heart racing as he watched her go.

What in bloody hell had just happened? The lass was utterly mad—fighting mad! Furious! Was it because she was deprived of sleep? He was inclined to think it was that, but he wasn't a complete cad—she wasn't a child who threw a tantrum because she'd missed her nap. Much of what she'd said had struck a chord inside him. She was no simple innocent to be hidden away and protected. Graham had underestimated her, perhaps. But Graham was not here to argue the point with.

"Ballocks," Craig growled under his breath.

He made a move to leave the room but was blocked by Eppy. "What did ye do to upset my lady?"

"I didna do anything, it was what I said." Craig let out a long-suffering sigh. "I think I insulted her."

Eppy bared her teeth. "How dare ye!"

The lass didn't even know what he'd said and she was on the attack. Then again, maybe she did. With Annie's voice raised a notch or two higher than normal, it would be within reason to believe the whole cottage had heard their exchange perfectly.

"I dared, aye. And I've been chastised for it."

"Ye dinna understand." Eppy shook her head as though he were an idiot, and he supposed that he was.

"I am starting to."

"Nay, ye dinna. And ye willna. Annie will no' stop until she's healed anyone and everyone in her path. And she willna ask for help. She'll push ye away, just like she tried to push me away."

Craig wanted to ask why, to learn everything he could about why Annie would drive herself into an early grave. But it wasn't Eppy's story to tell, and he didn't think she would anyway. She was fiercely loyal to her mistress. That didn't mean she couldn't offer him some advice, though.

"What should I do?" he asked.

"Talk to her. Understand her. Support her. Or leave her be."

He supposed he knew that answer already. It was just a matter of which choice he was going to make. Once he'd decided she needed to go stay with her cousin, he'd been set. He'd planned to take her there himself. Blind to her ambition and her own desires, he'd gone in there headstrong and been met with her ire. He fully deserved it, he could see that now. And he could also see that she wasn't going to just willingly go along with anything he said.

"Thank ye, Eppy."

The maid stepped aside, and as he entered the great room of the cottage, he was met with glowers from nearly every person in the room. He might have expected the wounded soldiers would side with their Doctor Annie, but Old Max, Lila, and their other sons had only just met her—how was it they already were willing to defend her? Craig had known her for months.

Which was why he should have known that to expect her to up and leave what she considered her ultimate duty was idiotic. The lass was not going to leave. She was going to do all she could to stay in the fight until the bitter end.

Wishing he could turn back time, he exited the cottage to find an empty glen. Where the hell had she gone? He circled the building, not seeing her. The barn proved empty as well.

"Where the hell are ye?" he asked the air.

She knew it wasn't safe to wander far, so why would she do it?

Circling the barn, he found her on the opposite side of the house in the family's garden, inspecting the tiny sprigs of green that were poking from the ground.

"Annie," he said softly, approaching her.

She didn't glance up, but she did purse her lips as if his presence put a sour taste in her mouth.

"I'm sorry. Truly I am." And he meant it.

She did glance at him then. "I thought ye knew me better."

"I do." He swallowed. "Ye remember when ye asked what I feared?"

Annie tilted her head up more, shielding her eyes. "Aye."

"I fear losing ye. I fear that when I told your brother I'd make sure ye were safe that I might have lied to a man I canna make amends to."

"Graham should never have asked it of ye."

"But he did, and there is nothing we can do to change that."

Annie nodded, looking down at her clasped hands. "What else did he ask of ye?"

Craig grinned. "He asked me no' to touch ye."

A short laugh escaped her. "Ye were willing to let that promise drop."

Craig would have laughed if it weren't so true. That promise had been more to himself, when he'd vowed she would be the last woman on this earth that he'd find an attachment to. And yet here he was, fully attached.

"I should have realized how important the cause was to ye."

"I made a pact with my friends. That may seem childish to ye, but to us it is verra serious. One we took a blood oath on. I'll no' go back on it."

"Your friends… Fiona? Jenny?"

"Aye. No' hard to guess, eh?"

"Ye mentioned Jenny's skill with a sword, and ye and Fiona are tight as thieves."

"We promised each other, swore on the graves of our fathers and grandfathers that we would see their cause through. That the rightful heir to the throne would be put in his rightful place at last. I wasn't there for my father nor my mother nor my brother. If I have to work myself to the bone to save every last soldier in Prince Charles's army, I will."

"How old were ye when ye made your vows?"

"Does it matter?"

"Nay." And it truly didn't. Whether it was last year or twenty years ago, she'd made a pledge to protect the prince, and this was how she was seeing it through. Who was he to stand in her way? "How can I help?"

Annie's brows lifted in question. "Help?"

"Aye." He would do anything she asked.

"Ye can return to the prince's service. Leave me to myself."

That cut deeper than the bullet that had lodged in his gut. But why? Returning to the prince's service had been his plan all along. Why did it feel so different when he heard Annie say that he needed to go?

"I think I might be better suited to act as your bodyguard for now."

Annie snorted. "Is this how ye will see through your promise to my brother? Acting as my governess?"

"Och, lass. I know nothing of manners and tutoring, I can assure ye. Anything I might be able to teach ye would no' be approved of by a governess." And likely not by her brother either. For everything he wanted to teach her had to do with kissing and getting naked...

Good God, man! Why the hell did his mind always stray in that direction? Was it the way her doe eyes glanced up at him? The pouty perfection of her pink, dewy lips? The slight flush of her cheeks that made him think of the last time he'd kissed her or the memory of her hands in his hair? The way she stared at his flesh as though she wanted to lick him? All of the above. Aye, every last damn reason.

"Ye're..." Her voice was breathless as she stood up to her full height.

"I'm..." he urged.

"Ye're wicked."

"How so?"

Annie's gaze slid down his body to rest on his boots.

"I dinna know, but when ye look at me like that...I *feel* wicked. So ye must be wicked, too."

Mo chreach. He was going to lose the battle he'd started inside. He was not going to be able to refrain from kissing her. Touching her.

Her gaze slid back up to his, and the desire he saw there was a flame that matched his own. Craig took a step toward her. Stopped. Annie took a step toward him. Stopped.

Something still hung in the air between them. An invisible block that kept them from completely embracing each other. One of them had to knock it down or solidify it.

"I shouldna kiss ye," he said.

"Why no'?"

"Because kissing is a distraction. Because I promised your brother I'd keep ye safe and treat ye as if ye were my own wee sister. Brothers and sisters dinna kiss."

"We are no' brother and sister, Craig. And I think even my brother would forgive ye for such if he knew...that I wanted ye to."

"We could be set upon at any moment."

"And if we were set upon at any moment, would ye no' want to have kissed me one last time?"

Craig groaned. "Och, but lass, I want to do more than kiss ye..."

Her eyes widened, and a little gasp escaped her. "What do ye want to do?"

She was a naughty lass, making him put voice to his desires, and dammit! He liked that. "I would lay ye out right here amongst the herbs and vegetables, and I would kiss every inch of your body. And I'd pray the whole time that the heavens would no' smite me for plucking an angel for my own."

Annie's breaths came quick, and the pulse in her neck leaped. He wanted to kiss that pulse point. To flick his tongue over it. Suck on it.

"That sounds verra tempting." Her voice was breathless.

"There is only one thing that is keeping me from doing it." Och, but he needed to be quiet, to cease this madness at once.

"What's that?"

"The cottage full of people at our backs."

"They canna see us with the barn in the way. What if we knew they wouldna come?"

"We'd no longer be talking… That is, if ye wished it to be so."

"I wish it."

Craig stumbled back, as though she'd shoved him. She wanted him, too.

Bloody hell. Time to throw caution to the wind.

Craig surged forward, his hands pressed to either side of her face, and he claimed her mouth for his. He slanted his lips over hers, nibbled at the lushness of them. She gasped with a passion matching his own, her arms coming around his body. He teased the corner of her mouth with his tongue, sliding across the length of her lower lip until she opened for him.

When he dove inside to taste her, it was glorious,

beyond glorious. Intoxicating. Her velvety tongue met his with enthusiasm, stroking, tasting, toying. She was a natural at kissing and, *mo chreach*, but he'd not been lying when he'd said there was only the cottage full of people keeping him from lying with her now. Not even the wound in his head or belly could keep him from making love to her, from showing her all the pleasure that was to be had between people.

He slid a hand from her face, over her neck, softly running his fingertips down the column to her collarbone, to her shoulder, down the length of her arm to her waist. He slid his palm up her ribs and rested it there just beneath her breast.

"Can I—" he started to say, but she thrust her breast into his hand, and he ended his request with a groan.

Annie's breast was the sweetest treasure, soft and full in the palm of his hand. He brushed a thumb over her taut nipple and drank in her gasp. With his other hand around the small of her back, he pulled her flush against him, his cock hard and pulsing against her belly. Annie let out a soft gasp of pleasure or surprise, he wasn't sure, but the sound of it set his blood to pounding. She had no idea how much he wanted her.

How much he dreaded the end of moments like this. She was clinging to him, her passionate kiss enough to make this world melt away. God, what he wouldn't do to be somewhere else, anywhere else, with her. That they might…

But nay, he wouldn't take her just like that. Wouldn't ruin her, even if she asked him to. A woman's virtue was the only currency she had, and he wasn't going to rob her of it. That was a right that belonged only to the man who would be her husband.

Craig stiffened at the thought of her with another man. His passion surged again at a new thought—perhaps the only man for her was himself. She could be his.

He slid his hand to her rear, the roundness of her bottom a delight to hold, and he tucked her even closer, desire pummeling his insides. This kiss could not last forever. The way she was running her fingers through the hair at the back of his neck, her hips thrust against his, he wasn't certain how much longer it would be before he told his self-control to bugger off.

Mine. The word repeated in his mind as he kissed her, stroked her breast, swallowed her gasps of pleasure. *Mine.*

Sixteen

Annie hadn't known that it was possible to be utterly possessed by a man's kiss. The sensations whipping through her body, the way she could barely catch her breath... She wanted to consume him. Then climb the length of his body and wrap herself about him. The only thing that was holding her back from doing just that was the fact that she'd likely hurt his wounds, and just as he'd said, there was a cottage full of people nearby.

But oh...if they were alone... She'd let him take her to the ground. Let him teach her everything his gaze had promised—pleasure beyond the pleasure of his hand at her breast. And her nipples... Goodness, but she never would have known there was sensation such as what he elicited from them. They'd only ever been irritating to her when they puckered at the slightest cold, and she'd assumed at some point she'd use them to feed any children she might have when the war was over.

But pleasure? Oh... And what if he were to put his mouth...? She gasped at the thought. He slid his mouth from hers, and she was about to protest until his lips trailed a path along the column of her neck, sending glorious ripples of pleasure through her limbs. A flick of his tongue against the place where her pulse leaped had her sighing and clutching onto him all the more. Then lower he went, bending toward her breast, his mouth hovering over the fabric and liquid heat seeping through the layers to her nipple, bringing her desire to life.

Aye, this, this was what she wanted and so much more.

He teased her nipple with his teeth through her gown and shift until she whimpered, and her back felt so bowed it would snap in half. She wasn't certain who started to go down to the ground first. Was it him laying her out or her pulling him down? And did it matter? The next thing she knew they were both prone, his body half covering hers.

"Your wounds," she mused between whimpers as he kissed his way back up her neck to her mouth.

"I'm fine…" He sucked on her lower lip. "I'd take a thousand bullets again and again if it meant I could lie here like this with ye."

"Oh, Craig." She threaded her hand through his hair, and he claimed her mouth once more, the hardness of his body rocking against hers.

Of her own volition she lifted a knee up by his hip, gasping at how his body so easily slid between her thighs and at the sensation of the hardness that pushed against her. Dear heavens… Pleasure. This was what pleasure was all about. Endless, deep, intoxicating…

"Och, lass, ye need to put your leg back down."

"What? Why?"

"Your heat… I can feel your heat against my cock, and it makes me want ye," he warned her in a low growl.

Oh, but he'd said…*cock*. The word was so incredibly wanton, it sent a shiver of need coursing through her, and she wanted to hear him say it again.

"I like the way it feels," she admitted, never one to mince words. "And I like the way ye talk."

Craig grinned down at her and rocked his hips into hers. "Do ye like this?"

"Aye." She bit her lip to stifle a moan. How was he making her feel so much all at once?

Craig bent to kiss her again, his hand at her breast and then sliding down over her ribs to her hip. Around the back he stroked to her arse, massaging her there, and then down her thigh to her knee where it pressed against his hip. Up her inner thigh his fingers trailed, slipping beneath her gown to slide over her bare flesh and then higher up, through the slit of her drawers until his fingers danced in the damp heat between her thighs.

Annie cried out, eyes flying open. Craig grinned down at her.

"Ye're wet for me, lass."

More of his wicked tongue. "I dinna know any other way to be."

He let out a short curse. "Never change, no' for me, no' for anyone. Your honesty is refreshing, and God, ye feel so good." A finger slid inside her as he said it. "So hot..."

So hot... Aye, she was aflame all over and shivering at the same time. Craig claimed her mouth, kissing her with a passion that made her want to scream with pleasure while his fingers danced in and out of her body, stroking between the folds and caressing over a certain spot that made her entire body ignite.

"Aye, there," she said, not even realizing what she was

saying or why but knowing she wanted him to touch her *there* over and over.

"Aye, there," he murmured back.

Stroke after stroke of his fingers, his tongue against hers, Annie thought she might explode. Her body was climbing higher and higher, and just when she thought the pleasure was too much, she went higher still—searching, seeking, wanting *something*. And then it came, whipping through her like an unexpected gust of wind, knocking the breath from her and shattering her insides. Everything shook. Everything *felt*. And that part in the center of her, where he touched—*rapture*. She cried out, and he swallowed the sound with his kiss as she rocked her hips against his hand. Through wave after wave she clung to him, until the sensations died down.

Craig rested his forehead against hers, tenderly kissing her lips, one soft peck at a time. "Ye liked that?" he asked.

"Oh aye… Did ye?"

"It was incredible."

"Did ye feel it too?"

"I felt your body pulsing around my fingers."

"I want to feel ye pulsing against my fingers."

Craig shuddered and let out a groan, his forehead falling to her shoulder. "Next time, lass, I promise ye."

When Craig started to pull away, she wanted to tug him closer. "Nay, no' yet. I dinna want to stop," she said.

"Neither do I," he said, resigned. "But we must. Eppy is certain to come looking for us. And she might—"

Annie grinned. "Knife ye."

Craig laughed softly, biting her lower lip. "I was going to say box my ears."

Annie laughed. "Aye, we're both mad." Though she was teasing, it was a good way to break this moment. Because as much as she didn't want to stop kissing and touching, as much as she wanted him to make good on his promise for her to touch him, she did not want them to be discovered in such a private position by anyone. And she also did not want to destroy the budding crops that Max's family would need to survive any more than they already had.

"Do ye know how beautiful ye are?"

Annie's smile faltered. "Ye dinna have to flatter me, Craig. I've already kissed ye."

"'Tis a fact, lass." He ran the backs of his fingers over her cheekbone. "Ye're beautiful."

Heat rose to her face, which was fortunately already flushed from their kisses. "Thank ye."

"Annie!" The call came from the front of the cottage, which meant it would only be a matter of moments before Eppy rounded the side of the barn to find them lying there, limbs entwined and faces flushed.

"Coming," Annie called.

Craig helped her up, and she wiped at the dirt from the garden on her skirt, ran her hands over her hair. There was not much she could do out here. Between the running, the nap, and Craig's hands, she was a thorough mess. "Thank ye for understanding that I've a calling and I canna ignore it."

"Lass, I will endeavor to aid ye in any way I can."

"I dinna need your help," she said softly, hoping he wouldn't take it as a rejection. They might have become intimate, but that didn't mean she was willing to give up everything to him. "I've gone this far on my own."

"Everyone needs help sometimes. Look at me." He held out his arms. "If no' for your help, I'd be a dead man."

Annie laughed. "I think ye're just stubborn enough that ye'd have figured out a way no' to have died out there."

"I dinna know whether to take insult at that or be delighted that ye think so highly of me."

Annie playfully slapped at his bicep and then threaded her arm around his elbow as they started to walk back toward the cottage. "Take it any way ye please."

They reached the cottage to find Eppy waiting by the door. Her shrewd gaze assessed them both, but she did not react in any way, though Annie knew there had to be something different in the way she looked because inside she was soaring. Her body still tingled, and her heart raced with excitement and anticipation for when they could next be alone. Oh, how she wished this war was over! Knowing that it was far from an end damped down her mood considerably.

"Bannocks are finished baking," Eppy said.

Annie's stomach growled in response. Between the fitful nap, the whisky, the anger, and then Craig's heated kisses, she'd completely forgotten about food. The scent of the oatcakes wafted from inside the cottage, mixing with the savory, herbed aroma of the pottage.

Inside, Lila was slathering butter and marmalade onto bannocks and passing them out to the men.

"Hold the marmalade for my lady," Eppy said. "But plenty of butter will do her some good."

Annie wanted to protest but didn't. Eppy was constantly getting on her about eating because more often than not she was running from one patient to another without any thought to herself. Besides, in her line of work, many of the things she saw took away one's appetite.

Craig gently tickled her back before putting some space between them, and she wanted to pull him to her side. To simply announce to everyone present that she was his and he was hers… Except they hadn't made any pledges to one another, had they? She felt the emptiness of his absence next to her keenly, and when Max's brother offered her his chair, she hesitated to take it but then couldn't refuse else he take offense.

But as soon as she was seated, Craig moved to stand behind her, his fingers brushing over her shoulder as he passed by, sending a warm shiver through her.

Annie accepted the warm, thick bannock from Lila, butter melting over the edges. She took a hearty bite, nearly groaning at the flavor and satisfaction of eating. It'd been an age since she'd had a fresh-baked bannock, or at least it felt that way. Devouring one piece, she was offered a second and didn't refuse.

While they ate, Old Max regaled the group with a story of battle from his youth, but Annie mostly let her mind wander, escaping to her memories of the moments behind the barn.

Craig, who'd remained standing behind her, knelt.

His breath caressed her ear, and he said, "I love the passion ye take while eating… Reminds me of the passion of your kiss."

With every word, the place between her legs pulsed as if her body were saying *Aye, give it to me again*. She nearly choked on the bite in her mouth. She glanced around to see if anyone had heard, but no one seemed to be paying them any attention. Chewing carefully, she swallowed and glanced behind her. What could she say? How did one respond to so obvious a flirtation? She looked back toward the gathered group, wishing it weren't impossible to somehow escape them.

Craig pulled up a vacated chair beside her, sitting in that way of men, arms crossed over his chest, legs taking up as much room as was allowed. Which meant his breeches-covered thigh was pressed to her own where she sat primly in her chair. The heat of his thigh pressed to hers sent frissons of desire racing through her all over again. Every minute of him lying on top of her came rushing back, the feeling of his thighs spreading hers. If there was no one here, she would remove herself from her chair at once and put herself where she belonged, which was in his lap.

Oh! The sheer wickedness of that thought alone…

How was she to continue with her duty if she kept behaving this way?

It had not been so very long ago when she had been sitting with her dear friend Jenny, in her bedchamber at Cnàmhan Broch, sipping wine and talking about Jenny's experience of the very same struggle. Albeit a wee bit different, given that at the time she was concerned Toran might have been a traitor, but all the same. She'd wanted him, desired him, accepted his kiss, and still struggled with the notion of taking it a step further. Jenny, too, had devoted herself to the cause, raising an army of hundreds of men for Prince Charles. To give any of that up for marriage had been unthinkable. But she hadn't had to give it up, had she? She'd been able to have both in the end.

Was it possible to have Craig *and* keep her duty to the prince? Could she hold both close to her heart? She bit her lip and slid him a glance. Men did not have to worry about such thoughts, did they? They could have it all.

"Is your sister wed?" she whispered.

Craig looked startled by the question. "She'd better no' be."

Annie giggled, which got them a few stares and a subtle hush as people were still trying to listen to Old Max's story.

"Is she much younger than ye?"

"Aye, she's nineteen."

"So ye're thinking she should be married soon then?"

"I'm thinking she'd be a perfect candidate for a nunnery. Why?"

Annie grinned. "Just wondering."

"Are ye attempting to play matchmaker?"

"Nay." She shook her head vehemently. She wasn't attempting to align his sister with anyone; she'd simply been trying to get an idea of what Craig thought about marriage. Which wasn't working. And she should have guessed that it wouldn't work that way. He was not one to pick up on subtle hints, and to be honest, she wasn't one to pass out subtle hints. She was normally much more straightforward. And why the hell was she thinking of marriage? They'd had a few encounters, but that didn't mean he'd want to align himself to her for life. And yet... she cherished the very idea.

So with a deep breath, she asked, "And what of ye?"

"I'm no' attempting to play matchmaker either. I'd be happy if she remained a wee lass all the rest of my days."

"Surely ye jest."

"Why would I jest?"

"Because every lass dreams of the day she'll wed."

"And ye? Do ye dream of it, Annie? I see no husband by your side, and if I had to guess, ye're several years older than my sister."

Annie touched the corners of her eyes where she imagined the first wrinkles of age would appear. "Do I look so much older already?"

"Haggard."

She whipped her head toward his, mouth open, prepared to let him have it, only to find him grinning at her and a wink flashed in her direction.

"Well, ye didna seem to mind kissing this haggard old crone."

Craig laughed aloud at that, and again several pairs of eyes flashed toward theirs.

"'Haps we'd best chat outside," he suggested.

"Please do," said several of the men present, chuckles in everyone's throats.

"My lady?" Craig stood and offered her his hand, which she readily accepted.

They stepped outside into the crisp spring air, one of the hounds following them out. Annie hadn't noticed the family hounds before; they'd been so well-behaved, lying at Old Max's feet.

Craig picked up a small twig and tossed it, the hound chasing after it.

"I think we may have been annoying them with our chatter," Annie said, taking the stick from the hound when he returned and throwing it herself.

"I think half of them were more interested in what we might be saying."

Annie giggled. "I think ye may be right." Talking with Craig somehow had the power to erase the chills and terrors of the past weeks and months. It felt so easy with him right now, tossing a stick to a hound. The air was clear without a hint of danger. She could almost pretend that they were in some other place and time, that this was their cottage and they were living a simple, happy life where dragoons did not exist. Where death and violence were not always lurking on the periphery.

They tossed the stick several more times until the hound got tired of chasing it and started to sniff around. Annie walked out toward the field, Craig beside her, needing to stretch her legs and ease the fullness in her belly. The hound followed, and once they were a fair distance from the cottage—not far enough away that they couldn't reach it in time if they heard horses but not close enough for their conversation to be heard by others—Annie stopped, bending to pluck a long piece of grass and coiling it around her finger.

The hound lay down where the sun hit just right. Annie followed suit, lying in a patch of sun, staring up at the sky, her fingers threading in the blades of grass. "I have no' lain in the grass like this in a long time. Mayhap since I was a lass."

Craig lay down beside her, his pinky finger brushing hers. Their hands clasped as they both stared at the sky, clouds dotting the blue.

"I was lying in the grass when ye found me, though no' by choice."

Annie rolled her eyes. "Ye're terrible."

"That was terrible, I agree." He chuckled to himself, and Annie found the sound to be entirely delightful.

"What did ye do for fun when ye were a lad?"

Craig stiffened beside her. Her question had not been overly intrusive, so why was he seizing up?

"I didna have much fun when I was a lad."

"Oh? Why no'?"

He shrugged. "I suppose ye could say I was no' the fun type."

"What child is no' the fun type?" Annie turned her head to look at him, studying his strong profile, the long line of his nose with a subtle bump at the bridge. He had prominent brows that were most certainly frowning, and she could see from how the hair of his beard shifted at the corner of his jaw that he was probably clenching his teeth. "'Tis all right," she conceded, "ye need no' feel ye must tell me. Forever more ye shall be deemed Craig, the Un-fun Child."

He laughed harshly, but though it was supposed to be a jovial sound, it didn't come out that way, and laughter did not fill his face. It was the exact opposite.

"I was no' a large child."

"Most children are no' large. I assumed ye were no' born the size ye are now."

He rolled his head toward hers and grinned. "I was much smaller than the other lads. A weakling."

Annie's smile faded, suddenly outraged on behalf of a younger Craig. "Who said ye were weak?"

"Everyone. And they were right."

Her heart clenched in her chest. Who could have had such a black heart that they'd have broken him as a child?

Craig let out a long-suffering sigh, and on that great exhale, his words spilled out in a torrent. It was as though he'd been holding them back since his childhood and she'd unlatched the gate and set them free.

"My da was a great warrior, the savior of our clan. Everyone looked to him for advice, for training, for fighting, for protection. When I was born, I was weak. Nearly died. My mother used to say I had a stubborn will and that is how I survived, but my da took a decidedly different opinion. He thought I should have been left in the woods. And so as I grew up, he took every opportunity he could to torment me. To prove to me that I was just a scrawny good-for-nothing."

Never in all of her life would she have guessed that the man sitting before her had ever been seen as scrawny or good for nothing. He was everything a soldier wanted to be. And he was tall, muscular in all the right places.

One look at him and ladies swooned. One glance and his enemies faltered. To think anyone could believe him to be less was simply…

“Clearly your da was mad.”

Seventeen

Craig stared at Annie, speechless for perhaps the first time in his life. Not that he was an incredibly talkative person to begin with, but speechless he was now nonetheless. The lass had not hesitated in naming his father a madman.

And until that moment, Craig had never considered it.

Annie's hands went to her cheeks. "Oh my, I'm so sorry. I didna mean to say it aloud."

But she had, and her words had been a gush of cold water on the hot anger he'd carried for years. He trusted her judgment otherwise; why not here? "Ye may be right," he found himself saying. "I'd never considered things that way. But what other reason could a man have to continuously put his only son into situations that would maim or even kill him?"

"None that I can think of. Battle, war, those are the duties of a soldier, aye, but a lad? Nay. He should have been teaching ye, protecting ye." She shook her head, her lips pursed. "I wish I'd been there. I'd have given him a piece of my mind. And perhaps the tip of my dagger."

Craig laughed. "And then he would have scorned me all the more to have a woman speaking up for me."

"I suppose ye're right." Annie sighed.

"My mother would have protected me, I think, but I'll never know. And my father didna have much to do with

Marielle. She was sent to live with an aunt of mine who had also borne a child around the same time."

"Too bad that *ye* were not also sent to live with your aunt."

"I agree." Craig let out a laugh that was half humor, half exasperation. "But perhaps I'd no' have turned out the way I am now."

"I dinna know if I believe that. Perhaps the truth is that ye were strong enough to triumph over your father's torment despite him, not because of him."

"Huh, 'haps I was."

She plucked a blade of grass and held it up, twirling it in the sunlight, the long thin green turning into a miniature whirlwind. "The faults of the father do no' have to be the faults of the son. When ye have a lad, and he's just as tiny—or perhaps twice your size, like our good hosts—ye'll know a different approach to take with him."

A son… *His* son…

He'd never allowed himself to go so far as thinking about the day he might have a son to carry on his name.

"Do ye want children?" The words were out of his mouth before he could halt them.

Annie turned to face him once more, surprise on her face. "I do. I'm just no' sure if I'll ever have them."

"And why's that?"

"Well, for one thing, I'm no' married."

"Ye do know a marriage is no' what brings a child, aye?" he teased. "In fact, earlier, we nearly…"

"Och, stop!" She rolled her eyes and tossed her blade of grass at him. "I am well aware of how it works, sir, and

I am also aware of the differences in the male and female bodies. In case ye'd forgotten, I am a healer and have even seen your…" She blushed crimson, her mouth left open and then slammed shut.

"Ye've seen my what?" Was she about to confess to having seen his cock? Oh, good God, but why did he have to have been unconscious for that? To see her eyes roving over his body… Just the mere thought of it had him growing hard, his cock pressing against the confines of his breeches. Craig shifted uncomfortably.

"Ye know what I mean." She bit her lip and looked toward the sky.

"I'm unsure."

"This is an incredibly improper conversation." She groaned, flopping her arm over her eyes.

That had him laughing. "Alas, ye're no' as proper as ye might be trying to portray. Ye're Doctor Annie, and ye've seen a hundred—" He stopped himself from saying *cocks*. "Ye've seen a hundred men as naked as the day they were born."

"That's a silly phrase. I've seen a hundred naked bairns, and I can tell ye, they do no' look the same as a man full grown."

Oh, she was a joy. He laughed all the harder.

"So ye were saying, lass, that ye've seen my—"

"Twig and berries," she said with a mischievous gleam in her eyes.

"Is that what ye think of… Och, never mind, though I must say I take offense to the way in which ye've diminished my parts."

Her hand flew to her mouth, and she suddenly looked very concerned.

"What is it?" Craig sat up, his gaze piercing the land all around them. But he saw and heard nothing. No dragoons, not a single flash of red.

"Ye're going to hate me now."

"What?" Craig returned his gaze to her. "Why would I hate ye?"

"I called ye small, *twig and berries,* but I didna mean it, I was teasing. Ye were no' small at all. Quite a bit larger than most." Now both of her hands were covering her cheeks, and her eyes were squeezed so tightly that her brow wrinkled. "Zounds, but I sound like a complete blubbering idiot. I need to stop talking."

It had taken him a few moments to understand what she meant, and when he had finally figured it out, Craig couldn't stop laughing. He fell back into the grass and howled until tears came to his eyes. "Lass, I never once thought ye were seriously calling my parts small, I promise," he said through fits of laughter.

She was mumbling, "Oh my, oh my, oh my," over and over, her hands over her eyes to shield out the world.

On impulse, Craig rolled toward her and tickled her ribs until she too was laughing. And then his fingers brushed her breast, and both of their laughter died, smiles still on their faces as he leaned up on his elbow and stared down at her. The sun had disappeared behind the gathering clouds now, dimming the daylight brightness into the hazy gray that often came when rain was imminent.

But he didn't want to move. Not from this spot so close to her, not from this moment that had been so carefree and full of joy. All he wanted in this very moment was to kiss her. To savor these few fleeting flashes of joy and mark them in his memory before heading back into the darkness of war. Before the redcoats descended upon them, which felt inevitable now. Especially since he'd decided he wouldn't make her go to her cousin's castle after all and that he would indeed follow her back to wherever the prince was hiding to resume the campaign.

Annie's hand came up, her fingers brushing over his chin. Her eyes scanned his face, her eyelids heavy with desire. "I like the way your beard tickles my skin."

"I like it when ye touch me," he confessed.

Heat thrummed in his veins, and his cock—which had been tamed briefly—was now pulsing again with the need to press against her. For her to touch him, to bring him to the point of release just like he'd said she could. To slide inside her. To claim her for his own.

Annie leaned up, and he didn't move. He wanted to feel her coming to him, pressing those tentative lips to his. And when she did—they were anything but tentative. Annie's mouth was fire and need, claiming him as she pressed into him, demanding he kiss her back. There was no hesitation in his response. He wanted to kiss her, to slide his tongue along hers, melting away from all the worries and fears.

Craig laid her gently back onto the grass, his mouth on hers, resting on one elbow to hold himself from lying on top of her. He slid his free hand up her arm, interlacing his fingers with hers beside her head. Her hand was small and rough in his and only made him want to devour her more, to know what those hands were capable of. Did she have any idea of the power she wielded?

For he was completely enthralled by her. There was no escaping. Even if she left him here now, told him she never wanted to see him again, the memory of her would haunt him.

"I love kissing ye," he murmured against her mouth.

"'Tis heaven," she whispered back, running her tongue over his lip.

Mo chreach, but he wanted her. Craig's lips skimmed the column of her neck, pressing to the hollow at her collarbone. His leg slung over her own and trapped her in place, his arousal pressed to her hip. *Pleasure,* his body and mind shouted in unison, *give her pleasure.* But there was too much risk in going further. They risked discovery. They risked what would happen if they were so distracted they didn't hear the enemy approach.

And yet he desperately wanted to make her his.

Och, but would she say *aye*?

His lips went back to hers, claiming her deep and hot. What he wouldn't give right now for four walls and a door...

"I want ye, lass," he murmured against her ear, teasing her earlobe with his teeth. "Ye have no idea what ye're doing to me. I've sworn off the company of women for going on two years now... And ye've the power to make me break that vow. The way ye came alive under my touch before, I want to feel it again."

She shifted beneath him so that his thigh fell between

her legs, and she hooked her calf over his. Entwined fingers, entwined legs, entwined tongues. They wrapped around each other in delicious splendor.

"I want ye, too. I want ye to have me."

"Dinna say it," he groaned. "I canna. We canna."

"I know." Disappointment filled her voice. "We've both made vows we must keep."

"I dinna need to keep my vow of abstinence," he said with a smile, tugging on her lower lip with his teeth. "But my vow to the prince is strong."

"As is mine." She let out a little whimper when he went to kiss her neck once more. "Is there a rule that two people vowed to see a king made canna...be together?"

"I think no'." Damnation, but he didn't want her to go any further, to offer her body to him. He wanted so much more, and yet he wasn't prepared to make her a proper offer, and he knew she wasn't either.

He was a soldier, the son of a soldier. He was not a laird or a titled man. And she was the daughter of a prominent laird, sister to another. What could he offer her?

Oddly enough, that thought had never crossed his mind until now. And he pulled away. Even if they were not bound by their duties to the prince, he could not have her. Though her father was gone and Graham had asked him to watch after her, that did not make him worthy of her hand. Logan would certainly not allow it. Already he'd taken things much too far with her. Touching her the way he had... God, it had been a sweet torment, and one he didn't want to take back. If anything, he could take that memory with him forever.

"But there are other rules," he said regrettably, untangling their mouths, their legs. But he kept her hand in his as he stared down at her.

"What?"

"Rules of daughters of great men and who they can and canna be with."

"Ah, but ye see, Lieutenant, I was born breaking the rules, and I dinna plan to start following them now." Her eyes gleamed up at him, and Craig realized in that moment that somehow along the way, he'd fallen in love with her.

Maybe he'd even been a little bit in love with her since the moment she'd first swung her blade in his direction.

"Are ye a rule breaker, Craig?"

His answer to that question would forever change them both. If he said *nay,* he'd have to disentangle himself from her completely; he'd have to issue his apologies for kissing her, for touching her, and he wasn't sorry at all. He wanted to touch her more. Kiss her until they were both breathless. And he didn't want to walk away. But if he said he was a rule breaker, then he'd be quietly committing to her... The idea of doing that was terrifying, even to a man as brave as he was.

But she was waiting for his answer, and the longer he took to make it, the more she would think his answer was a resounding *nay*. And it was the opposite, so far the opposite. "I would break any and every rule for ye, lass." It was as close to a confession as he could come. *I would do anything ye asked.*

Before she could respond, the hound growled and

leaped to his feet. They both stilled, listening for whatever it was the hound had heard.

"I dinna hear anything," Annie said.

"Me either," he whispered.

But the hound clearly still did and took off toward the woods, howling and barking. They both sat up, looking around. The front door of the cottage flew open, and Old Max appeared, his other hounds taking off after their mate.

The old man motioned them frantically forward, mouthing something they couldn't make out. On all fours, they crawled to standing and ran toward the cottage. Old Max tugged them inside. Each brother held a musket in his hands, and weapons were being passed out to the wounded. Energy flowed through Craig's veins, the same rush of battle he felt when he stood on the field. Ready to fight.

But a moment later the hounds returned and scratched at the door. When they were let in, they seemed not in the least bothered as they went to lie before the hearth, resuming watch over the fire.

"What in the bloody hell?" Craig rested the butt of his musket on the ground. He peered out the window but saw nothing amiss.

"Must have been a fox or wildcat." Old Max scratched his head.

"Or a scout who tossed a venison treat to the hounds and sent them on their way." Craig glanced toward the trio of animals lying quietly by the hearth. "Drugged venison."

At that pronouncement Annie marched over, kneeling before the hounds to check their eyes and sniff their breath.

"I dinna see any evidence of poison. Whatever set them off, it was warning enough," Annie said after a moment, stroking their heads. "We are no' safe here."

"Aye," Craig agreed. "If we could borrow your wagon and a couple horses, we'll make our way tomorrow."

Old Max shook his head, placing his musket up on his shoulders. "Ye'll no' do it alone. We'll help."

Annie stood by the hearth, worry creasing her brow. God, he hated to see that look on her face. He wanted to swoop in and make everything bad go away.

"I think tomorrow will be too late," Annie said. "And ye might consider no' coming back."

"I'm no' abandoning my home. If my other sons return, they'll no' know what's happened to us." Old Max put his hands on his hips and stared at each of them in the eyes. "Those bastards are no' going to take it from me."

"Then they will burn it, with ye and your family inside." Annie spoke softly, but her words sounded like a horn in the crofter's cottage, and everyone fell silent.

Eighteen

Annie watched the battle of emotions as they flickered over Mr. Gair's face. "I know ye dinna want to hear it, sir, but 'tis the truth. They burned my family's castle, Cullidunloch, no' three weeks ago while many of us were still inside." Emotion made her throat tight. "I know what it is to lose a home, all the memories that go along with it, but 'tis better than losing a life. Have we no' already lost enough?"

The old man nodded, his gaze falling on his wife and then his sons. "Aye. And there's a chance if we're gone they'll no' trouble with the cottage."

Annie nodded, though she knew the gesture was likely a lie. They'd been gone from the other croft when it burned. But the most important thing was that they all needed to get out of there before the hounds' warning was heeded too late.

"We should leave tonight."

"Aye, ye're right. We didna want to risk it, but first I think my sons and I should scout the property. See if anyone is skulking about. If 'tis only a couple of dragoons, my lads and I can take them."

Annie didn't like that idea at all, but no matter how she protested, Old Max was insistent. The men, even the wounded who did not want to be seen as invalids, insisted on taking the weapons they could round up and going outside to scout the property for anything amiss.

Even Max insisted he'd take a horse, and given that he planned to ride, she actually felt he might have a better chance of surviving than anyone else.

Discreetly, Annie approached Paul, who leaned against the wall near a window, keeping his weight on his good leg. "Paul," she said quietly, so as not to draw anyone else's attention. She peeled back the curtain, eyeing the meadow where not a quarter hour before she'd been lying in bliss. "Ye should ride too. With your hip shot up, another bout of running will do ye in."

He looked ready to protest when she glanced at him, but then he nodded, his gaze sliding suspiciously to the unnamed soldier.

"Leave him be," she ordered, and again he nodded, though with less conviction.

"I'll stay behind to protect the women," Craig volunteered. "And it will give me a chance to check your wagon."

"Good."

With that settled, the men left the cottage.

"Holler if ye see anything in the field," Craig said.

"I will." Annie stood on the threshold of the open door, the wind whipping up around her, stirring her skirts around her ankles and yanking hair from the carefully messy knot at the nape of her neck.

The sky looked ominous, the sun no longer winning any battles with the clouds. Leaves and other bits of debris swept past with each gust.

Behind her, Eppy and Lila were busy preparing supplies. Eppy exited the cottage juggling several canteens. "Help me fill these from the well?"

Annie grabbed two, and together they filled the canteens. Lila had already wrapped up bannocks and other foodstuffs, piling them onto the table when they returned.

"Is there a basket we can store these in?" Annie asked of the piles of food.

"I think so, in the cellar." Lila hitched her thumb toward a small wooden door that was flipped open on the floor.

The first few steps were visible from the room, but anything lower was not, so Annie took a candle from the table and gingerly made her way down. The shelves were filled with jars of canned goods, cooking supplies, and other household things. She found a sturdy basket that would hold the food and carried it upstairs to fill.

"We should douse the fire. By the time the redcoats arrive, they'll find the hearth cold and believe that no one has lived here for some time. Perhaps then they'll choose no' to burn it."

Lila nodded emphatically, and so Annie and Eppy made yet another trip to the well for water. Annie surveyed the landscape as far as she could see along the way but found that all seemed right in the world despite the blustery wind and the sky that threatened to open up at any minute.

A good rain would hopefully keep the dragoons at bay. Not that the bastards were afraid of water, but they tended to be lazy, and a good bit of rain often kept them indoors unless they'd been specifically ordered out. And this little cottage on the moor could not be a deliberate target.

Thick smoke billowed about the small main room of the cottage when they poured the water over the hearth flames, and Annie opened the door to let it out. Lucky for them it dissipated quickly, as eager for air as they were.

"Should we hide our things?" Lila stood in the center of the kitchen wringing her hands. She stared around the kitchen at dishes that looked like they'd been passed down from one generation to the next, precious items she was certain not to want to lose. It wasn't as if they had any silver, gold, or jewels more than a few precious family heirlooms, but what they did have held a lot of value to them nonetheless.

"That's a good idea," Annie agreed. "Have ye some extra linens we can wrap these in to keep them safe?"

"Aye, and in the cellar there are a couple of chests. If we pack them cleverly enough, they'll think 'tis just a bunch of old soiled linens."

"I like it. Anything to fake the rascals out."

Together they worked to collect any other items that looked to be of value and carried them down to the cellar, cleverly hiding everything in plain sight.

They chatted quietly as they worked, and Lila told them about when her mother had given her the dishes. They'd been passed down to her by her mother and her mother before that. Four generations back they went, and they were Lila's most prized possessions.

The door opened, startling the three of them, a spray of rain blown sideways and preceding Craig into the croft. He stepped inside, rain dripping from his hair and shoulders, and for the briefest moment, Annie allowed herself to stare at him. To be jealous of every drop of water that sluiced its way over his skin, dripping from his nose, lips, chin.

"I dinna like them being out there in the rain," Lila muttered. She crossed herself and looked toward the ceiling, pulling Annie from her reverie. "Pray they come back quick and dinna run into any trouble."

Annie, Eppy, and Craig followed suit.

"The wagon is only large enough to carry our supplies, with two men in the back and two on the driving bench. But 'tis in need of repair, and I canna do it alone." As Craig spoke, he leaned slightly, pressing at his side.

"Are ye all right?"

"Aye. Fine. Just bumped my ribs."

Annie narrowed her eyes at him, trying to picture his wound beneath his shirt.

He prodded again at his side.

"Seriously, what happened?" She approached him, pasting on her no-nonsense face. "Show me."

"I'm fine." He tried to bat away her probing hands, but he wasn't going to win this fight.

"Did ye say the wagon is broken?" Lila asked.

Annie's gaze shot up to Craig. She should have been paying closer attention. She'd been so concerned with his wounds that she'd not heard that part.

"Aye. The wagon's shot. Axle is broken, and when I tried to fix it, the yoke broke."

Lila crossed herself again, muttering a prayer. "We've no' used it yet this spring."

"Wood's rotted, and the iron's rusted. I tried to jimmy

it to work, but I couldna. The parts need to be completely repaired, and it will take some time."

Annie's heart lurched into her chest. What where they going to do if they couldn't use the wagon?

"How familiar is your husband with the mountains?" Annie asked, recalling a snippet of conversation from earlier.

"Verra. He grew up here. Played and hunted in the mountains, still does."

"I think 'tis best if we take the men up the mountain. There are caves we can take shelter in." Annie's hands started to shake, and she pinched them into her gown to keep anyone else from seeing them.

The situation was turning from bad to worse. Her home had been burned down, the prince's army had been massacred, her brother was dead, they were running for their lives, and now they were going to have to survive on a mountainside. The men were already exhausted from their journey that morning, and she hated to ask them to climb a rock face.

"There's no choice when we're sitting ducks. If surviving means we might have to live out of a cave, fighting off nature as well as redcoats, then so be it," she whispered. "We're survivors."

"Damn right we are, pardon me, madam." Craig dipped his chin to Lila.

"Damn the bastard redcoats," the older woman shouted. "Dinna pardon yourself for speaking your mind, sir."

From outside the door came the sound of a dog's whimper and a scratch upon the wood. The four of them froze. Why would only a single hound have returned? Annie's blood ran cold as every possible scenario went through her mind. Again, a whimper and a scratch. Lila skirted the table in a whirlwind headed for the door, but Craig quickly leaped in front of her.

"I'll get it, madam." His gaze met Annie's overtop of the other woman's head. "Perhaps ye'd all like to make sure everything is in order in the cellar?"

The way he said it was so casual, but the meaning behind his words was anything but.

"Eppy, go with Lila. I'll stay here."

"I insist—" Craig started, but Annie interrupted him.

"I'm no' leaving ye alone. Now prepare to open the door."

Lila and Eppy hurried down to the cellar, closing the wooden hatch behind them, and Annie tossed the rolled rug back over the top of it. She hurried to sit at the table, grabbing two cups and a jug of ale and hastily pouring out the glasses.

Craig opened the door to the croft slowly and then stilled so visibly that Annie's heart plummeted. A growl sounded from the other side of the door. A different growl than any of the hounds she'd become familiar with at the cottage since arriving that morning.

Nay...

Whatever animal stood on the other side of Craig, it wasn't one of Old Max's.

Annie couldn't see around Craig's enormous body, but the distinct sounds of metal chinking, of horse bridles, sword hilts scraping, spurs, were unmistakable and all an indication of one thing—*dragoons.*

She bit the inside of her cheek to keep back the moan that wanted to escape and rose from her chair. Metallic blood coated her tongue from how hard she'd bitten, and she forced herself to stop. The knife was still in her boot where she kept it. Within reach—and yet not, if they took her in hand.

Did they have time to run?

"Hands up and come out of the cottage," a deep male voice ordered from somewhere outside. It was hard to tell exactly where, with the wind howling, but it was clear he was most certainly speaking to Craig.

That was all the answer she needed to know that there wasn't time at all. The dragoons had come. They were caught. No escape. Annie choked on a sob of fear. All this time they'd been running and so very close to getting away. Until now.

She watched Craig's back stiffen, and she was grateful that they were all dressed in plain clothes and not kilts. If they were lucky, not a single white cockade would be found in the house, signs of allegiance to the true prince.

Craig didn't turn around, giving no indication to the men out front that there was anyone else in the cottage. He was trying to protect her, and while she found that valiant, she wasn't about to let him be taken by the enemy. Not when he'd be executed on the spot. Not when she could save him.

The moment he started to take a step forward she lurched into action and ducked beneath his arm where he'd planted his fist into the doorjamb.

"Praise be, Cumberland's men have arrived! Do ye

see that, my dear, they have answered our prayers." She glanced behind her at Craig's face, shuttered in every way but for his eyes. Still she could tell he was not happy with what she'd done, and she'd ask him for forgiveness later. Right now she had to save his life.

"And what prayers would those be, madam?" The man at the front of the pack stared her down, daring her to say the wrong thing.

"Prayers to King George, of course, that his men would scour the Highlands and scoop up the scum of the earth. We dinna need that rabble coming around here begging for bread."

"What rabble?" the dragoon asked.

Annie held her hand to the side of her mouth as if she were going to whisper a secret. "Jacobites."

"And you would profess loyalty to the king?" The dragoon sounded skeptical.

"What other?"

The dragoon in charge fixed his gaze on Craig. "And you, sir?"

Craig was so stiff behind her he could have been made of stone. She wanted to elbow him, to force him to answer, but still he stood stoic.

"It would seem your man is not of the same opinion as you, madam. Kindly step aside so we can assess him more fully."

"I assure ye he is." Annie whirled around, hands on her hips. "Tell them."

"She didna know," Craig said to the man, ignoring her completely.

Annie was so shocked her hands fell back to her sides, and she was struck dumb. What the bloody hell was he doing?

"She did not know what, sir?"

"That I am as ye say. A *Jacobite*." Craig growled the last, and she wanted to shout at the top of her lungs in frustration.

"A rebel, sir?" The dragoon grinned widely, hungrily, as though he'd just found a table set for a feast and he was starving.

"Aye, the verra rabble my wife believes haunts the place."

"Then I suggest you come out of the house. We've a need to have a word with you at the garrison."

Annie grabbed hold of Craig's arm as he tried to get past her. "What are ye doing?" she hissed. "Tell them the *truth*."

Her heart felt as though it were being ripped from her chest. Why was he doing this? Did he think to protect her by getting himself killed? Didn't he realize that by being honest he was signing his own death warrant?

"I am." To the man on horseback he said, "Leave my wife out of it, please. She didna know. I kept it a secret, given her family's been king's men for generations and she might have poisoned me while I slept."

Annie let out a gasp of affront that was both real and false at the same time.

"I see you have indeed thoroughly surprised your wife." The captain eyed her, piercing her with his pale-blue gaze. "Did you not ask your husband where he sustained these injuries? You are aware there was a battle near here not too long ago?"

"He said he hurt himself trying to fix the blasted wagon." Her words were breathless, her skin growing pale. Inside she screamed for him to come back, not to be a fool, a martyr.

"The fool is not worth your time," she said. "As his wife I will happily go in his place and vow to school him in the correct ways of loyalty."

The man laughed. "I appreciate your offer, my lady, but we only arrest and execute true rebels."

"Execute? Nay!" Annie rushed forward, grabbing onto Craig's arm, true fear in her eyes.

Two dragoons leaped from their horses, hauling her away from Craig. Their hold bit into her flesh, but she didn't care about the pain, didn't care about anything but the fact that the man she loved was being ripped from her. Damnation! She loved him!

"I warn you, madam, keep up that show and you'll be arrested alongside him."

"Go inside, wife," Craig growled, pleading in his blue-green gaze. "Let the men handle this."

Annie's entire body shook with fear now. She couldn't lose someone else she *loved*. "Nay, please, I beg ye. What can I offer ye to look the other way, Captain?"

The man in charge grinned cruelly, his lecherous gaze raking over her body, eyes glued to her chest where her breasts strained against the fabric of her gown thanks to the tight hold the men had on her arms. "What *can* you offer me?"

"She will offer ye nothing," Craig warned. "Wife, *go inside*."

Craig was purposefully not saying her name, protecting her. But didn't he realize she was trying to protect him too?

"Anything ye want, sir, please just let him be." She'd seen the suffering of countless women in this battle, and she was willing to suffer for the man she loved. Anything to keep him alive.

The cruel man chuckled. "It is not often I am offered anything I want." He licked his lips, giving her a very real idea of what exactly he had in mind.

"Dammit, woman, go inside. I'll no' have ye do this for me. Take me to the garrison," Craig demanded. "Else I'll be forced to start firing."

The men who'd held onto Annie leaped on Craig, tackling him to the ground, punching him in the face and kicking him in the ribs she knew were already sore. Annie screamed, racing toward them, wanting to pummel them with her fists, to kick *them* in the ribs. She reached for her boot, prepared to start injuring in the precise places she knew would kill.

Craig doubled over, still begging her to go inside. The handle of her knife skimmed her fingers.

"Do not do it, madam," the man on the horse warned, a pistol aimed her way. "Else you will suffer the same fate."

Nineteen

Annie held up her hands and took several steps backward. Her eyes stayed locked on him, filled with fear and with betrayal. Craig kept his face blank, but he wanted to lunge for her, break free of these bastards and grab her up in his arms. To tell her that he loved her. That he was sorry. That it had to be this way.

These moments were the last he'd ever know of her. The last time he'd look at her. The last time he'd hear her voice, and to know that the moment was filled with tragedy was enough to make even his knees go weak. The dragoons had stopped beating him for the moment, allowing him to stand, and he hoped that his gaze on her, steady, intense, would convey to her all of the things he could not say. Blood trickled warm from his nose, and he wiped it away with his shirt, purposefully lifting it enough that she could see that his bullet wound had not been broken open by their beating. She would take comfort in that, he knew.

Whatever happened from this moment forward, Craig would be able to live the last remaining moments of his life knowing that he'd saved the woman he loved and honored his dear friend's wishes to protect Annie.

The dragoons tied his hands with rope, nearly cutting off the circulation, but he did not protest. The pain they gave him was pain they weren't giving her. The sooner they had him out of there, the sooner he knew she would be safe. She could run then. The lads would be back soon and take her with them. He prayed fervently that they didn't come back sooner, decide to be heroes, and get themselves killed. There were three times as many dragoons as them. On a normal day any Highlander could take those odds, especially a Highlander with a musket, but this was not a normal day. And the men were half injured.

The dragoon in charge of this outfit was Captain Boyd. Craig didn't know him well but recognized his face. Boyd had been a torment to these parts for years, in charge of the dragoons and a garrison nearby. He ran a devilish lot.

Boyd stared at him now, eyes off Annie, and watching Craig very intently instead. Was he waiting for Craig to break, to say something? He dared not give the man the satisfaction.

Out of his peripheral vision, he could see that Annie was still slowly retreating. *Dinna go inside without me getting one last look at ye.*

She paused on the threshold as if she had heard him, or maybe she'd asked him to look at her, he couldn't tell. His mind was a tumult of anger, pain, and grief. Grief for a life he'd not gotten to live with her. And anger that once more he found himself in the middle of a gang of bullies with no true way out. But there was hope too, hope that she'd escape and find her brother in the east and be done with these bastards forever.

Craig watched her. Tears streamed down her beautiful face, and anguish turned her mouth down.

"Hush, love," he said softly. "Everything will be all right. Ye can shut the door."

"Aye, madam, he's in good hands," Boyd added, clear menace in his voice, and completely ruining the moment. But Craig couldn't leave her only with Boyd's promise of pain to remember him by. And he couldn't let that be the last thing he ever said to her.

"I love ye," he said.

"Rebels do not know how to love," Boyd said and then ordered his men to take him.

The fact that the bastard had once more tried to ruin the moment didn't matter because from the look on Annie's face, Boyd's words had bounced off the armor of her resolve.

She didn't say anything back, and though he longed to hear those words from her, he was glad she didn't speak. Already they were lucky as hell that Boyd hadn't tried to take her with him or allowed his men to violate her. For to confess her love for a rebel was quite a thing different than confessing she was wed to one. Marriages were forced all the time, but love? Love was an emotion that no one could force in the heart.

Oh God, how he loved her.

The men grappled him up, sitting him on Boyd's horse at the rear. With his arms bound, the only way to hold on was with his legs. This would be an uncomfortable ride. Every moment for him from here on out would be uncomfortable.

Boyd ordered the men to ride, and they whirled their horses about, but Craig kept his gaze on Annie, shifting every which way so as not to lose sight of her. She didn't shut the door, staying on the threshold, that expression of shock, grief, and—dare he hope it? Returned love?—still playing across her face and tears wetting her pale cheeks.

His love.

The only woman he'd ever met who challenged him, who made him smile. The only woman he'd ever deemed worthy of his love. What a wonderful wife she would have made. What a wonderful mother.

With every lope of the horse, her figure grew smaller and smaller until he could no longer make out the cottage at all.

The ride to Boyd's garrison was not long, several hours at most, but by the time they arrived, Craig's legs were cramping with the exertion they'd needed to hold on to the horse. There was no doubt that Boyd had ridden as hard as he could in hopes that Craig would fly off the back of the horse, perhaps break his neck. But Craig wasn't going to give him the satisfaction.

When he was yanked down off the horse in the center of the garrison's wide courtyard, it was at first difficult for him to find his footing. He stumbled, his legs screaming and his knees burning with the ache of having been in a single position for so long.

Boyd's men shoved at him as he swayed, keeping him unbalanced.

"Welcome to hell," Boyd said, walking toward him and removing his gloves. His lips peeled away from his teeth in what was probably supposed to be a smile but reminded Craig instead of a rabid wolf. "You can call me the devil."

"I'd prefer to call ye nothing at all," Craig taunted back. "Untie my hands and let's have a go at it. I know ye're hungry for it, and so am I."

"Oh, let's not make it easy on you, traitor." Boyd spat at Craig's feet. "Fight with your hands tied behind your back."

The men crowded around, nearly salivating in their excitement to see blood spilled. Craig strained his neck from side to side, cracking out the kinks, and blood flow returned to his limbs as he shook them out. Boyd wouldn't have anticipated it, but he'd been in this situation before. Dear Da had thought it was funny to watch Craig fight it out with the older boys without the use of his hands. The bastard had actually prepared him for something, go figure.

Craig grinned at Boyd. "I accept the challenge."

"The thing is," Boyd said, "it's not really a challenge. And you never get to win."

The man rushed forward then, punching Craig hard in the gut. Anticipating the move, Craig tightened his belly. The blow was rough, and even with his muscles taut, pain radiated through his body and he doubled over, the wind knocked out of him. There was definitely something different about an evil devil's fist than a lad's, wasn't there?

Instinct kicked in then. Quick to react, Craig snapped his head forward into Boyd's face, clipping him on the chin as he backed away. Boyd rubbed at the spot, his face growing red with anger and his eyes blazing. "You should not have done that."

"Is this no' a fight, Boyd?" Craig said. "Or was I supposed to stand here for a beating?"

"Oh, it's a fight." Boyd nodded his head at his men, and suddenly hands were pummeling Craig from all sides.

Again, not a new situation, besides the size of the men. He launched himself into action, knocking his head into anyone within butting distance. He used his feet, kicking men freely in the shins, the ballocks, and their guts. Bracing himself against one assailant, he launched his feet into those opposite.

They would eventually overpower him, he knew, and if they didn't, Boyd had only to send in fresh meat. But even knowing that the fight was futile, Craig wasn't giving up. He might be a dead man, but he was going to make a hell of a mess on his way out.

Annie slammed the door of the cottage closed, barred it, and ran to the cellar, shoving back the rug and flinging open the hatch.

"They took him," she said, her voice hysterical, tears making her vision blurry. "They *took* him."

I love ye. His words replayed in her head over and over again. They'd not been a ploy but an honest confession that she'd felt all the way down to the marrow of her bones. And her heart had sung out a returned call, but she'd dared not voice it for fear that Boyd would cleave Craig's head from his body at that very moment if only to torment them both. The man was a demon. A devil.

Jenny had told her about Boyd and the horrible, awful way in which he'd touched her when he'd come upon one of Jenny's secret headquarters. Many women had suffered a worse fate at his hands. And the way he treated his prisoners! Craig was not going to last long there. An execution was imminent. As soon as Boyd had his fun with him, the man would put Craig into an unconsecrated early grave. The very thought of it made her heart lurch.

He could not die. Not before she got to tell him how she felt. And hopefully not even then.

Eppy and Lila burst from the cellar. They grabbed her in their arms, wrapping her up in warmth and their own tears. Lila was shaking so badly that they both had to hold her up. "Oh God, Mary Mother, help us. My lads?"

"I didna see them," Annie tried to reassure her. "They are most likely safe."

"Did the redcoats hurt ye?" Eppy's voice cracked as she checked Annie for injury. "We thought ye were dead for certain."

"He's gone," Annie sobbed. "I have to save him."

Eppy yanked herself away, her gaze on Annie, suddenly hearing exactly what it was Annie was saying. "Nay. Ye canna. I'll tie ye up myself if I have to."

"'Tis too dangerous," Lila said.

The door to the cottage burst open, and Annie, expecting Boyd and his men returning, prepared to launch into a full-on attack. But it was the men returned from scouting, their faces ashen. A burgeoning bruise showed on the unnamed soldier's face, and Paul looked guilty as sin. She didn't have time to deal with their petty squabbles. Not when Craig had been taken.

"We saw what happened." Old Max rushed over. "But we were too far to help."

Annie shook her head. "Even if ye were close, to help would have only sealed your fates."

"I'm so sorry." Max hobbled toward her, grabbing her into a hug. All of her patients followed, surrounding her, holding her up. "What are we going to do?"

"I'm going to get him back." The men nodded slowly, but she suspected they didn't quite register what she meant. She knew that because they would think her crazy if they did. "I'm going to break into the garrison, and I need your help to do it."

"What?" Eppy gasped. "Nay, nay, nay. I willna allow it. I will tie ye up myself and toss ye into that cellar. Logan will kill me."

Annie ignored her maid and looked to Old Max. "I'll need ye waiting on the perimeter, hidden, of course, so that when we make our escape, we've a quick way to speed away."

"Aye," Old Max said without argument, which only prompted a volley of arguments, all in agreement with Eppy.

Max put his arm around Eppy's shoulders as she sobbed. Eppy knew Annie well enough by now to realize that she'd made up her mind and there was no going back.

"What? Nay, ye canna be thinking this is a good idea,"

Lila argued. "They will kill all of ye. Craig sacrificed himself for ye so that ye could escape."

Annie swallowed hard. "I know 'tis crazy, but I dinna want to live without him. He is one of the bright lights I've found in a world filled with darkness. I canna let him die for me when there is a chance I can save him."

Old Max looked his wife in the eye, took Lila's hand in his, and kissed her knuckles in a move so soft and chivalric it was completely unexpected of a man so burly, and it made Annie's eyes tear up.

"If it were me, love, would ye stay put?" he asked.

Lila shook her head. "Nay, I'd no' stay either. I'd try to help ye."

"And so we must help her any way we can."

"I'll help ye," Paul said.

"Me too," said their unknown soldier, flashing an irritated glance at Paul, who nodded, shockingly, with respect.

Max looked down at Eppy and then back at Annie. "I'd do it for love. I'll help ye."

Had Annie missed something? Were Eppy and Max... falling for each other? There was no time to contemplate what that might mean. There was no time for anything other than getting Craig back, and fast. "I'm going to need a pistol and a spare gown."

They eyed her with brows raised.

"I intend to smuggle him out as my lady's maid." Annie squared her shoulders.

"How?" Eppy asked. "They will see how big he is and know him to be a man."

"He can crouch or hobble."

"And his beard?"

"I'll bring a razor." As much as she loved his beard, that was one thing they'd know him for. Annie wrung her hands before her, meeting each person's concerned gaze. "I didna save him from the field of battle only to have him be taken prisoner by the Butcher's henchmen. Craig is an officer and has a better chance of being used as a bartering tool than a lesser man. Perhaps they won't kill him right away."

"And what if he's no' there?" Old Max asked.

An icy slice of fear speared her middle. That was a thought she didn't want to have. "He will be there."

"What is your plan?" Max asked. "How can we help?"

"Boyd is a nasty lot, but I happen to know a few of his movements. Tomorrow is Sunday, and he will visit the local kirks to torment those worshipping, as he, like King George, is anti-Catholic. Local women often go into the garrison to visit the prisoners and bring them food. I'll be a local woman, and without Boyd there, perhaps they won't recognize me so easily. We'll ease out when the other women leave and find ye with the wagon. Trust me." She pulled Fiona's velvet pouch from her boot, pinching the hard stones with her fingers. "And if need be, I'll use this to help. This will work."

It *had* to. There was no other way to get into the garrison that she alone could handle, and she wasn't going to ask any of the others to go inside with her. 'Twas too dangerous. But a lone woman? The guards would dismiss her, not seeing her as a viable threat at all. Lord, but they hadn't learned their lesson, had they?

All she had to do now was pray that Craig made it through the night.

Twenty

Pain radiated through Craig's body. But pain was good because pain meant that he was still alive, even if his existence had been relegated to a living hell.

He rolled over in his cell, one eye swollen shut, and stared through the slit of his other eye. The floor beneath him was cold stone. So he'd not been put into the dungeon, where the floors were dirt-packed and soaked through with God only knew what. And he was the only one in here, which was just as well, too. Then again, there would be no one to witness whatever it was Boyd had planned for him.

Alas, that might have been a blessing. Besides, none of them were getting out of here. Death was the only savior for them now.

Was this what being an officer had given him? A cell with a solid surface?

He tried to sit up, pain in his back and both sides. There were definitely a couple of ribs broken, he was certain, but his arms and legs appeared intact. He grabbed his ballocks, both of which were also still there. A man had to check, didn't he?

Sitting up, or rather pushing himself upright and slumping forward, he studied the empty cell as best he could through swollen eyes. A draft blew around his legs. He still had his boots, but there was a large tear in his breeches by his knee. The cell was barren, no furniture, no hearth, no other inmates. Just Craig, his broken body, and his thoughts. The door was wooden with a small square cut out near the top and iron bars lodged in place, as if anyone would ever be able to slip through the small opening. Only a rat or a cat could do that. A wooden slat had been shoved across the hole so he couldn't even see out, not that he was getting up to go look anyway.

Thinking of a cat only reminded him of Annie and her brother's dreadful pet. What *had* happened to Pinecone?

For that matter, where was his Annie now? Had she escaped as he'd hoped? Was she up the mountain? Or had they decided to head for Skye? Wherever it was, he prayed she was far away from here, safe and sound where no dragoon could get to her.

Och, he was a fool. When had Annie ever run away from anything? The lass was determined to be in the fight. Maybe she would change. Except he didn't want her to, had told her so when he'd lain with her in the garden. He closed his eyes, reliving those moments that they'd been together. Her soft smile, the flush of her cheeks, the way her lips grew rosier with each kiss. The passion in her gaze, her gasps of pleasure when he'd touched her.

Craig leaned his head back against the stone wall, intending to sleep and dream of her, but dammit, his head hurt something fierce. He let out a groan and rubbed the back of his head. There was a large knot at the base but fortunately no blood. His wounds from Culloden did not seem to have opened back up, thank the saints, but judging from the amount of pain throughout his body, he was covered in new bruises anyhow.

But he'd put up one hell of a fight. He'd likely blackened Boyd's eye by the end, and he wasn't the only one with a few broken ribs. He'd knocked one man unconscious and sent plenty of others howling for their mothers.

The bastards deserved every damn blow.

In the end they'd overpowered him, as he'd suspected they would, but the fight—it had been glorious. Craig grinned at the memory, wincing at the pain of a split lip. How furious Boyd had been that Craig had taken so long to fall. He might have lost in the end, but Craig still considered it a victory.

"Thanks, Da," he said bitterly to the walls, his voice sounding distant and his lips stinging with every syllable. He touched his mouth, feeling the crust of dried blood.

"What was that?" The slat was pulled from the tiny window on the door, and a man's face appeared in the small barred opening. "You want another round, savage?"

"Come in here, I dare ye," Craig taunted, waving the man in. He tried to stand but stumbled back and fell onto his arse as the door swung wide.

The guard marched forward with purpose. "You're an arrogant fool, and I'm going to teach you a lesson."

The words would have sounded more menacing if not for the stuffy English accent. Craig laughed, full aware he sounded a bit mad.

"I'd like to see ye try," Craig goaded. "I could take ye with my hands tied behind my back and your ma on my cock."

That earned him a punch right in the broken ribs but

also allowed him the moment he needed to reach for the bastard who'd dared get close enough. He grabbed his jailer by the ears, slamming the rascal's head into his knee and relishing in the sound of nose cartilage cracking.

Blood spurted from the guard's busted nose, and he screamed in pain, shouting curses that Craig couldn't hear over his own laughter.

"You fool, what the devil?" Several other guards rushed in, pulled the whoreson out, and then dragged Craig back to the wall. There they shackled him to chains that hung just high enough to be uncomfortable, stretching his arms up and straining the sockets of his shoulders.

"Come back and see me?" Craig called after the men, one of whom spat on the floor of the cell in answer.

Craig grinned at the fresh blood on his knee, for once not his own. They thought to rule him in hell, but they had no idea just whom they were dealing with. Craig had grown up in hell, and if they thought to master him now, well, then the devil was a bloody fool.

Dawn broke with a drizzle of rain, but Annie wasn't going to let the weather deter her from her plan. Today was the day she was getting Craig back. And if she died trying, then at least her death would be worth it. She'd shout out her love for him until they stole her last breath.

Annie lined the bottom of her basket with the altered gown she, Eppy, and Lila had spent the night enlarging so that it would fit Craig's frame. They'd also fashioned a special bonnet that could be pulled low over his brow and then wrapped it around the special bannock that contained a razor and a small vial of oil. They also included a scarf in case the shave did not go well, though muffling his face with it might draw more attention than a strapping Scotswoman with a slight beard.

On top of all that, the basket was filled with bannocks and jerky—food for the prisoners—as well as a pouch of coins that she could swipe from to offer any guards a bribe to clear her way forward. Tucked into her bodice was the jeweled brooch. The braid that curled into a bun at the nape of her neck was secured in place with pins she could use to pick any locks she needed to. She thanked the heavens for the training her da had given her and her brothers in lock-picking when they were young because she was fairly certain that today of all days, she was going to need that skill.

Beneath her gown she had hidden a pistol, wrapped in the folds of a cloak that she strapped to her waist that gave her middle some extra padding. She anticipated that getting a weapon into the garrison was going to be a lot trickier than it was to smuggle in a few bannocks.

Annie mentally checked off everything they'd prepared and then realized she was holding her breath. With a hand to her belly, she let it out. Everyone in the room was watching her, waiting. They'd been taking her lead, and she'd been dredging up every trick she could remember. This would work. If she started to think of all the ways in which their plan could go awry, then those events might actually occur. So all she had to do was believe in herself and their plan and be confident that soon she and Craig would be together.

No one dared voice their concerns, though she could practically hear their thoughts. They would support her in going forward, and they would support her if she chose to back down. The latter she would never do, but knowing how much they believed in her was enough to bolster her mood.

"Let's go."

Lila and Eppy were to remain at the cottage with Annie's patients, though the women argued against staying behind. Both had even suggested that they could go into the garrison with her, that they could help. But Annie couldn't ask them to put themselves in so much danger. It was one thing to help her prepare and be ready for the escape, but it was something entirely different to ask them to go inside a garrison full of the enemy and possibly get locked in forever.

Annie hugged everyone goodbye. Old Max had saddled up their aging nag so Annie wouldn't draw attention to herself in town or near the garrison by riding in on a well-bred horse. He and his strapping lads took the wagon, two other horses hitched to it.

They rode for several hours but not together. If their plan didn't work, they didn't want anyone who might later be called as a witness to be able to identify them as having been together. When they reached the village outside the garrison Annie slowed her pace, trying to fit in with the other women headed toward the massive fortress. Dark clouds filled the sky, threatening to open up and pour. The fortress looked stark, unforgiving. It had been a castle once, home to an earl, and was still surrounded by high, imposing stone walls with a portcullis at the gate. It was designed to keep people in as much as it was designed to keep them out. Dragoons marched on the walls, keeping watch over the town, but not in a way that felt like the townsfolk were being protected. In fact, quite the opposite.

'Twas a wonder at all that they let womenfolk in to see the prisoners, but she supposed they didn't want to waste their own coin feeding prisoners before they were executed, released, or traded. Thank goodness for that.

The closer she drew, the harder her heart pounded. Her palms were sweaty, making it difficult to hold the reins, and the old mare she rode flicked her tail with irritation every time Annie squeezed her thighs a little too hard out of nerves.

Halfway there, a slight figure caught Annie's attention. He was dressed in trews, cap low over the face, and approached Annie quickly, slinking against the wall. Was she about to get robbed? Of all days! This was the last thing she needed. The figure drew closer, staying close to the shadows of the walls, and Annie halted her horse, reaching into her boot. She was about to bring out a knife to protect herself when she realized it was not a male figure after all but one she was quite familiar with.

"Jenny?" she muttered.

She urged her horse toward the slim form. It looked so much like her dear friend, her gait unmistakable, but what was she doing here?

"Excuse me, sir," Annie asked.

Wide familiar green eyes met her gaze. It *was* Jenny.

"Have ye the time?" Annie kept her voice low, disinterested, and her face neutral.

Jenny made to pull out her pocket watch, coming closer to Annie's horse. "What are ye doing here?" Jenny asked in a whisper. "'Tis too dangerous for ye to be here alone."

"I'm going to the garrison."

Jenny looked stricken. "Nay, ye canna."

"I have no choice. They took Craig." God, saying the words still felt like a dagger to the heart.

"Who is Craig?"

"Remember that insufferable friend of Graham's?"

Jenny's lips thinned with sadness. "I'm so sorry about your brother." Jenny had come with her to bury Graham, but still the pain cut deep for them both. Graham had often teased Jenny when they were children, and their friendship had continued into adulthood.

"Graham always said he'd die of heartbreak that ye wouldna marry him," Annie offered, trying to lighten the mood.

Jenny smiled but quickly let it fall, glancing from the sides of her eyes at those who might be watching. "He was a good brother and a good friend. But what's this about his insufferable acquaintance?"

"Craig MacLean..." Tears pricked Annie's eyes. "I have fallen in love with him, and last night, Boyd took him."

"Boyd." Jenny spoke the name like a curse. "And ye plan to just waltz into the garrison and bring him out?"

"I've a plan." She explained what she meant to do, and Jenny nodded, snapping shut her timepiece and shoving it back in her pocket.

"'Tis about the right time. I'll create a distraction when they open the gates to allow ye in more easily." Jenny's brows rose and waggled slightly. "I do like to cause a distraction."

"Thank ye, my friend. Would it be better for ye to cause the disturbance when we're prepared to leave, though?"

"Hmm," Jenny said thoughtfully. "Aye. And it would give me a bit more time to put the plan into action. But I'll need a signal to know when to start."

"I'll give your bird call that ye use with your men when we reach the courtyard." Annie handed Jenny a bannock so their exchange would not seem so odd to anyone watching. "Thank ye, my friend."

"I would rather go in and get him myself." Jenny had always been the fearless one. No doubt she could easily gain access to Craig and bring him out, but his rescue was something Annie needed to do herself.

"I know. And I love ye for it."

Jenny took a bite of the bannock. "I love ye, too. Where will ye go?"

Annie worried her lower lip. "Fiona told me to meet her in Skye, but I've a need to see my brother and make certain he is all right before I rejoin the fight."

Jenny nodded. "Aye, ye should. I'll get a message to Fiona. Get yourselves to Nairn once ye're free from here. I've a contact there with a fishing boat. Tell him I sent ye, and he'll sail ye to Cluny Castle."

"Thank ye," Annie said gratefully.

"What are friends for?" Jenny winked, and then louder she said, "Garrison's down the road. Use caution, my friend."

Annie moved off, feeling more confident about her plan and the way of escape. Several horse posts stood outside the garrison, and other women were tying up their nags while they waited in line to get inside. Annie followed suit. She listened as the line of visitors gave their names to a man who was writing them on a list, ostensibly to make certain no one came out who hadn't gone in.

She listened to the other names given, committing several to memory that she could use for Craig on their way out if needed. Though hopefully Jenny would be able to create enough of a distraction that a borrowed name would not be necessary. Greater miracles had happened before.

Annie got into line, sweat rolling down her spine. It took all her efforts to still the trembling in her hands. Craig was inside. She had to remain strong. Pulling up the memories of Craig being hauled away helped to steady her resolve a bit. She was going to save him.

When it came her time to be inspected, the guards sifted through the jerky and bannocks. They made lascivious eyes at her as they slid their slimy hands over her legs, arms, and back for weapons, bypassing the thickness at her middle and stupidly not even checking her boot, too busy playing with the silk garters of her hose to pay attention.

The guard stood too close, grinning, and Annie feared

her experience was going to be different than the women who'd gone inside before her. "Name?"

"Mrs. Sullivan." She thanked Mrs. Sullivan one last time for her help. There had to be a hundred Mrs. Sullivans in Scotland, and for the moment there was one more.

"Prisoner?"

"I believe ye brought in my late husband's second cousin last evening." She tried to put him at as much of a distance to herself as possible. "A Lieutenant MacLean. I hoped to bring him a last meal before he is executed."

"Aye. Go." The man looked completely disgusted and shoved her forward, hard enough to throw off her balance but not hard enough to make her stumble.

And that was it? That easy? She passed through the gate, heart pounding and mouth dry. How had it been that easy? She was inside the fortress walls now, and even the act of stepping beyond the guard suddenly left her feeling heavy and oppressed, as though grief tugged at her limbs, dragging her down to the ground. What unknown tragedies happened within these walls? Annie tried to keep her gaze down, not looking around, wanting to appear small and unimportant.

Women hurried along to the main entrance, and Annie did, too, ducking her head in case any of the guards might recognize her from the night before. Once she was inside, another guard directed her to Craig's cell, where he opened a small viewing window high on the door and pointed for her to look.

"That him?" the guard asked.

Annie peered through the opening. Craig was there but chained to the wall, his head slumped against his chest. His clothes were torn, bloodied, and covered in filth. What had they done to him? Her heart skipped a beat, and for a fraction of a second, she feared she was too late. Her belly soured, and she swallowed hard against the bile that rose in her throat.

"Aye," she whispered.

"Five minutes, not a second more." The guard shoved the key in the lock, cranking it open, and it made an ear-piercing screeching noise.

Five minutes? That was all? She needed more than five minutes to shave his face and pick the shackle locks, and who knew how long it would take to get him in disguise and out of the blasted building? Annie reached into her basket, pulling out the first bribe she'd had to use.

Annie held out the flask of whisky toward the guard, fearful that he wouldn't be the type of man who accepted bribes. *Take it. Take it. Take it.* "For ye, sir. I know it gets a bit nippy in here for ye poor gents, and we dinna want ye to suffer." She offered a modest smile. "I willna tell, I promise."

The guard grinned and opened the flask, taking a large swig and passing her an appreciative smile. "Ten minutes," he amended, and Annie could have dropped to the floor to kiss the bastard's feet. He didn't leave her quite yet. The man remained at her back, and she had the sudden panic that he would shove her forward and lock the door behind her. Neither of them moved.

Craig stared at her from his one good eye, unmoved

as if he didn't recognize her. If he didn't, she'd chalk that up to the brutal beating it looked like he'd taken. His gaze slid to the guard, anger slicing across his bruised and swollen features. He opened his mouth, and she had the distinct gut feeling that he was going to demand she be taken away, so instead, she cut him off before he could speak.

"Are ye Lieutenant MacLean?" she asked.

He just stared at her, and she turned toward the guard. "Are ye certain this is he?"

"You don't recognize your own kin?" The guard took another long swig of whisky.

Annie shook her head. "I thought I did, but his face is…"

The man rolled his eyes. "It's him, all right. If he makes any sudden moves, holler." He exited the cell, leaving the door open a crack, placing too much trust in the locked shackles and his naive assumption that Craig would not be able to escape.

"I was married to your cousin," she said, in case the guard was still standing outside. "Though ye're a traitor, I wished to visit ye and give ye a last meal. Fresh-baked bannock."

She pulled the bonnet-wrapped bannock from the basket. As she stood on tiptoe to hand it to him, she whispered, "There's a razor and oil inside. I'll pretend to be feeding ye as I shave your face." Then louder, "Eat up, dinna argue, 'tis my mother-in-law's recipe, and she'd roll in her grave if ye insulted her by no' eating it on top of being a traitor."

Craig grunted but said nothing, which was probably

best. Annie popped a piece of bannock into his mouth. He chewed as she smoothed the shaving oil gently over his face. With every glide of her fingers, she flinched in fear of hurting him, but Craig made not a sound. In a panic she glanced behind her to make certain the guard wasn't watching through the small window in the door, but the slat was firmly in place.

When she was finished with the oil, she paused, her hands on his cheeks, desperate to lean up and kiss him, to confess her love, to tell him everything would be all right, but she dared not say anything, and she certainly dared not kiss him. Not with the guard possibly right outside.

Their gazes locked, and she tried not to read the pain in his questioning eyes. He wanted to know why she was here, why she hadn't saved herself. And those were answers she couldn't give him right now.

Annie touched the blade to his face, scraping softly, the hair coming away with ease and revealing another bruise along his jaw. She wiped the blade on the towel in her basket and went in for the second line. As she worked she kept up a string of boring, nonsensical chatter about the family, about their loyalty to King George, and when she finished shaving him, proud of the smoothness of his face, she stroked his cheeks, his lips.

How much time had passed? Five minutes? Seven? She glanced behind her, finding the doorway clear of the guard, and then she plucked two pins from her hair.

"Bend your knee, I'm going to need a leg up to reach the shackles," she whispered. "I'm sorry if I hurt ye." She bit her lip as she stepped onto his bent knee and hoisted herself up into the air. "When I was a wee lass," she murmured as she worked the pins in the shackles, "this was my favorite game."

Craig watched her with those intense eyes, not a single word leaving his lips. When she heard the click in the lock, she whispered, "Dinna move your hand, in case they peek into the cell before I'm done with the other." Of course they'd notice her on his knee and all would be over, but maybe there'd be enough warning for her to jump down.

As she worked the second lock, she told him of her process for drying jerky, which was just as boring as it sounded. Fortunately, the second lock popped quicker than the first. Success! Annie stepped down from his knee, wiping at the smudge of dirt she'd left behind and realizing just how ridiculous that was given his state.

"Let me tell ye about my second cousin Louisa and her four daughters' rabbits." She started on another long nonsensical story as she tugged the pistol out from beneath her gown.

Craig' eyes widened on the prize, his gaze glittering with merriment.

"They tried to get them to race a neighbor's bunnies, but all they kept trying to do was chase each other. If they'd let them win, they'd be in for a surprise a few weeks later when another litter arrived."

She shoved the bonnet over his head and then pulled the gown over his head too. "Make haste," she whispered and then, unable to stop herself, she brushed her lips over his. It was quick, not enough in the least, leaving her wanting so much more.

Even as bruised as he was, Craig managed to tug the gown over his clothes quickly. Annie wrapped the scarf around his neck to hide the thickness and then swung the cloak around his shoulders, tying it just beneath the scarf. Using some of the flour in the basket that had fallen from the bannocks, she gently patted his face to try and cover up some of the bruises. While it dulled some of the purple, it didn't work completely. He'd have to keep his head down and not make eye contact with anyone if this was going to work.

She walked over to the door then, still keeping up her inane chatter. She ran out of thoughts about rabbits and switched to chickens. A peek out into the corridor showed that two guards stood all the way at the end. They looked to be chatting and sharing the flask of whisky.

She closed the small slat that covered the iron bars, jammed a pin into the lock, and with the butt of the pistol broke it off to keep it there. She pulled the velvet pouch from her bodice. If the guards took note of two women coming out of the cell when only one had been let in, that would be the time to offer them a treasure they could never hope to afford in their lifetimes. The loss would be worth every bit if it were to save the two of them.

"Now," she mouthed to Craig, heart pounding. When he got closer to her, she gave him the basket, their fingers brushing. Somehow that simple touch gave her some reassurance. "Stoop like an old woman."

Which he did, somehow managing to make his bulk look nearly half the size. They exited the cell, and Craig hurried to the shadows and out of the line of sight of the guards who'd not yet noticed them. Annie closed the door as quietly as she could and jammed another pin into the lock, breaking it off as well. They'd not be able to see into the cell or get in, and that was just as well for her. But she still needed to stall them for time. If they didn't mark her leaving, they might go down to check and discover her handiwork with the cell door. No, it wouldn't do at all if they cried a warning to the other guards before she and Craig had a chance to effect their escape.

With Craig out of sight, she called down to the guards, "Thank ye, lads!"

Too busy with drink they raised their hands in dismissal, and she and Craig made their way silently down the stairs and out into the courtyard. They paused there for a moment, she to catch her bearings, and likely he needed to allow his eyes to adjust to the light. Even with the clouds looming overhead, it was brighter outside than it had been in that cell.

The courtyard was lined with soldiers, a few women coming and going here and there. Every eye felt like it was on them, boring into them, waiting for her to make a mistake. The guard by the gate turned to watch her, and his eyes narrowed at the sight of Craig. The air whooshed from her lungs, time suspended in air. Annie's heart did a flip. She needed to make the bird call to alert Jenny, but if she did it now, they would all see it come from her.

Annie pretended to trip and then looked down, acting as though her bootlace had come untied. She bent down, her head ducked, and pretended to lace it back up, making the bird call as she did.

On cue, a loud commotion began outside the gate, which turned all the guards' attention away from her and Craig.

"Come along, Granny," she muttered for the benefit of any passersby as they hurried through the courtyard and skated through the open gate, dragoons running past them. When they reached the old nag, she indicated for Craig to mount, but he shook his head. Annie stomped her foot. "Get on the damn horse."

"Ye really are my angel," Craig whispered as he climbed into the saddle and hunched over to make himself appear smaller. His large boots stuck out from the cloak, very obviously male, and she prayed Jenny's distraction lasted long enough for them to get to the edge of town where Old Max and his lads waited.

She glanced behind her to see the dragoons collecting in a massive horde, but fear propelled them forward. No time to see what brilliant plan Jenny had enacted—this was their only chance to escape. And they still weren't out of the woods.

Walking close to Craig's side, trying to hide his massive feet, she hurried them down the road and out of town.

Twenty-One

The escape had been so easy. *Too easy.*

As they rode through town, a major ruckus happening behind them, Craig couldn't help but imagine being overtaken by a gang of dragoons. The old nag they rode was slow enough that they'd be dragged off easily, maybe killed on the spot.

Annie encouraged the horse as they walked briskly toward the edge of town, heads down.

"Ye should be up here," he murmured.

"Dinna speak, should anyone hear ye..." Genuine fear laced her words, gripping tightly to Craig's heart.

He kept his mouth closed after that, not wanting to be the cause of them getting caught. Holy hell, he was proud of Annie. The woman had marched into the garrison with a smile on her face, gotten the guards drunk, and walked him right out of there. She had to have been terrified. How had she pulled it off? She was brilliant. She was brave. She was incredible. She was *his*.

Even if they were caught now, his opinion on that wouldn't change. He wanted to reach out to her, to hold her, to tell her how much he loved her, how proud he was.

Every step, every breath until they reached the road was excruciating—not physical pain as much as the fear of being caught. He kept his face down, knowing that one good look, or really one fleeting glance, would mean the end.

Beside him, Annie kept her hands on the reins and moved to block the view of his lower half from any passersby. She nodded and smiled to anyone they passed but otherwise was quiet. The panic riddling her right now had to be unimaginable. Each person they passed could be the one to call them out. They were marginally safer now, before the escape had been noticed, but everyone was still a danger to him. A danger to her.

Why had she risked her life for him? She should have been well away from here. And yet he was exceedingly grateful that she had. His heart was full with the love he felt for her.

The closer they got to the edge of town, the more he believed this might actually work. They might actually get away with this insane plot. Also, when had she become a lockpick? He imagined a tiny version of his Annie, dark hair framing a heart-shaped face, curious amber eyes narrowed in concentration as she picked a lock with her hairpin. Her favorite childhood game.

The crowd had thinned as they made their way to the outskirts of town. They were nearly there. A few more feet and their escape would be in sight. He spotted a cluster of people standing and talking around a wagon that had a few sacks in the back, as though they'd just been to market. It wasn't hard to recognize Old Max and his sons, massive, bearded crofters with a jovial spirit that could make anyone smile. Especially now.

Old Max raised his hand when he saw them, and they all jumped into action.

Craig was assisted off the horse, which he was slightly

grateful for given the pain in his ribs. Into the back of the wagon he went, lying down among the sacks.

"Good to see ye," he murmured to the lads. They chuckled as they covered him until he wasn't visible to anyone looking in.

"Let's go. Jenny's distraction will no' last long," Annie urged.

"Where to?" Old Max asked.

"Nairn. I've been given a contact there who'll sail us to my cousins at Cluny Castle." Annie slipped into the back of the wagon beside Craig, her long legs stretched out beside his.

"That's a far cry from Skye," Old Max pointed out, even as he started in that direction down the road, the wagon bouncing as he picked up speed.

Craig gritted his teeth against the pain, grateful for the throbbing ache. Every bouncing jolt forward meant they were farther from town, farther from Boyd, farther from death.

"'Twill only be for a short time, but I want to see my brother, and MacLean needs a wee bit more time to heal before he's thrust back into the fray."

"Aye, the rest of the lads will be happy to hear that he's alive," Max said.

"Ye know I can hear ye?" Craig chuckled. "I'm no' dead."

Annie's laughter tinkled through the grain sacks. "Ye will be if ye speak again."

Craig grinned, his blood still racing and nerves keeping him on edge. Was this going to work?

Nearly five hours later, his muscles cramping and his back screaming, they arrived in the seaport town of Nairn. Rain spilled on them all in droves. Craig had long since discarded the dress and bonnet, and once they were clear into the countryside he had been able to sit up to endure the ride with the rest of them. He told the story of his rescue to pass the time.

Their wagon bounced through the village toward the sea, where even in the rain, gulls squawked and flew overhead. They dismounted near a dock tavern, the lads going inside to discreetly inquire about fishermen who might know Mistress J. Craig remained with the wagon, lying in the back and pretending sleep.

Annie walked along the dock, stopping to chat with the few fishermen she came across. "My dear friend is in search of her uncle. Her name is Jenny. Might he be here?"

She made her plea over and over to every little boat she found until one man stood up.

"How is my wee J? I've no' seen her in an age," he said. His hair and beard had long since gone gray, and he wore a cap pulled down over his forehead. Dressed in loose trews and shirt and jacket that had seen better days, he beckoned her closer.

Annie took tentative steps, eyeing the man's fishing boat carefully. "She's well. In fact, she's asked me to invite ye for a visit."

"Is that so?"

"Aye. Might I trouble ye for a ride?"

He looked up toward the sky, the rain pelting down

from the dark clouds showing no signs of relenting. "Of course, a friend of my niece is a friend of mine. But the weather is not helping, my friend."

"Will this help?" Annie pulled out the pouch of coins and handed several to the old sailor.

He bit into the coins, his eyes lighting up. "Immensely."

Not five minutes later, Annie was hugging Old Max and his lads and bidding them farewell. She asked that they gather the others and bring them to Cluny Castle for safekeeping.

"We'll see ye there, Doc," Max said.

Craig climbed from the back of the wagon, and side by side, he and Annie walked down the dock to find the man who'd agreed to take them east. Every step, Annie worried more. She feared the fisherman would have taken off with her coin or perhaps told anyone who'd listen that she'd been asking after Jenny, a known rebel. Then the dragoons who had to be hiding about the town would come to find them, tackling them to the ground and tossing them into the water to watch them drown.

But none of that happened, and Jenny's fisherman compatriot was waiting gleefully for them at the end of the dock. He helped first Annie and then Craig over the side.

"Make yourselves comfortable. 'Tis chilly out on the water today."

They stepped over rigging, wove their way around barrels, and settled on a pile of discarded sacks near the rear of the boat. The fisherman made his preparations, and they chatted idly with him until they pushed off the dock.

He tossed them a plaid, which Craig caught.

"Stay warm. Dinna need ye catching your death on my watch."

Annie wrapped them both in the plaid, feeling their shared heat begin to ease the perpetual cold in her bones.

As they shoved off, putting distance between them and the land, she turned to Craig and grinned, finally feeling calm begin to settle over her for the first time in so long. "Hello."

"Hello, angel."

"We did it."

"*Ye* did it."

Annie shook her head. "I canna take all the credit, for I'd never have been able to do it alone."

Craig pushed himself to sit up, gritting his teeth. His arms went around her—not caring if the fisherman saw, not caring if anyone in the world saw—and he pulled her against him.

Annie sagged into his body, wrapping her arms gently around him. "I love ye," she whispered into his ear. "I realized when they were taking ye away that I canna live without ye."

"Och, lass, ye were the only thing keeping me alive. I love ye so damn much it hurts."

Annie pressed kisses gently to his bruised face and then his lips. What he wouldn't give at that moment to lay her out and make love to her, to let this world slip away. Forget his wounds, his bruises. Forget Boyd, the Butcher, and anyone else who wanted to do them harm.

The boat sailed swiftly through the water, going over a swell that jarred him enough to elicit a small moan.

"Ye're in pain." Annie pulled away.

"More pain when ye leave me."

She looked him over with assessing eyes, prodding fingers. "Oh dear," she said, lifting his shirt to inspect his old wound and finding his bruised ribs instead. "Ye've a couple of broken ribs, I'd wager."

"Aye, several." He pulled her against him, leaning back against the side of the boat with her in his arms. "Your presence makes the pain go away."

They lay in silence for a while, staring up at the sky and taking in the sounds of the sea.

"Why did ye change your mind about Skye?" he asked.

"I want to see my brother," she answered. "But I also need to make certain ye're safe. I already lost one man I love in this war, and I'm no' ready to lose another."

"I dinna want to lose ye, either. And I think we've got some time. The prince is on the run, from what I overheard at the garrison. They canna figure out where he's gone, and it's driving them all mad."

"Aye. And if we head straight for him now, we could lead his enemies there. Now that ye're an escaped prisoner."

"And ye'll be a wanted woman for helping me."

"Worth it."

"Completely." He kissed the top of her head, and she leaned up for a kiss on the lips, which he was more than happy to give. She was so warm and soft, and his chest swelled to the point of bursting. "Marry me, Annie."

"Nothing would give me more pleasure than to be

your wife. Well, save the end of the war," she teased. She snuggled deeper against him. "I love ye so much. I was beside myself when I thought they might kill ye. I could do nothing but get to ye. Even breathing was a chore."

"Och, lass, I went a bit mad when I thought they were going to take ye. But I'd no' have been able to live if they did."

"I'm so glad they didna kill ye right away. I was in a fair panic thinking I'd arrive too late."

"As am I, but I wasna making it easy for the bastards. Luckily, I was good sport for them, and they wanted to keep me around a little longer."

She grinned up at him, her amber eyes filled with hope. "I didna think ye would let them take ye down without a fight."

"Never."

His brushed his lips over hers once more, trying hard not to let his mind wander.

Several hours passed in peace with them holding each other in their arms.

"I'll drop ye at Cove Bay," the old fisherman said. "'Tis a bit south of Aberdeen, but fewer dragoons tend to wander those parts."

"Thank ye, sir. Ye've been a godsend to us," Annie said.

"We all have to do our part." He nodded. "I've a contact there, Mr. Downie. He's one of us. He'll get ye set up with a couple of horses and a place to stay for the night if ye need it."

Craig looked up at the sky, the light starting to fade. "It'll be dark soon," he said.

"Might be best to find a place to stay," Annie said. "And give ye a bit of time to rest."

But Craig wasn't thinking about resting. When he was with Annie, rest was the last thing on his mind. "Aye, rest," he agreed.

They sailed into Cove Bay, the docks empty for that time of night but the taverns full and men who'd had a bit too much ale falling out of them. The biggest difference between this port and others Annie had seen was the decided absence of red coats, at least for now. Thank heaven for small favors.

The fisherman helped them find Mr. Downie, who took them to his tavern. The place was attached to a stable, hopefully filled up with enough extra horses that they could borrow a couple for their journey to Cluny.

Downie led them into the tavern by a side door but paused before going up the stairs. He patted Craig heavily on the shoulder. "Old Salty says ye'll need a bed and a couple of horses."

"Aye." Craig stood tall, not grimacing from the pounding.

Downie eyed him. "And I think a new set of clothes."

Craig grinned. Though he'd removed the dress, his shirt and trews were torn and bloodied from his time in the garrison and caused him to stick out like a sore thumb. He was surprised Old Salty had not asked how he'd come across his injuries, but he supposed if he was aligned to Mistress J and often carried cargo, he'd gotten used to discretion.

"Ye'll no' be making any trouble for me, will ye?"

Mr. Downie tilted his head to the side, and tapped the handrail.

"None at all," Annie answered, passing the man several coins. "As a matter of fact, we'll be your best customers. We've just gotten married, and we're traveling to visit family to share the good news."

Craig had to hand it to her, the lass was a smooth talker and quick on her feet.

"Lovely! Newlyweds, my favorite." Mr. Downie pocketed the coins. "We'll be certain to get ye the best room we have, and my wife makes a delicious steak-and-ale pie."

Craig's mouth was already watering.

A loud round of laughter filtered from beyond the stairs inside the tavern. "Might want to avoid that room," Downie said knowingly. "Ye'll no' find friends in there. Let's get ye upstairs. We'll have a bath filled for ye."

Craig was grateful for the man's advice, and a moment later they were in a cozy room with a large bed, a small hearth, and a table for two.

Downie dragged a large tub into the room from somewhere down the hall, the massive basin resembling a trough for barn animals more than a bath. Annie and Craig's gazes locked, their lips twitching but forcing themselves not to laugh. A few minutes later three young lads hauled up steaming pots of water, pouring them into the tub.

Craig kept his back to the lads and stared out the window, not wanting to give them a good look at his face or any fodder for gossip with their mates. Annie fussed about the hearth, lighting the logs even after Downie'd said he'd do it for them later and Craig threatened to physically wrest her from the spot if she didn't stop. When she relented, he himself knelt to take care of the fire.

"Ye've saved my life a couple times now, lass. Allow me to do something for ye."

Soon enough the tub was filled, two meat pies were set on the table with a carafe of wine, fresh sets of clothes had been procured for them both, and the door was finally shut, leaving them alone. Craig couldn't decide what he wanted first.

"A bath, a pie, wine, or a kiss." He ticked off the choices on his fingers, walking closer to her with each word. "In what order should I take my pleasures?"

Annie laughed, her head tilting back, exposing the length of her throat. The sound was pure joy. "I should think pie and wine first, then a bath, and then a kiss. Or perhaps a kiss and then sustenance, a bath, and a second kiss."

"I like the way ye think, love." Craig winked and gathered her in his arms, pressing his lips to hers, ignoring the pain of his injuries in favor of the pleasure of her mouth on his.

Only when he pulled back she clung to him still, tears in her eyes.

"What is it?" Panic filled him. What had he missed?

"I thought I'd lost ye," she murmured, shaking her head and swiping at her tears. "I feel like a fool for crying."

"Ye're no fool." Craig smoothed away her tears. "I'd be lying if I said I didna have a tear or two upon seeing your face in that cell."

"I feel like this is a dream but one that will end in a nightmare."

"Let us enjoy the dream then, pushing the demons as far away as we can." He brushed his lips over hers one more time before leading her to the table and pouring them each a glass of wine. "To our forever."

Annie raised her glass. "Forever." They drank then, each of them eyeing each other over the rims. "The pies smell divine."

"So damn good. Shall we say kiss, wine, food, bath, kiss?"

Annie laughed and pulled out her chair, settling in and passing him a pie and fork. They dove into the ale pies with gusto, leaving not a trace of sauce or crumb of crust behind, and downed the wine like water. As they ate, both finally began to relax a little.

"What made ye want to become a healer? Ye've told me about your pact to join the rebels, but why this?"

Annie took a sip of her wine and then set it carefully down. "My da was not able to be saved. The healer was out of reach, and nobody knew how to help him. He died."

"That is tragic."

"Aye. More so was when my mother became ill some years later. Though I'd started my training, I had no' the skills to help her, either. I was able to help my brother Logan, but Graham…" She shook her head, tears coming to her eyes. "I couldna help him."

"Ye couldna have helped him had ye been right there on the battlefield when he was hit, lass. His wound was fatal. Likely, he passed on impact."

She nodded, swiping angrily at the tears. "I know this, but still it feels like everyone I love, who I care about, gets hurt and I am helpless."

"Och, lass, ye give so much of yourself and ask for so little in return. Look at all ye've done for the men ye saved on the field. They would be dead without ye, as would countless men ye've helped to heal. Me included. Ye're an incredible woman. A talented healer. Ye must forgive yourself for whatever transgressions ye fear ye've made."

"I know." She let out a long-suffering sigh, and he reached for her hand, squeezing gently.

"Do ye want to indulge in the bath first?" Craig offered. "I'll turn my back."

Annie shook her head. "I couldna. I'm no' the one who's been in prison. Ye should go first."

"That is exactly why I want to go last. Ye've no idea how disgusting it is to lie in a cell. I'd no' be able to live with myself if ye sank into the filth I left behind."

"Ye know I care naught, other than I dinna want to take the warmth of the water away from ye. But if it bothers ye, I'll be fine washing with the basin. Ye enjoy the tub."

Back and forth they went a few times, and finally Craig went to the door, making certain it was locked. He turned and said, "Now that ye're my *wife*, why do ye no' share the bath with me?"

Annie's eyes widened, and she slowly dragged her gaze from him to the tub and back again. Her brows lifted in curiosity. "Is that something a wife might do?"

Craig nodded slowly, his mouth going dry at the

thought of the two of them in the bath together, their wet bodies slipping and sliding in the warm water. But first he needed to wash off some of the grime in the basin, fearing he'd dirty the water enough to disgust her.

"All right." Her voice was breathless, setting his blood to thrumming in his veins. She had agreed—*to be naked* with him.

Craig blinked. Had he heard her correctly? He swallowed hard and said softly, "All right. Let me wash up a bit first."

Standing before her, eyes locked on each other, he removed his shirt and stilled. It had been the same way he'd stood before her the first time they'd kissed, his chest bared. Could she see the pounding of his heart? He took a cloth and dipped it into the basin, wiping away the grime on his face, neck, and torso.

Annie took off her cloak, adding it to the growing pile of dirty clothes. He removed his boots and hose, and she did the same. Then she reached behind her and started to work on the laces of her gown, her beautiful amber eyes fixed on him as he finished washing away the grime.

"Allow me." Craig tossed the rag and closed the distance between them, stroking his fingers over her arms.

Annie turned slowly, tugging her hair over her shoulder to expose the back of her neck, where he couldn't help but place a kiss. With nimble fingers he unlaced and unbuttoned her gown, running a finger down her spine. She shivered.

Craig leaned forward, pressing another kiss to the back of her neck. "Are ye cold?" he whispered.

"Never when I'm with ye."

He smoothed his hands over her shoulders, sliding the gown slowly off her until it rested at her waist and then lower until it pooled at her feet. She stepped out of it and turned around to face him in her thin chemise. He could see everything through the fine linen, the outline of her curves, the roundness of her breasts, the taut pink nipples that pressed against the fabric, the outline of her belly, and a thatch of dark curls in a perfect triangle between her thighs. It was a vision he hadn't forgotten, and yet it was all the more intense seeing it now.

Craig swallowed, lifting the gown from the floor and tossing it aside. He had to do something with his hands to keep from reaching for her and terrifying her with his frantic ardor.

"If ye want, ye can bathe in your chemise," he offered, not wanting to frighten her away from him.

"Are ye going to bathe in your trews?" she asked, nodding to the fabric still clinging to his body, noticeably tighter in the center and growing tighter by the minute.

"Nay." He shook his head but didn't make a move to unbutton his trews just yet.

"Then I will no' remain in my chemise."

Craig swallowed hard as her fingers untied the drawstring at her throat, opening the chemise just enough to give him a hint of skin between her breasts. *Mo chreach*, he wanted to taste her. When last he'd had his mouth at her breast, there had been layers of fabric between his tongue and her sweet flesh.

Craig undid two buttons on his trews, peeling down

the flap and then pausing. He wanted nothing more than to be standing there before her naked. His nudity would be nothing new to her and yet, in this context, so incredibly different.

"Are ye certain, love?" His voice was low, and desire thrummed thick and wild through his veins. "I'll keep going if ye still wish it. Or ye can turn around and we can go on as if there's been no change at all between us."

Twenty-Two

If she still wished it…

Oh, Annie wished it. She wished it very much. Wanted to see him fully naked. To touch his skin. Wanted to feel once more the pleasure he'd given her in the field, wanted to give him back that same pleasure. She licked her lips, staring at the way the fabric on the front of his trews folded down from where he'd unbuttoned them, how a trail of ginger hair teased his skin and her imagination with what lay beneath the rest of that flap.

Annie took two steps forward, surprised by how closing the distance between them wasn't as frightening as she thought it might be. That saying *aye* to what she wanted, to the man she wanted, hadn't caused lightning to strike or dragoons to attack. But she'd always been bolder than she should be, always been the one to take the lead, to do as she pleased. And why should this be any different? The man she loved was standing before her asking if she wanted him, asking if she wished him to continue undressing, and it was all she could do not to shout that *aye,* she *verra much* wanted him to remove every stitch of fabric on his body.

"I want ye," she said softly. Lightly she rested her hands on his muscled, warm chest, spreading her fingers wide, reaching up on tiptoe to kiss his lips.

Her hands slid down to the waistband of his trews, to the center where the remaining buttons blocked her from what was hidden beneath. Craig remained still except for his lips moving slowly against hers, his tongue teasing the tip of hers.

She flicked open a button and he sucked the breath from her mouth, all the air leaving her lungs—as though he'd taken it all away with that shallow hiss.

"Ye dinna know how much those words give me pleasure." Craig's chest rumbled beneath her fingers.

"Oh, pleasure," she murmured. "I want it all."

He was no longer still then, his hands skimming to the front of her chemise and finishing the untying she'd abandoned in her desire to do away with his trews. The soft linen whispered down her shoulders, the chill in the room snaking over her heated skin as the garment settled around her hips, exposing her back, her breasts, her stomach.

With a shuddering breath, she reached the final button on his trews, the heat of his body singeing her skin. All she had to do was reach inside to free his arousal, but she wasn't certain she was that bold yet. Aye, she'd seen him when she bathed him after bringing him to the croft, but seeing him helpless and unconscious was one thing—and knowing right now that the part of him that would bring her pleasure would be engorged with desire made her feel suddenly timid. Then again, she'd wanted to do this in the field days ago, and he had said that she could the next time they were together. Hands on his hips, she slipped her fingers beneath his waistband, skimming over the heat of his hips, around to his rear, the taut muscles of his arse flexing beneath her touch.

"I like the way ye touch me," Craig growled against her lips. "I want ye to touch me everywhere. I want to touch ye everywhere..."

Oh...my...aye...

That was exactly what she needed to bolster her courage. Annie dragged her fingernails lightly around to the front of his hips, pausing only for the briefest moment before she reached for the length of him. She wrapped her fingers around the smooth, velvet hardness of his shaft.

Craig groaned, deepening their kiss, exciting her to the point she nearly forgot what she was doing. But she wanted to hear him moan again.

"Tell me what to do." She slid her palm up, over the smooth tip and back down, marveling at how his body could be soft and hard all at once.

"That, I like that."

He liked it... She liked it... Annie's heart pounded as she stroked him, the delicious weight of his arousal in her palm as he kissed her breath away. His hands were on her bare back, trailing up and down her spine, gripping her arse. She skimmed her thumb over the soft head once more, feeling a drop of moisture. Curious, she pulled away from their kiss to stare down at him, the shaft that she held so gloriously upright in her fist.

"Ye're wet, too," she said.

"Good God, Annie..." He moaned. "I want to touch ye."

His lips trailed a path from her lips down to her neck and then lower until he hovered above her breasts.

"Perfection," he murmured as he flicked his tongue over her skin.

Annie gasped at the feel of his heated, velvet tongue, there and gone again just as swiftly. He took a step back, but she didn't let go of his shaft, not wanting him to retreat fully. His eyes met hers, heat and fire swirling around in their blue-green depths. He wrapped his hand around hers, moving her grip up and down his shaft, his forehead falling forward against her, a ragged breath tearing from his throat.

"I need ye to stop," he said, but he kept leading her up and down. "Please. Too good."

Too good...

"I need to last. Please stop." He captured her mouth with his, pressing his body hard into hers, their hands entwined around his velvet shaft crushing into the apex at her thighs.

Annie gasped at the shocking pleasure of it. "Ye like it."

"Too much." He tore his mouth away from her, peeled her hand off him. "I want to see ye."

Eyes on her, he slid her chemise past her hips, and it fell off the rest of the way, giving her enough of a boost in boldness to do the same to his trews. She smoothed her hands down toward his thighs, taking the garment with her, freeing his member more fully. It landed hard and satiny against her belly, and she stopped moving altogether then, relishing for a moment in that heated, sensual touch.

Only an inch or two of air separated them, save for that part of him resting against her, and she wanted to feel it all. To wrap herself around him and never be apart from him again.

Craig slid his hands around to her bottom, and then he was lifting her up, his mouth covering hers as he carried her toward the bath. He climbed inside, settling her on his lap facing away from him.

"Am I hurting ye?" she asked, suddenly worried about his bruised ribs.

"Everything is perfect when I'm with ye." He trailed his fingers along her arm, leaving gooseflesh rising in his path. Everywhere tingled with anticipation of his touch, with excitement that they were together, naked.

Craig took up a linen cloth and ran it over her arm, her shoulders, gently pushing her forward as he rubbed it along the length of her spine.

"I should be washing ye," she said.

"Nay, lass. Let me take care of ye."

Allowing someone else to take care of her was a concept Annie had a hard time accepting. She was supposed to be the caregiver, and yet the feel of him washing her, the warm water sluicing over her skin, the scent of the lemon and thyme soap, was exhilarating.

Perhaps in this she could let him have his way...

His lips touched the back of her neck, the wet, soapy cloth brushing over her breasts. Her nipples hard, the place between her thighs was aching. His arousal pressed against her back, thick and hard, and she wanted to touch him again. But then he slid the cloth down her belly and between her thighs, and she lost track of her thoughts completely.

He stroked the cloth against the most private part of her, his teeth scraping over her ear while his other hand massaged her breast. "This bath is torture," he confessed.

Annie leaned back against him, her legs parting and a sigh on her lips. "Exquisite."

The cloth disappeared, and his fingers were on her directly, gently sliding between her folds and over the nub that sparked with pleasure. Exquisite didn't even begin to describe what she was feeling right now. How did he know just the right spot to touch?

In a slow circle, he stroked between her thighs, and with every swirl of his fingers, she felt the flame inside her growing until she was hot all over and writhing against him. Annie tilted her head back against his shoulder, turning just enough that she could see his face. He pressed his lips to hers, his tongue teasing her mouth in the same delicious way as his fingers danced expertly over her skin.

She had the urge to turn around, to crawl over him.

"Och, lass, I love the way ye respond to me," he murmured against her lips. "I want all of ye."

"Aye, I'm yours."

Craig's fingers withdrew, leaving her feeling cold, vacant, lost. Then he was standing up behind her, lifting her into the cold air of the room. He drew her toward the bed, where he sat down wet on the edge and pulled her closer, his lips capturing one turgid nipple in his mouth. She moaned, thrusting her fingers into his hair, her body immediately responding with the intense need and want that he drew from her. She lifted a knee beside his hip, needing to be closer.

He was quick to change their position so that she was now sitting on the edge of the bed and he stood before her. His mouth lingering on hers, he slowly knelt before her, spreading her legs wide, hands splayed on her thighs.

Annie arched her back, her breasts scraping over his muscled chest.

"I'm going to kiss ye," he said, mouth still on hers, "here." His fingers slid toward her center, stroking through the curls.

Annie opened her mouth to protest but found herself completely speechless when she opened her eyes to see him looking up at her from between her thighs. The scene was wicked and so very delicious all at once. And she decided she wanted him, very much, to do just what he'd described. She nodded, and Craig smiled, a satisfied and devious grin on his handsome face.

Annie held her breath while he parted her folds, his lips coming closer, and then he kissed her. Just a gentle brush of his lips at first, enough to make her legs twitch and for her to gasp. Then his tongue flicked out, stroking upward between her folds, and Annie cried out as pleasure seemed to scorch every inch of her body.

To think that one tiny stroke—but that thought was interrupted by another and another stroke of his wicked tongue. Pleasure thrummed through her relentlessly. She gripped his hair. Craig reached up and gently pressed her chest until she lay back. Spreading her thighs wider, he hooked them over his shoulders and continued his assault of pleasure on her sex. Good God, the man's tongue…

Annie gripped the sheets, lips parted as she moaned. He whipped her senses up into a frenzy, bringing her to the brink of satisfaction before pulling back to tease her with his lips on her inner thigh. He nipped gently with his teeth before diving back in to torment her some more.

When he tried to pull away again, she squeezed him with her thighs. "Please," she begged. "I want it… All of it."

Craig growled, the strokes of his tongue growing more insistent, the pressure more firm, until she danced right there on the edge of the precipice.

"Aye, sweetheart, that's it, ye're almost there," he murmured against her heat. "Let it come, let go."

Annie moaned, her hips rising to meet his mouth. And then she felt it, that first frisson of release like a spark against a cannon's fuse. It fired her into an explosion that rocked her to the core. Pleasure washed over her, wave after wave, and she rode it out with every mad, relentless lash of his tongue.

When her legs fell apart, shaking and spent, Craig kissed the inside of her thigh and crawled up the length of her body. The satisfied grin on his face brought out a satiated grin of her own. He kissed her hard on the mouth, her scent surrounding him, her essence on his tongue.

"I want to love ye the same way," she said.

Craig groaned, his forehead resting on hers. "Aye, love, aye, but no' tonight. I could barely handle your hand. If ye put your tongue on me… If ye take me into your mouth…" He muttered an expletive. "Next time."

She was about to protest, but he consumed her with another kiss, his body settling against her, the weight and thickness of his arousal pressed to the very heat of her. And though she'd thought the release she'd just experienced would have left her empty, the flame of her desire sparked once more.

Craig slid his hands beneath her buttocks, raising her to meet him more fully, his erection cradled against her sex. He smoothed her legs around his hips and rocked back and forth against her until she was moaning.

"I want ye, all of ye," he said, sliding a finger inside her.

Annie could barely speak as he touched her. "Aye, please."

Craig skimmed his teeth along her neck, sucking gently on her collarbone and then flicking his tongue over her nipple as he stroked in and out of her, the pad of his thumb circling the nub of her pleasure.

"Ye're ready for me," he groaned against her breast.

"I've been ready."

For whatever reason, her words made him groan all the more. He dipped his head, continuing his attention to her breasts, and she arched her back, allowing pleasure to take her. His fingers withdrew from her body, and she wanted very much for him to put them back, to fill her. But he gripped his arousal and slid it gently back and forth against her, sending spirals of pleasure unfurling from her limbs. Oh, aye, this would do just as well...

"Kiss me," she said, and he obeyed, his mouth on hers, tongue dancing in and out, stroking as he'd just done moments ago to her core.

"I canna wait any longer," he moaned against her mouth. "Your body is ready for me. Is your heart?"

"Aye, aye, aye," she sighed. Kissing him harder and wrapping her arms around his neck, she lifted her hips.

Craig thrust forward, taking her in one long stroke and a low growl in his throat. There was a small pinch of pain, but she barely had time to think on it as he continued to kiss her, his fingers dancing between their bodies to stroke that part of her that sparked.

"Are ye all right?"

"Aye," she moaned, "dinna stop."

"I love ye," he murmured as he withdrew and thrust in again. "My Annie lass."

"I love ye, too." Annie followed her instinct, her hips rising and falling with his thrusts. She clung to him, wrapped around him in the way she'd wanted to be. Every stroke of his body inside her own brought her to the same heights of passion as he'd evoked moments ago. Pleasure, pure and wonderful, radiated around her. Love compounded inside her, so strong and intense, until she felt she was going to explode both inside and out.

"Oh, Annie," he groaned, his mouth at her neck, on her breast, and back up to her lips. "Does it feel good?"

"So good."

"I want to please ye."

"Ye please me more than I could have ever dreamed."

"Good, so verra good."

Annie moaned softly, tugging on his lower lip with her teeth until he claimed her mouth in a searing kiss, his body rocking into hers. Again and again they came together, drew apart, the sensations between her thighs decadent, until she felt that flame ignite once more. It shattered her.

She clung to him, riding out the pleasure, wave after rapturous wave.

"Och, my God, Annie, ye… That was…" But Craig appeared speechless, breathless even as he let out a long growl and surged faster, harder against her. His body tightened and a massive shudder rocked his entire form as he drove against her, into her.

Annie clung to him as he moved, the pleasure of feeling him come apart as gratifying as her own release. He slowed to stop, lying atop her, their bodies slick from the bath and perspiration. Her legs still trembled, her entire body buzzing.

"That was amazing," she said, pressing her lips to his forehead and then the pink pucker of his scar.

"Incredible." He rolled to the side, pulling her with him, wrapping them up in the blanket.

Annie curled against him, feeling warm, sated, and the happiest she'd ever been. "Did I hurt ye?" she asked, running a hand over his bruised chest, drawing a circle over his heart.

"Ye, hurt me?" He chuckled. "Nay, lass, 'tis I who should be asking that."

"Oh." She felt her face flush and a shy, silly smile on her lips. "I'm perfect."

"Aye, ye are. Everything I ever wanted." Craig pressed his lips to hers once more, taking her breath away.

Twenty-Three

Annie woke in the night, her back warm with Craig's body draped over her. She snuggled deeper against him, surprised she'd been able to fall asleep so easily, knowing exactly what was at stake.

She listened to the sounds of the tavern. The boisterous crowd who'd been carousing when they'd arrived seemed to have calmed down. The wind blew in gusts against the walls and windows outside. One of the windows must have been open a crack because with every gust, a breeze blew over her exposed skin. The tavern's skeleton creaked and groaned with every shift of the wind. And in the moments when the wind died down, she swore she heard a slight tinkling on the breeze. Like the wind on a bridle.

And that was when she bolted upright.

"Craig," she whispered in a panic, shaking him. "They're here."

Craig leaped out of bed, rushing naked to the window where he peeled back the drape just a crack to peer outside.

"Get dressed." The grim tone of his voice told her all she needed to know. They'd been found.

Annie and Craig dressed quickly. *Too easy.* All of it had been too easy. But she also believed wholeheartedly that it had been worth it, if only just to have had this night to relish. However long they had left, she would remember the way it felt to make love to him, to hear him say the words and see the moment on his face when his body had shattered into hers.

Annie tugged on her clothes, thrust her feet into her boots, and grabbed her cloak, tossing it over her shoulders as they left the chamber. Craig held his pistol in front of him and she her dagger. If it came to blows, which it very well might, this time she wouldn't let anyone take him away from her without a real fight.

The door to the tavern thundered just as they reached the top of the stairs, someone pounding hard on the other side.

Too late.

Annie grabbed Craig's hand, holding on as if that would keep him beside her always.

A door at the end of the hall opened, and Mr. Downie stepped out, holding up a candle, his eyes wide, mouth slack.

"Dragoons," Craig said tersely.

"This way." Downie waved them down the hall toward his chamber. "We've a way out in case of fire. Or in case someone needs to make their escape."

With her hand firmly in Craig's grasp, Annie followed him down the corridor and into the tavern owner's chamber, where he pointed to a small window.

"There." Downie rummaged through a wardrobe, handing them a rope ladder. "Use this."

Craig took the makeshift ladder, giving it a few yanks to test its strength.

"I was a sailor." Downie shrugged as if in explanation.

Clustered around his wife were the lads who'd helped them with the bath and three small lasses, all staring at Annie and Craig as though they were specters in the night. Perhaps they were soon to become just that.

Craig flung open the window and hooked the ladder on the nails that looked to have been driven in the wall for that exact purpose. "I'll go down first, but if they take me, Annie, ye stay put. Dinna come for me this time."

Annie nodded, lying in that simple gesture. How could he expect that she would do anything differently? She would come for him every time.

Craig lifted himself out the window, the front door to the tavern rattling with the pounding of the dragoons' fists.

"I'll have to answer it soon," Mr. Downie said, "afore they break it down completely."

"We understand," Annie said, watching Craig's speedy descent. "Ye've a family to protect."

She shoved the dagger into her sleeve and hauled herself out the window, just as Downie left the chamber with a lit candle to answer the door.

She'd barely made it to the ground when the sound of marching boots charging through the tavern filtered through the open window. Then the window was slammed shut, filtering out the sounds, though they echoed.

Craig grasped her hips to pull her down just as the rope gave way, likely cut from the inside to keep the dragoons from seeing it. Good God, she hoped the bastards didn't burn the tavern down. If so, they'd used the family's last means to escape.

But nay, they wouldn't do so without cause. Och, who was she kidding? The dragoons had no hearts. They didn't see anyone as human, caring only for slaughter and brutality.

"We canna leave them," Annie whispered harshly.

Craig wrapped his hand around hers. "We have to."

She swallowed hard, tears of fear sparking in her eyes. "But—"

"He's been through this before. He knows what to do."

Annie had to believe that. Old Salty, Mr. Downie, and any number of others across the land were secretly involved in the transport of wanted Jacobites, trying to hide them from the reaching arms of Cumberland's men. They knew what they were doing. No doubt they had plans in place and contingency plans should those first plans get tossed out the door.

Darkness surrounded them, save for a few candles lit inside the tavern. Clouds covered most of the stars and moon above. While the lack of light made it hard to navigate toward the stable, it also made it hard for the dragoons to see them. They entered the stable quietly through the back, the scents of hay and leather strong.

"Can ye ride bareback?" Craig asked.

Annie shook her head.

"Now's a good time to learn. We'll ride together. We've no' time to saddle a horse." No doubt the stables were the next place the bastards would look for them.

He took the first horse he could find, slipping on a bridle and leading it outside. Craig helped her up onto the horse and then climbed up behind her. His heat and solid strength at her back were a comfort. This time, if it came to that point, they would go down together.

Rather than gallop away as they wanted to, they had to keep the horse going slowly so as not to draw attention. Every leaping shadow was a dragoon lurching toward them. Every gust of wind was the enemy's breath at their neck.

Pray get us out of town…

But they didn't make it far. Not this time. The dragoons must have anticipated their escape, and they'd not made it more than a few hundred yards down the street before they heard galloping behind them.

"Go," Annie cried. "We've been seen."

Craig urged the horse into a gallop, and shots rang out behind them, dirt kicking up at their sides as bullets riddled the road. She clung to the horse's mane, waiting for the pain of a musket shot to tear into her.

Annie tried to see behind them in the blackness of night, dark shadows racing closer and closer. "They are gaining on us." The earth felt as though it were trembling like mad with the hoofbeats of a hundred dragoons, even though it was probably fewer than a dozen.

"Hold tight, love, lean low," Craig instructed. "This nag is no' going to get us far, but we're going to give it all she's got."

But the whizzing bullets and gaining pursuers put the fear of death in the poor animal because it hauled itself up short and reared up onto its hind legs. Annie held on for dear life, barely keeping her seat. As soon as the horse's hooves were back on the ground, Craig leaped off and dragged her down with him. The terrified mount took off, bucking at the darkness.

They stood frozen in the center of the road, the dragoons tugging their horses to a stop. They could run, but they'd be shot immediately.

"What do we have here?" Though she didn't recognize the speaker, his English accent was undeniable.

She supposed she should be grateful that he was unfamiliar. It *could* mean the men didn't know who she and Craig were. If it were Boyd chasing them or any of the men from the garrison where they'd escaped, they would be executed on sight. That didn't mean these men wouldn't try to cause them harm—in fact, she was quite certain they would enjoy doing just that.

"What did Old Salty bring us?" one of the men sneered.

So they knew Old Salty. Craig muttered an expletive at the exact moment she did the same. The man's cover was blown, unless he'd been paid to give them up. Either way, Annie would have to somehow let Jenny know, else anyone else she sent the fisherman's way would be given up too. Unless Old Salty wasn't even the man Jenny had sent her to…

Oh God, what about Downie and his family?

She looked behind them at the town beyond.

"Do not worry about them." The dragoon who'd spoken before waved away her clear concern. "We pay well for anyone willing to give up a Jacobite spy."

"We're no' spies," Annie said, conviction in her voice. "I'm a healer."

"A witch, no doubt," the bastard replied.

To accuse a woman of witchcraft was a dangerous thing. Nearly four thousand women, men, and children had been burned at the stake in Scotland in less than two hundred years. She didn't want to think about Bonnie Prince Charlie's ancestor James VI, the king who'd been the catalyst for such tragic and horrifying actions.

"Dinna curse her for a witch," Craig said. "She's the furthest thing from it."

The leader grinned as though he found the whole thing very funny, and Annie clenched her fist around a handful of Craig's shirt, trying to keep herself from flying at the bastard in a mad rage that would end with a bullet between her eyes.

"Protecting your little witch, are ye? Has she put a spell on ye?"

"Dinna speak of my wife that way." There was a warning edge to Craig's voice she'd not heard before, and it sent a shiver down her spine.

There was no way that he could take on all these men, even if he were fully healed. By her count, there were at least nine redcoats, and all mounted. Even if she were able to dispatch one, which she wasn't entirely certain she could, that still left eight for him.

More riders sounded behind them, coming through the village gates at great speed, and the dragoons shifted their attention behind Annie and Craig, pointing their pistols toward the newcomers. Reinforcements for the dragoons, no doubt, but the ones in front of her didn't look as though they'd been expecting company.

"What the bloody hell?" the dragoon leader exclaimed.

Annie whirled to see men, Scottish men, on horseback, a group at least twenty-five strong. She gasped as they reined in their horses.

"Leave my sister alone."

Sister?

Annie squinted her eyes in the darkness, trying to make out the shadows of the men. There sitting in the center of the group was her brother Logan—tall, healthy, and fierce.

"Oh, look here, boys, the witch has her own army."

The dragoons were so drunk on power, Annie supposed, that they didn't realize that there were now more than twice as many Scots as English. After the massacre at Culloden, they must truly have believed they would always have the upper hand.

"Ye do realize ye're outnumbered?" Logan asked, clearly thinking the same thing as Annie.

"We were outnumbered at Culloden and look what happened."

That was enough to send Annie into a fit of rage. Culloden was where they'd killed Graham, slaughtered thousands more, and this bastard had just admitted to being there. He could have been the one to strike that final blow that took Graham away. She reached for the knife in her sleeve, leaping forward to do damage to anything, anyone! But she was stopped mid-launch by Craig's arm around her middle.

"Stop," he growled into her ear. "I canna lose ye."

She whipped her head around, anger making her

blood boil. "And I canna lose ye. They will no' take ye. I'll knife every one of them."

He kissed her temple, whispered against her ear. "There ye are, love, the madwoman I fell for." But he soothed her with those words rather than send her into a tirade. It was then she noticed he was slowly walking them backward until Logan and his men were surrounding them in a tightly knit circle of Scottish power.

"We'll be leaving now, unless ye want to prove ye can win against our numbers yet again," Logan tested the men, and she wanted to shout for him to stop, but he was in charge now. Overriding him would take away his independence, his strength, and hadn't that been done to him enough already?

"We do not need to prove anything. We will be victorious," the dragoon spat.

The arrogance coming from that side of the road was astounding! The dragoons truly thought this was going to be a fight they could win.

The energy from the Highlanders surrounding her and Craig was palpable. They were itching to wipe the near-frozen ground with their enemies. And Annie would be lying if she said she didn't want to see that happen.

"We accept your challenge," Logan said.

"Give us the name of the man we're about to kill," the dragoon leader demanded.

"I'll tell ye my name right before I thrust my blade through your black heart." Logan pulled his sword from his scabbard with one hand and held his pistol in the other.

Annie's heart lurched up into her throat. "Logan," she whispered. "Please dinna."

But her brother couldn't hear her even if she'd spoken louder because he was bellowing a battle cry.

She kept expecting the dragoons to come to their senses and disperse, but they did not seem so inclined. And though Logan needed a chance to prove himself, she wanted that to be the last thing he was doing right now. And then Craig was thrusting her behind him and asking the warrior beside him, "Hand me a sword."

He was going to fight? *Nay, nay, nay!*

"Craig, please, dinna do this." She clutched at his back, holding tight.

He turned to face her, sword in one hand, and touched her face with the other. "Lass, if I do nothing and something were to happen to ye, then I would have to live the rest of my days knowing that I was the reason ye were harmed. I will protect ye, always."

"But—"

Craig kissed her then, stopping her from begging him further. Surrounded by their countrymen, their fellow rebels, he kissed her breathless, and she felt his love all the way to the tips of her toes and back again.

She wanted to hold onto him forever, to never let go and never let him be in harm's way again. That was the whole reason that she'd followed him to the garrison, she didn't want him to be hurt, wanted him away from danger. But if anything, she'd led him right into another trap.

There was no safe place in all of Scotland. Dragoons

swarmed every moor, village, and mountain and everything in between.

If this was the way it had to be, then she wouldn't let him be the only one doing the protecting. She slid her dagger from her sleeve.

"I'm no' going to let anyone hurt ye."

Craig narrowed his gaze, and she could tell he wanted to argue with her.

"Ye canna be the only one meant to protect. I've spent my entire life saving people, and if this is the way in which I am meant to do it at this moment, then so be it. I will."

The argument she was expecting to happen did not. Instead he swooped in and kissed her once more, as Logan and his men lurched into action.

In an incredible Highland charge at close range, the dragoons would never come out on top. The sheer savagery of the charge always terrified the dragoons to no end. Highlanders were not afraid of death, and even when facing the devil himself, they kept on fighting.

The redcoats fired their pistols almost immediately, shots whizzing past the Scotsmen's heads. One of the Highlanders was winged by a bullet to the shoulder, jolting him backward on his horse. Another had his cap blown off, lucky not to have had it be a bullet to the head. But every other shot missed.

Logan and his men's aim was truer, felling several dragoons from their mounts. Shot used up, the men converged on each other with blades clashing, sparks flying from the force of striking steel.

All at once Annie felt herself pulled in multiple

directions. Did she run to her brother, help him fend off the man attempting to hack at him with a blade, or leap in front of Craig when a dragoon thrust a bayonet toward his chest? Or did she leave the fighting to those better suited and rush to aid the Highlander who'd been shot? Even though his wound was not particularly bad, she still felt the need to make certain he was cared for.

But almost as soon as she wrestled with the thoughts they were gone, as the clashing suddenly drew to a halt. The battle noise faded away, and she was left only with the blowing wind and a few men moaning in pain.

Logan stood over the man who'd egged him on, his heel on the man's chest and his blade at his neck. "So that ye know the name of the man who killed ye, I'm Logan MacPherson, chief of my clan."

Craig tossed the lifeless man who'd tried to gut him to the ground, whirled around, and marched toward her. He gathered her in his arms, both he and Annie heaving sighs of relief, bodies shuddering as they clung to one another. Annie buried her face in his chest, tears streaming down her face, hands shaking. She trembled all over with blessed relief.

Craig tipped her face up toward his. "We won."

"I love ye." Annie wrapped her arms around his neck, rising up on tiptoe, kissing him in full view of everyone, and not giving a damn who saw.

Twenty-Four

Four months later
Cullidunloch Castle

Annie stared up at the tower keep, where the sun shone down on the newly repaired roof. Black soot still marred the keep walls in places, though the clan members had worked themselves hard to scrub away at the charring. The damage, though extensive, had not been as bad as she'd first thought on that dreadful night. They'd spent three months at Cluny Castle, healing, loving, and plotting their next moves, and while they'd been away, MacPhersons had come and gone trying to repair what they could and salvage what was inside, including the large armada chest that her father had let her and her brothers practice lock-picking with.

Already the wooden floors inside the castle that had collapsed had been replaced, and of the tapestries from the great hall that she'd cherished, two had survived with only the edges charred. Lucky for them, the rain on the night of the blaze had been what saved most of their things.

Annie jumped at a tickle of fur around her ankles. Pinecone curled herself around Annie's legs, as she'd been doing since Annie's return. Strangely enough, the cat had greeted Annie with kisses and purrs and never a mean scratch yet, though Annie fully expected the temperamental animal to change her mind at some point. But right now, she would take the love and acceptance from Graham's pet.

Annie bent down and picked up Pinecone, letting the animal snuggle against her neck. She closed her eyes and smiled, imagining that somehow Graham had managed to get a message to the cat that she was to be loved.

"I must admit, I'm jealous of that blasted cat." Craig sidled up beside her, wrapping his arm around her shoulders. "I want to rub around your legs and snuggle your neck."

Annie laughed and leaned into her husband, savoring the strength and breadth of him. He'd been working hard since his wounds had fully healed, building up his strength, and it felt as though he'd gotten bigger, if that were possible. Oh, did she love to wrap herself around that strength.

Luckily for him Pinecone did not retaliate at his affection for Annie, jumping down instead with a sweet meow to curl herself around Craig's legs. Annie turned into him and tilted her head up, beckoning him silently for a kiss. He bent to press his lips to hers, brushing them softly as he inhaled deeply. "Mmm. Ye smell of lavender."

"And ye smell of..." She pinched her nose playfully and laughed when he looked down at her in shock. "I jest. Ye smell delicious. Like sun and leather." Annie wrapped her arms around his middle, rising up on tiptoe to kiss him some more.

She hadn't grown tired of kissing, touching. Truth

was she never grew tired of *him*. Every moment they had together was a blessing, even when they disagreed, because there had been more times than one that death had nearly taken them from each other. Annie was determined to make each day until the end of their time together a good one, no matter what. "I love ye," she murmured against his lips.

"Och, lass, I—"

"Captain?"

Captain MacLean now, no longer a lieutenant. Word had come from the prince, who was still on the run, for certain officers in his army to be raised in rank, and Craig had been honored to accept the new title.

Craig turned with a slight frown on his face to reply to Seamus and Jameson, who approached holding stacks of folded kilts. Jenny had managed to put together a ransom payment for a number of men being held in the garrison, Seamus and the other MacPherson lads included. Annie was beyond relieved that they'd made it out alive and were finally back home at Cullidunloch where they belonged. Seamus and Jameson were once more at each other's side. Where they were free to be themselves.

Annie turned around to face the men fully. She might have been annoyed at the interruption, except that she and Craig were often found in this position, and the only way for anyone to get anything done was to interrupt them.

"Kilts are all ready, sir," Jameson said, hefting the load of plaid in his arms.

"Good, for tonight we celebrate in style." Craig waggled his brows at Annie, a playful grin on his lips.

"'Tis a dangerous game the lot of ye play." The rebels grew bolder, looking for various ways in which to thwart those who would suppress them. Underground organizations abounded, to which they belonged and gave their support.

"Our chief is fully behind it," Seamus argued, speaking of Logan.

"Aye, 'tis true," Craig added. "If the government thinks to tell us we canna wear our kilts, then we'll wear them with relish. In fact, we'll dance in them and gladly bend over in order for them to better kiss our bare arses."

Over the past few months, the dragoons had increased their patrols and violence, still searching for the hidden prince, and one edict after another had come crashing down on Scottish heads.

First, no one was to wear a kilt. King George seemed to think of the plaid as a symbol of the rebellion rather than the clothes they'd been wearing for centuries. Additionally, he'd stripped away the power chiefs held over their people, making them nothing more than landlords. Anyone found to be out of order was to be arrested. More often than not, depending on whose orders the arresting officers took, execution was meted out.

It was all rubbish. The people on MacPherson lands would never do anything but respect their chief as chief. They'd continue to come to him for justice for their grievances, continue to pay their taxes in exchange for protection. As long as the dragoons were still pillaging the lands, there would be a need for protection. And rebels weren't giving up. Their rightful prince was still out there.

This was the reason they'd all followed Logan back to Cullidunloch, why Craig had eagerly accepted Logan's offer to lead their men together—Logan as their clan chief and Craig as their war chief. King George's government could try to stifle them, to push them down, and while they'd go along with it on the surface, the king could never cut them down like he wanted to. The Highlands were in their blood. Their way of life was ingrained in their souls, and they weren't just going to give it up because some foreign king said they must.

Nay, their prince would rise up again. And they would help him rise.

And tonight, a celebration feast would be had in honor of Craig's sister's arrival at Cullidunloch. The beautiful Marielle had many admirers among the men, and Logan happened to be one of the most ardent.

With his arm still around Annie's shoulders, Craig steered her toward the castle. He bent to whisper in her ear. "There's something I need to discuss with ye, love."

The heat of his breath on her ear sent a warm shiver racing through her. "What is it?"

"I think we'd best discuss it in private."

Annie glanced up at Craig and the mischievous grin curling his lips. "As a matter of fact, I too have something that needs discussing. *Privately*." Which was theoretically true, but she also very much wanted to get him alone because when that door shut, she was going to demand he get naked.

Craig's fingers laced with hers, and they hurried inside, only to be stopped short by the sight of Max bending down to kiss Eppy square on the lips. Max and his family had come to join the rebellion at Cullidunloch, as had the other soldiers Annie had rescued from Culloden.

Jenny and Toran were expected to arrive soon, though Fiona had sent her regrets. Apparently she was on a very important mission, which left them all wondering exactly *what* she was delivering. Annie had not seen her dear friend since they'd parted at the cottage months before, but they had exchanged several exciting letters, and Fiona had even sent her and Craig a wedding gift—a new treasure chest with a lock Annie had been working to pick for the last several evenings. She planned to hide the pin that Fiona had given her inside once she got it open.

Max and Eppy leaped apart at the same moment, exclaiming at the same time, "My lady" and "Doc Annie."

"Carry on," Annie said with a wave of her hand. Who was she to stand in the way of love? The two of them had been dancing for months around that flirtation that had begun in Mrs. Sullivan's cottage.

Besides, she had somewhere to be and a very handsome husband to seduce. Annie and Craig skirted around the couple and raced up the stairs toward their chamber, only to hear a demonic screeching behind them. They jerked to a halt, whipping around and bumping into each in a way that had them falling against the wall in nearly the same spot they'd found themselves months before.

Pinecone raced past them up the stairs, and Annie rolled her eyes.

"Damn cat." The cat had claimed Graham's chamber as her own, and no one had argued with her about it. If the feline wanted to spend the rest of her days with the ghost of the man she'd loved, who was Annie—or anyone else—to stop her?

Annie started back up the stairs, but Craig stopped her. He tugged her back toward him, shifting until he leaned Annie into the wall, her back flat against the stone, arms going around his neck. He really did smell delicious. So delicious she wanted to lick him.

His hands settled warmly at her hips, and he grinned down at her. "Have I told ye yet today just how beautiful ye are?"

"Aye, but a lass never gets sick of hearing such things."

"Ye're beautiful." He pressed his lips to hers. "Brilliant. Brave. And ye have the best"—his hands slid up over her ribs to cup the round swells on her chest—"breasts I've ever seen."

Annie giggled, tugging at the back of his neck for a kiss. With a growl, Craig captured her mouth in a kiss full of carnal intent. His body slid against hers, his tongue stroking deep, and Annie moaned against him, lifting her leg to hook around his hip. Goodness, if he didn't take her upstairs right now—

"Och, for the love of all that's holy, could ye no' do that in your chamber instead of the stairs the rest of us have to traverse?"

The two of them broke apart languidly, rolling their eyes toward Logan, who stood just a few stairs above them, one hand on a hip, the other on his cane, and a frown on his face. Her brother looked hale and hearty, with barely any sign of the beating he'd taken at the

Butcher's hands months before. He walked confidently now on his wooden foot, and with that confidence came a lot of attention from eligible ladies looking for a husband.

"I'll remind ye that ye said that when next I catch ye with my sister," Craig warned.

Annie's hand flew to her chest in shock. "Caught him with your sister?" She turned her stunned eyes toward Logan, whose face was flushing red. "What does he mean?"

Logan groaned. "Ye caught nothing."

"No' yet," Craig admitted with a smirk. "But I know what a lass looks like when she's been...ravished."

"Ye know nothing," Logan said and then glanced at Annie and frowned. "Fine, ye may know something. But I'll have ye know I wish to—"

"Wed!" Marielle bounced down the stairs behind Logan.

Her plaid gown looked a bit wrinkled, and her ginger hair was mussed. The flush of her cheeks made the blue in her eyes stand out. *Ravished indeed.* She truly was lovely and sweet as honey. And a wedding? Annie was pleased to call her sister—and to finally *have* a sister.

"Where the hell were ye?" Craig growled, and all Annie could do was widen her eyes.

Logan and Marielle had clearly been together... *upstairs.*

"Cullidunloch has become a house of debauchery," Annie murmured with a light laugh, which only drew a growl from Craig.

Her husband started to reach for Logan, grabbing the front of his shirt. "If ye so much as—wait, did ye say *wed*?"

"Oh, please say aye," Marielle begged. "I love him so."

Craig let go of Logan's shirt. The two men stared at each other for a long time, neither of them saying a word and neither of them showing in their expressions what might be going through their heads.

"Do ye love her?" Craig asked.

"Aye," Logan answered.

"Ye should have asked me permission afore ye...did whatever ye were doing." Craig frowned.

"I could say the same of ye," Logan said with a raise of his brow.

"A wedding," Annie sighed, pressing her hand to her belly.

Marielle glanced down at where Annie's hand rested, and her own hand slapped against her chest. "Are ye with child?"

Craig jerked his gaze back to Annie's, the frown missing now and astonishment taking over his features. Annie didn't even have time to hide her surprise at Marielle's clever guess. She'd only suspected for about a month but had been waiting to be certain to tell Craig. She'd thought to have told him upstairs, but now it seemed the moment had come.

"A bairn?" Craig came back down a step toward her, his gaze sliding down her body.

Annie nodded, pressing both hands over her belly. "Aye."

Craig swooped in, pressing his lips to hers in a deep kiss, neither of them fully aware of the moment when Logan and Marielle slipped past them. It was just as well because there was nothing more Annie wanted to say to them at that moment. She only wanted to celebrate with her husband the life they'd created, both inside her and outside.

Craig lifted her into his arms and carried her the rest of the way upstairs into their bedchamber, the very one that he'd first entered to sew her up. He laid her down on the bed, then marched back toward the door, and put the bar in place.

"No more damned interruptions," he said, tearing off his shirt and tugging off his boots.

"Thank God for that." Annie sat up and kicked off her own shoes, rolled down her hose.

Craig crawled onto the bed beside her, wearing only his kilt. He undid the buttons at her back, and she yanked at all the fabric of her clothes until she was fully nude, lying beside her husband.

"Our bairn." He pressed his hand to her belly, still flat save for the tiniest little lump.

Annie trailed her fingers over his knee, beneath his kilt and up his thigh. "Another generation of stubborn to be born into our family lines."

Craig laughed and lifted her up so that she straddled his lap. He stroked his fingers over her abdomen and leaned toward her belly to whisper, "Hello in there. I've a feeling ye're going to drive us truly mad."

Annie burst into fits of laughter at that. "As if we are no' already."

"I'm mad about ye, love, and only ye." Craig brought his mouth to hers, tender, full of love, and he showed her just how much.

Read on for a sneak peek at the next in
Eliza Knight's Prince Charlie's Angels series

You've Got Plaid

Available May 2021 from Sourcebooks Casablanca

April, 1746
Dòchas Keep, Scottish Highlands

"Dinna leave the castle," Ian MacBean, interim chief of the clan, demanded from the bailey, armed to the teeth for battle.

Fiona MacBean stared hard at her brother, taking in the way his lips were pressed so tight, they were nearly white. His red hair, the same fiery color as her own, was tucked beneath his feathered cap at a jaunty angle, softening the hard lines of his face, and determined furrow of his brow.

Fiona tossed her hair back with a slight shake of her head. There was no way in hell she was staying in the castle when there was vital information to be gathered, and intelligence to be shared. Hell, the reason Ian was even headed off to war was because of her, which made her feel doubly guilty.

Ian's departure and subsequent insistence she stay home was rooted in a message she'd delivered to her brother Gus several months prior. It had informed him that their baby sister Leanna's betrothed had hightailed it to the eastern shores of America with the dowry Gus had so graciously imparted on him early. A hefty amount of coin they couldn't afford to lose. *Bastard.*

The news was so mortifying to their clan that they'd kept it mostly secret, telling those who needed to know that Gus had escorted Leanna at the summons of her betrothed so they might settle somewhere in Maryland, rather than that they were chasing him down. Which meant that Ian was now in charge of everyone in their clan—including her.

"Fiona, I mean it. Gus entrusted your safety and that of the clan to me while he's gone."

Ian didn't understand. He never had. And he'd spent entirely too much time looking up to Gus for answers rather than forming any of his own. Her work as a spy courier was as integral to their support of Prince Charlie as his work on the battlefield.

A shiver of fear raced down her spine. Her only consolation about him going to war was that he'd be with Jenny Mackintosh, Laird of Clan Mackintosh and charmingly named the Colonel by Bonnie Prince Charlie, after she'd raised arms and her men had succeeded in warding off the Jacobites who wanted to take the prince's head.

It wasn't that Ian wasn't skilled at fighting—if anything, he was a damned beast on the field—but she would feel better knowing he was with people she trusted, and not some fools who might turn tail and run when the going got tough.

"Fiona?" Ian let go of his horse's reins and marched toward her. He reached her, pressing his hands to her shoulders, his deep green eyes piercing into hers. "Please, for the love of all things holy, bloody well stay here. I canna have ye running about the countryside when I'm preoccupied with war."

"I've already *been* running about the countryside and ye know it."

Fiona knew how to protect herself. Had made it her business to learn to fight against men bigger than her, so she'd not be made a victim. She was well versed in the use of daggers and knew which spots to hit to fell a man. The pins in her hair were sturdy and sharp enough to inflict damage. More often than not, she could be found with daggers hidden horizontally in the layered leather of her belt, as well as her boots. One could never be too prepared.

"Aye, but at least then, I could come to your aid if ye needed me." He pressed his lips together, and the recollection of how close they'd come to attack by dragoons over the years sat heavy between them. "I canna save ye if I'm in a bloody battle."

She didn't need saving, but she wasn't about to make him worry about her while he had dragoon pistols pointed at him. Better to placate her brother now and apologize later.

"Aye, fine, Ian. I'll stay put. But ye better come back, else I'll be angrier than a stuck pig that ye made me rot in this keep while ye went away to have all the fun."

Ian sighed with great relief and rolled his eyes. "I'll come back, I promise."

"Good. Because if ye die, I swear I'll kill ye all over again."

Ian laughed at the line the four siblings had been repeating to one another since their first encounter with dragoons in the woods so long ago.

"Until we meet again, wee sister."

"I'm older than ye." Fiona slugged him in the chest, not hard enough to hurt.

Ian grinned. "But ye're still smaller." He danced backward away from her, out of reach of her swinging hands.

"I'll spare ye the energy now, because we both know the Colonel is going to run ye ragged, but when ye return, brother, we're going to spar."

Ian pointed at her and nodded. "Ye can count on it." He leapt up onto his horse and issued orders to their men.

The summons to join Jenny's army had directed them not too far from MacBean lands. Prince Charles Stuart—the regent for his exiled father, and rightful heir to the Scottish throne which had been usurped by Hanoverians—had set up camp at Culloden House. This had forced Duncan Forbes, owner of the house, to either rally with the Jacobites or run. Fiona couldn't understand why a Scot *wouldn't* want their natural king to take his place.

Having grown up surrounded by men focused on the return of the Stuart line, it came naturally to her. So unsurprisingly, she'd kept up a childhood pact made with her two dearest friends to do everything in their power to make certain he regained his rightful place.

Jenny was a natural leader and soldier. Annie a healer. And Fiona...well, she'd learned subterfuge early on, and she had an excellent memory. Relaying messages from one Jacobite camp to another had been a skill honed as a girl, and now earned her the nickname of Phantom. She was proud of the work she'd done for the prince. Proud that he'd taken note of it.

"Be well!" Fiona called out to the men as they crossed under the gate, waving her arm, and watching until the very last of them had disappeared down the road.

She waited an hour.

That seemed a sufficient amount of time to allow to pass before she changed out of her day gown and into her sturdier traveling wool.

"Going, my lady?" Beitris had been her lady's maid since they were both fifteen years old. There was an eager look about her eyes, as she'd begged on more than one occasion to go with Fiona, but the risk was too great. Traveling through the woods alone was dangerous enough. Taking a maid along would slow her down. There was also the fact that even the sight of a wee mouse had Beitris screaming and running for the nearest chair.

"Aye. The duty of a postmistress calls." Of course, being a postmistress was the perfect position from which to conduct business of a more clandestine nature. The dragoons tended to leave her be if they saw her delivering mail, as she was officially appointed by the royal government. It allowed her to roam freely, but it wasn't always a safeguard—especially since she used it as a cover to deliver rebel messages.

"What of your brother's order?"

Fiona raised a brow. "The prince himself named me

one of his most loyal messengers." And he'd given her a ring to prove it. She glanced down at the simple round cabochon emerald on her right middle finger. Any message delivered from the prince clearly could not contain his signature or seal, but a simple presentation of this ring denoted that she carried his official business.

Which was why she had to get herself to Culloden House and the battlefield.

"Stay safe, my lady. Ye've told your brother much the same, but as ye oft leave in secret, no one has been able to tell ye as much."

"I will." Fiona pulled Beitris in for a hug. "I've kept myself alive this long, have I no'?"

"This is true."

Like everyone else in their clan, Beitris worried what ill could befall Fiona while on the road. The royal postmistress badge could only take her so far, and wasn't a guaranteed free pass from a ruffian, be he an outlaw, a dragoon or a drunkard.

However, Fiona feared not the repercussions for herself, but instead for what the men in her life might do to protect her honor. Her father—God rest his soul—had been horrified when she first took the position, and passed his fears on to her brothers. Any of them would go to battle and die for her; and their deaths would be forever on her head, which was why she was damn careful whenever she left the house.

She didn't want men to die for her. She wanted them to fight for the *cause*. And so she'd bid her father and her siblings to allow her to keep her postmistress position for the sake of their country. They'd agreed, on one condition, and that was if she ever found herself at the end of a dragoon's pistol, she would quit. Fiona agreed, and she didn't regret that decision. Nor did she regret not telling them when such occasions occurred. They all had to do their part, and this was hers.

Remaining quiet had allowed her father to fight many a battle, keeping their family safe, until he'd finally fallen on a beach in the north when a government ship fired a cannon at the gathered warriors.

Destroyed by the loss of her husband, Fiona's mother had withdrawn even from her own children, and several summers past went to live with her sister in Orkney. She didn't even write, not wanting a memory of her life at Dòchas, which Fiona tried not to take personally, though in truth she felt quite abandoned. The loss of both of her parents so quickly had put her into a melancholy that she couldn't seem to pull herself out of.

It was actually a missive that Gus brought her from her old friend Aes that caused her to rise up and believe in herself once more.

Over the mountain of fear is your dream attained.

Aes would never know how that simple phrase changed her life. How she lived every day with it racing through her brain. Because, though she was brave and though she risked much, she was not without fear. Not reckless, as some might accuse her of being. She was crossing the *mountain of fear,* and reaching for her dream—a better, safer Scotland, ruled by the Stuart line as it should have been since before she was born.

So although she understood fear, she wasn't going to be ruled by it.

She'd made a pact with her friends, with herself, to stand up to the blasted dragoons and wouldn't let a little thing like fear stand in the way. And so, she'd traveled to the secret meetings of the lairds, though her da was no longer present. She offered her services as a courier to them, and with the help of Aes, and out of respect for her departed da, had made it happen. Though most of the men at first thought to send her on fool's errands, she quickly proved she was not the wee idiot many believed her to be.

With a thick cloak, gloves, an extra pair of hose covering her feet, and in sturdy boots, Fiona slipped out of the castle unnoticed. The air was frigid and the sky gray. Soon it would either snow or pelt frozen ice onto their heads. She was guessing the latter. She slinked around the guard's blind spots until she crossed the forest edge.

Normally, she'd have taken a horse, but given she didn't want anyone to know she'd left right after her brother's very public proclamation that she should stay, and given her destination was only a few hours' walk away, she chose to take the path on foot.

To some, a forest was a vast and haunting place, dark and shadowed, littered with two- and four-legged creatures that could just as easily do harm as ignore a body's presence. In the wood there were spaces to hide, places to leap out from. There were nooks to curl up inside of and high-altitude places from which to observe the world. The forest was as peaceful as it was chilling.

Fiona felt at home in the forest, even when the green of the pines had turned into glistening gray icicles. The place housed her greatest triumphs and had the potential to harbor her worst nightmares.

Having grown up with a wood surrounding her clan, she'd become intimate with the way roots looped from the ground, and which trees would give her hives, and which would give her shelter. She knew paths to get to the surrounding clans and could peer through the leaves at the top even in the height of summer, to see which direction to take.

Since she was a girl, she'd expanded her forest knowledge, recognizing landmarks and remembering events that happened there. For example, the route from Dòchas Keep to Cnàmhan Broch, the castle of her dear friend Jenny, held a path she'd not traversed since she was twelve years old, the day they'd run into the dragoons.

And she hadn't let running the forest end when she'd become a woman. If anything, she considered herself an expert in forestry. An expert in people, too.

When danger was afoot, Fiona either made herself invisible, or she made the ones who messed with her disappear. Sometimes, just from her own memory.

There was a reason she'd been gifted the name of Phantom.

Fiona was well-versed at keeping herself hidden, even when in plain sight. She was a master at her trade and had dozens of costumes that she could don, voices that she could use, and various personas that she plucked out of her basket. But when she wasn't dressed in costume, she was aware of how she turned heads. It was one of the reasons she kept her fiery hair in a cap. The flaming red color often gathered notice, as did her unusual eyes, a shade of blue that was nearly violet.

Men and women alike called her beautiful. And she wanted to be flattered by that, but in the end, she also didn't want anyone to remember her.

Thinking of that, Fiona shoved her red hair farther into her cap. Powder smeared on her face paled the natural flush to her skin and hid the smattering of freckles over her nose that everyone thought was adorable. She'd smeared coal beneath her eyes to give her a more tired look, not that it was truly needed. She sported exhausted circles any time of day or night, for she only slept in short snatches. When this war was over, when Prince Charles was back on the throne, she'd sleep for days.

Until that time, she had to keep moving forward.

Never stop.

Tonight, she was dressed as a healer, her woolen frock torn in a few places, stains on the front apron to look as though she'd been elbows deep in a man's guts, and a basket looped over her arm filled with herbs and vials. Inside the tiny bottles were various tinctures that she had mixed herself—poisons, if truth be told. If she were to administer these tinctures to anyone, they would find themselves feeling a bit ill. Or dead.

Fiona wasn't a violent type, despite the knives and

poisons. She would much prefer to avoid any sort of conflict or confrontation whatsoever.

If she were stopped by a dragoon along her postmistress route, she typically would plead her duty to the mail, bat her lashes, and be on her way. But that was by day. During the night, things were a bit different, hence the costume. If caught now, they'd question why she was traveling alone at night, and she'd say because the ill did not wait for sunup, and she couldn't wait for an escort when someone could be dying.

At night the darkness helped to keep her hidden. Not that they'd have an easy time finding her during the day. Fiona's costumes were always muted browns and greens to help her blend in with the foliage of the forest or hedges lining a road, and the moors if she were lying in the thick grasses.

As a child, she'd been an expert at playing seek and find. In fact, her siblings could not get her to come out even when their mother was demanding their return. One of her favorite games was to sneak out of her hiding spot while they were in a panic, rush home, and be seated at the table having a bite to eat when one of them finally reappeared. This used to drive them all crazy, and she rather liked doing that—well, at least driving her brothers into a rage. More often than not, she tried to spare Leanna.

Wasn't that the job of every younger child? To make one's older sibling go a bit mad?

She smiled at the thought as Culloden House finally came into view.

Straightening her shoulders, she prepared to present herself to Prince Charles. The men recognized her as she walked through the courtyard and into the house, nodding with respect, and she greeted them in turn.

The prince was at the dining room table, which was spread with maps, scouring the area.

"This ground here." He pointed to a spot on the map.

"'Tis surrounded by bogs," his advisor Murray responded.

The prince grinned, showing off a bonnie dimple in his cheek. "All the better for the dragoons to get stuck in."

Murray, it appeared, was immune to the smile that made many women swoon. "But it may end up hindering our men as well."

The prince looked up then, his blue eyes alighting on Fiona. He truly was a bonnie fellow, almost too soft-looking to be planning a battle. The prince straightened, and Fiona curtsied.

"You've returned, mistress. Good. I've a stack of messages awaiting your dispatch."

"Your Highness," she said.

"MacDougall, give her the coin pouch."

One of the prince's men approached with a heavy purse, her payment for services rendered.

"Any news?" the prince asked.

"Cumberland's men are on the move. They've been sighted near the Grampians."

The prince nodded. "Good. Then he brings his men to their death." He came forward and presented her with his hand, and Fiona bent to kiss his ring.

When she rose, he was grinning at her, a dazzling smile that would no doubt win over many a woman, but not her. Fiona was about one thing—the mission. Falling for a man, especially one as unattainable as the prince, would be disastrous.

"You have been instrumental in all of this, Mistress MacBean. We could not be where we are without you. Do not forget that. Your loyalty has been noted and you will be rewarded."

The heavy coin pouch was in her hand, and knowing she was helping to thwart dragoons was payment enough. But if the prince wanted to give her more, perhaps offer her and her brothers a place at his court when he was finally sitting on the throne in Edinburgh and London, she would not dissuade him.

Three days later...

Fiona hopped over a fallen log, slick with ice, and then stilled at a movement some distance to her left. Gingerly, she eased toward the sound, peering through thick lines of pine. A troop of men—but not dragoons, rather Highlanders. They thought themselves silent, and they mostly were to anyone of normal aptitude for spying and hiding, but not Fiona.

She crouched down, closed her eyes, and turned her face toward the sky.

Men were on the move, slowly but deliberately,

heading back toward Culloden if she were to hazard a guess. But they shouldn't be. That was not the plan. Why were they headed that way?

She'd been given a missive from the prince to deliver to the men at Nairn, that reinforcements were catching up but had been waylaid. From the sounds of it, the army from Nairn was returning before she'd had a chance to deliver the news. She'd not been dallying either. Something must have happened.

"Blast it all," she muttered under her breath.

Fiona darted to her left, ducking beneath tree limbs, dodging roots and fallen branches, and yanking her skirts from clawing brambles, pausing every so often to listen to the sounds of the men. She finally spied them, moving shadows mixed with the other obscurities of the night.

She searched their chests for glints of moonlight on brass buttons that would indicate she'd come across a troop of dragoons instead of the Highlanders she'd assumed to be there. But there was no glint, solidifying her fear that they were Jacobites who had turned around from Nairn.

Even so, she remained careful as she orchestrated a path to collide with theirs in a way that seemed completely natural, to avoid being fired upon or in case she was wrong about who they were. And believing them to be rebels, she plucked the Royal Postmistress pin from her jacket so as not to confuse them, be they strangers to her.

Fiona met the soldiers at the front, standing in the center of the road like an apparition. The lot of them drew up at the sight of her there, a few gasping. Most wore kilts and boots, and even in the night, she could make out the shape of caps on their heads. Definitely Highlanders. Most likely Jacobites.

"Is it a sprite?" one man asked, followed by jeers, and a few whispered confirmations.

Fiona rolled her eyes, knowing that in the dark they'd not be able to see quite that well.

When no other men stepped forward, Fiona opened her mouth to speak, only to see a tall Highlander shift from a few men back and come to stand before the group.

"What are ye doing in the road?" His voice was low, gravelly. Tired, and irritated.

Was he the leader of this pack?

"I could ask ye the same thing." This was not the response the man would be expecting, and that was all right. She didn't often do what people were expecting, and she still stood strong.

"Move aside, we've no business with a woman roaming in the middle of the night. Ye could only be up to one thing—and we're no' interested."

Fiona suppressed a derisive snort. It would not be the first time someone had accused her of being a whore, or tried to make her into one.

"'Tis a good thing my house is no' on fire, or my entire family massacred, for ye'd be of no help." She tossed her head gently, feigning affront.

The man's stance shifted, a sign of guilt, but he said nothing. Lord, he was big. A head taller than most of the other men, and easily twice as broad as herself.

Though it was hard to see just where he was looking, or the expression on his face, the way the hair on the back of her nape prickled, she instinctively knew he was staring her down. Examining her as hard as she was examining him.

"Did they send ye?" he asked.

This was a tough question, because he could mean the men who had actually sent her, or the dragoons she'd just alluded to.

"Who would send me to ye? Do I know ye, sir?"

The man grunted, a sound that was both an answer at the same time it wasn't.

"We've no' met afore," he said. "I dinna know of any women who roam the forest at night."

She would have brought up the healer disguise, except that doing so might lead to him asking for help and any help she gave would be more detrimental to his men than not. Though she'd watched Annie work on men any number of times, she'd never quite picked up the skills for healing. And she didn't really care to. She could sew a stitch if needed, but the lines would be jagged, and she'd have nothing to ease the pain, nor any salves to make sure infection didn't set in.

Well, they'd wasted enough time with unpleasantries. She had about thirty seconds or less to establish trust with this stranger in order to relay her message.

"It is no' without purpose that we meet upon the road, though I expected it to be closer to Nairn," she started.

A few men drew their swords, immediately jumping to the wrong conclusion.

Acknowledgments

As always, I must thank my amazing family. I am extremely fortunate to have such a supportive husband and three wonderful daughters. During the creation of this book they endured many "forage for yourselves" nights as I crammed in the last of my word count and "forgot" to make dinner (they even brought me little foraged gifts which sustained me in the trenches), and then they gracefully endured my bursts of cooking afterward and dutifully tried all my new recipes. Thank you to my agent, Kevan Lyon, for believing in me and being my pillar. Many thanks to the team at Sourcebooks, especially my editor, Deb Werksman, for their excitement about the series and continued support. And last but never least, a shout-out to the most incredible writer friends a gal could have who helped me plot, read pages, offered advice, traveled with me for research, and handed me glasses of wine. Listed in no particular order: Andrea Snider, Brenna Ash, Madeline Martin, Lori Ann Bailey, Christi Barth, and my #MorningWriterChicks. Dreams happen when we believe in ourselves and persist no matter what.

About the Author

Eliza Knight is an award-winning and *USA Today* bestselling author of over fifty sizzling historical romances. Under the name E. Knight, she's known for riveting tales that cross landscapes around the world. Her love of history began as a young girl when she traipsed the halls of Versailles and ran through the fields in Southern France. While not reading, writing, or researching her latest book, she chases after her three children. In her spare time (if there is such a thing...) she likes daydreaming, wine tasting, traveling, hiking, staring at the stars, watching movies, shopping, and visiting with family and friends. She lives atop a small mountain with her own knight in shining armor, three princesses, and two very naughty Newfies.

Visit Eliza at elizaknight.com or her historical blog History Undressed: historyundressed.com.